"I SOMETIMES THINK THAT ONE'S PAST LIFE IS WRITTEN IN
A FOREIGN LANGUAGE," SAID MRS. BOWRING,
SHUTTING THE BOOK SHE HELD.

—*Adam Johnstone's Son.*

THE COMPLETE WORKS OF
F. MARION CRAWFORD

In Thirty-two Volumes ❧ *Authorized Edition*

Adam Johnstone's Son

A Rose of Yesterday

BY

F. MARION CRAWFORD

WITH FRONTISPIECE

P. F. COLLIER & SON
NEW YORK

THE COMPLETE WORKS OF F. MARION CRAWFORD

—26—

ADAM JOHNSTONE'S SON

ADAM JOHNSTONE'S SON

CHAPTER I

"I SOMETIMES think that one's past life is written in a foreign language," said Mrs. Bowring, shutting the book she held, but keeping the place with one smooth, thin forefinger, while her still, blue eyes turned from her daughter's face towards the hazy hills that hemmed the sea thirty miles to the southward. "When one wants to read it, one finds ever so many words which one cannot understand, and one has to look them out in a sort of unfamiliar dictionary, and try to make sense of the sentences as best one can. Only the big things are clear."

Clare glanced at her mother, smiling innocently and half mechanically, without much definite expression, and quite without curiosity. Youth can be in sympathy with age, while not understanding it, while not suspecting, perhaps, that there is anything to understand beyond the streaked hair and the pale glance and the little torture-lines which paint the portrait of fifty years for the eyes of twenty.

1

Every woman knows the calendar of her own face. The lines are years, one for such and such a year, one for such and such another; the streaks are months, perhaps, or weeks, or sometimes hours, where the tear-storms have bleached the brown, the black, or the gold. " This little wrinkle — it was so very little then !" she says. "It came when I doubted for a day. There is a shadow there, just at each temple, where the cloud passed, when my sun went out. The bright hair grew lower on my forehead. It is worn away, as though by a crown, that was not of gold. There are hollows there, near the ears, on each side, since that week when love was done to death before my eyes and died — intestate — leaving his substance to be divided amongst indifferent heirs. They wrangle for what he has left, but he himself is gone, beyond hearing or caring, and, thank God, beyond suffering. But the marks are left."

Youth looks on and sees alike the ill-healed wounds of the martyrdom and the rough scars of sin's scourges, and does not understand. Clare Bowring smiled, without definite expression, just because her mother had spoken and seemed to ask for sympathy; and then she looked away for a few moments. She had a bit of work in her hands, a little bag which she was making out of a piece of old Italian damask, to hold a needle-case and thread and scissors. She had stopped sewing, and instinctively waited before beginning again, as though to acknowledge by a little affectionate deference that her mother had said something serious and had a right to expect attention. But she did not answer, for she could not understand.

Her own young life was vividly clear to her; so very vividly clear, that it sometimes made her think of a tiresome chromolithograph. All the facts and thoughts of it were so near that she knew them by heart, as people come to know the patterns of the wall-paper in the room they inhabit. She had nothing to hide, nothing to regret, nothing which she thought she should care very much to recall, though she remembered everything. A girl is very young when she can recollect distinctly every frock she has had, the first long one, and the second, and the third; and the first ball gown, and the second, and no third, because that is still in the future, and a particular pair of gloves which did not fit, and a certain pair of shoes she wore so long because they were so comfortable, and the precise origin of every one of the few trinkets and bits of jewellery she possesses. That was Clare Bowring's case. She could remember everything and everybody in her life. But her father was not in her memories, and there was a little motionless grey cloud in the place where he should have been. He had been a soldier, and had been killed in an obscure skirmish with black men, in one of England's obscure but expensive little wars. Death is always very much the same thing, and it seems unfair that the guns of Balaclava should still roar "glory" while the black man's quick spear-thrust only spells "dead," without comment. But glory in death is even more a matter of luck than fame in life. At all events, Captain Bowring, as brave a gentleman as ever faced fire, had perished like so many other brave gentlemen of his kind, in a quiet way, without any fuss, beyond killing half a dozen or so of his assailants, and had left his widow the glory of receiving a small pension in return for his blood, and that was all. Some day, when the dead are reckoned, and the manner of their death noted, poor Bowring may count for more than some of his friends who died at home from a constitutional inability to enjoy all the good things fortune set before them, complicated by a disposition incapable of being satisfied with only a part of the feast. But at the time of this tale they counted for more than he; for they had been constrained to leave behind them what they could not consume, while he, poor man, had left very little besides the aforesaid interest in the investment of his blood, in the form of a pension to his widow, and the small grey cloud in the memory of his girl-child, in the place where he should have been. For he had been killed when she had been a baby.

The mother and daughter were lonely, if not alone in the world ; for when one has no money to speak of, and no relations at all, the world is a lonely place, regarded from the ordinary point of view — which is, of course, the true one. They had no home in England, and they gener- ally lived abroad, more or less, in one or another of the places of society's departed spirits, such as Florence. They had not, however, entered into Limbo without hope, since they were able to return to the social earth when they pleased, and to be alive again, and the people they met abroad sometimes asked them to stop with them at home, recognising the fact that they were still socially living and casting shadows. They were sure of half a hundred friendly faces in London and of half a dozen hospitable houses in the country ; and that is not little for people who have nothing wherewith to buy smiles and pay for invitations. Clare had more than once met women of her mother's age and older, who had looked at her rather thoughtfully and longer than had seemed quite natural, saying very quietly that her father had been " a great friend of theirs." But those were not the women

whom her mother liked best, and Clare sometimes wondered whether the little grey cloud
in her memory, which represented her father,
might not be there to hide away something
more human than an ideal. Her mother spoke
of him, sometimes gravely, sometimes with a
far-away smile, but never tenderly. The smile
did not mean much, Clare thought. People
often spoke of dead people with a sort of faint
look of uncertain beatitude — the same which
many think appropriate to the singing of hymns.
The absence of anything like tenderness meant
more. The gravity was only natural and decent.

"Your father was a brave man," Mrs. Bowring sometimes said. "Your father was very
handsome," she would say. "He was very
quick-tempered," she perhaps added.

But that was all. Clare had a friend whose
husband had died young and suddenly, and her
friend's heart was broken. She did not speak
as Mrs. Bowring did. When the latter said that
her past life seemed to be written in a foreign
language, Clare did not understand, but she
knew that the something of which the transla-
tion was lost, as it were, belonged to her father.
She always felt an instinctive desire to defend
him, and to make her mother feel more sympathy for his memory. Yet, at the same time,
she loved her mother in such a way as made her

feel that if there had been any trouble, her father must have been in the wrong. Then she was quite sure that she did not understand, and she held her tongue, and smiled vaguely, and waited a moment before she went on with her work.

Besides, she was not at all inclined to argue anything at present. She had been ill, and her mother was worn out with taking care of her, and they had come to Amalfi to get quite well and strong again in the air of the southern spring. They had settled themselves for a couple of months in the queer hotel, which was once a monastery, perched high up under the still higher overhanging rocks, far above the beach and the busy little town; and now, in the May afternoon, they sat side by side under the trellis of vines on the terraced walk, their faces turned southward, in the shade of the steep mountain behind them; the sea was blue at their feet, and quite still, but farther out the westerly breeze that swept past the Conca combed it to crisp roughness; then it was less blue to southward, and gradually it grew less real, till it lost colour and melted into a sky-haze that almost hid the southern mountains and the lizard-like head of the far Licosa.

A bit of coarse faded carpet lay upon the ground under the two ladies' feet, and the shady

air had a soft green tinge in it from the young
vine-leaves overhead. At first sight one would
have said that both were delicate, if not ill.
Both were fair, though in different degrees, and
both were pale and quiet, and looked a little
weary.

The young girl sat in the deep straw chair,
hatless, with bare white hands that held her
work. Her thick flaxen hair, straightly parted
and smoothed away from its low growth on the
forehead, half hid small fresh ears, unpierced.
Long lashes, too white for beauty, cast very
faint light shadows as she looked down; but
when she raised the lids, the dark-blue eyes were
bright, with wide pupils and a straight look,
quick to fasten, slow to let go, never yet quite
softened, and yet never mannishly hard. But,
in its own way, perhaps, there is no look so
hard as the look of maiden innocence can be.
There can even be something terrible in its unconscious stare. There is the spirit of God's
own fearful directness in it. Half quibbling
with words perhaps, but surely with half truth,
one might say that youth "is," while all else
"has been"; and that youth alone possesses the
present, too innocent to know it all, yet too selfish even to doubt of what is its own — too sure
of itself to doubt anything, to fear anything, or
even truly to pray for anything. There is no

equality and no community in virtue; it is only
original sin that makes us all equal and human.
Old Lucifer, fallen, crushed, and damned, knows
the worth of forgiveness — not young Michael,
flintily hard and monumentally upright in his
steel coat, a terror to the devil himself.   And
youth can have something of that archangelic
rigidity.   Youth is not yet quite human.

But there was much in Clare Bowring's face
which told that she was to be quite human some
day.   The lower features were not more than
strong enough — the curved lips would be fuller
before long, the small nostrils, the gentle chin,
were a little sharper than was natural, now, from
illness, but round in outline and not over promi-
nent; and the slender throat was very delicate
and feminine.   Only in the dark-blue eyes there
was still that unabashed, quick glance and long-
abiding straightness, and innocent hardness, and
the unconscious selfishness of the uncontami-
nated.

Standing on her feet, she would have seemed
rather tall than short, though really but of average height.   Seated, she looked tall, and her
glance was a little downward to most people's
eyes.   Just now she was too thin, and seemed
taller than she was.   But the fresh light was
already in the young white skin, and there was
a soft colour in the lobes of the little ears, as

the white leaves of daisies sometimes blush all round their tips.

The nervous white hands held the little bag lightly, and twined it and sewed it deftly, for Clare was clever with her fingers.   Possibly they looked even a little whiter than they were, by contrast with the dark stuff of her dress, and illness had made them shrink at the lower part, robbing them of their natural strength, though not of their grace.   There is a sort of refinement, not of taste, nor of talent, but of feeling and thought, and it shows itself in the hands of those who have it, more than in any feature of the face, in a sort of very true proportion between the hand and its fingers, between each finger and its joints, each joint and each nail; a something which says that such a hand could not do anything ignoble, could not take meanly, nor strike cowardly, nor press falsely; a quality of skin neither rough and coarse, nor over smooth like satin, but cool and pleasant to the touch as fine silk that is closely woven.   The fingers of such hands are very straight and very elastic, but not supple like young snakes, as some fingers are, and the cushion of the hand is not over full nor heavy, nor yet shrunken and undeveloped as in the wasted hands of old Asiatic races.

In outward appearance there was that sort of inherited likeness between mother and daughter which is apt to strike strangers more than persons of the same family. Mrs. Bowring had been beautiful in her youth — far more beautiful than Clare — but her face had been weaker, in spite of the regularity of the features and their faultless proportion. Life had given them an acquired strength, but not of the lovely kind, and the complexion was faded, and the hair had darkened, and the eyes had paled. Some faces are beautified by suffering. Mrs. Bowring's face was not of that class. It was as though a thin, hard mask had been formed and closely moulded upon it, as the action of the sea overlays some sorts of soft rock with a surface thin as paper but as hard as granite. In spite of the hardness, the features were not really strong. There was refinement in them, however, of the same kind which the daughter had, and as much, though less pleasing. A fern — a spray of maiden's-hair — loses much of its beauty but none of its refinement when petrified in limestone or made fossil in coal.

As they sat there, side by side, mother and daughter, where they had sat every day for a week or more, they had very little to say. They had exhausted the recapitulation of Clare's illness, during the first days of her convalescence. It was not the first time that they had been in Amalfi, and they had enumerated its beauties to

each other, and renewed their acquaintance with
it from a distance, looking down from the terrace upon the low-lying town, and the beach
and the painted boats, and the little crowd that
swarmed out now and then like ants, very busy
and very much in a hurry, running hither and
thither, disappearing presently as by magic, and
leaving the shore to the sun and the sea.   The
two had spoken of a little excursion to Ravello,
and they meant to go thither as soon as they
should be strong enough ; but that was not yet.
And meanwhile they lived through the quiet
days, morning, meal times, evening, bed time,
and round again, through the little hotel's pro-
gramme of possibility ; eating what was offered
them, but feasting royally on air and sunshine
and spring sweetness; moistening their lips
in strange southern wines, but drinking deep
draughts of the rich southern air-life ; watching the people of all sorts and of many conditions, who came and stayed a day and went
away again, but social only in each other's lives,
and even that by sympathy rather than in speech.
A corner of life's show was before them, and
they kept their places on the vine-sheltered terrace and looked on.   But it seemed as though
nothing could ever possibly happen there to
affect the direction of their own quietly moving
existence.

Seeing that her daughter did not say anything in answer to the remark about the past being written in a foreign language, Mrs. Bowring looked at the distant sky-haze thoughtfully for a few moments, then opened her book again where her thin forefinger had kept the place, and began to read. There was no disappointment in her face at not being understood, for she had spoken almost to herself and had expected no reply. No change of expression softened or accentuated the quiet hardness which overspread her naturally gentle face. But the thought was evidently still present in her mind, for her attention did not fix itself upon her book, and presently she looked at her daughter, as the latter bent her head over the little bag she was making.

The young girl felt her mother's eyes upon her, looked up herself, and smiled faintly, almost mechanically, as before. It was a sort of habit they both had — a way of acknowledging one another's presence in the world. But this time it seemed to Clare that there was a question in the look, and after she had smiled she spoke.

"No," she said, "I don't understand how anybody can forget the past. It seems to me that I shall always remember why I did things, said things, and thought things. I should, if I lived a hundred years, I'm quite sure."

"Perhaps you have a better memory than
I," answered Mrs. Bowring. "But I don't think
it is exactly a question of memory either. I
can remember what I said, and did, and thought,
well — twenty years ago. But it seems to me
very strange that I should have thought, and
spoken, and acted, just as I did. After all isn't
it natural? They tell us that our bodies are
quite changed in less time than that."

"Yes — but the soul does not change," said
Clare with conviction.

"The soul — "

Mrs. Bowring repeated the word, but said
nothing more, and her still, blue eyes wandered
from her daughter's face and again fixed themselves on an imaginary point of the far southern
distance.

"At least," said Clare, "I was always taught
so."

She smiled again, rather coldly, as though
admitting that such teaching might not be infalli-
ble after all.

"It is best to believe it," said her mother
quietly, but in a colourless voice. "Besides,"
she added, with a change of tone, "I do believe
it, you know. One is always the same, in the
main things. It is the point of view that
changes. The best picture in the world does
not look the same in every light, does it?"

" No, I suppose not. You may like it in one light and not in another, and in one place and not in another."

" Or at one time of life, and not at another," added Mrs. Bowring, thoughtfully.

" I can't imagine that." Clare paused a moment. " Of course you are thinking of people," she continued presently, with a little more animation. " One always means people, when one talks in that way. And that is what I cannot quite understand. It seems to me that if I liked people once I should always like them."

Her mother looked at her.

" Yes — perhaps you would," she said, and she relapsed into silence.

Clare's colour did not change. No particular person was in her thoughts, and she had, as it were, given her own general and inexperienced opinion of her own character, quite honestly and without affectation.

" I don't know which are the happier," said Mrs. Bowring at last, " the people who change, or the people who can't."

" You mean faithful or unfaithful people, I suppose," observed the young girl with grave innocence.

A very slight flush rose in Mrs. Bowring's thin cheeks, and the quiet eyes grew suddenly

hard, but Clare was busy with her work again
and did not see.

"Those are big words," said the older woman
in a low voice.

"Well — yes — of course!" answered Clare.
"So they ought to be! It is always the main
question, isn't it? Whether you can trust a
person or not, I mean."

"That is one question. The other is, whether
the person deserves to be trusted."

"Oh — it's the same thing!"

"Not exactly."

"You know what I mean, mother. Besides,
I don't believe that any one who can't trust is
really to be trusted. Do you?"

"My dear Clare!" exclaimed Mrs. Bowring.
"You can't put life into a nutshell, like that!"

"No. I suppose not, though if a thing is true
at all it must be always true."

"Saving exceptions."

"Are there any exceptions to truth?" asked
Clare incredulously. "Truth isn't grammar —
nor the British Constitution."

"No. But then, we don't know everything.
What we call truth is what we know. It is
only what we know. All that we don't know,
but which is, is true, too — especially, all that
we don't know about people with whom we
have to live."

"Oh — if people have secrets!" The young girl laughed idly. "But you and I, for instance, mother — we have no secrets from each other, have we? Well? Why should any two people who love each other have secrets? And if they have none, why, then, they know all that there is to be known about one another, and each trusts the other, and has a right to be trusted, because everything is known — and everything is the whole truth. It seems to me that is simple enough, isn't it?"

Mrs. Bowring laughed in her turn. It was rather a hard little laugh, but Clare was used to the sound of it, and joined in it, feeling that she had vanquished her mother in argument, and settled one of the most important questions of life for ever.

"What a pretty steamer!" exclaimed Mrs. Bowring suddenly.

"It's a yacht," said Clare after a moment. "The flag is English, too. I can see it distinctly."

She laid down her work, and her mother closed her book upon her forefinger again, and they watched the graceful white vessel as she glided slowly in from the Conca, which she had rounded while they had been talking.

"It's very big, for a yacht," observed Mrs. Bowring. "They are coming here."

c

"They have probably come round from Naples to spend a day," said Clare. "We are sure to have them up here. What a nuisance!"

"Yes. Everybody comes up here who comes to Amalfi at all. I hope they won't stay long."

"There is no fear of that," answered Clare. "I heard those people saying the other day that this is not a place where a vessel can lie any length of time. You know how the sea sometimes breaks on the beach."

Mrs. Bowring and her daughter desired of all things to be quiet. The visitors who came, stayed a few days at the hotel, and went away again, were as a rule tourists or semi-invalids in search of a climate, and anything but noisy. But people coming in a smart English yacht would probably be society people, and as such Mrs. Bowring wished that they would keep away. They would behave as though the place belonged to them, so long as they remained; they would get all the attention of the proprietor and of the servants for the time being; and they would make everybody feel shabby and poor.

The Bowrings were poor, indeed, but they were not shabby. It was perhaps because they were well aware that nobody could mistake them for average tourists that they resented the coming of a party which belonged to what is called society. Mrs. Bowring had a strong aversion to making new acquaintances, and even disliked being thrown into the proximity of people who might know friends of hers, who might have heard of her, and who might talk about her and her daughter. Clare said that her mother's shyness in this respect was almost morbid; but she had unconsciously caught a little of it herself, and, like her mother, she was often quite uselessly on her guard against strangers, of the kind whom she might possibly be called upon to know, though she was perfectly affable and at her ease with those whom she looked upon as undoubtedly her social inferiors.

They were not mistaken in their prediction that the party from the yacht would come up to the Cappuccini. Half an hour after the yacht had dropped anchor the terrace was invaded. They came up in twos and threes, nearly a dozen of them, men and women, smart-looking people with healthy, sun-burnt faces, voices loud from the sea as voices become on a long voyage — or else very low indeed. By contrast with the frequenters of Amalfi they all seemed to wear overpoweringly good clothes and perfectly new hats and caps, and their russet shoes were resplendent. They moved as though everything belonged to them, from the wild crests of the hills above to the calm blue water below, and

the hotel servants did their best to foster the
agreeable illusion.   They all wanted chairs, and
tables, and things to drink, and fruit.   One very
fair little lady with hard, restless eyes, and clad
in white serge, insisted upon having grapes, and
no one could convince her that grapes were not
ripe in May.

"It's quite absurd!" she objected.   "Of course
they're ripe !   We had the most beautiful grapes
at breakfast at Leo Cairngorm's the other day,
so of course they must have them here.   Brook !
Do tell the man not to be absurd !"

"Man !" said the member of the party she
had last addressed.   "Do not be absurd !"

"Sì, Signore," replied the black-whiskered
Amalfitan servant with alacrity.

"You see !" cried the little lady triumphantly.
"I told you so !   You must insist with these
people.   You can always get what you want.
Brook, where's my fan?"

She settled upon a straw chair — like a white
butterfly.   The others walked on towards the
end of the terrace, but the young man whom she
called Brook stood beside her, slowly lighting a
cigarette, not five paces from Mrs. Bowring and
Clare.

"I'm sure I don't know where your fan is,"
he said, with a short laugh, as he threw the end
of the match over the wall.

"Well then, look for it!" she answered, rather sharply. "I'm awfully hot, and I want it."

He glanced at her before he spoke again.

"I don't know where it is," he said quietly, but there was a shade of annoyance in his face.

"I gave it to you just as we were getting into the boat," answered the lady in white. "Do you mean to say that you left it on board?"

"I think you must be mistaken," said the young man. "You must have given it to somebody else."

"It isn't likely that I should mistake you for any one else — espetially to-day."

"Well — I haven't got it. I'll get you one in the hotel, if you'll have patience for a moment."

He turned and strode along the terrace towards the house. Clare Bowring had been watching the two, and she looked after the man as he moved rapidly away. He walked well, for he was a singularly well-made young fellow, who looked as though he were master of every inch of himself. She had liked his brown face and bright blue eyes, too, and somehow she resented the way in which the little lady ordered him about. She looked round and saw that her mother was watching him too. Then, as he disappeared, they both looked at the lady. She too had followed him with her eyes, and as she

turned her face sideways to the Bowrings Clare
thought that she was biting her lip, as though
something annoyed her or hurt her. She kept
her eyes on the door. Presently the young man
reappeared, bearing a palm-leaf fan in his hand
and blowing a cloud of cigarette smoke into the
air. Instantly the lady smiled, and the smile
brightened as he came near.

" Thank you — dear," she said as he gave her
the fan.

The last word was spoken in a lower tone, and
could certainly not have been heard by the other
members of the party, but it reached Clare's ears,
where she sat.

"Not at all," answered the young man
quietly.

But as he spoke he glanced quickly about
him, and his eyes met Clare's. She fancied
that she saw a look of startled annoyance
in them, and he coloured a little under his tan.
He had a very manly face, square and strong.
He bent down a little and said something in
a low voice. The lady in white half turned her
head, impatiently, but did not look quite round.
Clare saw, however, that her expression had
changed again, and that the smile was gone.

" If I don't care, why should you ? " were the
next words Clare heard, spoken impatiently and
petulantly.

The man who answered to the name of Brook said nothing, but sat down on the parapet of the terrace, looking out over his shoulder to seaward. A few seconds later he threw away his half-smoked cigarette.

"I like this place," said the lady in white, quite audibly. " I think I shall send on board for my things and stay here."

The young man started as though he had been struck, and faced her in silence. He could not help seeing Clare Bowring beyond her.

" I'm going indoors, mother," said the young girl, rising rather abruptly. " I'm sure it must be time for tea. Won't you come too?"

The young man did not answer his companion's remark, but turned his face away again and looked seaward, listening to the retreating footsteps of the two ladies.

On the threshold of the hotel Clare felt a strong desire to look back again and see whether he had moved, but she was ashamed of it and went in, holding her head high and looking straight before her.

CHAPTER II

THE people from the yacht belonged to that class of men and women whose uncertainty, or indifference, about the future leads them to take possession of all they can lay hands on in the present, with a view to squeezing the world like a lemon for such enjoyment as it may yield. So long as they tarried at the old hotel, it was their private property. The Bowrings were forgotten; the two English old maids had no existence; the Russian invalid got no more hot water for his tea; the plain but obstinately inquiring German family could get no more information; even the quiet young French couple — a honeymoon couple — sank into insignificance. The only protest came from an American, whose wife was ill and never appeared, and who staggered the landlord by asking what he would sell the whole place for on condition of vacating the premises before dinner.

"They will be gone before dinner," the proprietor answered.

But they did not go. When it was already late somebody saw the moon rise, almost full,

and suggested that the moonlight would be very
fine, and that it would be amusing to dine at
the hotel table and spend the evening on the
terrace and go on board late.

" I shall," said the little lady in white serge,
" whatever the rest of you do. Brook ! Send
somebody on board to get a lot of cloaks and
shawls and things. I am'sure it is going to be
cold. Don't go away ! I want you to take me
for a walk before dinner, so as to be nice and
hungry, you know."

For some reason or other, several of the party
laughed, and from their tone one might have
guessed that they were in the habit of laughing,
or were expected to laugh, at the lady's speeches.
And every one agreed that it would be much
nicer to spend the evening on the terrace, and
that it was a pity that they could not dine out
of doors because it would be far too cool. Then
the lady in white and the man called Brook
began to walk furiously up and down in the
fading light, while the lady talked very fast in
a low voice, except when she was passing within
earshot of some of the others, and the man
looked straight before him, answering occasionally in monosyllables.

Then there was more confusion in the hotel,
and the Russian invalid expressed his opinion
to the two English old maids, with whom he

fraternised, that dinner would be an hour late, thanks to their compatriots. But they assumed an expression appropriate when speaking of the peerage, and whispered that the yacht must belong to the Duke of Orkney, who, they had read, was cruising in the Mediterranean, and that the Duke was probably the big man in grey clothes who had a gold cigarette case. But in all this they were quite mistaken. And their repeated examinations of the hotel register were altogether fruitless, because none of the party had written their names in it. The old maids, however, were quite happy and resigned to waiting for their dinner. They presently retired to attempt for themselves what stingy nature had refused to do for them in the way of adornment, for the dinner was undoubtedly to be an occasion of state, and their eyes were to see the glory of a lord.

The party sat together at one end of the table, which extended the whole length of the high and narrow vaulted hall, while the guests staying in the hotel filled the opposite half. Most of the guests were more subdued than usual, and the party from the yacht seemed noisy by contrast. The old maids strained their ears to catch a name here and there. Clare and her mother talked little. The Russian invalid put up a single eyeglass, looked long and curi-

ously at each of the new comers in turn, and
then did not vouchsafe them another glance.
The German family criticised the food severely,
and then got into a fierce discussion about Bismarck and the Pope, in the course of which they
forgot the existence of their fellow-diners, but
not of their dinner.

Clare could not help glancing once or twice
at the couple that had attracted her attention,
and she found herself wondering what their relation to each other could be, and whether they
were engaged to be married. Somebody called
the lady in white " Mrs. Crosby." Then somebody else called her " Lady Fan " — which was
very confusing. " Brook " never called her anything. Clare saw him fill his glass and look at
Lady Fan very hard before he drank, and then
Lady Fan did the same thing. Nevertheless
they seemed to be perpetually quarrelling over
little things. When Brook was tired of being
bullied, he calmly ignored his companion, turned
from her, and talked in a low tone to a dark
woman who had been a beauty and was the
most thoroughly well-dressed of the extremely
well-dressed party. Lady Fan bit her lip for a
moment, and then said something at which all
the others laughed — except Brook and the
advanced beauty, who continued to talk in
undertones.

To Clare's mind there was about them all, except Brook, a little dash of something which was not "quite, quite," as the world would have expressed it. In her opinion Lady Fan was distinctly disagreeable, whoever she might be — as distinctly so as Brook was the contrary. And somehow the girl could not help resenting the woman's way of treating him. It offended her oddly and jarred upon her good taste, as something to which she was not at all accustomed in her surroundings. Lady Fan was very exquisite in her outward ways, and her speech was of the proper smartness. Yet everything she did and said was intensely unpleasant to Clare.

The Bowrings and the regular guests finished their dinner before the yachting party, and rose almost in a body, with a clattering of their light chairs on the tiled floor. Only the English old maids kept their places a little longer than the rest, and took some more filberts and half a glass of white wine, each. They could not keep their eyes from the party at the other end of the table, and their faces grew a little redder as they sat there. Clare and her mother had to go round the long table to get out, being the last on their side, and they were also the last to reach the door. Again the young girl felt that strong desire to turn her

head and look back at Brook and Lady Fan.
She noticed it this time, as something she had
never felt until that afternoon, but she would
not yield to it. She walked on, looking straight
at the back of her mother's head. Then she
heard quick footsteps on the tiles behind her,
and Brook's voice.

"I beg your pardon," he was saying, "you
have dropped your shawl."

She turned quickly, and met his eyes as he
stopped close to her, holding out the white
chudder which had slipped to the floor unnoticed when she had risen from her seat. She
took it mechanically and thanked him. Instinctively looking past him down the long hall, she
saw that the little lady in white had turned in
her seat and was watching her. Brook made a
slight bow and was gone again in an instant.
Then Clare followed her mother and went out.

"Let us go out behind the house," she said
when they were in the broad corridor. "There
will be moonlight there, and those people will
monopolise the terrace when they have finished
dinner."

At the western end of the old monastery there
is a broad open space, between the buildings and
the overhanging rocks, at the base of which
there is a deep recess, almost amounting to a
cave, in which stands a great black cross planted

in a pedestal of whitewashed masonry. A few
steps lead up to it. As the moon rose higher
the cross was in the shadow, while the platform
and the buildings were in the full light.

The two women ascended the steps and sat
down upon a stone seat.

"What a night!" exclaimed the young girl
softly.

Her mother silently bent her head; but neither
spoke again for some time. The moonlight before them was almost dazzling, and the air was
warm. Beyond the stone parapet, far below,
the tideless sea was silent and motionless under
the moon. A crooked fig-tree, still leafless,
though the little figs were already shaped on it,
cast its intricate shadow upon the platform.
Very far away, a boy was singing a slow minor
chant in a high voice. The peace was almost
disquieting — there was something intensely ex-
pectant in it, as though the night were in love,
and its heart beating.

Clare sat still, her hand upon her mother's
thin wrist, her lips just parted a little, her eyes
wide and filled with moon-dreams. She had
almost lost herself in unworded fancies when
her mother moved and spoke.

"I had quite forgotten a letter I was writing,"
she said. "I must finish it. Stay here, and I
will come back again presently."

She rose, and Clare watched her slim dark figure and the long black shadow that moved with it across the platform towards the open door of the hotel. But when it had disappeared the white fancies came flitting back through the silent light, and in the shade the young eyes fixed themselves quietly to meet the vision and see it all, and to keep it for ever if she could.

She did not know what it was that she saw, but it was beautiful, and what she felt was on a sudden as the realisation of something she had dimly desired in vain. Yet in itself it was nothing realised; it was perhaps only the certainty of longing for something all heart and no name, and it was happiness to long for it. For the first intuition of love is only an exquisite foretaste, a delight in itself, as far from the bitter hunger of love starving as a girl's faintness is from a cruel death. The light was dazzling, and yet it was full of gentle things that smiled, somehow, without faces. She was not very imaginative, perhaps, else the faces might have come too, and voices, and all, save the one reality which had as yet neither voice nor face, nor any name. It was all the something that love was to mean, somewhere, some day — the airy lace of a maiden life-dream, in which no figure was yet wrought amongst the fancy-threads that the May moon was weaving in the soft spring night.

There was no sadness in it, at all, for there was no memory, and without memory there can be no sadness, any more than there can be fear where there is no anticipation, far or near. Most happiness is really of the future, and most grief, if we would be honest, is of the past.

The young girl sat still and dreamed that the old world was as young as she, and that in its soft bosom there were exquisite sweetnesses untried, and soft yearnings for a beautiful unknown, and little pulses that could quicken with foretasted joy which only needed face and name to take angelic shape of present love. The world could not be old while she was young.

And she had her youth and knew it, and it was almost all she had. It seemed much to her, and she had no unsatisfiable craving for the world's stuff in which to attire it. In that, at least, her mother had been wise, teaching her to believe and to enjoy, rather than to doubt and criticise, and if there had been anything to hide from her it had been hidden, even beyond suspicion of its presence. Perhaps the armour of knowledge is of little worth until doubt has shaken the heart and weakened the joints, and broken the terrible steadfastness of perfect innocence in the eyes. Clare knew that she was young, she felt that the white dream was sweet, and she believed that the world's heart was clean and good. All good was natural and eternal, lofty and splendid as an archangel in the light. God had made evil as a background of shadows to show how good the light was. Every one could come and stand in the light if he chose, for the mere trouble of moving. It seemed so simple. She wondered why everybody could not see it as she did.

A flash of white in the white moonlight disturbed her meditations. Two people had come out of the door and were walking slowly across the platform side by side. They were not speaking, and their footsteps crushed the light gravel sharply as they came forward. Clare recognised Brook and Lady Fan. Seated in the shadow on one side of the great black cross and a little behind it, she could see their faces distinctly, but she had no idea that they were dazzled by the light and could not see her at all in her dark dress. She fancied that they were looking at her as they came on.

The shadow of the rock had crept forward upon the open space, while she had been dreaming. The two turned, just before they reached it, and then stood still, instead of walking back.

" Brook — " began Lady Fan, as though she were going to say something.

But she checked herself and looked up at him quickly, chilled already by his humour. Clare

D

thought that the woman's voice shook a little, as she pronounced the name. Brook did not turn his head nor look down.

"Yes?" he said, with a sort of interrogation. "What were you going to say?" he asked after a moment's pause.

She seemed to hesitate, for she did not answer at once. Then she glanced towards the hotel and looked down.

"You won't come back with us?" she asked, at last, in a pleading voice.

"I can't," he answered. "You know I can't. I've got to wait for them here."

"Yes, I know. But they are not here yet. I don't believe they are coming for two or three days. You could perfectly well come on to Genoa with us, and get back by rail."

"No," said Brook quietly, "I can't."

"Would you, if you could?" asked the lady in white, and her tone began to change again.

"What a question!" he laughed drily.

"It is an odd question, isn't it, coming from me?" Her voice grew hard, and she stopped. "Well — you know what it means," she added abruptly. "You may as well answer it and have it over. It is very easy to say you would not, if you could. I shall understand all the rest, and you will be saved the trouble of saying things — things which I should think you would find it rather hard to say."

"Couldn't you say them, instead?" he asked slowly, and looking at her for the first time. He spoke gravely and coldly.

"I!" There was indignation, real or well affected, in the tone.

"Yes, you," answered the man, with a shade less coldness, but as gravely as before. "You never loved me."

Lady Fan's small white face was turned to his instantly, and Clare could see the fierce, hurt expression in the eyes and about the quivering mouth. The young girl suddenly realised that she was accidentally overhearing something which was very serious to the two speakers. It flashed upon her that they had not seen her where she sat in the shadow, and she looked about her hastily in the hope of escaping unobserved. But that was impossible. There was no way of getting out of the recess of the rock where the cross stood, except by coming out into the light, and no way of reaching the hotel except by crossing the open platform.

Then she thought of coughing, to call attention to her presence. She would rise and come forward, and hurry across to the door. She felt that she ought to have come out of the shadows as soon as the pair had appeared, and that she had done wrong in sitting still. But then, she told herself with perfect justice that they were strangers, and that she could not possibly have foreseen that they had come there to quarrel.

They were strangers, and she did not even know their names. So far as they were concerned, and their feelings, it would be much more pleasant for them if they never suspected that any one had overheard them than if she were to appear in the midst of their conversation, having evidently been listening up to that point. It will be admitted that, being a woman, she had a choice; for she knew that if she had been in Lady Fan's place she should have preferred never to know that any one had heard her. She fancied what she should feel if any one should cough unexpectedly behind her when she had just been accused by the man she loved of not loving him at all. And of course the little lady in white loved Brook — she had called him "dear" that very afternoon. But that Brook did not love Lady Fan was as plain as possible.

There was certainly no mean curiosity in Clare to know the secrets of these strangers. But all the same, she would not have been a human girl, of any period in humanity's history, if she had not been profoundly interested in the fate of the woman before her. That afternoon she would have thought it far more probable that the woman should break the man's heart than

that she should break her own for him. But
now it looked otherwise. Clare thought there
was no mistaking the first tremor of the voice,
the look of the white face, and the indignation
of the tone afterwards. With a man, the question of revealing his presence as a third person
would have been a point of honour. In Clare's
case it was a question of delicacy and kindness
as from one woman to another.

Nevertheless, she hesitated, and she might
have come forward after all. Ten slow seconds
had passed since Brook had spoken. Then Lady
Fan's little figure shook, her face turned away,
and she tried to choke down one small bitter
sob, pressing her handkerchief desperately to
her lips.

"Oh, Brook!" she cried, a moment later, and
her tiny teeth tore the edge of the handkerchief audibly in the stillness.

"It's not your fault," said the man, with
an attempt at gentleness in his voice. "I
couldn't blame you, if I were brute enough to
wish to."

"Blame me! Oh, really — I think you're
mad, you know!"

"Besides," continued the young man, philosophically, "I think we ought to be glad, don't
you?"

"Glad?"

"Yes — that we are not going to break our hearts now that it's over."

Clare thought his tone horribly business-like and indifferent.

"Oh no! We sha'n't break our hearts any more! We are not children." Her voice was thin and bitter, with a crying laugh in it.

"Look here, Fan!" said Brook suddenly. "This is all nonsense. We agreed to play together, and we've played very nicely, and now you have to go home, and I have got to stay here, whether I like it or not. Let us be good friends and say good-bye, and if we meet again and have nothing better to do, we can play again if we please. But as for taking it in this tragical way — why, it isn't worth it."

The young girl crouching in the shadow felt as though she had been struck, and her heart went out with indignant sympathy to the little lady in white.

"Do you know? I think you are the most absolutely brutal, cynical creature I ever met!" There was anger in the voice, now, and something more — something which Clare could not understand.

"Well, I'm sorry," answered the man. "I don't mean to be brutal, I'm sure, and I don't think I'm cynical either. I look at things as they are, not as they ought to be. We are not

angels, and the millennium hasn't come yet.
I suppose it would be bad for us if it did,
just now. But we used to be very good friends
last year. I don't see why we shouldn't be
again."

" Friends! Oh no!"

Lady Fan turned from him and made a step
or two alone, out through the moonlight, towards
the house. Brook did not move. Perhaps he
knew that she would come back, as indeed she
did, stopping suddenly and turning round to face
him again.

" Brook," she began more softly, " do you
remember that evening up at the Acropolis — at
sunset? Do you remember what you said?"

" Yes, I think I do."

" You said that if I could get free you would
marry me."

" Yes." The man's tone had changed suddenly.

" Well — I believed you, that's all."

Brook stood quite still, and looked at her
quietly. Some seconds passed before she spoke
again.

" You did not mean it?" she asked sorrow-
fully.

Still he said nothing.

" Because you know," she continued, her eyes
fixed on his, " the position is not at all impossi-

ble. All things considered, I suppose I could
have a divorce for the asking."

Clare started a little in the dark. She was
beginning to guess something of the truth she
could not understand. The man still said nothing, but he began to walk up and down slowly,
with folded arms, along the edge of the shadow
before Lady Fan as she stood still, following
him with her eyes.

"You did not mean a word of what you said
that afternoon? Not one word?" She spoke
very slowly and distinctly.

He was silent still, pacing up and down before
her. Suddenly, without a word, she turned from
him and walked quickly away, towards the
hotel. He started and stood still, looking after
her — then he also made a step.

"Fan!" he called, in a tone she could hear,
but she went on. "Mrs. Crosby!" he called
again.

She stopped, turned, and waited. It was
clear that Lady Fan was a nickname, Clare
thought.

"Well?" she asked.

Clare clasped her hands together in her excitement, watching and listening, and holding
her breath.

"Don't go like that!" exclaimed Brook, going
forward and holding out one hand.

" Do you want me?" asked the lady in white, very gently, almost tenderly. Clare did not understand how any woman could have so little pride, but she pitied the little lady from her heart.

Brook went on till he came up with Lady Fan, who did not make a step to meet him. But just as he reached her she put out her hand to take his. Clare thought he was relenting, but she was mistaken. His voice came back to her clear and distinct, and it had a very gentle ring in it.

"Fan, dear," he said, "we have been very fond of each other in our careless way. But we have not loved each other. We may have thought that we did, for a moment, now and then. I shall always be fond of you, just in that way. I'll do anything for you. But I won't marry you, if you get a divorce. It would be utter folly. If I ever said I would, in so many words — well, I'm ashamed of it. You'll forgive me some day. One says things — sometimes — that one means for a minute, and then, afterwards, one doesn't mean them. But I mean what I am saying now."

He dropped her hand, and stood looking at her, and waiting for her to speak. Her face, as Clare saw it, from a distance now, looked whiter than ever. After an instant she turned from

him with a quick movement, but not towards
the hotel.

She walked slowly towards the stone parapet
of the platform. As she went, Clare again saw
her raise her handkerchief and press it to her
lips, but she did not bend her head. She went
and leaned on her elbows on the parapet, and
her hands pulled nervously at the handkerchief
as she looked down at the calm sea far below.
Brook followed her slowly, but just as he was
near, she, hearing his footsteps, turned and
leaned back against the low wall.

"Give me a cigarette," she said in a hard
voice. "I'm nervous — and I've got to face
those people in a moment."

Clare started again in sheer surprise. She
had expected tears, fainting, angry words, a passionate appeal — anything rather than what she
heard. Brook produced a silver case which
gleamed in the moonlight. Lady Fan took a
cigarette, and her companion took another. He
struck a match and held it up for her in the
still air. The little flame cast its red glare into
their faces. The young girl had good eyes, and
as she watched them she saw the man's expression was grave and stern, a little sad, perhaps,
but she fancied that there was the beginning
of a scornful smile on the woman's lips. She
understood less clearly then than ever what

manner of human beings these two strangers might be.

For some moments they smoked in silence, the lady in white leaning back against the parapet, the man standing upright with one hand in his pocket, holding his cigarette in the other, and looking out to sea. Then Lady Fan stood up, too, and threw her cigarette over the wall.

"It's time to be going," she said, suddenly. "They'll be coming after us if we stay here."

But she did not move. Sideways she looked up into his face. Then she held out her hand.

"Good-bye, Brook," she said, quietly enough, as he took it.

"Good-bye," he murmured in a low voice, but distinctly.

Their hands stayed together after they had spoken, and still she looked up to him in the moonlight. Suddenly he bent down and kissed her on the forehead — in an odd, hasty way.

"I'm sorry, Fan, but it won't do," he said.

"Again!" she answered. "Once more, please!" And she held up her face.

He kissed her again, but less hastily, Clare thought, as she watched them. Then, without another word, they walked towards the hotel, side by side, close together, so that their hands almost touched. When they were not ten paces from the door, they stopped again and looked at each other.

At that moment Clare saw her mother's dark figure on the threshold. The pair must have heard her steps, for they separated a little and instantly went on, passing Mrs. Bowring quickly. Clare sat still in her place, waiting for her mother to come to her. She feared lest, if she moved, the two might come back for an instant, see her, and understand that they had been watched. Mrs. Bowring went forward a few steps.

" Clare ! " she called.

" Yes," answered the young girl softly. " Here I am."

" Oh — I could not see you at all," said her mother. " Come down into the moonlight."

The young girl descended the steps, and the two began to walk up and down together on the platform.

" Those were two of the people from the yacht that I met at the door," said Mrs. Bowring. " The lady in white serge, and that good-looking young man."

" Yes," Clare answered. " They were here some time. I don't think they saw me."

She had meant to tell her mother something of what had happened, in the hope of being told that she had done right in not revealing her presence. But on second thoughts she re-

solved to say nothing about it. To have told
the story would have seemed like betraying a
confidence, even though they were strangers to
her.

"I could not help wondering about them this
afternoon," said Mrs. Bowring. "She ordered him
about in a most extraordinary way, as though
he had been her servant. I thought it in very
bad taste, to say the least of it. Of course I
don't know anything about their relations, but
it struck me that she wished to show him off, as
her possession."

"Yes," answered Clare, thoughtfully. "I
thought so too."

"Very foolish of her! No man will stand
that sort of thing long. That isn't the way to
treat a man in order to keep him."

"What is the best way?" asked the young
girl idly, with a little laugh.

"Don't ask me!" answered Mrs. Bowring
quickly, as they turned in their walk. "But I
should think — " she added, a moment later,
"I don't know — but I should think — " she
hesitated.

"What?" inquired Clare, with some curiosity.

"Well, I was going to say, I should think
that a man would wish to feel that he is holding, not that he is held. But then people are so
different! One can never tell. At all events,

it is foolish to wish to show everybody that you own a man, so to say."

Mrs. Bowring seemed to be considering the question, but she evidently found nothing more to say about it, and they walked up and down in silence for a long time, each occupied with her own thoughts. Then all at once there was a sound of many voices speaking English, and trying to give orders in Italian, and the words "Good-bye, Brook!" sounded several times above the rest. Little by little, all grew still again.

"They are gone at last," said Mrs. Bowring, with a sigh of relief.

CHAPTER III

CLARE BOWRING went to her room that night feeling as though she had been at the theatre. She could not get rid of the impression made upon her by the scene she had witnessed, and over and over again, as she lay awake, with the moonbeams streaming into her room, she went over all she had seen and heard on the platform. It had, at least, been very like the theatre. The broad, flat stage, the somewhat conventionally picturesque buildings, the strip of far-off sea, as flat as a band of paint, the unnaturally bright moonlight, the two chief figures going through a love quarrel in the foreground, and she herself calmly seated in the shadow, as in the darkened amphitheatre, and looking on unseen and unnoticed.

But the two people had not talked at all as people talked on the stage in any piece Clare had ever seen. What would have been the "points" in a play had all been left out, and instead there had been abrupt pauses and awkward silences, and then, at what should have been the supreme moment, the lady in white

47

had asked for a cigarette. And the two hasty
little kisses that had a sort of perfunctory air,
and the queer, jerky " good-byes," and the last
stop near the door of the hotel — it all had an
air of being very badly done. It could not have
been a success on the stage, Clare thought.

And yet this was a bit of life, of the real,
genuine life of two people who had been in love,
and perhaps were in love still, though they
might not know it. She had been present at
what must, in her view, have been a great crisis
in two lives. Such things, she thought, could
not happen more than once in a lifetime — twice,
perhaps. Her mother had been married twice,
so Clare admitted a second possibility. But not
more than that.

The situation, too, as she reviewed it, was
nothing short of romantic. Here was a young
man who had evidently been making love to a
married woman, and who had made her believe
that he loved her, and had made her love him
too. Clare remembered the desperate little sob,
and the handkerchief twice pressed to the pale
lips. The woman was married, and yet she actually loved the man enough to think of divorcing her husband in order to marry him. Then,
just when she was ready, he had turned and
told her in the most heartless way that it had
been all play, and that he would not marry her

under any circumstances. It seemed monstrous
to the innocent girl that they should even have
spoken of marriage, until the divorce was accomplished. Then, of course, it would have
been all right. Clare had been brought up with
modern ideas about divorce in general, as being
a fair and just thing in certain circumstances.
She had learned that it could not be right to let
an innocent woman suffer all her life because
she had married a brute by mistake. Doubtless
that was Lady Fan's case. But she should have
got her divorce first, and then she might have
talked of marriage afterwards. It was very
wrong of her.

But Lady Fan's thoughtlessness — or wickedness, as Clare thought she ought to call it —
sank into insignificance before the cynical heartlessness of the man. It was impossible ever to
forget the cool way in which he had said she
ought not to take it so tragically, because it was
not worth it. Yet he had admitted that he had
promised to marry her if she got a divorce. He
had made love to her, there on the Acropolis, at
sunset, as she had said. He even granted that
he might have believed himself in earnest for a
few moments. And now he told her that he
was sorry, but that "it would not do." It had
evidently been all his fault, for he had found
nothing with which to reproach her. If there

E

had been anything, Clare thought, he would have brought it up in self-defence. She could not suspect that he would almost rather have married Lady Fan, and ruined his life, than have done that. Innocence cannot even guess at sin's code of honour — though sometimes it would be in evil case without it. Brook had probably broken Lady Fan's heart that night, thought the young girl, though Lady Fan had said with such a bitter, crying laugh that they were not children and that their hearts could not break.

And it all seemed very unreal, as she looked back upon it. The situation was certainly romantic, but the words had been poor beyond her imagination, and the actors had halted in their parts, as at a first rehearsal.

Then Clare reflected that of course neither of them had ever been in such a situation before, and that, if they were not naturally eloquent, it was not surprising that they should have expressed themselves in short, jerky sentences. But that was only an excuse she made to herself to account for the apparent unreality of it all. She turned her cheek to a cool end of the pillow and tried to go to sleep.

She tried to bring back the white dreams she had dreamt when she had sat alone in the shadow before the other two had come out to quarrel. She did her best to bring back that vague, soft joy of yearning for something beautiful and unknown. She tried to drop the silver veil of fancy-threads woven by the May moon between her and the world. But it would not come. Instead of it, she saw the flat platform, the man and woman standing in the unnatural brightness, and the woman's desperate little face when he had told her that she had never loved him. The dream was not white any more.

So that was life. That was reality. That was the way men treated women. She thought she began to understand what faithlessness and unfaithfulness meant. She had seen an unfaithful man, and had heard him telling the woman he had made love him that he never could love her any more. That was real life.

Clare's heart went out to the little lady in white. By this time she was alone in her cabin, and her pillow was wet with tears. Brook doubtless was calmly asleep, unless he were drinking or doing some of those vaguely wicked things which, in the imagination of very simple young girls, fill up the hours of fast men, and help sometimes to make those very men " interesting." But after what she had seen Clare felt that Brook could never interest her under imaginable circumstances. He was simply a " brute," as the lady in white had told him, and Clare wished that some woman could make him suffer for his sins and expiate the misdeeds which had made that little face so desperate and that short laugh so bitter.

She wished, though she hardly knew it, that she had done anything rather than have sat there in the shadow, all through the scene. She had lost something that night which it would be hard indeed to find again. There was a big jagged rent in the drop-curtain of illusions before her life-stage, and through it she saw things that troubled her and would not be forgotten.

She had no memory of her own of which the vivid brightness or the intimate sadness could diminish the force of this new impression. Possibly, she was of the kind that do not easily fall in love, for she had met during the past two years more than one man whom many a girl of her age and bringing up might have fancied. Some of them might have fallen in love with her, if she had allowed them, or if she had felt the least spark of interest in them and had shown it. But she had not. Her manner was cold and over-dignified for her years, and she had very little vanity together with much pride — too much of the latter, perhaps, to be ever what is called popular. For "popular" persons are generally those who wish to be such; and pride and the love of popularity are at opposite poles of the character-world. Proud characters

set love high and their own love higher, while a
vain woman will risk her heart for a compliment, and her reputation for the sake of having
a lion in her leash, if only for a day. Clare
Bowring had not yet been near to loving, and
she had nothing of her own to contrast with this
experience in which she had been a mere spec-
tator. It at once took the aspect of a generality.
This man and this woman were probably not
unlike most men and women, if the truth were
known, she thought. And she had seen the real
truth, as few people could ever have seen it —
the supreme crisis of a love-affair going on before
her very eyes, in her hearing, at her feet, the
actors having no suspicion of her presence. It
was, perhaps, the certainty that she could not
misinterpret it all which most disgusted her, and
wounded something in her which she had never
defined, but which was really a sort of belief
that love must always carry with it something
beautiful, whether joyous, or tender, or tragic.
Of that, there had been nothing in what she had
seen. Only the woman's face came back to her,
and hurt her, and she felt her own heart go out
to poor Lady Fan, while it hardened against
Brook with an exaggerated hatred, as though
he had insulted and injured all living women.

It was probable that she was to see this man
during several days to come. The idea struck

her when she was, almost asleep, and it waked
her again, with a start. It was quite certain
that he had stayed behind, when the others had
gone down to the yacht, for she had heard the
voices calling out " Good-bye, Brook ! " Besides
he had said repeatedly to the lady in white that
he must stay. He was expecting his people. It
was quite certain that Clare must see him during
the next day or two. It was not impossible that
he might try to make her mother's acquaintance
and her own. The idea was intensely disagreeable to her. In the first place, she hated him
beforehand for what he had done, and, secondly,
she had once heard his secret. It was one thing,
so long as he was a total stranger. It would be
quite another, if she should come to know him.
She had a vague thought of pretending to be ill,
and staying in her room as long as he remained
in the place. But in that case she should have
to explain matters to her mother. She should
not like to do that. The thought of the difficulty disturbed her a little while longer. Then,
at last, she fell asleep, tired with what she had
felt, and seen, and heard.

The yacht sailed before daybreak, and in the
morning the little hotel had returned to its normal state of peace. The early sun blazed upon
the white walls above, and upon the half-moon
beach below, and shot straight into the recess in

the rocks where Clare had sat by the old black
cross in the dark. The level beams ran through
her room, too, for it faced south-east, looking
across the gulf; and when she went to the window and stood in the sunshine, her flaxen hair
looked almost white, and the good southern
warmth brought soft colour to the northern
girl's cheeks. She was like a thin, fair angel,
standing there on the high balcony, looking to
seaward in the calm air. That, at least, was
what a fisherman from Praiano thought, as he
turned his hawk-eyes upwards, standing to his
oars and paddling slowly along, topheavy in his
tiny boat. But no native of Amalfi ever mistook
a foreigner for an angel.

Everything was quiet and peaceful again, and
there seemed to be neither trace nor memory of
the preceding day's invasion. The English old
maids were early at their window, and saw with
disappointment that the yacht was gone. They
were never to know whether the big man with
the gold cigarette case had been the Duke of
Orkney or not. But order was restored, and
they got their tea and toast without difficulty.
The Russian invalid was slicing a lemon into his
cup on the vine-sheltered terrace, and the German family, having slept on the question of the
Pope and Bismarck, were ruddy with morning
energy, and were making an early start for a

place in the hills where the Professor had heard
that there was an inscription of the ninth
century.

The young girl stood still on her balcony,
happily dazed for a few moments by the strong
sunshine and the clear air. It is probably the
sensation enjoyed for hours together by a dog
basking in the sun, but with most human beings
it does not last long — the sun is soon too hot
for the head, or too bright for the eyes, or there
is a draught, or the flies disturb one. Man is
not capable of as much physical enjoyment as
the other animals, though perhaps his enjoyment
is keener during the first moments. Then comes
thought, restlessness, discontent, change, effort,
and progress, and the history of man's superior-
ity is the journal of his pain.

For a little while, Clare stood blinking in the
sunshine, smitten into a pleasant semi-conscious-
ness by the strong nature around her. Then she
thought of Brook and the lady in white, and of
all she had been a witness of in the evening, and
the colour of things changed a little, and she
turned away and went between the little white
and red curtains into her room again. Life was
certainly not the same since she had heard and
seen what a man and a woman could say and be.
There were certain new impressions, where there
had been no impression at all, but only a maiden

readiness to receive the beautiful. What had come was not beautiful, by any means, and the thought of it darkened the air a little, so that the day was not to be what it might have been. She realised how she was affected, and grew impatient with herself. After all, it would be the easiest thing in the world to avoid the man, even if he stayed some time. Her mother was not much given to making acquaintance with strangers.

And it would have been easy enough, if the man himself had taken the same view. He, however, had watched the Bowrings on the preceding evening, and had made up his mind that they were "human beings," as he put it; that is to say, that they belonged to his own class, whereas none of the people at the upper end of the table had any claim to be counted with the social blessed. He was young, and though he knew how to amuse himself alone, and had all manner of manly tastes and inclinations, he preferred pleasant society to solitude, and his experience told him that the society of the Bowrings would in all probability be pleasant. He therefore determined that he would try to know them at once, and the determination had already been formed in his mind when he had run after Clare to give her the shawl she had dropped.

He got up rather late, and promptly marched out upon the terrace under the vines, smoking a briar-root pipe with that solemn air whereby the Englishman abroad proclaims to the world that he owns the scenery. There is something almost phenomenal about an Englishman's solid self-satisfaction when he is alone with his pipe. Every nation has its own way of smoking. There is a hasty and vicious manner about the Frenchman's little cigarette of pungent black tobacco; the Italian dreams over his rat-tail cigar; the American either eats half of his Havana while he smokes the other, or else he takes a frivolous delight in smoking delicately and keeping the white ash whole to the end; the German surrounds himself with a cloud, and, god-like, meditates within it; there is a sacrificial air about the Asiatic's narghileh, as the thin spire rises steadily and spreads above his head; but the Englishman's short briar-root pipe has a powerful individuality of its own. Its simplicity is Gothic, its solidity is of the Stone Age, he smokes it in the face of the higher civilisation, and it is the badge of the conqueror. A man who asserts that he has a right to smoke a pipe anywhere, practically asserts that he has a right to everything. And it will be admitted that Englishmen get a good deal.

Moreover, as soon as the Englishman has

finished smoking he generally goes and does
something else. Brook knocked the ashes out
of his pipe, and immediately went in search of
the head waiter, to whom he explained with
some difficulty that he wished to be placed next
tô the two ladies who sat last on the side away
from the staircase at the public table. The
waiter tried to explain that the two ladies,
though they had been some time in the hotel,
insisted upon being always last on that side because there was more air. But Brook was firm,
and he strengthened his argument with coin,
and got what he wanted. He also made the
waiter point out to him the Bowrings' name on
the board which held the names of the guests.
Then he asked the way to Ravello, turned up
his trousers round his ankles, and marched off
at a swinging pace down the steep descent towards the beach, which he had to cross before
climbing the hill to the old town. Nothing in
his outward manner or appearance betrayed that
he had been through a rather serious crisis on
the preceding evening.

That was what struck Clare Bowring when,
to her dismay, he sat down beside her at the
midday meal. She could not help glancing at
him as he took his seat. His eyes were bright,
his face, browned by the sun, was fresh and
rested. There was not a line of care or thought

on his forehead. The young girl felt that she
was flushing with anger. He saw her colour,
and took it for a sign of shyness. He made a
sort of apologetic movement of the head and
shoulders towards her which was not exactly a
bow — for to an Englishman's mind a bow is
almost a familiarity — but which expressed a
kind of vague desire not to cause any incon-
venience.

The colour deepened a little in Clare's face,
and then disappeared. She found something to
say to her mother, on her other side, which it
would hardly have been worth while to say at
all under ordinary circumstances. Mrs. Bowring
had glanced at the man while he was taking his
seat, and her eyebrows had contracted a little.
Later she looked furtively past her daughter at
his profile, and then stared a long time at her
plate. As for him, he began to eat with conscious strength, as healthy young men do, but he
watched his opportunity for doing or saying anything which might lead to a first acquaintance.

To tell the truth, however, he was in no
hurry. He knew how to make himself comfortable, and it was an important element in his
comfort to be seated next to the only persons in
the place with whom he should care to associate.
That point being gained, he was willing to wait
for whatever was to come afterwards. He did

not expect in any case to gain more than the chance of a little pleasant conversation, and he was not troubled by any youthful desire to shine in the eyes of the fair girl beside whom he found himself, beyond the natural wish to appear well before women in general, which modifies the conduct of all natural and manly young men when women are present at all.

As the meal proceeded, however, he was surprised to find that no opportunity presented itself for exchanging a word with his neighbour. He had so often found it impossible to avoid speaking with strangers at a public table that he had taken the probability of some little incident for granted, and caught himself glancing surreptitiously at Clare's plate to see whether there were nothing wanting which he might offer her. But he could not think of anything. The fried sardines were succeeded by the regulation braised beef with the gluey brown sauce which grows in most foreign hotels. That, in its turn, was followed by some curiously dry slices of spongecake, each bearing a bit of pink and white sugar frosting, and accompanied by fresh orange marmalade, which Brook thought very good, but which Clare refused. And then there was fruit — beautiful oranges, uncanny apples, and walnuts — and the young man foresaw the near end of the meal, and wished that something would happen. But still nothing happened at all.

He watched Clare's hands as she prepared an orange in the Italian fashion, taking off the peel at one end, then passing the knife twice completely round at right angles, and finally stripping the peel away in four neat pieces. The hands were beautiful in their way, too thin, perhaps, and almost too white from recent illness, but straight and elastic, with little blue veins at the sides of the finger-joints and exquisite nails that were naturally polished. The girl was clever with her fingers, she could not help seeing that her neighbour was watching her, and she peeled the orange with unusual skill and care. It was a good one, too, and the peel separated easily from the deep yellow fruit.

" How awfully jolly ! " exclaimed the young man, unconsciously, in genuine admiration.

He was startled by the sound of his own voice, for he had not meant to speak, and the blood rushed to his sunburnt face. Clare's eyes flashed upon him in a glance of surprise, and the colour rose in her cheeks also. She was evidently not pleased, and he felt that he had been guilty of a breach of English propriety. When an Englishman does a tactless thing he generally hastens to make it worse, becomes suddenly shy, and flounders.

"I — I beg your pardon," stammered Brook. "I really didn't mean to speak — that is — you did it so awfully well, you know!"

"It's the Italian way," Clare answered, beginning to quarter the orange.

She felt that she could not exactly be silent after he had apologised for admiring her skill. But she remembered that she had felt some vanity in what she had been doing, and had done it with some unnecessary ostentation. She hoped that he would not say anything more, for the sound of his voice reminded her of what she had heard him say to the lady in white, and she hated him with all her heart.

But the young man was encouraged by her sufficiently gracious answer, and was already glad of what he had done.

"Do all Italians do it that way?" he asked boldly.

"Generally," answered the young girl, and she began to eat the orange.

Brook took another from the dish before him.

"Let me see," he said, turning it round and round. "You cut a slice off one end." He began to cut the peel.

"Not too deep," said Clare, "or you will cut into the fruit."

"Oh — thanks, awfully. Yes, I see. This way?"

He took the end off, and looked at her for
approval.   She nodded gravely, and then turned
away her eyes.   He made the two cuts round
the peel, crosswise, and looked to her again, but
she affected not to see him.

"Oh — might I ask you —" he began.   She
looked at his orange again, without a smile.
" Please don't think me too dreadfully rude,"
he said.   " But it was so pretty, and I'm tremendously anxious to learn.   Was it this way?"

His fingers teased the peel, and it began to
come off.   He raised his eyes with another look
of inquiry.

" Yes.   That's all right," said Clare calmly.

She was going to look away again, when she
reflected that since he was so pertinacious it
would be better to see the operation finished
once for all.   Then she and her mother would
get up and go away, as they had finished.   But
he wished to push his advantage.

" And now what does one do ? " he asked, for
the sake of saying something.

" One   eats it," answered Clare, half impatiently.

He stared at her a moment and then broke
into a laugh, and Clare, very much to her own
surprise and annoyance, laughed too, in spite of
herself.   That broke the ice.   When two people
have laughed together over something one of

them has said, there is no denying the acquaintance.

"It was really awfully kind of you!" he exclaimed, his eyes still laughing. "It was horridly rude of me to say anything at all, but I really couldn't help it. If I could get anybody to introduce me, so that I could apologise properly, I would, you know, but in this place — "

He looked towards the German family and the English old maids, in a helpless sort of way, and then laughed again.

"I don't think it's necessary," said Clare rather coldly.

"No — I suppose not," he answered, growing graver at once. "And I think it is allowed — isn't it ? — to speak to one's neighbour at a table d'hôte, you know. Not but what it was awfully rude of me, all the same," he added hastily.

"Oh no. Not at all."

Clare stared at the wall opposite and leaned back in her chair.

"Oh! thanks awfully! I was afraid you might think so, you know."

Mrs. Bowring leaned forward as her daughter leaned back. Seeing that the latter had fallen into conversation with the stranger, she was too much a woman of the world not to speak to him at once in order to avoid any awkwardness when they next met, for he could

F

not possibly have spoken first to her across the
young girl.

" Is it your first visit to Amalfi? " she inquired,
with as much originality as is common in such
cases.

Brook leaned forward too, and looked over at
the elder woman.

" Yes," he answered, " I was with a party,
and they dropped me here last night.   I was to
meet my people here, but they haven't turned up
yet, so I'm seeing the sights.   I went up to Ravello this morning — you know, that place on the
hill.   There's an awfully good view from there,
isn't there ? "

Clare thought his fluency developed very
quickly when he spoke to her mother.   As he
leaned forward she could not help seeing his
face, and she looked at him closely, for the first
time, and with some curiosity.   He was handsome, and had a wonderfully frank and good-
humoured expression.   He was not in the least
a " beauty " man — she thought he might be a
soldier or a sailor, and a very good specimen of
either.   Furthermore, he was undoubtedly a gentleman, so far as a man is to be judged by his outward manner and appearance.   In her heart she
had already set him down as little short of a villain.   The discrepancy between his looks and
what she thought of him disturbed her.   It was

unpleasant to feel that a man who had acted as
he had acted last night could look as fresh, and
innocent, and unconcerned as he looked to-day.
It was disagreeable to have him at her elbow.
Either he had never cared a straw for poor Lady
Fan, and in that case he had almost broken her
heart out of sheer mischief and love of selfish
amusement, or else, if he had cared for her at all,
he was a pitiably fickle and faithless creature —
something much more despicable in the eyes of
most women than the most heartless cynic. One
or the other he must be, thought Clare. In either
case he was bad, because Lady Fan was married,
and it was wicked to make love to married
women. There was a directness about Clare's
view which would either have made the man
laugh or would have hurt him rather badly.
She wondered what sort of expression would
come over his handsome face if she were suddenly to tell him what she knew. The idea
took her by surprise, and she smiled to herself
as she thought of it.

Yet she could not help glancing at him again
and again, as he talked across her with her
mother, making very commonplace remarks
about the beauty of the place. Very much in
spite of herself, she wished to know him better,
though she already hated him. His face attracted
her strangely, and his voice was pleasant, close

to her ear.   He had not in the least the look of
the traditional lady-killer, of whom the tradition
seems to survive as a moral scarecrow for the
education of the young, though the creature is
extinct among Anglo-Saxons.   He was, on the
contrary, a manly man, who looked as though he
would prefer tennis to tea and polo to poetry —
and men to women for company, as a rule.   She
felt that if she had not heard him talking with
the lady in white she should have liked him
very much.   As it was, she said to herself that
she wished she might never see him again — and
all the time her eyes returned again and again
to his sunburnt face and profile, till in a few
minutes she knew his features by heart.

CHAPTER IV

A CHANCE acquaintance may, under favourable circumstances, develop faster than one brought about by formal introduction, because neither party has been previously led to expect anything of the other. There is no surer way of making friendship impossible than telling two people that they are sure to be such good friends, and are just suited to each other. The law of natural selection applies to almost everything we want in the world, from food and climate to a wife.

When Clare and her mother had established themselves as usual on the terrace under the vines that afternoon, Brook came and sat beside them for a while. Mrs. Bowring liked him and talked easily with him, but Clare was silent and seemed absent-minded. The young man looked at her from time to time with curiosity, for he was not used to being treated with such perfect indifference as she showed to him. He was not spoilt, as the phrase goes, but he had always been accustomed to a certain amount of attention, when he met new people, and, without

being in the least annoyed, he thought it strange
that this particular young lady should seem not
even to listen to what he said.

Mrs. Bowring, on the other hand, scarcely
took her eyes from his face after the first ten
minutes, and not a word he spoke escaped her.
By contrast with her daughter's behaviour, her
earnest attention was very noticeable. By degrees she began to ask him questions about himself.

"Do you expect your people to-morrow?"
she inquired.

Clare looked up quickly. It was very unlike
her mother to show even that small amount of
curiosity about a stranger. It was clear that
Mrs. Bowring had conceived a sudden liking for
the young man.

"They were to have been here to-day," he
answered indifferently. "They may come this
evening, I suppose, but they have not even
ordered rooms. I asked the man there — the
owner of the place, I suppose he is."

"Then of course you will wait for them,"
suggested Mrs. Bowring.

"Yes. It's an awful bore, too. That is — "
he corrected himself hastily — "I mean, if I were
to be here without a soul to speak to, you know.
Of course, it's different, this way."

"How?" asked Mrs. Bowring, with a brighter

smile than Clare had seen on her face for a long
time.

"Oh, because you are so kind as to let me
talk to you," answered the young man, without
the least embarrassment.

"Then you are a social person?" Mrs. Bowring laughed a little. "You don't like to be
alone?"

"Oh no! Not when I can be with nice people.
Of course not. I don't believe anybody does.
Unless I'm doing something, you know — shooting, or going up a hill, or fishing. Then I don't
mind. But of course I would much rather be
alone than with bores, don't you know? Or —
or — well, the other kind of people."

"What kind?" asked Mrs. Bowring.

"There are only two kinds," answered Brook,
gravely. "There is our kind — and then there
is the other kind. I don't know what to call
them, do you? All the people who never seem
to understand exactly what we are talking about
nor why we do things — and all that. I call
them 'the other kind.' But then I haven't a
great command of language. What should you
call them?"

"Cads, perhaps," suggested Clare, who had
not spoken for a long time.

"Oh no, not exactly," answered the young
man, looking at her. "Besides, 'cads' doesn't

include women, does it? A gentleman's son
sometimes turns out a most awful cad, a regular
'bounder.' It's rare, but it does happen sometimes. A mere cad may know, and understand'
all right, but he's got the wrong sort of feeling inside of him about most things. For instance — you don't mind? A cad may know
perfectly well that he ought not to 'kiss and
tell' — but he will all the same. The 'other
kind,' as I call them, don't even know. That
makes them awfully hard to get on with."

"Then, of the two, you prefer the cad?" inquired Clare coolly.

"No. I don't know. They are both pretty
bad. But a cad may be very amusing, sometimes."

"When he kisses and tells?" asked the
young girl viciously.

Brook looked at her, in quick surprise at her
tone.

"No," he answered quietly. "I didn't mean
that. The clowns in the circus represent amusing cads. Some of them are awfully clever,
too," he added, turning the subject. "Some of
those fiddling fellows are extraordinary. They
really play very decently. They must have a
lot of talent, when you think of all the different
things they do besides their feats of strength —
they act, and play the fiddle, and sing, and
dance — "

"You seem to have a great admiration for clowns," observed Clare in an indifferent tone.

"Well — they are amusing, aren't they? Of course, it isn't high art, and that sort of thing, but one laughs at them, and sometimes they do very pretty things. One can't be always on one's hind legs, doing Hamlet, can one? There's a limit to the amount of tragedy one can stand during life. After all, it is better to laugh than to cry."

"When one can," said Mrs. Bowring thoughtfully.

"Some people always can, whatever happens," said the young girl.

"Perhaps they are right," answered the young man. "Things are not often so serious as they are supposed to be. It's like being in a house that's supposed to be haunted — on All Hallow E'en, for instance — it's awfully gruesome and creepy at night when the wind moans and the owls screech. And then, the next morning, one wonders how one could have been such an idiot. Other things are often like that. You think the world's coming to an end — and then it doesn't, you know. It goes on just the same. You are rather surprised at first, but you soon get used to it. I suppose that is what is meant by losing one's illusions."

"Sometimes the world stops for an individual

and doesn't go on again," said Mrs. Bowring,
with a faint smile.

"Oh, I suppose people do break their hearts
sometimes," returned Brook, somewhat thoughtfully. "But it must be something tremendously
serious," he added with instant cheerfulness.
"I don't believe it happens often. Most people
just have a queer sensation in their throat for a
minute, and they smoke a cigarette for their
nerves, and go away and think of something
else."

Clare looked at him, and her eyes flashed
angrily, for she remembered Lady Fan's cigarette and the preceding evening. He remembered it too, and was thinking of it, for he
smiled as he spoke and looked away at the hori-
zon as though he saw something in the air. For
the first time in her life the young girl had a
cruel impulse. She wished that she were a great
beauty, or that she possessed infinite charm, that
she might revenge the little lady in white and
make the man suffer as he deserved. At one
moment she was ashamed of the wish, and then
again it returned, and she smiled as she thought
of it.

She was vaguely aware, too, that the man
attracted her in a way which did not interfere
with her resentment against him. She would
certainly not have admitted that he was inter-

esting to her on account of Lady Fan — but
there was in her a feminine willingness to play
with the fire at which another woman had
burned her wings. Almost all women feel that,
until they have once felt too much themselves.
The more innocent and inexperienced they are,
the more sure they are, as a rule, of their own perfect safety, and the more ready to run any risk.

Neither of the women answered the young
man's rather frivolous assertion for some moments. Then Mrs. Bowring looked at him
kindly, but with a far-away expression, as
though she were thinking of some one else.

"You are young," she said gently.

"It's true that I'm not very old," he answered.
"I was five-and-twenty on my last birthday."

"Five-and-twenty," repeated Mrs. Bowring
very slowly, and looking at the distance, with
the air of a person who is making a mental cal-
culation.

"Are you surprised?" asked the young man,
watching her.

She started a little.

"Surprised? Oh dear no! Why should I be?"

And again she looked at him earnestly, until,
realising what she was doing, she suddenly shut
her eyes, shook herself almost imperceptibly, and
took out some work which she had brought out
with her.

"Oh!" he exclaimed. "I thought you might fancy I was a good deal older or younger. But I'm always told that I look just my age."

"I think you do," answered Mrs. Bowring, without looking up.

Clare glanced at his face again. It was natural, under the circumstances, though she knew his features by heart already. She met his eyes, and for a moment she could not look away from them. It was as though they fixed her against her will, after she had once met them. There was nothing extraordinary about them, except that they were very bright and clear. With an effort she turned away, and the faint colour rose in her face.

"I am nineteen," she said quietly, as though she were answering a question.

"Indeed?" exclaimed Brook, not thinking of anything else to say.

Mrs. Bowring looked at her daughter in considerable surprise. Then Clare blushed painfully, realising that she had spoken without any intention of speaking, and had volunteered a piece of information which had certainly not been asked. It was very well, being but nineteen years old; but she was oddly conscious that if she had been forty she should have said so in just the same absent-minded way, at that moment.

"Nineteen and six are twenty-five, aren't they?" asked Mrs. Bowring suddenly.

"Yes, I believe so," answered the young man, with a laugh, but a good deal surprised in his turn, for the question seemed irrelevant and absurd in the extreme. "But I'm not good at sums," he added. "I was an awful idiot at school. They used to call me Log. That was short for logarithm, you know, because I was such a log at arithmetic. A fellow gave me the nickname one day. It wasn't very funny, so I punched his head. But the name stuck to me. Awfully appropriate, anyhow, as it turned out."

"Did you punch his head because it wasn't funny?" asked Clare, glad of the turn in the conversation.

"Oh — I don't know — on general principles. He was a diabolically clever little chap, though he wasn't very witty. He came out Senior Wrangler at Cambridge. I heard he had gone mad last year. Lots of those clever chaps do, you know. Or else they turn parsons and take pupils for a living. I'd much rather be stupid, myself. There's more to live for, when you don't know everything. Don't you think so?"

Both women laughed, and felt that the man was tactful. They were also both reflecting, of themselves and of each other, that they were not generally silly women, and they wondered how they had both managed to say such foolish things, speaking out irrelevantly what was passing in their minds.

"I think I shall go for a walk," said Brook, rising rather abruptly. "I'll go up the hill for a change. Thanks awfully. Good-bye!"

He lifted his hat and went off towards the hotel. Mrs. Bowring looked after him, but Clare leaned back in her seat and opened a book she had with her. The colour rose and fell in her cheeks, and she kept her eyes resolutely bent down.

"What a nice fellow!" exclaimed Mrs. Bowring when the young man was out of hearing. "I wonder who he is."

"What difference can it make, what his name is?" asked Clare, still looking down.

"What is the matter with you, child?" Mrs. Bowring asked. "You talk so strangely to-day!"

"So do you, mother. Fancy asking him whether nineteen and six are twenty-five!"

"For that matter, my dear, I thought it very strange that you should tell him your age, like that."

"I suppose I was absent-minded. Yes! I know it was silly, I don't know why I said it. Do you want to know his name? I'll go and see. It must be on the board by this time, as he is stopping here."

She rose and was going, when her mother called her back.

" Clare ! Wait till he is gone, at all events ! Fancy, if he saw you ! "

" Oh ! He won't see me ! If he comes that way I'll go into the office and buy stamps."

Clare went in and looked over the square board with its many little slips for the names of the guests. Some were on visiting cards and some were written in the large, scrawling, illiterate hand of the head waiter. Some belonged to people who were already gone. It looked well, in the little hotel, to have a great many names on the list. Some seconds passed before Clare found that of the new-comer.

" Mr. Brook Johnstone."

Brook was his first name, then. It was uncommon. She looked at it fixedly. There was no address on the small, neatly engraved card. While she was looking at it a door opened quietly behind her, in the opposite side of the corridor. She paid no attention to it for a moment ; then, hearing no footsteps, she instinctively turned. Brook Johnstone was standing on the threshold watching her. She blushed violently, in her annoyance, for he could not doubt but that she was looking for his name. He saw and understood, and came forward naturally, with a smile. He had a stick in his hand.

"That's me," he said, with a little laugh, tapping his card on the board with the head of his stick. "If I'd had an ounce of manners I should have managed to tell you who I was by this time. Won't you excuse me, and take this for an introduction? Johnstone — with an E at the end — Scotch, you know."

"Thanks," answered Clare, recovering from her embarrassment. "I'll tell my mother." She hesitated a moment. "And that's us," she added, laughing rather nervously and pointing out one of the cards. "How grammatical we are, aren't we?" she laughed, while he stooped and read the name which chanced to be at the bottom of the board.

"Well — what should one say? 'That's we.' It sounds just as badly. And you can't say 'we are that,' can you? Besides, there's no one to hear us, so it makes no difference. I don't suppose that you — you and Mrs. Bowring — would care to go for a walk, would you?"

"No," answered Clare, with sudden coldness. "I don't think so, thank you. We are not great walkers."

They went as far as the door together. Johnstone bowed and walked off, and Clare went back to her mother.

"He caught me," she said, in a tone of annoyance. "You were quite right. Then he showed

me his name himself, on the board. It's Johnstone — Mr. Brook Johnstone, with an E — he
says that he is Scotch. Why — mother! Johnstone! How odd! That was the name of — "

She stopped short and looked at her mother,
who had grown unnaturally pale during the last
few seconds.

" Yes, dear. That was the name of my first
husband."

Mrs. Bowring spoke in a low voice, looking
down at her work. But her hands trembled
violently, and she was clearly making a great
effort to control herself. Clare watched her
anxiously, not at all understanding.

" Mother dear, what is it ? " she asked. " The
name is only a coincidence — it's not such an
uncommon name, after all — and besides — "

" Oh, of course," said Mrs. Bowring, in a dull
tone. " It's a mere coincidence — probably no
relation. I'm nervous, to-day."

Her manner seemed unaccountable to her
daughter, except on the supposition that she
was ill. She very rarely spoke of her first husband, by whom she had no children. When she
did, she mentioned his name gravely, as one
speaks of dead persons who have been dear, but
that was all. She had never shown anything
like emotion in connection with the subject, and
the young girl avoided it instinctively, as most

children, of whose parents the one has been twice married, avoid the mention of the first husband or wife, who was not their father or mother.

"I wish I understood you!" exclaimed Clare.

"There's nothing to understand, dear," said Mrs. Bowring, still very pale. "I'm nervous — that's all."

Before long she left Clare by herself and went indoors, and locked herself into her room. The rooms in the old hotel were once the cells of the monks, small vaulted chambers in which there is barely space for the most necessary furniture. During nearly an hour Mrs. Bowring paced up and down, a beat of fourteen feet between the low window and the locked door. At last she stopped before the little glass, and looked at herself, and smoothed her streaked hair.

"Nineteen and six — are twenty-five," she said slowly in a low voice, and her eyes stared into their own reflection rather wildly.

CHAPTER V

BROOK JOHNSTONE's people did not come on the next day, nor on the day after that, but he expressed no surprise at the delay, and did not again say that it was a bore to have to wait for them. Meanwhile he spent a great deal of his time with the Bowrings, and the acquaintance ripened quickly towards intimacy, without passing near friendship, as such acquaintance sometimes will, when it springs up suddenly in the shallow ground of an out-of-the-way hotel on the Continent.

"For Heaven's sake don't let that man fall in love with you, Clare!" said Mrs. Bowring one morning, with what seemed unnecessary vehemence.

Clare's lip curled scornfully as she thought of poor Lady Fan.

"There isn't the slightest danger of that!" she answered. "Any more than there is of my falling in love with him," she added.

"Are you sure of that?" asked her mother. "You seem to like him. Besides, he is very nice, and very good-looking."

" Oh yes — of course he is. But one doesn't necessarily fall in love with every nice and good-looking man one meets."

Thereupon Clare cut the conversation short by going off to her own room. She had been expecting for some time that her mother would make some remark about the growing intimacy with young Johnstone. To tell the truth, Mrs. Bowring had not the slightest ground for anxiety in any previous attachment of her daughter. She was beginning to wonder whether Clare would ever show any preference for any man.

But she did not at all wish to marry her at present, for she felt that life without the girl would be unbearably lonely. On the other hand, Clare had a right to marry. They were poor. A part of their little income was the pension that Mrs. Bowring had been fortunate enough to get as the widow of an officer killed in action, but that would cease at her death, as poor Captain Bowring's allowance from his family had ceased at his death. The family had objected to the marriage from the first, and refused to do any-thing for his child after he was gone. It would go hard with Clare if she were left alone in the world with what her mother could leave her. On the other hand, that little, or the prospect of it, was quite safe, and would make a great difference to her, as a married woman. The

two lived on it, with economy. Clare could
certainly dress very well on it if she married a
rich man, but she could as certainly not afford
to marry a poor one.

As for this young Johnstone, he had not volunteered much information about himself, and,
though Mrs. Bowring sometimes asked him questions, she was extremely careful not to ask any
which could be taken in the nature of an inquiry as to his prospects in life, merely because
that might possibly suggest to him that she was
thinking of her daughter. And when an Englishman is reticent in such matters, it is utterly
impossible to guess whether he be a millionaire
or a penniless younger son. Johnstone never
spoke of money, in any connection. He never
said that he could afford one thing or could not
afford another. He talked a good deal of shooting and sport, but never hinted that his father
had any land. He never mentioned a family
place in the country, nor anything of the sort.
He did not even tell the Bowrings to whom the
yacht belonged in which he had come, though
he frequently alluded to things which had been
said and done by the party during a two months'
cruise, chiefly in eastern waters.

The Bowrings were quite as reticent about
themselves, and each respected the other's silence.
Nevertheless they grew intimate, scarcely know-

ing how the intimacy developed. That is to say, they very quickly became accustomed, all three, to one another's society. If Johnstone was out of the hotel first, of an afternoon, he moped about with his pipe in an objectless way, as though he had lost something, until the Bowrings came out. If he was writing letters and they appeared first, they talked in detached phrases and looked often towards the door, until he came and sat down beside them.

On the third evening, at dinner, he seemed very much amused at something, and then, as though he could not keep the joke to himself, he told his companions that he had received a telegram from his father, in answer to one of his own, informing him that he had made a mistake of a whole fortnight in the date, and must amuse himself as he pleased in the interval.

"Just like me!" he observed. "I got the letter in Smyrna or somewhere — I forget — and I managed to lose it before I had read it through. But I thought I had the date all right. I'm glad, at all events. I was tired of those good people, and it's ever so much pleasanter here."

Clare's gentle mouth hardened suddenly as she thought of Lady Fan. Johnstone had been thoroughly tired of her. That was what he meant when he spoke of "those good people."

"You get tired of people easily, don't you?"
she inquired coldly.

"Oh no — not always," answered Johnstone.

By this time he was growing used to her
sudden changes of manner and to the occasional
scornful speeches she made. He could not understand them in the least, as may'be imagined,
and having considerable experience he set them
down to the score of a certain girlish shyness,
which showed itself in no other way. He had
known women whose shyness manifested itself
in saying disagreeable things for which they
were sometimes sorry afterwards.

"No," he added reflectively. "I don't think
I'm a very fickle person."

Clare turned upon him the terrible innocence
of her clear blue eyes. She thought she knew
the truth about him too, and that he could not
look her in the face. But she was mistaken.
He met her glance fearlessly and quietly, with a
frank smile and a little wonder at its fixed
scrutiny. She would not look away, rude
though she might seem, nor be stared out of
countenance by a man whom she believed to be
false and untrue. But his eyes were very bright,
and in a few seconds they began to dazzle her,
and she felt her eyelids trembling violently. It
was a new sensation, and a very unpleasant one.

It seemed to her that the man had suddenly got some power over her. She made a strong effort and turned away her face, and again she blushed with annoyance.

"I beg your pardon," Johnstone said quickly, in a very low voice. "I didn't mean to be so rude."

Clare said nothing as she sat beside him, but she looked at the opposite wall, and her hand made an impatient little gesture as the fingers lay on the edge of the table. Possibly, if her mother had not been on her other side, she might have answered him. As it was, she felt that she could not speak just then. She was very much disturbed, as though something new and totally unknown had got hold of her. It was not only that she hated the man for his heartlessness, while she felt that he had some sort of influence over her, which was more than mere attraction. There was something beyond, deep down in her heart, which was nameless, and painful, but which she somehow felt that she wanted. And aside from it all, she was angry with him for having stared her out of countenance, forgetting that when she had turned upon him she had meant to do the same by him, feeling quite sure that he could not look her in the face.

They spoke little during the remainder of the

meal, for Clare was quite willing to show that
she was angry, though she had little right to be.
After all, she had looked at him, and he had
looked at her. After dinner she disappeared,
and was not seen during the remainder of the
evening.

When she was alone, however, she went over
the whole matter thoughtfully, and she made up
her mind that she had been hasty. For she was
naturally just. She said to herself that she
had no claim to the man's secrets, which she
had learned in a way of which she was not at
all proud; and that if he could keep his own
counsel, he, on his side, had a right to do so.
The fact that she knew him to be heartless and
faithless by no means implied that he was also
indiscreet, though when an individual has done
anything which we think bad we easily suppose
that he may do every other bad thing imaginable.
Johnstone's discretion, at least, was admirable,
now that she thought of it. His bright eyes and
frank look would have disarmed any suspicion
short of the certainty she possessed. There had
not been the least contraction of the lids, the
smallest change in the expression of his mouth,
not the faintest increase of colour in his young
face.

So much the worse, thought the young girl
suddenly. He was not only bad. He was also

an accomplished actor.   No doubt his eyes had
been as steady and bright and his whole face as
truthful when he had made love to Lady Fan at
sunset on the Acropolis.   Somehow, the allusion
to that scene had produced a vivid impression on
Clare's mind, and she often found herself wondering what he had said, and how he had looked
just then.

Her resentment against him increased as she
thought it all over, and again she felt a longing
to be cruel to him, and to make him suffer just
what he had made Lady Fan endure.

Then she was suddenly and unexpectedly over-
come by a shamed sense of her inability to accom-
plish any such act of justice.   It was as though
she had already tried, and had failed, and he
had laughed in her face and turned away.   It
seemed to her that there could be nothing in
her which could appeal to such a man.   There
was Lady Fan, much older, with plenty of experience, doubtless; and she had been deceived, and
betrayed, and abandoned, before the young girl's
very eyes.   What chance could such a mere girl
possibly have?   It was folly, and moreover it
was wicked of her to think of such things.   She
would be willingly lowering herself to his level,
trying to do the very thing which she despised
and hated in him, trying to outwit him, to out-
deceive him, to out-betray him.   One side of

her nature, at least, revolted against any such scheme. Besides, she could never do it.

She was not a great beauty; she was not extraordinarily clever — not clever at all, she said to herself in her sudden fit of humility; she had no "experience." That last word means a good deal more to most young girls than they can find in it after life's illogical surprises have taught them the terrible power of chance and mood and impulse.

She glanced at her face in the mirror, and looked away. Then she glanced again. The third time she turned to the glass she began to examine her features in detail. Lady Fan was a fair woman, too. But, without vanity, she had to admit that she was much better-looking than Lady Fan. She was also much younger and fresher, which should be an advantage, she thought. She wished that her hair were golden instead of flaxen; that her eyes were dark instead of blue; that her cheeks were not so thin, and her throat a shade less slender. Nevertheless, she would have been willing to stand any comparison with the little lady in white. Of course, compared with the famous beauties, some of whom she had seen, she was scarcely worth a glance. Doubtless, Brook Johnstone knew them all.

Then she gazed into her own eyes. She did

not know that a woman, alone, may look into her own eyes and blush and turn away. She looked long and steadily, and quite quietly. After all, they looked dark, for the pupils were very large and the blue iris was of that deep colour which borders upon violet. There was something a little unusual in them, too, though she could not quite make out what it was. Why did not all women look straight before them as she did? There must be some mysterious reason. It was a pity that her eyelashes were almost white. Yet they, too, added something to the peculiarity of that strange gaze.

"They are like periwinkles in a snowstorm!" exclaimed Clare, tired of her own face; and she turned from the mirror and went to bed.

CHAPTER VI

THE first sign that two people no longer stand
to each other in the relation of mere acquaintances is generally that the tones of their voices
change, while they feel a slight and unaccountable constraint when they happen to be left
alone together.

Two days passed after the little incident
which had occurred at dinner before Clare and
Johnstone were momentarily face to face out of
Mrs. Bowring's sight. At first Clare had not
been aware that her mother was taking pains to
be always present when the young man was
about, but when she noticed the fact she at once
began to resent it. Such constant watchfulness
was unlike her mother, un-English, and almost
unnatural. When they were all seated together
on the terrace, if Mrs. Bowring wished to go indoors to write a letter or to get something she
invented some excuse for making her daughter
go with her, and stay with her till she came out
again. A French or Italian mother could not
have been more particular or careful, but a
French or Italian girl would have been accus-

tomed to such treatment, and would not have seen anything unusual in it. But Mrs. Bowring had never acted in such a way before now, and it irritated the young girl extremely. She felt that she was being treated like a child, and that Johnstone must see it and think it ridiculous. At last Clare made an attempt at resistance, out of sheer contrariety.

"I don't want to write letters!" she answered impatiently. "I wrote two yesterday. It is hot indoors, and I would much rather stay here!"

Mrs. Bowring went as far as the parapet, and looked down at the sea for a moment. Then she came back and sat down again.

"It's quite true," she said. "It is hot indoors. I don't think I shall write, after all."

Brook Johnstone could not help smiling a little, though he turned away his face to hide his amusement. It was so perfectly evident that Mrs. Bowring was determined not to leave Clare alone with him that he must have been blind not to see it. Clare saw the smile, and was angry. She was nineteen years old, she had been out in the world, the terrace was a public place, Johnstone was a gentleman, and the whole thing was absurd. She took up her work and closed her lips tightly.

Johnstone felt the awkwardness, rose suddenly, and said he would go for a walk. Clare raised

her eyes and nodded as he lifted his hat. He
was still smiling, and her resentment deepened.
A moment later, mother and daughter were
alone. Clare did not lay down her work, nor
look up when she spoke.

"Really, mother, it's too absurd!" she exclaimed, and a little colour came to her cheeks.

"What is absurd, my dear?" asked Mrs.
Bowring, affecting not to understand.

"Your abject fear of leaving me for five
minutes with Mr. Johnstone. I'm not a baby.
He was laughing. I was positively ashamed!
What do you suppose could have happened, if
you had gone in and written your letters and
left us quietly here? And it happens every
day, you know! If you want a glass of water,
I have to go in with you."

"My dear! What an exaggeration!"

"It's not an exaggeration, mother — really.
You know that you wouldn't leave me with him
for five minutes, for anything in the world."

"Do you wish to be left alone with him, my
dear?" asked Mrs. Bowring, rather abruptly.

Clare was indignant.

"Wish it? No! Certainly not! But if it should
happen naturally, by accident, I should not get
up and run away. I'm not afraid of the man,
as you seem to be. What can he do to me?
And you have no idea how strangely you behave,

and what ridiculous excuses you invent for me.
The other day you insisted on my going in to
look for a train in the time-tables when you
know we haven't the slightest intention of going
away for ever so long. Really — you're turning
into a perfect duenna. I wish you would behave
naturally, as you always used to do."

" I think you exaggerate," said Mrs. Bowring.
"I never leave you alone with men you hardly
know — "

" You can't exactly say that we hardly know
Mr. Johnstone, when he has been with us, morning, noon, and night, for nearly a week, mother."

" My dear, we know nothing about him — "

" If you are so anxious to know his father's
Christian name, ask him. It wouldn't seem at
all odd. I will, if you like."

" Don't ! " cried Mrs. Bowring, with unusual
energy. "I mean," she added in a lower tone
and looking away, " it would be very rude —
he would think it very strange. In fact, it is
merely idle curiosity on my part — really, I
would much rather not know."

Clare looked at her mother in surprise.

" How oddly you talk ! " she exclaimed. Then
her tone changed. " Mother dear — is anything
the matter ? You don't seem quite — what shall
I say ? Are you suffering, dearest ? Has anything happened ? "

She dropped her work, and leaned forward, her hand on her mother's, and gazing into her face with a look of anxiety.

"No, dear," answered Mrs. Bowring. "No, no — it's nothing. Perhaps I'm a little nervous — that's all."

"I believe the air of this place doesn't suit you. Why shouldn't we go away at once?"

Mrs. Bowring shook her head and protested energetically.

"No — oh no! I wouldn't go away for anything. I like the place immensely, and we are both getting perfectly well here. Oh no! I wouldn't think of going away."

Clare leaned back in her seat again. She was devotedly fond of her mother, and she could not but see that something was wrong. In spite of what she said, Mrs. Bowring was certainly not growing stronger, though she was not exactly ill. The pale face was paler, and there was a worn and restless look in the long-suffering, almost colourless eyes.

"I'm sorry I made such a fuss about Mr. Johnstone," said Clare softly, after a short pause.

"No, darling," answered her mother instantly. "I dare say I have been a little over careful. I don't know — I had a sort of presentiment that you might take a fancy to him."

"I know. You said so the first day. But I

sha'n't, mother. You need not be at all afraid.
He is not at all the sort of man to whom I should
ever take a fancy, as you call it."

"I don't see why not," said Mrs. Bowring
thoughtfully.

"Of course — it's hard to explain." Clare
smiled. "But if that is what you are afraid of,
you can leave us alone all day. My 'fancy'
would be quite, quite different."

"Very well, darling. At all events, I'll try
not to turn into a duenna."

Johnstone did not appear again until dinner,
and then he was unusually silent, only exchanging a remark with Clare now and then, and not
once leaning forward to say a few words to Mrs.
Bowring as he generally did. The latter had
at first thought of exchanging places with her
daughter, but had reflected that it would be
almost a rudeness to make such a change after
the second day.

They went out upon the terrace, and had
their coffee there. Several of the other people
did the same, and walked slowly up and down
under the vines. Mrs. Bowring, wishing to destroy as soon as possible the unpleasant impression she had created, left the two together,
saying that she would get something to put
over her shoulders, as the air was cool.

Clare and Johnstone stood by the parapet and

looked at each other. Then Clare leaned with her elbows on the wall and stared in silence at the little lights on the beach below, trying to make out the shapes of the boats which were hauled up in a long row. Neither spoke for a long time, and Clare, at least, felt unpleasantly the constraint of the unusual silence.

"It is a beautiful place, isn't it?" observed Johnstone at last, for the sake of hearing his own voice.

"Oh yes, quite beautiful," answered the young girl in a half-indifferent, half-discontented tone, and the words ended with a sort of girlish sniff.

Again there was silence. Johnstone, standing up beside her, looked towards the hotel, to see whether Mrs. Bowring were coming back. But she was anxious to appear indifferent to their being together, and was in no hurry to return. Johnstone sat down upon the wall, while Clare leaned over it.

"Miss Bowring!" he said suddenly, to call her attention.

"Yes?" She did not look up; but to her own amazement she felt a queer little thrill at the sound of his voice, for it had not its usual tone.

"Don't you think I had better go to Naples?" he asked.

Clare felt herself start a little, and she waited a moment before she said anything in reply. She did not wish to betray any astonishment in her voice. Johnstone had asked the question under a sudden impulse; but a far wiser and more skilful man than himself could not have hit upon one better calculated to precipitate intimacy. Clare, on her side, was woman enough to know that she had a choice of answers, and to see that the answer she should choose must make a difference hereafter. At the same time, she had been surprised, and when she thought of it afterwards it seemed to her that the question itself had been an impertinent one, merely because it forced her to make an answer of some sort. She decided in favour of making everything as clear as possible.

"Why?" she asked, without looking round.

At all events she would throw the burden of an elucidation upon him. He was not afraid of taking it up.

"It's this," he answered. "I've rather thrust my acquaintance upon you, and, if I stay here until my people come, I can't exactly change my seat and go and sit at the other end of the table, nor pretend to be busy all day, and never 'come out here and sit with you, after telling you repeatedly that I have nothing on earth to do. Can I?"

"Why should you?"

"Because Mrs. Bowring doesn't like me."

Clare rose from her elbows and stood up, resting her hands upon the wall, but still looking down at the lights on the beach.

"I assure you, you're quite mistaken," she answered, with quiet emphasis. "My mother thinks you're very nice."

"Then why—" Johnstone checked himself, and crumbled little bits of mortar from the rough wall with his thumbs.

"Why what?"

"I don't know whether I know you well enough to ask the question, Miss Bowring."

"Let's assume that you do—for the sake of argument," said Clare, with a short laugh, as she glanced at his face, dimly visible in the falling darkness.

"Thanks awfully," he answered, but he did not laugh with her. "It isn't exactly an easy thing to say, is it? Only—I couldn't help noticing—I hope you'll forgive me, if you think I'm rude, won't you? I couldn't help noticing that your mother was most awfully afraid of leaving us alone for a minute, you know—as though she thought I were a suspicious character, don't you know? Something of that sort. So, of course, I thought she didn't like me. Do you see? Tremendously cheeky of me to talk in this way, isn't it?"

"Do you know ? It is, rather." Clare was more inclined to laugh than before, but she only smiled in the dark.

"Well, it would be, of course, if I didn't happen to be so painfully respectable."

"Painfully respectable! What an expression!" This time, Clare laughed aloud.

"Yes. That's just it. Well, I couldn't exactly tell Mrs. Bowring that, could I? Besides, one isn't vain of being respectable. I couldn't say, Please, Mrs. Bowring, my father is Mr. Smith, and my mother was a Miss Brown, of very good family, and we've got five hundred a year in Consols, and we're not in trade, and I've been to a good school, and am not at all dangerous. It would have sounded so — so uncalled for, don't you know? Wouldn't it?"

"Very. But now that you've explained it to me, I suppose I may tell my mother, mayn't I? Let me see. Your father is Mr. Smith, and your mother was a Miss Brown — "

"Oh, please — no!" interrupted Johnstone. "I didn't mean it so very literally. But it is just about that sort of thing — just like anybody else. Only about our not being in trade, I'm not so sure of that. My father is a brewer. Brewing is not a profession, so I suppose it must be a trade, isn't it?"

"You might call it a manufacture," suggested Clare.

"Yes. It sounds better. But that isn't the question, you know. You'll see my people when they come, and then you'll understand what I mean — they really are tremendously respectable."

"Of course!" assented the young girl. "Like the party you came with on the yacht. That kind of people."

"Oh dear no!" exclaimed Johnstone. "Not at all those kind of people. They wouldn't like it at all, if you said so."

"Ah! indeed!" Clare was inclined to laugh again.

"The party I came with belong rather to a gay set. Awfully nice, you know," he hastened to add, "and quite the people one knows at home. But my father and mother — oh no! they are quite different — the difference between whist and baccarat, you know, if you understand that sort of thing — old port and brandy and soda — both very good in their way, but quite different."

"I should think so."

"Then —" Johnstone hesitated again. "Then, Miss Bowring — you don't think that your mother really dislikes me, after all?"

"Oh dear no! Not in the least. I've heard her say all sorts of nice things about you."

"Really? Then I think I'll stay here. I didn't want to be a nuisance, you know — always in the way."

"You're not in the way," answered Clare.

Mrs. Bowring came back with her shawl, and the rest of the evening passed off as usual. Later, when she was alone, the young girl remembered all the conversation, and she saw that it had been in her power to make Johnstone leave Amalfi. While she was wondering why she had not done so, since she hated him for what she knew of him, she fell asleep, and the question remained unanswered. In the morning she told the substance of it all to her mother, and ended by telling her that Johnstone's father was a brewer.

"Of course," answered Mrs. Bowring absently. "I know that." Then she realised what she had said, and glanced at Clare with an odd, scared look.

Clare uttered an exclamation of surprise.

"Mother! Why, then — you knew all about him! Why didn't you tell me?"

A long silence followed, during which Mrs. Bowring sat with her face turned from her daughter. Then she raised her hand and passed it slowly over her forehead, as though trying to collect her thoughts.

"One comes across very strange things in

life, my dear," she said at last. " I am not sure
that we had not better go away, after all. I'll
think about it."

Beyond this Clare could get no information,
nor any explanation of the fact that Mrs. Bowring should have known something about Brook
Johnstone's father. The girl made a guess, of
course. The elder Johnstone must be a relation
of her mother's first husband ; though, considering that Mrs. Bowring had never seen Brook
before now, and that the latter had never told
her anything about his father, it was hard to
see how she could be so sure of the fact. Possibly, Brook strongly resembled his father's family.
That, indeed, was the only admissible theory.
But all that Clare knew and could put together
into reasonable shape could not explain why her
mother so much disliked leaving her alone with
the man, even for five minutes.

In this, however, Mrs. Bowring changed suddenly, after the first evening when she had left
them on the terrace. She either took a totally
different view of the situation, or else she was
ashamed of seeming to watch them all the
time, and the consequence was that during the
next three or four days they were very often
together without her.

Johnstone enjoyed the young girl's society,
and did not pretend tŏ deny the fact in his own

thoughts. Whatever mischief he might have
been in while on the yacht, his natural instincts
were simple and honest. In a certain way, Clare
was a revelation to him of something to which
he had never been accustomed, and which he
had most carefully avoided. He had no sisters,
and as a boy he had not been thrown with girls.
He was an only. son, and his mother, a very
practical woman, had warned him as he grew
up that he was a great match, and had better
avoid young girls altogether until he saw one
whom he should like to marry, though how he
was to see that particular one, if he avoided all
alike, was a question into which his mother did
not choose to enter. Having first gone into
society upon this principle, however, and having
been at once taken up and made much of by an
extremely fashionable young woman afflicted
with an elderly and eccentric husband, it was
not likely that Brook would return to the
threshold of the schoolroom for women's society.
He went on as he had begun in his first "salad"
days, and at five-and-twenty he had the reputation of having done more damage than any of
his young contemporaries, while he had never
once shown the slightest inclination to marry.
His mother, always a practical woman, did not
press the question of marriage, deeming that
with his disposition he would stand a better

chance of married peace when he had expended
a good deal of what she called his vivacity;
and his father, who came of very long-lived
people, always said that no man should take a
wife before he was thirty. As Brook did not
gamble immoderately, nor start a racing stable,
nor propose to manage an opera troupe, the
practical lady felt that he was really a very good
young man. His father liked him for his own
sake; but as Adam Johnstone had been gay in
his youth, in spite of his sober Scotch blood,
even beyond the bounds of ordinary "fastness,"
the fact of his being fond of Brook was not of
itself a guarantee that the latter was such a very
good young man as his mother said that he was.
Somehow or other Brook had hitherto managed
to keep clear of any entanglement which could
hamper his life, probably by virtue of that hardness which he had shown to poor Lady Fan, and
which had so strongly prejudiced Clare Bowring
against him. His father said cynically that
the lad was canny. Hitherto he had certainly
shown that he could be selfish; and perhaps
there is less difference between the meanings of
the Scotch and English words than most people
suppose.

Daily and almost hourly intercourse with
such a young girl as Clare was a totally new
experience to Brook Johnstone, and there were

moments when he hardly recognised himself for the man who had landed from the yacht ten days earlier, and who had said good-bye to Lady Fan on the platform behind the hotel.

Hitherto he had always known in a day or two whether he was inclined to make love to a woman or not. An inclination to make love and the satisfaction of it had been, so far, his nearest approach to being in love at all. Nor, when he had felt the inclination, had he ever hesitated. Like a certain great English states-man of similar disposition, he had sometimes been repulsed, but he never remembered having given offence. For he possessed that tactful intuition which guides some men through life in their intercourse with women. He rarely spoke the first word too soon, and if he were going to speak at all he never spoke too late — which error is, of the two, by far the greater. He was young, perhaps, to have had such experi-ence; but in the social world of to-day it is especially the fashion for men to be extremely young, even to youthfulness, and lack of years is no longer the atrocious crime which Pitt would neither attempt to palliate or deny. We have just emerged from a period of wrinkles and paint, during which we were told that age knew everything and youth nothing. The ex-plosion into nonsense of nine tenths of all we

were taught at school and college has given
our children a terrible weapon against us; and
women, who are all practical in their own way,
prefer the blundering whole-heartedness of youth
to the skilful tactics and over-effective effects
of the middle-aged love-actor. In this direction,
at least, the breeze that goes before the dawn of
a new century is already blowing. Perhaps it
is a good sign — but a sign of some sort it
certainly is.

Brook Johnstone felt that he was in an unfamiliar position, and he tried to analyse his own
feelings. He was perfectly honest about it, but
he had very little talent for analysis. On the
other hand, he had a very keen sense of what
we roughly call honour. Clare was not Lady
Fan, and would probably never get into that
category. Clare belonged amongst the women
whom he respected, and he respected them all,
with all his heart. They included all young
girls, and his mother, and all young women who
were happily married. It will be admitted that,
for a man who made no pretence to higher vir-
tues, Brook was no worse than his contemporaries, and was better than a great many.

Be that as it may, in lack of any finer means
of discrimination, he tried to define his own
position with regard to Clare Bowring very simply and honestly. Either he was falling in love,

or he was not. Secondly, Clare was either the
kind of girl whom he should like to marry,
spoken of by his practical mother — or she was
not.

So far, all was extremely plain. The trouble
was that he could not find any answers to the
questions. He could not in the least be sure
that he was falling in love, because he knew
that he had never really been in love in his life.
And as for saying at once that Clare was, or
was not, the girl whom he should like to marry,
how in the world could he tell that, unless he
fell in love with her? Of course he did not
wish to marry her unless he loved her. But he
conceived it possible that he might fall in love
with her and then not wish to marry her after
all, which, in his simple opinion, would have
been entirely despicable. If there were any
chance of that, he ought to go away at once.
But he did not know whether there were any
chance of it or not. He could go away in any
case, in order to be on the safe side ; but then,
there was no reason in the world why he should
not marry her, if he should love her, and if she
would marry him. The question became very
badly mixed, and under the circumstances he
told himself that he was splitting hairs on the
mountains he had made of his molehills. He
determined to stay where he was. At all events,

judging from all signs with which he was acquainted, Clare was very far indeed from being
in love with him, so that in this respect his sense
of honour was perfectly safe and undisturbed.

Having set his mind at rest in this way, he
allowed himself to talk with her as he pleased.
There was no reason why he should hamper himself in conversation, so long as he said nothing
calculated to make an impression — nothing
which could come under the general head of
"making love." The result was that he was
much more agreeable than he supposed. Clare's
innocent eyes watched him, and her mind was
divided about him.

She was utterly young and inexperienced, but
she was a woman, and she believed him to be
false, faithless, and designing. She had no idea
of the broad distinction he drew between all good
and innocent women like herself, and all the rest
whom he considered lawful prey. She concluded
therefore, very rashly, that he was simply pur-
suing his usual tactics, a main part of which
consisted in seeming perfectly unaffected and
natural while only waiting for a faint sign of
encouragement in order then to play the part of
the passionate lover.

The generalisations of youth are terrible.
What has failed once is despicably damned for
ever. What is true to-day is true enough to-

morrow to kill all other truths outright. The
man whose hand has shaken once is a coward;
he who has fought one battle is to be the hero
of seventy. Life is a forest of inverted pyra-
mids, for the young; upon every point is bal-
anced a gigantic weight of top-heavy ideals,
spreading base-upwards.

To Clare, everything Johnstone said or did
was the working of a faithless intention towards
its end. It was clear enough that he sought her
and stayed with her as long as he could, day by
day. Therefore he intended to make love to her,
sooner or later, and then, when he was tired, he
would say good-bye to her just as he had said
good-bye to Lady Fan, and break her heart, and
have one story more to laugh over when he was
alone. It was quite clear that he could not mean
anything else, after what she had seen.

All the same, he pleased her when he was
with her, and attracted her oddly. She told herself that unless he had some unusual qualities
he could not possibly break hearts for pastime,
as he undoubtedly did, from year's end to year's
end. She studied the question, and reached the
conclusion that his strength was in his eyes.
They were the most frank, brave, good-hu-
moured, clear, unaffected eyes she had ever
seen, but she could not look at them long. There
was no reason why she should, indeed, but she

hated to feel that she could not, if she chose. Whenever she tried, she at once had the feeling that he had power over her, to make her do things she did not wish to do. That was probably the way in which he had influenced Lady Fan and the other women, probably a dozen, thought Clare. If they were really as honest as they seemed, she thought she should have been able to meet them without the least sensation of nervousness.

One day she caught herself wishing that he had never done the thing she so hated. She was too honest to attribute to him outward defects which he did not possess, and she could not help thinking what a fine fellow he would be if he were not so bad. She might have liked him very much, then. But as it was, it was impossible that she should ever not hate him. Then she smiled to herself, as she thought how surprised he would be if he could guess what she thought of him.

But there was no probability of that, for she felt that she had no right to know what she knew, and so she treated him always, as she thought, with the same even, indifferent civility. But not seldom she knew that she was wickedly wishing that he might really fall in love with her and find out that men could break their hearts as well as women. She should like to

fight with him, with his own weapons, for the
glory of all her sex, and make him thoroughly
miserable for his sins.   It could not be wrong
to wish that, after what she had seen, but it
would be very wrong to try and make him fall in
love, just with that intention.   That would be
almost as bad as what he had done; not quite
so bad, of course, because it would serve him
right, but yet a deed which she might be
ashamed to remember.

She herself felt perfectly safe.   She was neither
sentimental nor susceptible, for if she had been
one or the other she must by this time have had
some "experience," as she vaguely called it.
But she had not.   She had never even liked
any man so much as she liked this man whom
she hated.   This was not a contradiction of
facts, which, as Euclid teaches us, is impossible.
She liked him for what she saw, and she hated
him for what she knew.

One day, when Mrs. Bowring was present, the
conversation turned upon a recent novel in which
the hero, after making love to a woman, found
that he had made a mistake, and promptly
made love to her sister, whom he married in
the end.

"I despise that sort of man!" cried Clare,
rather vehemently, and flashing her eyes upon
Johnstone.

For a moment she had thought that she could surprise him, that he would look away, or change colour, or in some way betray his most guilty conscience. But he did not seem in the least disturbed, and met her glance as calmly as ever.

"Do you?" he asked with an indifferent laugh. "Why? The fellow was honest, at all events. He found that he didn't love the one to whom he was engaged, and that he did love the other. So he set things straight before it was too late, and married the right one. He was a very sensible man, and it must have taken courage to be so honest about it."

"Courage!" exclaimed the young girl in high scorn. "He was a brute and a coward!"

"Dear me!" laughed Brook. "Don't you admit that a man may ever make a mistake?"

"When a man makes a mistake of that sort, he should either cut his throat, or else keep his word to the woman and try to make her happy."

"That's a violent view — really! It seems to me that when a man has made a mistake the best thing to do is to go and say so. The bigger the mistake, the harder it is to acknowledge it, and the more courage it needs. Don't you think so, Mrs. Bowring?"

"The mistake of all mistakes is a mistake in marriage," said the elder woman, looking away. "There is no remedy for that, but death"

"Yes," answered Clare. "But don't you think that I'm right? It's what you say, after all —"

"Not exactly, my dear. No man who doesn't love a woman can make her happy for long."

"Well — a man who makes a woman think that he loves her, and then leaves her for some one else, is a brute, and a beast, and a coward, and a wretch, and a villain — and I hate him, and so do all women!"

"That's categorical!" observed Brook, with a laugh. "But I dare say you are quite right in theory, only practice is so awfully different, you know. And a woman doesn't thank a man for pretending to love her."

Clare's eyes flashed almost savagely, and her lip curled in scorn.

"There's only one right," she said. "I don't know how many wrongs there are — and I don't want to know!"

"No," answered Brook, gravely enough. "And there is no reason why you ever should."

CHAPTER VII

"You seemed to be most tremendously in earnest yesterday, when we were talking about that book," observed Brook on the following afternoon.

"Of course I was," answered Clare. "I said just what I thought."

They were walking together along the high road which leads from Amalfi towards Salerno. It is certainly one of the most beautiful roads in Europe, and in the whole world. The chain of rocky heights dashes with wild abruptness from its five thousand feet straight to the dark-blue sea, bristling with sharp needles and spikes of stone, rough with a chaos of brown boulders, cracked from peak to foot with deep torn gorges. In each gorge nestles a garden of orange and lemons and pomegranates, and out of the stones there blows a perfume of southern blossom through all the month of May. The sea lies dark and clear below, ever tideless, often still as a woodland pool; then, sometimes, it rises suddenly in deep-toned wrath, smiting the face of the cliff, booming through the low-mouthed caves, curling its great green curls and combing them out to frothing ringlets along the strips of beach, winding itself about the rock of Conca in a heavily gleaming sheet and whirling its wraith of foam to heaven, the very ghost of storm.

And in the face of those rough rocks, high above the water, is hewn a way that leads round the mountain's base, many miles along it, over the sharp-jutting spurs, and in between the boulders and the needles, down into the gardens of the gorges and past the dark towers whence watchmen once descried the Saracen's ill-boding sail and sent up their warning beacon of smoke by day and fire by night.

It is the most beautiful road in the world, in its infinite variety, in the grandeur above and the breadth below, and the marvellous rich sweetness of the deep gardens — passing as it does out of wilderness into splendour, out of splendour into wealth of colour and light and odour, and again out to the rugged strength of the loneliness beyond.

Clare and Johnstone had exchanged idle phrases for a while, until they had passed Atrani and the turn where the new way leads up to Ravello, and were fairly out on the road. They were both glad to be out together and walking, for Clare had grown stronger, and was weary of always sitting on the terrace, and

Johnstone was tired of taking long walks alone, merely for the sake of being hungry afterwards, and of late had given it up altogether. Mrs. Bowring herself was glad to be alone for once, and made little or no objection, and so the two had started in the early afternoon.

Johnstone's remark had been premeditated, for his curiosity had been aroused on the preceding day by Clare's words and manner. But after she had given him her brief answer she said no more, and they walked on in silence for a few moments.

"Yes," said Johnstone at last, as though he had been reflecting, "you generally say what you think. I didn't doubt it at the time. But you seem rather hard on the men. Women are all angels, of course — "

"Not at all!" interrupted Clare. "Some of us are quite the contrary."

"Well, it's a generally accepted thing, you know. That's what I mean. But it isn't generally accepted that men are. If you take men into consideration at all, you must make some allowances."

"I don't see why. You are much stronger than we are. You all think that you have much more pride. You always say that you have a sense of honour which we can't understand. I should think that with all those advantages you would be much too proud to insist upon our making allowances for you."

"That's rather keen, you know," answered Brook, with a laugh. "All the same, it's a woman's occupation to be good, and a man has a lot of other things to do besides. That's the plain English of it. When a woman isn't good she falls. When a man is bad, he doesn't — it's his nature."

"Oh — if you begin by saying that all men are bad! That's an odd way out of it."

"Not at all. Good men and bad women are the exceptions, that's all — in the way you mean goodness and badness."

"And how do you think I mean goodness and badness? It seems to me that you are taking a great deal for granted, aren't you?"

"Oh, I don't know," said Brook, growing vague on a sudden. "Those are rather hard things to talk about."

"I like to talk about them. How do you think I understand those two words?"

"I don't know," repeated Johnstone, still more vaguely. "I suppose your theory is that men and women are exactly equal, and that a man shouldn't do what a woman ought not to do — and all that, you know. I don't exactly know how to put it."

"I don't see why what is wrong for a woman

should be right for a man," said Clare. "The law doesn't make any difference, does it? A man goes to prison for stealing or forging, and so does a woman. I don't see why society should make any distinction about other things. If there were a law against flirting, it would send the men to prison just like the women, wouldn't it?"

"What an awful idea!" laughed Brook.

"Yes, but in theory —"

"Oh, in theory it's all right. But in practice we men are not wrapped in cotton and tied up with pink ribbons from the day we are born to the day we are married. I — I don't exactly know how to explain what I mean, but that's the general idea. Among poor people — I believe one mustn't say the lower classes any more — well, with them it isn't quite the same. The women don't get so much care and looking after, when they are young, you know — that sort of thing. The consequence is, that there's much more equality between men and women. I believe the women are worse, and the men are better — it's my opinion, at all events. I dare say it isn't worth much. It's only what I see at home, you know."

"But the working people don't flirt!" exclaimed Clare. "They drink, and that sort of thing —"

"Yes, lots of them drink, men and women. And as for flirting — they don't call it flirting, but in their way I dare say it's very much the same thing. Only, in our part of the country, a man who flirts, if you call it so, gets just as bad a name as a woman. You see, they have all had about the same bringing up. But with us it's quite different. A girl is brought up in a cage, like a turtle dove, with nothing to do except to be good, while a boy is sent to a public school when he is eleven or twelve, which is exactly the same as sending him to hell, except that he has the certainty of getting away."

"But boys don't learn to flirt at Eton," observed the young girl.

"Well — no," answered Johnstone. "But they learn everything else, except Latin and Greek, and they go to a private tutor to learn those things before they go to the university."

"You mean that they learn to drink and gamble, and all that?" asked Clare.

"Oh — more or less — a little of everything that does no good — and then you expect us afterwards to be the same as you are, who have been brought up by your mothers at home. It isn't fair, you know."

"No," answered Clare, yielding. "It isn't fair. That strikes me as the best argument you have used yet. But it doesn't make it right, for all that. And why shouldn't men be brought up to be good, just as women are?"

Brook laughed.

"That's quite another matter. Only a paternal government could do that — or a maternal government. We haven't got either, so we have to do the best we can. I only state the fact, and you are obliged to admit it. I can't go back to the reason. The fact remains. In certain ways, at a certain age, all men as a rule are bad, and all women, on the whole, are good. Most of you know it, and you judge us accordingly and make allowances. But you yourself don't seem inclined to be merciful. Perhaps you'll be less hard-hearted when you are older."

"I'm not hard-hearted!" exclaimed Clare, indignantly. "I'm only just. And I shall always be the same, I'm sure."

"If I were a Frenchman," said Brook, "I should be polite, and say that I hoped so. As I'm not, and as it would be rude to say that I didn't believe it, I'll say nothing. Only to be what you call just, isn't the way to be liked, you know."

"I don't want to be liked," Clare answered, rather sharply. "I hate what are called popular people!"

"So do I. They are generally awful bores, don't you know? They want to keep the thing up and be liked all the time."

"Well — if one likes people at all, one ought to like them all the time," objected Clare, with unnecessary contrariety.

"That was the original point," observed Brook. "That was your objection to the man in the book — that he loved first one sister and then the other. Poor chap! The first one loved him, and the second one prayed for him! He had no luck!"

"A man who will do that sort of thing is past praying for!" retorted the young girl. "It seems to me that when a man makes a woman believe that he loves her, the best thing he can do is to be faithful to her afterwards."

"Yes — but supposing that he is quite sure that he can't make her happy —"

"Then he had no right to make love to her at all."

"But he didn't know it at first. He didn't find out until he had known her a long time."

"That makes it all the worse," exclaimed Clare with conviction, but without logic.

"And while he was trying to find out, she fell in love with him," continued Brook. "That was unlucky, but it wasn't his fault, you know —"

"Oh yes, it was — in that book at least. He asked her to marry him before he had half made up his mind. Really, Mr. Johnstone," she continued, almost losing her temper, "you defend the man almost as though you were defending yourself!"

"That's rather a hard thing to say to a man, isn't it?"

Johnstone was young enough to be annoyed, though he was amused.

"Then why do you defend the man?" asked Clare, standing still at a turn of the road and facing him.

"I won't, if we are going to quarrel about a ridiculous book," he answered, looking at her. "My opinion's not worth enough for that."

"If you have an opinion at all, it's worth fighting for."

"I don't want to fight, and I won't fight with you," he answered, beginning to laugh.

"With me or with any one else — "

"No — not with you," he said with sudden emphasis.

"Why not with me?"

"Because I like you very much," he answered boldly, and they stood looking at each other in the middle of the road.

Clare had started in surprise, and the colour rose slowly to her face, but she would not take her eyes from his. For the first time it seemed to her that he had no power over her.

"I'm sorry," she answered. "For I don't like you."

"Are you in earnest?" He could not help laughing.

"Yes." There was no mistaking her tone.

Johnstone's face changed, and for the first time in their acquaintance he was the one to turn his eyes away.

"I'm sorry too," he said quietly. "Shall we turn back?" he asked after a moment's pause.

"No, I want to walk," answered Clare.

She turned from him, and began to walk on in silence. For some time neither spoke. Johnstone was puzzled, surprised, and a little hurt, but he attributed what she had said to his own roughness in telling her that he liked her, though he could not see that he had done anything so very terrible. He had spoken spontaneously, too, without the least thought of producing an impression, or of beginning to make love to her. Perhaps he owed her an apology. If she thought so, he did, and it could do no harm to try.

"I'm very sorry, if I have offended you just now," he said gently. "I didn't mean to."

"You didn't offend me," answered Clare. "It isn't rude to say that one likes a person."

"Oh — I beg your pardon — I thought perhaps —"

He hesitated, surprised by her very unexpected answer. He could not imagine what she wanted.

"Because I said that I didn't like you?" she asked.

"Well — yes."

"Then it was I who offended you," answered the young girl. "I didn't mean to, either. Only, when you said that you liked me, I thought you were in earnest, you know, and so I wanted to be quite honest, because I thought it was fairer. You see, if I had let you think that I liked you, you might have thought we were going to drift into being friends, and that's impossible, you know — because I never did like you, and I never shall. But that needn't prevent our walking together, and talking, and all that. At least, I don't mean that it should. That's the reason why I won't turn back just yet —"

"But how in the world can you enjoy walking and talking with a man you don't like?" asked Johnstone, who was completely at sea, and began to think that he must be dreaming.

"Well — you are awfully good company, you know, and I can't always be sitting with my mother on the terrace, though we love each other dearly."

"You are the most extraordinary person!"
exclaimed Johnstone, in genuine bewilderment.
"And of course your mother dislikes me too,
doesn't she?"

"Not at all," answered Clare. "You asked
me that before, and I told you the truth. Since
then, she likes you better and better. She is
always saying how nice you are."

"Then I had better always talk to her," suggested Brook, feeling for a clue.

"Oh, I shouldn't like that at all!" cried the
young girl, laughing.

"And yet you don't like me. This is like
twenty questions. You must have some very
particular reason for it," he added thoughtfully.
"I suppose I must have done some awful thing
without knowing it. I wish you would tell me.
Won't you, please? Then I'll go away."

"No," Clare answered. "I won't tell you.
But I have a reason. I'm not capricious. I
don't take violent dislikes to people for nothing.
Let it alone. We can talk very pleasantly
about other things. Since you are good enough
to like me, it might be amusing to tell me why.
If you have any good reason, you know, you
won't stop liking me just because I don't like
you, will you?"

She glanced sideways at him as she spoke,
and he was watching her and trying to under-

stand her, for the revelation of her dislike had
come upon him very suddenly. She was on the
right as they walked, and he saw her against
the light sky, above the line of the low parapet.
Perhaps the light behind her dazzled him; at
all events, he had a strange impression for a
moment. She seemed to have the better of him,
and to be stronger and more determined than he.
She seemed taller than she was, too, for she was
on the higher part of the road, in the middle
of it. For an instant he felt precisely what
she so often felt with him, that she had power
over him. But he did not resent the sensation
as she did, though it was quite as new to him.

Nevertheless, he did not answer her, for she
had spoken only half in earnest, and he himself
was not just then inclined to joke for the mere
sake of joking. He looked down at the road
under his feet, and he knew all at once that
Clare attracted him much more than he had
imagined. The sidelong glance she had be-
stowed upon him had fascination in it. There
was an odd charm about her girlish contrariety
and in her frank avowal that she did not like
him. Her dislike roused him. He did not
choose to be disliked by her, especially for some
absurd trifle in his behaviour, which he had not
even noticed when he had made the mistake,
whatever it might be.

He walked along in silence, and he was aware of her light tread and the soft sound of her serge skirt as she moved. He wished her to like him, and wished that he knew what to do to change her mind. But that would not be easy, since he did not know the cause of her dislike. Presently she spoke again, and more gravely.

"I should not have said that. I'm sorry. But of course you knew that I wasn't in earnest."

"I don't know why you should not have said it," he answered. "As a matter of fact, you are quite right. I don't like you any the less because you don't like me. Liking isn't a bargain with cash on delivery. I think I like you all the more for being so honest. Do you mind?"

"Not in the least. It's a very good reason." Clare smiled, and then suddenly looked grave again, wondering whether it would not be really honest to tell him then and there that she had overheard his last interview with Lady Fan.

But she reflected that it could only make him feel uncomfortable.

"And another reason why I like you is because you are combative," he said thoughtfully. "I'm not, you know. One always admires the qualities one hasn't oneself."

"And you are not combative? You don't like to be in the opposition?"

" Not a bit ! I'm not fond of fighting. I
systematically avoid a row."

"I shouldn't have thought that," said Clare,
looking at him again. "Do you know? I think
most people would take you for a soldier."

"Do I look as though I would seek the bubble
reputation at the cannon's mouth?" Brook
laughed. " Am I full of strange oaths?"

" Oh, that's ridiculous, you know !" exclaimed
Clare. " I mean, you look as though you would
fight."

"I never would if I could help it. And so
far I have managed 'to help it' very well. I'm
naturally mild, I think. You are not, you know.
I don't mean to be rude, but I think you are
pugnacious — 'combative' is prettier."

" My father was a soldier," said the girl, with
some pride.

" And mine is a brewer. There's a lot of in-
heritable difference between handling gunpowder
and brewing mild ale. Like father, like son.
I shall brew mild ale too. If you could have
charged at Balaclava, you would. By the way,
it isn't the beer that you object to ? Please
tell me. I shouldn't mind at all, and I'd much
rather know that it was only that."

" How absurd !" cried Clare with scorn. " As
though it made any difference !"

" Well — what is it, then?" asked Brook with

sudden impatience. "You have no right to hate me without telling me why."

"No right?" The young girl turned on him half fiercely, and then laughed. "You haven't a standing order from Heaven to be liked by the whole human race, you know!"

"And if I had, you would be the solitary exception, I suppose," suggested Johnstone with a rather discontented smile.

"Perhaps."

"Is there anything I could do to make you change your mind? Because, if it were anything in reason, I'd do it."

"It's rather a pity that you should put in the condition of its being in reason," answered Clare, as her lip curled. "But there isn't anything. You may just as well give it up at once."

"I won't."

"It's a waste of time, I assure you. Besides, it's mere vanity. It's only because everybody likes you — so you think that I should too."

"Between us, we are getting at my character at last," observed Brook with some asperity. "You've discovered my vanity, now. By-and-by we shall find out some more good qualities."

"Perhaps. Each one will be a step in our acquaintance, you know. Steps may lead down, as well as up. We are walking down hill on

this road just now, and it's steep. Look at that
unfortunate mule dragging that cart up hill
towards us! That's like trying to be friends,
against odds. I wish the man would not beat
the beast like that, though! What brutes these
people are!"

Her dark blue eyes fixed themselves keenly
on the sight, and the pupils grew wide and
angry. The cart was a hundred yards away,
coming up the road, piled high with sacks of
potatoes, and drawn by one wretched mule.
The huge carter was sprawling on the front
sacks, yelling a tuneless chant at the top of his
voice. He was a black-haired man, with a hideous mouth, and his face was red with wine.
As he yelled his song he flogged his miserable
beast with a heavy whip, accenting his howls
with cruel blows. Clare grew pale with anger
as she came nearer and saw it all more distinctly. The mule's knees bent nearly double
at every violent step, its wide eyes were bright
red all round, its white tongue hung out, and it
gasped for breath. The road was stony, too,
besides being steep, for it had been lately mended
and not rolled.

"Brute!" exclaimed Clare, in a low voice, and
her face grew paler.

Johnstone said nothing, and his face did not
change as they advanced.

"Don't you see?" cried the young girl. "Can't you do anything? Can't you stop him?"

"Oh yes. I think I can do that," answered Brook indifferently. "It is rather rough on the mule."

"Rough! It's brutal, it's beastly, it's cowardly, it's perfectly inhuman!"

At that moment the unfortunate animal stumbled, struggled to recover itself as the lash descended pitilessly upon its thin flanks, and then fell headlong and tumbled upon its side. The heavy cart pulled back, half turning, so that the shafts were dragged sideways across the mule, whose weight prevented the load from rolling down hill. The carrier stopped singing and swore, beating the beast with all his might, as it lay still gasping for breath.

"Ah, assassin! Ah, carrion! I will teach thee! Curses on the dead of thy house!" he roared.

Brook and Clare were coming nearer.

"That's not very intelligent of the fellow," observed Johnstone indifferently. "He had much better get down."

"Oh, stop it, stop it!" cried the young girl, suffering acutely for the helpless creature.

But the man had apparently recognised the impossibility of producing any impression unless he descended from his perch. He threw the whip to the ground and slid off the sacks. He

stood looking at the mule for a moment, and
then kicked it in the back with all his might.
Then, just as Johnstone and Clare came up, he
went round to the back of the cart, walking unsteadily, for he was evidently drunk. The two
stopped by the parapet and looked on.

"He's going to unload," said Johnstone.
"That's sensible, at all events."

The sacks, as usual in Italy, were bound to
the cart by cords, which were fast in front, but
which wound upon a heavy spindle at the back.
The spindle had three holes in it, in which staves
were thrust as levers, to turn it and hold the
ropes taut. Two of the staves were tightly
pressed against the load, while the third stood
nearly upright in its hole.

The man took the third stave, a bar of elm
four feet long and as thick as a man's wrist,
and came round to the mule again on the side
away from Clare and Johnstone. He lifted the
weapon high in air, and almost before they
realised what horror he was perpetrating he
had struck three or four tremendous blows upon
the creature's back, making as many bleeding
wounds. The mule kicked and shivered violently, and its eyes were almost starting from
its head.

Johnstone came up first, caught the stave in
air as it was about to descend again, wrenched

it out of the man's hands, and hurled it over
Clare's head, across the parapet and into the
sea. The man fell back a step, and his face grew
purple with rage. He roared out a volley of
horrible oaths, in a dialect perfectly incompre-
hensible even to Clare, who knew Italian well.

" You needn't yell like that, my good man,"
said Johnstone, smiling at him.

The man was big and strong, and drunk. He
clenched his fists, and made for his adversary,
head down, in the futile Italian fashion. The
Englishman stepped aside, landed a left-handed
blow behind his ear, and followed it up with a
tremendous kick, which sent the fellow upon
his face in the ditch under the rocks. Clare
looked on, and her eyes brightened singularly,
for she had fighting blood in her veins. The
man seemed stunned, and lay still where he had
fallen. Johnstone turned to the fallen mule,
which lay bleeding and gasping under the shafts,
and he began to unbuckle the harness.

" Could you put a big stone behind the wheel?"
he asked, as Clare tried to help him.

He knew that the cart must roll back if it
were not blocked, for he had noticed how it
stood. Clare looked about for a stone, picked
one up by the roadside, and went to the back of
the cart, while Johnstone patted the mule's head,
and busied himself with the buckles of the har-

ness, bending low as he did so. Clare also bent down, trying to force the stone under the wheel, and did not notice that the carter was sitting up by the roadside, feeling for something in his pocket.

An instant later he was on his feet. When Clare stood up, he was stepping softly up behind Johnstone. As he moved, she saw that he had an open clasp-knife in his right hand. Johnstone was still bending down unconscious of his danger. The young girl was light on her feet and quick, and not cowardly. The man was before her, halfway between her and Brook. She sprang with all her might, threw her arms round the drunken man's neck from behind, and dragged him backward. He struck wildly behind him with the knife, and roared out curses.

"Quick!" cried Clare, in her high, clear voice. "He's got a knife! Quick!"

But Johnstone had heard their steps, and was already upon him from before, while the young girl's arms tightened round his neck from behind. The fellow struck about him wildly with his blade, staggering backwards as Clare dragged upon him.

"Let go, or you'll fall!" Brook shouted to her.

As he spoke, dodging the knife, he struck the man twice in the face, left and right, in an earnest, business-like way. Clare caught herself

by the wheel of the cart as she sprang aside, almost falling under the man's weight. A moment later, Brook was kneeling on his chest,
having the knife in his hand and holding it near
the carter's throat.

"Lie still!" he said rather quietly, in English.
"Give me the halter, please!" he said to Clare,
without looking up. "It's hanging to the shaft
there in a coil."

Kneeling on the man's chest — to tell the
truth, he was badly stunned, though not unconscious — Brook took two half-hitches with the
halter round one wrist, passed the line under
his neck as he lay, and hauled on it till the arm
came under his side, then hitched the other
wrist, passed the line back, hauled on it, and
finally took two turns round the throat. Clare
watched the operation, very pale and breathing
hard.

"He's drunk," observed Johnstone. "Otherwise I wouldn't tie him up, you know. Now, if
you move," he said in English to his prisoner,
"you'll strangle yourself."

Thereupon he rose, forced the fellow to roll
over, and hitched the fall of the line round both
wrists again, and made it fast, so that the man
lay, with his head drawn back by his own hands,
which he could not move without tightening the
rope round his neck.

"He's frightened now," said Brook. "Let's get the poor mule out of that."

In a few minutes he got the wretched beast free. It was ready enough to rise as soon as it felt that it could do so, and it struggled to its feet, badly hurt by the beating and bleeding in many places, but not seriously injured. The carter watched them as he lay on the road, half strangled, and cursed them in a choking voice.

"And now, what in the world are we going to do with them?" asked Brook, rubbing the mule's nose. "It's a pretty bad case," he continued, thoughtfully. "The mule can't draw the load, the carter can't be allowed to beat the mule, and we can't afford to let the carter have his head. What the dickens are we to do?"

He laughed a little. Then he suddenly looked hard at Clare, as though remembering something.

"It was awfully plucky of you to jump on him in that way," he said. "Just at the right moment, too, by Jove! That devil would have got at me if you hadn't stopped him. Awfully plucky, upon my word! And I'm tremendously obliged, Miss Bowring, indeed I am!"

"It's nothing to be grateful for, it seems to me," Clare answered. "I suppose there's nothing to be done but to sit down and wait until somebody comes. It's a lonely road, of course, and we may wait a long time."

" I say," exclaimed Johnstone, "you've torn your frock rather badly! Look at it!"

She drew her skirt round with her hand. There were long, clean rents in the skirt, on her right side.

" It was his knife," she said, thoughtfully surveying the damage. " He kept trying to get at me with it. I'm sorry, for I haven't another serge skirt with me."

Then she felt herself blushing, and turned away.

" I'll just pin it up," she said, and she disappeared behind the cart rather precipitately.

" By Jove! You have pretty good nerves!" observed Johnstone, more to himself than to her. " Shut up!" he cried to the carter, who was swearing again. " Stop that noise, will you?"

He made a step angrily towards the man, for the sight of the slit frock had roused him again, when he thought what the knife might have done. The fellow was silent instantly, and lay quite still, for he knew that he should strangle himself if he moved.

" I'll have you in prison before night," continued Johnstone, speaking English to him. " Oh yes! the *carabinieri* will come, and you will go to *galera* — do you understand that?"

He had picked up the words somewhere. The man began to moan and pray.

"Stop that noise!" cried Brook, with slow emphasis.

He was not far wrong in saying that the carabineers would come. They patrol the roads day and night, in pairs, as they patrol every high road and every mountain path in Italy, all the year round. And just then, far up the road down which Johnstone and Clare had come, two of them appeared in sight, recognisable a mile away by their snow-white crossbelts and gleaming accoutrements. There are twelve or fourteen thousand of them in the country, trained soldiers and picked men, by all odds the finest corps in the army. Until lately no man could serve in the carabineers who could not show documentary evidence that neither he nor his father nor his mother had ever been in prison even for the smallest offence. They are feared and respected, and it is they who have so greatly reduced brigandage throughout the country.

Clare came back to Johnstone's side, having done what she could to pin the rents together.

"It's all right now," she cried. "Here come the carabineers. They will take the man and his cart to the next village. Let me talk to them — I can speak Italian, you know."

She was pale again, and very quiet. She had

noticed that her hands trembled violently when she was pinning her frock, though they had been steady enough when they had gone round the man's throat.

When the patrol men came up, she stepped forward and explained what had happened, clearly and briefly. There was the bleeding mule, Johnstone standing before it and rubbing its dusty nose; there was the knife; there was the man. With a modest gesture she showed them where her frock had been cut to shreds. Johnstone made remarks in English, reflecting upon the Italian character, which she did not think fit to translate.

The carabineers were silent fellows with big moustaches — the one very dark, the other as fair as a Swede — they were clean, strong, sober men, with frank eyes, and they said very little. They asked the strangers' names, and Johnstone, at Clare's request, wrote her name on his card, and the address in Amalfi. One of them knew the carter for a bad character.

"We will take care of him and his cart," said the dark man, who was the superior. "The signori may go in quiet."

They untied the rope that bound the man. He rose trembling, and stood on his feet, for he knew that he was in their power. But they showed no intention of putting him in handcuffs.

"Turn the cart round!" said the dark man.

They helped the carter to do it, and blocked it with stones.

"Put in the mule!" was the next order, and the carabineers held up the shafts while the man obeyed.

Then both saluted Johnstone and Clare, and shouldered their short carbines, which had stood against the parapet.

"Forward!" said the dark man, quietly.

The carter took the mule by the head and started it gently enough. The creature understood, and was glad to go down hill; the wheels creaked, the cart moved, and the party went off, one of the carabineers marching on either side.

Clare drew a long breath as she stood looking after them for a moment.

"Let us go home," she said at last, and turned up the road.

For some minutes they walked on in silence.

"I think you probably saved my life at the risk of yours, Miss Bowring," said Johnstone, at last, looking up. "Thank you very much."

"Nonsense!" exclaimed the young girl, and she tried to laugh.

"But you were telling me that you were not combative — that you always avoided a fight, you know, and that you were so mild, and all that. For a very mild man, Mr. Johnstone, who hates fighting, you are a good 'man of your hands,' as they say in the *Morte d'Arthur*."

"Oh, I don't call that a fight!" answered Johnstone, contemptuously. "Why, my collar isn't even crumpled. As for my hands, if I could find a spring I would wash them, after touching that fellow."

"That's the advantage of wearing gloves," observed Clare, looking at her own.

They were both very young, and though they knew that they had been in great danger they affected perfect indifference about it to each other, after the manner of true Britons. But each admired the other, and Brook was suddenly conscious that he had never known a woman whom, in some ways, he thought so admirable as Clare Bowring, but both felt a singular constraint as they walked homeward.

"Do you know?" Clare began, when they were near Amalfi, "I think we had better say nothing about it to my mother — that is, if you don't mind."

"By all means," answered Brook. "I'm sure I don't want to talk about it."

"No, and my mother is very nervous — you know — about my going off to walk without her. Oh, not about you — with anybody. You see, I'd been very ill before I came here."

CHAPTER VIII

In obedience to Clare's expressed wish, Johnstone made no mention that evening of the rather serious adventure on the Salerno road. They had fallen into the habit of shaking hands when they bade each other good-night. When it was time, and the two ladies rose to withdraw, Johnstone suddenly wished that Clare would make some little sign to him — the least thing to show that this particular evening was not precisely what all the other evenings had been, that they were drawn a little closer together, that perhaps she would change her mind and not dislike him any more for that unknown reason at which he could not even guess.

They joined hands, and his eyes met hers. But there was no unusual pressure — no little acknowledgment of a common danger past. The blue eyes looked at him straight and proudly, without softening, and the fresh lips calmly said good-night. Johnstone remained alone, and in a singularly bad humour for such a good-tempered man. He was angry with Clare for being so cold and indifferent, and he was

ashamed of himself for wishing that she would
admire him a little for having knocked down a
tipsy carter. It was not much of an exploit.
What she had done had been very much more
remarkable. The man would not have killed
him, of course, but he might have given him a
very dangerous wound with that ugly clasp-
knife. Clare's frock was cut to pieces on one
side, and it was a wonder that she had escaped
without a scratch. He had no right to expect
any praise for what he had done, when she had
done so much more.

To tell the truth, it was not praise that he
wanted, but a sign that she was not indifferent
to him, or at least that she no longer disliked
him. He was ashamed to own to himself that
he was half in love with a young girl who had
told him that she did not like him and would
never even be his friend. Women had not
usually treated him in that way, so far. But
the fact remained, that she had got possession
of his thoughts, and made him think about his
actions when she was present. It took a good
deal to disturb Brook Johnstone's young sleep,
but he did not sleep well that night.

As for Clare, when she was alone, she regretted
that she had not just nodded kindly to him, and
nothing more, when she had said good-night.
She knew perfectly well that he expected some-

thing of the sort, and that it would have been
natural, and quite harmless, without any possibility of consequence. She consoled herself by
repeating that she had done quite right, as the
vision of Lady Fan rose distinctly before her in
a flood of memory's moonlight. Then it struck
her, as the vision faded, that her position was a
very odd one. Personally, she liked the man.
Impersonally, she hated and despised him. At
least she believed that she did, and that she
should, for the sake of all women. To her, as
she had known him, he was brave, kind, gentle
in manner and speech, boyishly frank. As she
had seen him that once, she had thought him
heartless, cowardly, and cynical. She could not
reconcile the two, and therefore, in her thoughts,
she unconsciously divided him into two indi-
vidualities — her Mr. Johnstone and Lady Fan's
Brook. There was very little resemblance between them. Oddly enough, she felt a sort of
pang for him, that he could ever have been the
other man whom she had first seen. She was
getting into a very complicated frame of mind.

They met in the morning and exchanged
greetings with unusual coldness. Brook asked
whether she were tired; she said that she had done
nothing to tire her, as though she resented the
question; he said nothing in answer, and they
both looked at the sea and thought it extremely

dull. Presently Johnstone went off for a walk
alone, and Clare buried herself in a book for the
morning. She did not wish to think, because
her thoughts were so very contradictory. It
was easier to try and follow some one else's
ideas. She found that almost worse than thinking, but, being very tenacious, she stuck to it
and tried to read.

At the midday meal they exchanged common-
places, and neither looked at the other. Just as
they left the dining-room a heavy thunderstorm
broke overhead with a deluge of rain. Clare
said that the thunder made her head ache, and
she disappeared on pretence of lying down.
Mrs. Bowring went to write letters, and Johnstone hung about the reading-room, and smoked
a pipe in the long corridor, till he was sick of
the sound of his own footsteps. Amalfi was all
very well in fine weather, he reflected, but when
it rained it was as dismal as penny whist, Sunday in London, or a volume of sermons — or
all three together, he added viciously, in his
thoughts. The German family had fallen back
upon the guide book, Mommsen's *History of
Rome*, and the *Gartenlaube*. The Russian invalid was presumably in his room, with a teapot,
and the two English old maids were reading a
violently sensational novel aloud to each other
by turns in the hotel drawing-room. They

stopped reading and got very red, when Johnstone looked in.

It was a dreary afternoon, and he wished that something would happen. The fight on the preceding day had stirred his blood — and other things perhaps had contributed to his restless state of mind. He thought of Clare's torn frock, and he wished he had killed the carter outright. He reflected that, as the man was attacking him with a knife, he himself would have been acquitted.

Late in the afternoon the sky cleared and the red light of the lowering sun struck the crests of the higher hills to eastward. Brook went out and smelled the earth-scented air, and the damp odour of the orange-blossoms. But that did not please him either, so he turned back and went through the long corridor to the platform at the back of the hotel. To his surprise he came face to face with Clare, who was walking briskly backwards and forwards, and saw him just as he emerged from the door. They both stood still and looked at each other with an odd little constraint, almost like anxiety, in their faces. There was a short, awkward silence.

"Well?" said Clare, interrogatively, and raising her eyebrows a very little, as though wondering why he did not speak.

"Nothing," Johnstone answered, turning his face seaward. "I wasn't going to say anything."

"Oh! — you looked as though you were."

"No," he said. "I came out to get a breath of air, that's all."

"So did I. I — I think I've been out long enough. I'll go in." And she made a step towards the door.

"Oh, please, don't!" he cried suddenly. "Can't we walk together a little bit? That is, if you are not tired."

"Oh no! I'm not tired," answered the young girl with a cold little laugh. "I'll stay if you like — just a few minutes."

"Thanks, awfully," said Brook in a shy, jerky way.

They began to walk up and down, much less quickly than Clare had been walking when alone. They seemed to have nothing to say to each other. Johnstone remarked that he thought it would not rain again just then, and after some minutes of reflection Clare said that she remembered having seen two thunderstorms within an hour, with a clear sky between, not long ago. Johnstone also thought the matter over for some time before he answered, and then said that he supposed the clouds must have been somewhere in the meantime — an observation which did not strike either Clare or even himself as particularly intelligent.

"I don't think you know much about thunderstorms," said Clare, after another silence.

"I? No — why should I?"

"I don't know. It's supposed to be just as well to know about things, isn't it?"

"I dare say," answered Brook, indifferently. "But science isn't exactly in my line, if I have any line."

They recrossed the platform in silence.

"What is your line — if you have any?" Clare asked, looking at the ground as she walked, and perfectly indifferent as to his answer.

"It ought to be beer," answered Brook, gravely. "But then, you know how it is — one has all sorts of experts, and one ends by taking their word for granted about it. I don't believe I have any line — unless it's in the way of out-of-door things. I'm fond of shooting, and I can ride fairly, you know, like anybody else."

"Yes," said Clare, "you were telling me so the other day, you know."

"Yes," Johnstone murmured thoughtfully, "that's true. Please excuse me. I'm always repeating myself."

"I didn't mean that." Her tone changed a

little. "You can be very amusing when you like, you know."

"Thanks, awfully. I should like to be amusing now, for instance, but I can't."

"Now? Why now?"

"Because I'm boring you to madness, little by little, and I'm awfully sorry too, for I want you to like **me** — though you say you never will — and of course you can't like a bore, can you? I say, Miss Bowring, don't you think we could strike some sort of friendly agreement — to be friends without 'liking,' somehow? I'm beginning to hate the word. I believe it's the colour of my hair or my coat — or something — that you dislike so. I wish you'd tell me. It would be much kinder. I'd go to work and change it —"

"Dye your hair?" Clare laughed, glad that the ice was broken again.

"Oh yes — if you like," he answered, laughing too. "Anything to please you."

"Anything 'in reason' — as you proposed yesterday."

"No — anything in reason or out of it. I'm getting desperate!" He laughed again, but in his laughter there was a little note of something new to the young girl, a sort of understreak of earnestness.

"It isn't anything you can change," said

Clare, after a moment's hesitation. "And it certainly has nothing to do with your appearance, or your manners, or your tailor," she added.

"Oh well, then, it's evidently something I've done, or said," Brook murmured, looking at her.

But she did not return his glance, as they walked side by side; indeed, she turned her face from him a little, and she said nothing, for she was far too truthful to deny his assertion.

"Then I'm right," he said, with an interrogation, after a long pause.

"Don't ask me, please! It's of no importance after all. Talk of something else."

"I don't agree with you," Brook answered. "It is very important to me."

"Oh, nonsense!" Clare tried to laugh. "What difference can it make to you, whether I like you or not?"

"Don't say that. It makes a great difference — more than I thought it could, in fact. One — one doesn't like to be misjudged by one's friends, you know."

"But I'm not your friend."

"I want you to be."

"I can't."

"You won't," said Brook, in a lower tone, and almost angrily. "You've made up your mind against me, on account of something you've guessed at, and you won't tell me what it is, so I can't possibly defend myself. I haven't the least idea what it can be. I never did anything particularly bad, I believe, and I never did anything I should be ashamed of owning. I don't like to say that sort of thing, you know, about myself, but you drive me to it. It isn't fair. Upon my word, it's not fair play. You tell a man he's a bad lot, like that, in the air, and then you refuse to say why you think so. Or else the whole thing is a sort of joke you've invented — if it is, it's awfully one-sided, it seems to me."

"Do you really think me capable of anything so silly?" asked Clare.

"No, I don't. That makes it all the worse, because it proves that you have — or think you have — something against me. I don't know much about law, but it strikes me as something tremendously like libel. Don't you think so yourself?"

"Oh no! Indeed I don't. Libel means saying things against people, doesn't it? I haven't done that —"

"Indeed you have! I mean, I beg your pardon for contradicting you like that —"

"Rather flatly," observed Clare, as they turned in their walk, and their eyes met.

"Well, I'm sorry, but since we are talking

about it, I've got to say what I think. After
all, I'm the person attacked. I have a right to
defend myself."

" I haven't attacked you," answered the young
girl, gravely.

" I won't be rude, if I can help it," said Brook,
half roughly. " But I asked you if you disliked
me for something I had done or said, and you
couldn't deny it. That means that I have done
or said something bad enough to make you say
that you will never be my friend — and that
must be something very bad indeed."

"Then you think I'm not squeamish? It
would have to be something very, very bad."

" Yes."

" Thank you. Well, I thought it very bad.
Anybody would, I should fancy."

" I never did anything very, very bad, so
you must be mistaken," answered Johnstone,
exasperated.

Clare said nothing, but walked along with
her head rather high, looking straight before
her. It had all happened before her eyes, on
the very ground under her feet, on that platform. Johnstone knew that he had spoken
roughly.

" I say," he began, " was I rude? I'm awfully
sorry." Clare stopped and stood still.

" Mr. Johnstone, we sha'n't agree. I will

never tell you, and you will never be satisfied unless I do. So it's a dead-lock."

"You are horribly unjust," answered Brook, very much in earnest, and fixing his bright eyes on hers. "You seem to take a delight in tormenting me with this imaginary secret. After all, if it's something you saw me do, or heard me say, I must know of it and remember it, so there's no earthly reason why we shouldn't discuss it."

There was again that fascination in his eyes, and she felt herself yielding.

"I'll say one thing," she said. "I wish you hadn't done it!"

She felt that she could not look away from him, and that he was getting her into his power. The colour rose in her face.

"Please don't look at me!" she said suddenly, gazing helplessly into his eyes, but his steady look did not change.

"Please — oh, please look away!" she cried, half-frightened and growing pale again.

He turned from her, surprised at her manner.

"I'm afraid you're not in earnest about this, after all," he said, thoughtfully. "If you meant what you said, why shouldn't you look at me?"

She blushed scarlet again.

"It's very rude to stare like that!" she said,

in an offended tone. "You know that you've
got something — I don't know what to call it —
one can't look away when you look at one. Of
course you know it, and you ought not to do it.
It isn't nice."

"I didn't know there was anything peculiar
about my eyes," said Brook. "Indeed I didn't!
Nobody ever told me so, I'm sure. By Jove!"
he exclaimed, "I believe it's that! I've probably done it before — and that's why you —" he
stopped.

"Please don't think me so silly," answered
Clare, recovering her composure. "It's nothing
of the sort. As for that — that way you have
of looking — I dare say I'm nervous since my
illness. Besides —" she hesitated, and then
smiled. "Besides, do you know? If you had
looked at me a moment longer I should have
told you the whole thing, and then we should
both have been sorry."

"I should not, I'm sure," said Brook, with
conviction. "But I don't understand about my
looking at you. I never tried to mesmerise any
one —"

"There is no such thing as mesmerism. It's
all hypnotism, you know."

"I don't know what they call it. You know
what I mean. But I'm sure it's your imagination."

"Oh yes, I dare say," answered the young girl with affected carelessness. "It's merely because I'm nervous."

"Well, so far as I'm concerned, it's quite unconscious. I don't know — I suppose I wanted to see in your eyes what you were thinking about. Besides, when one likes a person, one doesn't think it so dreadfully rude to look at them — at him — I mean, at you — when one is in earnest about something — does one?"

"I don't know," said Clare. "But please don't do it to me. It makes me feel awfully uncomfortable somehow. You won't, will you?" she asked, with a sort of appeal. "You would make me tell you everything — and then I should hate myself."

"But I shouldn't hate you."

"Oh yes, you would! You would hate me for knowing."

"By Jove! It's too bad!" cried Brook. "But as for that," he added humbly, "nothing would make me hate you."

"Nothing? You don't know!"

"Yes, I do! You couldn't make me change my mind about you. I've grown to — to like you a great deal too much for that in this short time — a great deal more than is good for me, I believe," he added, with a sort of rough impulsiveness. "Not that I'm at all surprised, you know," he continued with an attempt at a laugh. "One can't see a person like you, most of the day, for ten days or a fortnight, without — well, you know, admiring you most tremendously — can one? I dare say you think that might be put into better English. But it's true all the same."

A silence followed. The warm blood mantled softly in the girl's fair cheeks. She was taken by surprise with an odd little breath of happiness, as it were, suddenly blowing upon her, whence she knew not. It was so utterly new that she wondered at it, and was not conscious of the faint blush that answered it.

"One gets awfully intimate in a few days," observed Brook, as though he had discovered something quite new.

She nodded, but said nothing, and they still walked up and down. Then his words made her think of that sudden intimacy which had probably sprung up between him and Lady Fan on board the yacht, and her heart was hardened again.

"It isn't worth while to be intimate, as you call it," she said at last, with a little sudden sharpness. "People ought never to be intimate, unless they have to live together — in the same place, you know. Then they can't exactly help it, I suppose."

"Why should they? One can't exactly in-

trench oneself behind a wall with pistols and say
'Be my friend if you dare.' Life would be very
uncomfortable, I should think."

"Oh, you know what I mean! Don't be so
awfully literal."

"I was trying to understand," said Johnstone,
with unusual meekness. "I won't, if you don't
want me to. But I don't agree with you a bit.
I think it's very jolly to be intimate — in this
sort of way — or perhaps a little more so."

"Intimate enemies? Enemies can be just as
intimate as friends, you know."

"I'd rather have you for my intimate enemy
than not know you at all," said Brook.

"That's saying a great deal, Mr. Johnstone."

Again she was pleased in a new way by what
he said. And a temptation came upon her una-
wares. It was perfectly clear that he was beginning to make love to her. She thought of her
reflections after she had seen him alone with
Lady Fan, and of how she had wished that she
could break his heart, and pay him back with
suffering for the pain he had given another
woman. The possibility seemed nearer now
than then. At least, she could easily let him
believe that she believed him, and then laugh at
him and his acting. For of course it was acting.
How could such a man be earnest? All at once
the thought that he should respect her so little

as to pretend to make love to her incensed her.

" What an extraordinary idea ! " she exclaimed rather scornfully. " You would rather be hated, than not known ! "

" I wasn't talking generalities — I was speaking of you. Please don't misunderstand me on purpose. It isn't kind."

" Are you in need of kindness just now? You don't exactly strike one in that way, you know. But your people will be coming in a day or two, I suppose. I've no doubt they'll be kind to you, as you call it — whatever that may mean. One speaks of being kind to animals and servants, you know — that sort of thing."

Nothing can outdo the brutality of a perfectly unaffected young girl under certain circumstances.

" I don't class myself with either, thank you," said Brook, justly offended. " You certainly manage to put things in a new light sometimes. I feel rather like that mule we saw yesterday."

" Oh — I thought you didn't class yourself with animals ! " she laughed.

" Have you any particular reason for saying horridly disagreeable things ? " asked Brook coldly.

There was a pause.

" I didn't mean to be disagreeable — at least

not so disagreeable as all that," said Clare at
last. "I don't know why it is, but you have a
talent for making me seem rude."

"Force of example," suggested Johnstone.

"No, I'll say that for you — you have very
good manners."

"Thanks, awfully. Considering the provocation, you know, that's an immense compliment."

"I thought I would be 'kind' for a change.
By the bye, what are we quarrelling about?"
She laughed. "You began by saying something
very nice to me, and then I told you that you
were like the mule, didn't I? It's very odd!
I believe you hypnotise me, after all."

"At all events, if we were not intimate, you
couldn't possibly say the things you do," observed Brook, already pacified.

"And I suppose you would not take the
things I say, so meekly, would you?"

"I told you I was a very mild person," said
Johnstone. "We were talking about it yesterday, do you remember?"

"Oh yes! And then you illustrated your
idea of meekness by knocking down the first
man we met."

"It was your fault," retorted Brook. "You
told me to stop his beating the mule. So I did.
Fortunately you stopped him from sticking a
knife into me. Do you know? You have

awfully good nerves. Most women would have screamed and run up a tree — or something. They would have got out of the way, at all events."

"I think most women would have done precisely what I did," said Clare. "Why should you say that most women are cowards?"

"I didn't," answered Brook. "But I refuse to quarrel about it. I meant to say that I admired you — I mean, what you did — well, more than anything."

"That's a sweeping sort of compliment. Am I to return it?" She glanced at him and smiled.

"You couldn't, with truth."

"Of course I could. I don't remember ever seeing anything of that sort before, but I don't believe that anybody could have done it better. I admired you more than anything just then, you know." She laughed once more as she added the last words.

"Oh, I don't expect you to go on admiring me. I'm quite satisfied, and grateful, and all that."

"I'm glad you're so easily satisfied. Couldn't we talk seriously about something or other? It seems to me that we've been chaffing for half an hour, haven't we?"

"It hasn't been all chaff, Miss Bowring," said Johnstone. "At least, not on my side."

"Then I'm sorry," Clare answered. They relapsed into silence, as they walked their beat, to and fro. The sun had gone down, and it was already twilight on that side of the mountains. The rain had cooled the air, and the far land to southward was darkly distinct beyond the purple water. It was very chilly, and Clare was without a shawl, and Johnstone was hatless, but neither of them noticed that it was cool. Johnstone was the first to speak.

"Is this sort of thing to go on for ever, Miss Bowring?" he asked gravely.

"What?" But she knew very well what he meant.

"This — this very odd footing we are on, you and I — are we never going to get past it?"

"Oh — I hope not," answered Clare, cheerfully. "I think it's very pleasant, don't you? And most original. We are intimate enough to say all sorts of things, and I'm your enemy, and you say you are my friend. I can't imagine any better arrangement. We shall always laugh when we think of it — even years hence. You will be going away in a few days, and we shall stay here into the summer and we shall never see each other again, in all probability. We shall always look back on this time — as something quite odd, you know."

"You are quite mistaken if you think that we shall never meet again," said Johnstone.

"I mean that it's very unlikely. You see we don't go home very often, and when we do we stop with friends in the country. We don't go much into society. And the rest of the time we generally live in Florence."

"There is nothing to prevent me from coming to Florence — or living there, if I choose."

"Oh no — I suppose not. Except that you would be bored to death. It's not very amusing, unless you happen to be fond of pictures, and you never said you were."

"I should go to see you."

"Oh — yes — you could call, and of course if we were at home we should be very glad to see you. But that would only occupy about half an hour of one day. That isn't much."

"I mean that I should go to Florence simply for the sake of seeing you, and seeing you often — all the time, in fact."

"Dear me! That would be a great deal, wouldn't it? I thought you meant just to call, don't you know?"

"I'm in earnest, though it sounds very funny, I dare say," said Johnstone.

"It sounds rather mad," answered Clare, laughing a little. "I hope you won't do anything of the kind, because I wouldn't see you

more than once or twice. I'd have headaches
and colds and concerts — all the things one has
when one isn't at home to people. But my
mother would be delighted. She likes you tremendously, you know, and you could go about
to galleries together and read Ruskin and Browning — do you know the Statue and the Bust?
And you could go and see Casa Guidi, where the
Brownings lived, and you could drive up to San
Miniato, and then, you know, you could drive
up again and read more Browning and more
Ruskin. I'm sure you would enjoy it to any
extent. But I should have to go through a ter-
rific siege of colds and headaches. It would be
rather hard on me."

"And harder on me," observed Brook, "and
quite fearful for Mrs. Bowring."

"Oh no! She would enjoy every minute of it.
You forget that she likes you."

"You are afraid I should forget that you
don't."

"I almost — oh, a long way from quite! I
almost liked you yesterday when you thrashed
the carter and tied him up so neatly. It was
beautifully done — all those knots! I suppose
you learned them on board of the yacht, didn't
you?"

"I've yachted a good deal," said Brook.

"Generally with that party?" inquired Clare.

"No. That was the first time. My father has an old tub he goes about in, and we sometimes go together."

" Is he coming here in his ' old tub ' ? "

" Oh no — he's lent her to a fellow who has taken her off to Japan, I believe."

" Japàn! Is it safe ? In an ' old tub ' ! "

" Oh, well — that's a way of talking, you know. She's a good enough boat, you know. My father went to New York in her, last year. She's a steamer, you know. I hate steamers. They are such dirty noisy things ! But of course if you are going a long way, they are the only things."

He spoke in a jerky way, annoyed and discomfited by her forcing the conversation off the track. Though he was aware that he had gone further than he intended, when he proposed to spend the winter in Florence. Moreover, he was very tenacious by nature, and had rarely been seriously opposed during his short life. Her persistent refusal to tell him the cause of her deep-rooted dislike exasperated him, while her frank and careless manner and good-fellowship fascinated him more and more.

" Tell me all about the yacht," she said. " I'm sure she is a beauty, though you call her an old tub."

" I don't want to talk about yachts," he an-

swered, returning to the attack in spite of her.
" I want to talk about the chances of seeing you
after we part here."

" There aren't any," replied the young girl
carelessly. " What is the name of the yacht?"

" Very commonplace — ' Lucy,' that's all. I'll
make chances if there are none —"

" You mustn't say that ' Lucy' is commonplace. That's my mother's name."

" I beg your pardon. I couldn't know that.
It always struck me that it wasn't much of a
name for a yacht, you know. That was all I
meant. He's a queer old bird, my father; he
always says he took it from the Bride of Lam-
mermoor, Heaven knows why. But please — I
really can't go away and feel that I'm not to see
you again soon. You seem to think that I'm
chaffing. I'm not. I'm very serious. I like
you very much, and I don't see why one should
just meet and then go off, and let that be the
end — do you?"

" I don't see why not," exclaimed Clare, hating
the unexpected longing she felt to agree with
him, and tell him to come and stay in Florence
as much as he pleased. " Come — it's too cold
here. I must be going in."

CHAPTER IX

BROOK JOHNSTONE had never been in the habit of observing his sensations nor of paying any great attention to his actions. He was not at all an actor, as Clare believed him to be, and the idea that he could ever have taken pleasure in giving pain would have made him laugh. Possibly, it would have made him very angry, but it certainly had no foundation at all in fact. He had been liked, loved, and made much of, not for anything he had ever taken the trouble to do, but partly for his own sake, and partly on account of his position. Such charm as he had for women lay in his frankness, good humour, and simplicity of character. That he had appeared to be changeable in his affection was merely due to the fact that he had never been in love. He vaguely recognised the fact in his inner consciousness, though he would have said that he had been in love half a dozen times; which only amounted to saying that women he had liked had been in love with him or had thought that they were, or had wished to have it thought that he loved them or had per-

haps, like poor Lady Fan, been willing to risk a
good deal on the bare chance of marrying one
of the best of society's matches in the end.   He
was too young to look upon such affairs very
seriously.   When he had been tired of the game
he had not lacked the courage to say so, and in
most cases he had been forgiven.   Lady Fan
might prove an exception, but he hoped not.
He was enormously far removed from being a
saint, it is true, but it is due to him to repeat
that he had drawn the line rigidly at a certain
limit, and that all women beyond that line had
been to him as his own mother, in thought and
deed.   Let those who have the right to cast
stones — and the cruelty to do so — decide for
themselves whether Brook Johnstone was a bad
man at heart, or not.   It need not be hinted
that a proportion of the stone-throwing Pharisees owe their immaculate reputation to their
conspicuous lack of attraction; the little band
has a place apart and they stand there and
lapidate most of us, and secretly wish that they
had ever had the chance of being as bad as we
are without being found out.   But the great
army of the pure in heart are mixed with us
sinners in the fight, and though they may pray
for us, they do not carp at our imperfections —
and occasionally they get hit by the Pharisees
just as we do, being rather whiter than we and

therefore offering a more tempting mark for a jagged stone or a handful of pious mud. You may know the Pharisee by his intimate knowledge of the sins he has never committed.

Besides, though the code of honour is not worth much as compared with the Ten Commandments, it is notably better than nothing, in the way of morality. It will keep a man from lying and evil speaking as well as from picking and stealing, and if it does not force him to honour all women as angels, it makes him respect a very large proportion of them as good women and therefore sacred, in a very practical way of sacredness. Brook Johnstone always was very careful in all matters where honour and his own feeling about honour were concerned. For that reason he had told Clare that he had never done anything very bad, whereas what she had seen him do was monstrous in her eyes. She had not reflected that she knew nothing about Lady Fan; and if she had heard half there was to be known she would not have understood. That night on the platform Lady Fan had given her own version of what had taken place on the Acropolis at sunset, and Brook had not denied anything. Clare did not reflect that Lady Fan might very possibly have exaggerated the facts very much in her statement of them, and that at such a time Brook was certainly not the man to argue

the case, since it had manifestly been his only
course to take all the apparent blame on himself. Even if he had known that Clare had
heard the conversation, he could not possibly
have explained the matter to her — not even if
she had been an old woman — without telling
all the truth about Lady Fan, and he was too
honourable a man to do that, under any conceiv-
able circumstances.

He was decidedly and really in love with the
girl. He knew it, because what he felt was not
like anything he had ever felt before. It was
anything but the pleasurable excitement to
which he was accustomed. There might have
been something of that if he had received even
the smallest encouragement. But, do what he
would, he could find none. The attraction increased, and the encouragement was daily less,
he thought. Clare occasionally said things which
made him half believe that she did not wholly
dislike him. That was as much as he could say.
He cudgelled his brains and wrung his memory
to discover what he could have done to offend
her, and he could not remember anything —
which was not surprising. It was clear that she
had never heard of him before he had come to
Amalfi. He had satisfied himself of that by
questions, otherwise he would naturally enough
have come near the truth and guessed that she

must have known of some affair in which he had been concerned, which she judged harshly from her own point of view.

He was beginning to suffer, and he was not accustomed to suffering, least of all to any of the mental kind, for his life had always gone smoothly. He had believed hitherto that most people exaggerated, and worried themselves unnecessarily, but when he found it hard to sleep, and noticed that he had a dull, unsatisfied sort of misery with him all day long, he began to understand. He did not think that Clare could really enjoy teasing him, and, besides, it was not like mere teasing, either. She was evidently in earnest when she repeated that she did not like him. He knew her face when she was chaffing, and her tone, and the little bending of the delicate, swan-like throat, too long for perfect beauty, but not for perfect grace. When she was in earnest, her head rose, her eyes looked straight before her, and her voice sank to a graver note. He knew all the signs of truth, for with her it was always very near the surface, dwelling not in a deep well, but in clear water, as it were, open to the sky. Her truth was evidently truth, and her jesting was transparent as a child's.

It looked a hopeless case, but he had no intention of considering it without hope, nor any inclination to relinquish his attempts. He did not tell himself in so many words that he wished to marry her, and intended to marry her, and would marry her, if it were humanly possible, and he assuredly made no such promises to himself. Nor did he look at her as he had looked at women in whom he had been momentarily interested, appreciating her good points of face and figure, cataloguing and compiling her attractions so as to admire them all in turn, forget none, and receive their whole effect.

He had a restless, hungry craving that left him no peace, and that seemed to desire only a word, a look, the slightest touch of sympathy, to be instantly satisfied. And he could not get from her one softened glance, nor one sympathetic pressure of the hand, nor one word spoken more gravely than another, except the assurance of her genuine dislike.

That was the only thing he had to complain of, but it was enough. He could not reproach her with having encouraged him, for she had told him the truth from the first. He had not quite believed her. So much the worse for him. If he had, and if he had gone to Naples to wait for his people, all this would not have happened, for he had not fallen in love at first sight. A fortnight of daily and almost hourly intercourse was very good and reasonable ground for being in love.

He grew absent-minded, and his pipe went out unexpectedly, which always irritated him, and sometimes he did not take the trouble to light it again. He rose at dawn and went for long walks in the hills, with the idea that the early air and the lofty coolness would do him good, and with the acknowledged intention of doing his walking at an hour when he could not possibly be with Clare. For he could not keep away from her, whether Mrs. Bowring were with her or not. He was too much a man of the world to sit all day long before her, glaring at her in shy silence, as a boy might have done, and as he would have been content to do; so he took immense pains to be agreeable, when her mother was present, and Mrs. Bowring liked him, and said that he had really a most extraordinary talent for conversation. It was not that he ever said anything very memorable; but he talked most of the time, and always pleasantly, telling stories about people and places he had known, discussing the lighter books of the day, and affecting that profound ignorance of politics which makes some women feel at their ease, and encourages amusing discussion.

Mrs. Bowring watched him when she was there with a persistency which might have made him nervous if he had not been wholly absorbed in her daughter. She evidently saw something in him which reminded her of some one or something. She had changed of late, and Clare was beginning to think that she must be ill, though she scouted the suggestion, and said that she was growing daily stronger. She had altogether relaxed her vigilance with regard to the two young people, and seemed willing that they should go where they pleased together, and sit alone together by the hour.

"I dare say I watched him a good deal at first," she said to her daughter. "But I have made up my mind about him. He's a very good sort of young fellow, and I'm glad that you have a companion. You see I can't walk much, and now that you are getting better you need exercise. After all, one can always trust the best of one's own people. He's not falling in love with you, is he, dear? I sometimes fancy that he looks at you as though he were."

"Nonsense, mother!" and Clare laughed intentionally. "But he's very good company."

"It would be very unfortunate if he did," said Mrs. Bowring, looking away, and speaking almost to herself. "I am not sure that we should not have gone away—"

"Really! If one is to be turned out of the most beautiful place in the world because a young Englishman chooses to stop in the same hotel! Besides, why in the world should he

fall in love with me? He's used to a very
different kind of people, I fancy."

"What do you mean?"

"Oh — the gay set — 'a' gay set, I suppose,
for there are probably more than one of them.
They are quite different from us, you know."

"That is no reason. On the contrary — men
like variety and change — change, yes," repeated
Mrs. Bowring, with an odd emphasis. "At all
events, child, don't take a fancy to him!" she
added. "Not that I'm much afraid of that.
You are anything but 'susceptible,' my dear!"
she laughed faintly.

"You need not be in the least afraid," answered Clare. "But, after all, mother — just
supposing the case — I can't see why it should
be such an awful calamity if we took a fancy to
each other. We belong to the same class of
people, if not to the same set. He has enough
money, and I'm not absolutely penniless, though
we are as poor as church mice —"

"For Heaven's sake, don't suggest such a
thing!" cried Mrs. Bowring.

Her face was white, and her lips trembled.
There was a frightened look in her pale eyes,
and she turned her face quickly to her daughter,
and quickly away again.

"Mother!" exclaimed the young girl, in surprise. "What in the world is the matter? I

was only laughing — besides — " she stopped,
puzzled. " Tell me the truth, mother," she continued suddenly. " You know about his people —
his father is some connection of — of your first
husband — there's some disgraceful story about
them — tell me the truth. Why shouldn't I
know ? "

" I hope you never will ! " answered Mrs. Bowring, in a low voice that had a sort of horror
in it.

" Then there is something ? " Clare herself
turned a little paler as she asked the question.

" Don't ask me — don't ask me ! "

" Something disgraceful ? " The young girl
leaned forward as she spoke, and her eyes were
wide and anxious, forcing her mother to speak.

" Yes — no," faltered Mrs. Bowring. " Nothing to do with this one — something his father
did long ago."

" Dishonourable ? " asked Clare, her voice sinking lower and lower.

" No — not as men look at it — oh, don't ask
me ! Please don't ask me — please don't, darling ! "

" Then his yacht is named after you," said
the young girl in a flash of intelligence.

" His yacht ? " asked the elder woman ex-
citedly. " What ? I don't understand."

" Mr. Johnstone told me that his father had a

big steam yacht called the 'Lucy'—mother, that man loved you, he loves you still."

"Me? Oh no — no, he never loved me!" She laughed wildly, with quivering lips. "Don't, child — don't! For God's sake don't ask questions — you'll drive me mad! It's the secret of my life — the only secret I have from you — oh, Clare, if you love me at all — don't ask me!"

"Mother, sweet! Of course I love you!"

The young girl, very pale and wondering, kneeled beside the elder woman and threw her arms round her and drew down her face, kissing the white cheeks and the starting tears and the faded flaxen hair. The storm subsided, almost without breaking, for Mrs. Bowring was a brave woman and, in some ways, a strong woman, and whatever her secret might be, she had kept it long and well from her daughter.

Clare knew her, and inwardly decided that the secret must have been worth keeping. She loved her mother far too well to hurt her with questions, but she was amazed at what she herself felt of resentful curiosity to know the truth about anything which could cast a shadow upon the man she disliked, as she thought so sincerely. Her mind worked like lightning, while her voice spoke softly and her hands sought those thin, familiar, gentle fingers which were an integral part of her world and life.

Two possibilities presented themselves. Johnstone's father was a brother or near connection
of her mother's first husband. Either she had
loved him, been deceived in him, and had married the brother instead ; or,- having married,
this man had hated her and fought against her,
and harmed her, because she was his elder
brother's wife, and he coveted the inheritance.
In either case it was no fault of Brook's. The
most that could be said would be that he might
have his father's character. She inclined to the
first of her theories. Old Johnstone had made
love to her mother and had half broken her heart,
before she had married his brother. Brook was
no better — and she thought of Lady Fan. But
she was strangely glad that her mother had said
" not dishonourable, as men look at it." It had
been as though a cruel hand had been taken
from her throat, when she had heard that.

" But, mother," she said presently, " these
people are coming to-morrow or the next day —
and they mean to stay, he says. Let us go away,
before they come. We can come back afterwards — you don't want to meet them."

Mrs. Bowring was calm again, or appeared to
be so, whatever was passing in her mind.

"I shall certainly not run away," she answered
in a low, steady voice. " I will not run away
and leave Adam Johnstone's son to tell his father

that I was afraid to meet him, or his wife," she added, almost in a whisper. " I've been weak, sometimes, my dear — " her voice rose to its natural key again, " and I've made a mistake in life.   But I won't be a coward — I don't believe I am, by nature, and if I were I wouldn't let myself be afraid now."

" It would not be fear, mother. Why should you suffer, if you are going to suffer in meeting him ? We had much better go away at once. When they have all left, we can come back."

" And you would not mind going away to-morrow, and never seeing Brook Johnstone again?" asked Mrs. Bowring, quietly.

" I ?   No !   Why should I ? "

Clare meant to speak the truth, and she thought that it was the truth.   But it was not. She grew a little paler a moment after the words had passed her lips, but her mother did not see the change of colour.

" I'm glad of that, at all events," said the elder woman.   " But I won't go away.   No — I won't," she repeated, as though spurring her own courage.

" Very well," answered the young girl.   " But we can keep very much to ourselves all the time they are here, can't we ?   We needn't make their acquaintance — at least — " she stopped short, realising that it would be impossible to

avoid knowing Brook's people if they were stopping in the same hotel.

"Their acquaintance!" Mrs. Bowring laughed
bitterly at the idea.

"Oh — I forgot," said Clare. "At all events,
we need not meet unnecessarily. That's what I
mean, you know."

There was a short pause, during which her
mother seemed to be thinking.

"I shall see him alone, for I have something
to say to him," she said at last, as though she
had come to a decision. "Go out, my dear,"
she added. "Leave me alone a little while. I
shall be all right when it is time for luncheon."

Her daughter left her, but she did not go out
at once. She went to her own room and sat
down to think over what she had seen and
heard. If she went out she should probably
find Johnstone waiting for her, and she did not
wish to meet him just then. It was better to be
alone. She would find out why the idea of not
seeing him any more had hurt her after she had
spoken.

But that was not an easy matter at all. So
soon as she tried to think of herself and her
own feelings, she began to think of her mother.
And when she endeavoured to solve the mystery
and guess the secret, her thoughts flew off suddenly to Brook, and she wished that she were

outside in the sunshine talking to him. And
again, as the probable conversation suggested itself to her, she was glad that she was not with
him, and she tried to think again. Then she
forced herself to recall the scene with Lady Fan
on the terrace, and she did her best to put him
in the worst possible light, which in her opinion
was a very bad light indeed. And his father
before him — Adam — her mother had told her
the name for the first time, and it struck her as
an odd one — old Adam Johnstone had been a
heart-breaker, and a faith-breaker, and a betrayer
of women before Brook was in the world at all.
Her theory held good, when she looked at it
fairly, and her resentment grew apace. It was
natural enough, for in her imagination she had
always hated that first husband of her mother's
who had come and gone before her father; and
now she extended her hatred to this probable
brother, and it had much more force, because the
man was alive and a reality, and was soon to come
and be a visible talking person. There was one
good point about him and his coming. It helped
her to revive her hatred of Brook and to colour it
with the inheritance of some harm done to her
own mother. That certainly was an advantage.

But she should be very sorry not to see Brook
any more, never to hear him talk to her again,
never to look into his eyes — which, all the

same, she so unreasonably dreaded. It was beyond her powers of analysis to reconcile her like
and dislike. All the little logic she had said
that it was impossible to like and dislike the
same person at the same time. She seemed to
have two hearts, and the one cried " Hate,"
while the other cried " Love." That was absurd, and altogether ridiculous, and quite contemptible.

There they were, however, the two hearts,
fighting it out, or at least altercating and threatening to fight and hurt her. Of course " love "
meant " like " — it was a general term, well
contrasting with " hate." As for really caring,
beyond a liking for Brook Johnstone, she was
sure that it was impossible. But the liking was
strong. She exploded her difficulty at last with
the bomb of a splendidly youthful quibble. She
said to herself that she undoubtedly hated him
and despised him, and that he was certainly the
very lowest of living men for treating Lady Fan
so badly — besides being a black sinner, a point
which had less weight. And then she told herself that the cry of something in her to " like "
instead of hating was simply the expression of
what she might have felt, and should have felt,
and should have had a right to have felt, had it
not been for poor Lady Fan ; but also of something which she assuredly did not feel, never

could feel, and never meant to feel. In other words, she should have liked Brook if she had not had good cause to dislike him. She was satisfied with this explanation of her feelings, and she suddenly felt that she could go out and see him and talk to him without being inconsistent. She had forgotten to explain to herself why she wished him not to go away. She went out accordingly, and sat down on the terrace in the soft air.

She glanced up and down, but Johnstone was not to be seen anywhere, and she wished that she had not come out after all. He had probably waited some time and had then gone for a walk by himself. She thought that he might have waited just a little longer before giving it up, and she half unconsciously made up her mind to requite him by staying indoors after luncheon. She had not even brought a book or a piece of work, for she had felt quite sure that he would be walking up and down as usual, with his pipe, looking as though he owned the scenery. She half rose to go in, and then changed her mind. She would give him one more chance and count fifty, before she went away, at a good quick rate.

She began to count. At thirty-five her pace slackened. She stopped a long time at forty-five, and then went slowly to the end. But Johnstone did not come. Once again, she reluctantly

decided — and she began slowly; and again she
slackened speed and dragged over the last ten
numbers. But he did not come.

" Oh, this is ridiculous ! " she exclaimed aloud
to herself, as she rose impatiently from her
seat.

She felt injured, for her mother had sent her
away, and there was no one to talk to her, and
she did not care to think any more, lest the
questions she had decided should again seem
open and doubtful. She went into the hotel
and walked down the corridor. He might be in
the reading-room. She walked quickly, because
she was a little ashamed of looking for him when
she felt that he should be looking for her. Suddenly she stopped, for she heard him whistling
somewhere. Whistling was his solitary accom-
plishment, and he did it very well. There was
no mistaking the shakes and runs, and pretty
bird-like cadences. She listened, but she bit her
lip. He was light-hearted, at all events, she
thought.

The sound came nearer, and Brook suddenly
appeared in the corridor, his hat on the back of
his head, his hands in his pockets. As he caught
sight of Clare the shrill tune ceased, and one
hand removed the hat.

" I've been looking for you everywhere, for
the last two hours," he cried as he came along.

"Good morning," he said as he reached her. "I was just going back to the terrace in despair."

"It sounded more as though you were whistling for me," answered Clare, with a laugh, for she was instantly happy, and pacified, and peaceful.

"Well — not exactly!" he answered. "But I did hope that you would hear me and know that I was about — wishing you would come."

"I always come out in the morning," she replied with sudden demureness. "Indeed — I wondered where you were. Let us go out, shall we?"

"We might go for a walk," suggested Brook.

"It is too late."

"Just a little walk — down to the town and across the bridge to Atrani, and back. Couldn't we?"

"Oh, we could, of course. Very well — I've got a hat on, haven't I? All right. Come along!"

"My people are coming to-day," said Brook, as they passed through the door. "I've just had a telegram."

"To-day!" exclaimed Clare in·surprise, and somewhat disturbed.

"Yes, you know I have been expecting them at any moment. I fancy they have been knock-

ing about, you know — seeing Pæstum and
all that. They are such queer people. They
always want to see everything — as though it
mattered!"

"There are only the two? Mr. and Mrs.
Johnstone?"

"Yes — that's all." Brook laughed a little
as though she had said something amusing.

"What are you laughing at?" asked Clare,
naturally enough.

"Oh, nothing. It's ridiculous — but it sounded
funny — unfamiliar, I mean. My father has
fallen a victim to knighthood, that's all. The
affliction came upon him some time ago, and his
name is Adam — of all the names in the world."

"It was the first," observed Clare reassur-
ingly. "It doesn't sound badly either — Sir
Adam. I beg his pardon for calling him 'Mr.'"
She laughed in her turn.

"Oh, he wouldn't mind," said Brook. "He's
not at all that sort. Do you know? I think
you'll like him awfully. He's a fine old chap
in his way, though he is a brewer. He's much
bigger than I am, but he's rather odd, you
know. Sometimes he'll talk like anything, and
sometimes he won't open his lips. We aren't
at all alike in that way. I talk all the time, I
believe — rain or shine. Don't I bore you
dreadfully sometimes?"

"No — you never bore me," answered Clare with perfect truth.

"I mean, when I talk as I did yesterday afternoon," said Johnstone with a shade of irritation.

"Oh, that — yes! Please don't begin again, and spoil our walk!"

But the walk was not destined to be a long one. A narrow, paved footway leads down from the old monastery to the shore, in zigzag, between low whitewashed walls, passing at last under some houses which are built across it on arches.

Just as they came in sight a tall old man emerged from this archway, walking steadily up the hill. He was tall and bony, with a long grey beard, shaggy bent brows, keen dark eyes, and an eagle nose. He wore clothes of rough grey woollen tweed, and carried a grey felt hat in one long hand.

A moment after he had come out of the arch he caught sight of Brook, and his rough face brightened instantly. He waved the grey hat and called out.

"Hulloa, my boy! There you are, eh!"

His voice was thin, like many Scotch voices, but it carried far, and had a manly ring in it. Brook did not answer, but waved his hat.

"That's my father," he said in a low tone to

Clare. "May I introduce him? And there's
my mother — being carried up in the chair."

A couple of lusty porters were carrying Lady
Johnstone up the steep ascent. She was a fat
lady with bright blue eyes, like her son's, and a
much brighter colour. She had a parasol in
one hand and a fan in the other, and she shook
a little with every step the porters made. In
the rear, a moment later, came other porters,
carrying boxes and bags of all sizes. Then a
short woman, evidently Lady Johnstone's maid,
came quietly along by herself, stopping occasionally to look at the sea.

Clare looked curiously at the party as they
approached. Her first impulse had been to leave
Brook and go back alone to warn her mother.
It was not far. But she realised that it would
be much better and wiser to face the introduction at once. In less than five minutes Sir
Adam had reached them. He shook hands
with Brook vigorously, and looked at him as a
man looks who loves his son. Clare saw the
glance, and it pleased her.

"Let me introduce you to Miss Bowring," said
Brook. "Mrs. Bowring and Miss Bowring are
staying here, and have been awfully good to
me."

Sir Adam turned his keen eyes to Clare, as
she held out her hand.

"I beg your pardon," he said, "but are you a daughter of Captain Bowring who was killed some years ago in Africa?"

"Yes." She looked up to him inquiringly and distrustfully.

His face brightened again and softened — then hardened singularly, all at once. She could not have believed that such features could change so quickly.

"And my son says that your mother is here! My dear young lady — I'm very glad! I hope you mean to stay."

The words were cordial. The tone was cold. Brook stared at his father, very much surprised to find that he knew anything of the Bowrings, for he himself had not mentioned them in his letters. But the porters, walking more slowly, had just brought his mother up to where the three stood, and waited, panting a little, and the chair swinging slightly from the shoulder-straps.

"Dear old boy!" cried Lady Johnstone. "It is good to see you. No — don't kiss me, my dear — it's far too hot. Let me look at you."

Sir Adam gravely introduced Clare. Lady Johnstone's fat face became stony as a red granite mummy case, and she bent her apoplectic neck stiffly.

"Oh!" she ejaculated. "Very glad, I'm sure.

Were you going for a walk?" she asked, turning to Brook, severely.

"Yes, there was just time. I didn't know when to expect you. But if Miss Bowring doesn't mind, we'll give it up, and I'll install you. Your rooms are all ready."

It was at once clear to Clare that Lady Johnstone had never heard the name of Bowring, and that she resented the idea of her son walking alone with any young girl.

CHAPTER X

CLARE went directly to her mother's room. She had hardly spoken again during the few minutes while she had necessarily remained with the Johnstones, climbing the hill back to the hotel. At the door she had stood aside to let Lady Johnstone go in, Sir Adam had followed his wife, and Brook had lingered, doubtless hoping to exchange a few words more with Clare. But she was preoccupied, and had not vouchsafed him a glance.

"They have come," she said, as she closed Mrs. Bowring's door behind her.

Her mother was seated by the open window, her hands lying idly in her lap, her face turned away, as Clare entered. She started slightly, and looked round.

"Oh!" she exclaimed. "Already! Well — it had to come. Have you met?"

Clare told her all that had happened.

"And he said that he was glad?" asked Mrs. Bowring, with the ghost of a smile.

"He said so — yes. His voice was cold. But

193

when he first heard my name and asked about my father his face softened."

"His face softened," repeated Mrs. Bowring. to herself, just above a whisper, as the ghost of the smile flitted about her pale lips.

"He seemed glad at first, and then he looked displeased. Is that it?" she asked, raising her voice again.

"That was what I thought," answered Clare. "Why don't you have luncheon in your room, mother?" she asked suddenly.

"He would think I was afraid to meet him," said the elder woman.

A long silence followed, and Clare sat down on a stiff straw chair, looking out of the window. At last she turned to her mother again.

"You couldn't tell me all about it, could you, mother dear?" she asked. "It seems to me it would be so much easier for us both. Perhaps I could help you. And I myself — I should know better how to act."

"No. I can't tell·you. I only pray that I may never have to. As for you, darling — be natural. It is a very strange position to be in, but you cannot know it — you can't be supposed to know it. I wish I could have kept my secret better — but I broke down when you told me about the yacht. You can only help me in one way — don't ask me questions, dear. It would

be harder for me, if you knew — indeed it would.
Be natural. You need not run after them, you
know —"

"I should think not!" cried Clare indignantly.

"I mean, you need not go and sit by them
and talk to them for long at a time. But don't
be suddenly cold and rude to their son. There's
nothing against — I mean, it has nothing to do
with him. You mustn't think it has, you know.
Be natural — be yourself."

"It's not altogether easy to be natural under
the circumstances," Clare answered, with some
truth, and a great deal of repressed curiosity
which she did her best to hide away altogether
for her mother's sake.

At luncheon the Johnstones were all three
placed on the opposite side of the table, and
Brook was no longer Clare's neighbour. The
Bowrings were already in their places when the
three entered, Sir Adam giving his arm to his
wife, who seemed to need help in walking, or at
all events to be glad of it. Brook followed at a
little distance, and Clare saw that he was looking at her regretfully, as though he wished himself at her side again. Had she been less young
and unconscious and thoroughly innocent, she
must have seen by this time that he was seriously in love with her.

Sir Adam held his wife's chair for her, with

somewhat old-fashioned courtesy, and pushed it
gently as she sat down. Then he raised his
head, and his eyes met Mrs. Bowring's. For a
few moments they looked at each other. Then
his expression changed and softened, as it had
when he had first met Clare, but Mrs. Bowring's
face grew hard and pale. He did not sit down,
but to his wife's surprise walked quietly all round
the end of the table and up the other side to
where Mrs. Bowring sat. She knew that he
was coming, and she turned a little to meet
his hand. The English old maids watched the
proceedings with keen interest from the upper
end.

Sir Adam held out his hand, and Mrs. Bowring took it.

"It is a great pleasure to me to meet you
again," he said slowly, as though speaking with
an effort. "Brook says that you have been very
good to him, and so I want to thank you at
once. Yes — this is your daughter — Brook
introduced me. Excuse me — I'll get round to
my place again. Shall we meet after luncheon?"

"If you like," said Mrs. Bowring in a con
strained tone. "By all means," she added ner.
vously.

"My dear," said Sir Adam, speaking across
the table to his wife, "let me introduce you to

my old friend Mrs. Bowring, the mother of this young lady whom you have already met," he added, glancing down at Clare's flaxen head.

Again Lady Johnstone slightly bent her apoplectic neck, but her expression was not stony, as it had been when she had first looked at Clare. On the contrary, she smiled very pleasantly and naturally, and her frank blue eyes looked at Mrs. Bowring with a friendly interest.

Clare thought that she heard a faint sigh of relief escape her mother's lips just then. Sir Adam's heavy steps echoed upon the tile floor, as he marched all round the table again to his seat. The table itself was narrow, and it was easy to talk across it, without raising the voice. Sir Adam sat on one side of his wife, and Brook on the other, last on his side, as Clare was on hers.

There was very little conversation at first. Brook did not care to talk across to Clare, and Sir Adam seemed to have said all he meant to say for the present. Lady Johnstone, who seemed to be a cheerful, conversational soul, began to talk to Mrs. Bowring, evidently attracted by her at first sight.

"It's a beautiful place when you get here," she said. "Isn't it? The view from my window is heavenly! But to get here! Dear me! I was carried up by two men, you know, and I

thought they would have died. I hope they are
enjoying their dinner, poor fellows! I'm sure
they never carried such a load before ! "

And she laughed, with a sort of frank, half
self-commiserating amusement at her own proportions.

" Oh, I fancy they must be used to it," said
Mrs. Bowring, reassuringly, for the sake of saying something.

" They'll hate the sight of me in a week!"
said Lady Johnstone. " I mean to go everywhere, while I'm here — up all the hills, and
down all the valleys. I always see everything
when I come to a new place. It's pleasant to sit
still afterwards, and feel that you've done it
all, don't you know ? I shall ruin you in porters,
Adam," she added, turning her large round face
slowly to her husband.

" Certainly, certainly," answered Sir Adam,
nodding gravely, as he dissected the bones out of
a fried sardine.

" You're awfully good about it," said Lady
Johnstone, in thanks for unlimited porters to
come.

Like many unusually stout people, she ate
very little, and had plenty of time for talking.

" You knew my husband a long time ago,
then ! " she began, again looking across at Mrs.
Bowring.

Sir Adam glanced at Mrs. Bowring sharply from beneath his shaggy brows.

"Oh yes," she said calmly. "We met before he was married."

The grey-headed man slowly nodded assent, but said nothing.

"Before his first marriage?" inquired Lady Johnstone gravely. "You know that he has been married twice."

"Yes," answered Mrs. Bowring. "Before his first marriage."

Again Sir Adam nodded solemnly.

"How interesting!" exclaimed Lady Johnstone. "Such old friends! And to meet in this accidental way, in this queer place!"

"We generally live abroad," said Mrs. Bowring. "Generally in Florence. Do you know Florence?"

"Oh yes!" cried the fat lady enthusiastically. "I dote on Florence. I'm perfectly mad about pictures, you know. Perfectly mad!"

The vision of a woman cast in Lady Johnstone's proportions and perfectly mad might have provoked a smile on Mrs. Bowring's face at any other time.

"I suppose you buy pictures, as well as admire them," she said, glad of the turn the conversation had taken.

"Sometimes," answered the other. "Some-

times. I wish I could buy more. But good
pictures are getting to be most frightfully dear.
Besides, you are hardly ever sure of getting an
original, unless there are all the documents —
and that means thousands, literally thousands of
pounds. But now and then I kick over the
traces, you know."

Clare could not help smiling at the simile, and
bent down her head. Brook was watching her,
he understood and was annoyed, for he loved his
mother in his own way.

" At all events you won't be able to ruin yourself in pictures here," said Mrs. Bowring.

" No — but how about the porters ? " suggested
Sir Adam.

" My dear Adam," said Lady Johnstone, " unless they are all Shylocks here, they won't exact a ducat for every pound of flesh. If they
did, you would certainly never get back to England."

It was impossible not to laugh. Lady Johnstone did not look at all the sort of person to
say witty things, though she was the very incarnation of good humour — except when she
thought that Brook was in danger of being married. And every one laughed, Sir Adam first,
then Brook, and then the Bowrings. The effect
was good. Lady Johnstone was really afflicted
with curiosity, and her first questions to Mrs.

Bowring had been asked purely out of a wish to make advances. She was strongly attracted by the quiet, pale face, with its excessive refinement and delicately traced lines of suffering. She felt that the woman had taken life too hard, and it was her instinct to comfort her, and warm her and take care of her, from the first. Brook understood and rejoiced, for he knew his mother's tenacity about her first impressions, and he wished to have her on his side.

After that the ice was broken and the conversation did not flag. Sir Adam looked at Mrs. Bowring from time to time with an expression of uncertainty which sat strangely on his determined features, and whenever any new subject was broached he watched her uneasily until she had spoken. But Mrs. Bowring rarely returned his glances, and her eyes never lingered on his face even when she was speaking to him. Clare, for her part, joined in the conversation, and wondered and waited. Her theory was strengthened by what she saw. Clearly Sir Adam felt uncomfortable in her mother's presence; therefore he had injured her in some way, and doubted whether she had ever forgiven him. But to the girl's quick instinct it was clear that he did not stand to Mrs. Bowring only in the position of one who had harmed her. In some way of love or friendship, he had once been very fond of her.

The youngest woman cannot easily mistake the signs of such bygone intercourse.

When they rose, Mrs. Bowring walked slowly, on her side of the table, so as not to reach the door before Lady Johnstone, who could not move fast under any circumstances. They all went out together upon the terrace.

"Brook," said the fat lady, "I must sit down, or I shall die. You know, my dear — get me one that won't break!"

She laughed a little, as Brook went off to find a solid chair. A few minutes later she was enthroned in safety, her husband on one side of her and Mrs. Bowring on the other, all facing the sea.

"It's too perfect for words!" she exclaimed, in solid and peaceful satisfaction. "Adam, isn't it a dream? You thin people don't know how nice it is to come to anchor in a pleasant place after a long voyage!"

She sighed happily and moved her arms so that their weight was quite at rest without an effort.

Clare and Johnstone walked slowly up and down, passing and repassing, and trying to talk as though neither were aware that there was something unusual in the situation, to say the least of it. At last they stopped at the end farthest away from the others.

"I had no idea that my father had known your mother long ago," said Brook suddenly. "Had you?"

"Yes — of late," answered Clare. "You see my mother wasn't sure, until you told me his first name," she hastened to add.

"Oh — I see. Of course. Stupid of me not to try and bring it into the conversation sooner, wasn't it? But it seems to have been ever so long ago. Don't you think so?"

"Yes. Ever so long ago."

"When they were quite young, I suppose. Your mother must have been perfectly beautiful when she was young. I dare say my father was madly in love with her. It wouldn't be at all surprising, you know, would it? He was a tremendous fellow for falling in love."

"Oh! Was he?" Clare spoke rather coldly.

"You're not angry, are you, because I suggested it?" asked Brook quickly. "I don't see that there's any harm in it. There's no reason why a young man as he was shouldn't have been desperately in love with a beautiful young girl, is there?"

"None whatever," answered Clare. "I was only thinking — it's rather an odd coincidence — do you mind telling me something?"

"Of course not! What is it?"

"Had your father ever a brother — who died?"

"No. He had a lot of sisters — some of them are alive still. Awful old things, my aunts are, too. No, he never had any brother. Why do you ask?"

"Nothing — it's a mere coincidence. Did I ever tell you that my mother was married twice? My father was her second husband. The first had your name."

"Johnstone, with an E on the end of it?"

"Yes — with an E."

"Gad! that's funny!" exclaimed Brook. "Some connection, I dare say. Then we are connected too, you and I, not much though, when one thinks of it. Step-cousin by marriage, and ever so many degrees removed, too."

"You can't call that a connection," said Clare with a little laugh, but her face was thoughtful. "Still, it is odd that she should have known your father well, and should have married a man of the same name — with the E — isn't it?"

"He may have been an own cousin, for all I know," said Brook. "I'll ask. He's sure to remember. He never forgets anything. And it's another coincidence too, that my father should have been married twice, just like your mother, and that I should be the son of the second marriage, too. What odd things happen, when one comes to compare notes!"

While they had walked up and down, Lady Johnstone had paid no attention to them, but she had grown restless as soon as she had seen that they stood still at a distance to talk, and her bright blue eyes turned towards them again and again, with sudden motherly anxiety. At last she could bear it no longer.

"Brook!" she cried. "Brook, my dear boy!" Brook and Clare walked back towards the little group.

"Brook, dear," said Lady Johnstone. "Please come and tell me the names of all the mountains and places we see from here. You know, I always want to know everything as soon as I arrive."

Sir Adam rose from his chair.

"Should you like to take a turn?" he asked, speaking to Mrs. Bowring and standing before her.

She rose in silence and stepped forward, with a quiet, set face, as though she knew that the supreme moment had come.

"Take our chairs," said Sir Adam to Clare and Brook. "We are going to walk about a little."

Mrs. Bowring turned in the direction whence the young people had come, towards the end of the terrace. Sir Adam walked erect beside her.

"Is there a way out at that end?" he asked

in a low voice, when they had gone a little
distance.

" No."

" We can't stand there and talk.   Where can
we go ?   Isn't there a quiet place somewhere ? "

" Do you want to talk to me ? " asked Mrs.
Bowring, looking straight before her.

" Yes, please," answered Sir Adam, almost
sharply, but still in a low tone.   " I've waited
a long time," he added.

Mrs. Bowring said nothing in answer.   They
reached the end of the walk, and she turned
without pausing.

" The point out there is called the Conca,"
she said, pointing to the rocks far out below.
" It curls round like a shell, you know.   Conca
means a sea-shell, I think.   It seems to be a
great place for fishing, for there are always
little boats about it in fine weather."

" I remember," replied Sir Adam.   " I was
here thirty years ago.   It hasn't changed much.
Are there still those little paper-mills in the val-
ley on the way to Ravello ?   They used to be
very primitive."

They kept up their forced conversation as
they passed Lady Johnstone and the young
people.   Then they were silent again, as they
went towards the hotel.

" We'll go through the house," said Mrs.

Bowring, speaking low again. "There's a quiet place on the other side — Clare and your son will have to stay with your wife."

"Yes, I thought of that, when I told them to take our chairs."

In silence they traversed the long tiled corridor with set faces, like two people who are going to do something dangerous and disagreeable together. They came out upon the platform before the deep recess of the rocks in which stood the black cross. There was nobody there.

"We shall not be disturbed out here," said Mrs. Bowring, quietly. "The people in the hotel go to their rooms after luncheon. We will sit down there by the cross, if you don't mind — I'm not so strong as I used to be, you know."

They ascended the few steps which led up to the bench where Clare had sat on that evening which she could not forget, and they sat down side by side, not looking at each other's faces.

A long silence followed. Once or twice Sir Adam shifted his feet uneasily, and opened his mouth as though he were going to say something, but suddenly changed his mind. Mrs. Bowring was the first to speak.

"Please understand," she said slowly, glancing at him sideways, "I don't want you to say anything, and I don't know what you can have

to say. As for my being here, it's very simple.
If I had known that Brook Johnstone was your
son before he had made our acquaintance, and
that you were coming here, I should have gone
away at once. As soon as I knew him I suspected who he was. You must know that he is
like you as you used to be — except your eyes.
Then I said to myself that he would tell you
that he had met us, and that you would of course
think that I had been afraid to meet you. I'm
not. So I stayed. I don't know whether I did
right or wrong. To me it seemed right, and
I'm willing to abide the consequences, if there
are to be any."

"What consequences can there be?" asked
the grey-bearded man, turning his eyes slowly
to her face.

"That depends upon how you act. It might
have been better to behave as though we had
never met, and to let your son introduce you to
me as he introduced you to Clare. We might
have started upon a more formal footing, then.
You have chosen to say that we are old friends.
It's an odd expression to use — but let it stand.
I won't quarrel with it. It does well enough.
As for the position, it's not pleasant for me, but
it must be worse for you. There's not much to
choose. But I don't want you to think that I
expect you to talk about old times unless you

like. If you have anything which you wish to say, I'll hear it all without interrupting you. But I do wish you to believe that I won't do anything nor say anything which could touch your wife. She seems to be happy with you. I hope she always has been and always will be. She knew what she was doing when she married you. God knows, there was publicity enough. Was it my fault? I suppose you've always thought so. Very well, then — say that it was my fault. But don't tell your wife who I am unless she forces you to it out of curiosity."

"Do you think I should wish to?" asked Sir Adam, bitterly.

"No — of course not. But she may ask you who I was and when we met, and all about it. Try and keep her off the subject. We don't want to tell lies, you know."

"I shall say that you were Lucy Waring. That's true enough. You were christened Lucy Waring. She need never know what your last name was. That isn't a lie, is it?"

"Not exactly — under the circumstances."

"And your daughter knows nothing, of course? I want to know how we stand, you see."

"No — only that we have met before. I don't know what she may suspect. And your son?"

"Oh, I suppose he knows. Somebody must have told him."

"He doesn't know who I am, though," said
Mrs. Bowring, with conviction. "He seems to
be more like his mother than like you. He
couldn't conceal anything long."

"I wasn't particularly good at that either, as
it turned out," said Sir Adam, gravely.

"No, thank God!"

"Do you think it's something to be thankful
for? I don't. Things might have gone better
afterwards —"

"Afterwards!" The suffering of the woman's
life was in the tone and in her eyes.

"Yes, afterwards. I'm an old man, Lucy, and
I've seen a great many things since you and I
parted, and a great many people. I was bad
enough, but I've seen worse men since, who have
had another chance and have turned out well."

"Their wives did not love them. I am almost
old, too. I loved you, Adam. It was a bad
hurt you gave me, and the wound never healed.
I married — I had to marry. He was an honest gentleman. Then he was killed. That hurt
too, for I was very fond of him — but it did not
hurt as the other did. Nothing could."

Her voice shook, and she turned away her
face. At least, he should not see that her lip
trembled.

"I didn't think you cared," said Sir Adam,
and his own voice was not very steady.

She turned upon him almost fiercely, and there was a blue light in her faded eyes.

"I! You thought I didn't care? You've no right to say that — it's wicked of you, and it's cruel. Did you think I married you for your money, Adam? And if I had — should I have given it up to be divorced because you gave jewels to an actress? I loved you, and I wanted your love, or nothing. You couldn't be faithful — commonly, decently faithful, for one year — and I got myself free from you, because I would not be your wife, nor eat your bread, nor touch your hand, if you couldn't love me. Don't say that you ever loved me, except my face. We hadn't been divorced a year when you married again. Don't say that you loved me! You loved your wife — your second wife — perhaps. I hope so. I hope you love her now — and I dare say you do, for she looks happy — but don't say that you ever loved me — just long enough to marry me and betray me!"

"You're hard, Lucy. You're as hard as ever you were twenty years ago," said Adam Johnstone.

As he leaned forward, resting an elbow on his knee, he passed his brown hand across his eyes, and then stared vaguely at the white walls of the old hotel beyond the platform.

"But you know that I'm right," answered

Mrs. Bowring. "Perhaps I'm hard, too. I'm sorry. You said that you had been mad, I remember — I don't like to think of all you said, but you said that. And I remember thinking that I had been much more mad than you, to have married you, but that I should soon be really mad — raving mad — if I remained your wife. I couldn't. I should have died. Afterwards I thought it would have been better if I had died then. But I lived through it. Then, after the death of my old aunt, I was alone. What was I to do? I was poor and lonely, and a divorced woman, though the right had been on my side. Richard Bowring knew all about it, and I married him. I did not love you any more, then, but I told him the truth when I told him that I could never love any one again. He was satisfied — so we were married."

"I don't blame you," said Sir Adam.

"Blame me! No — it would hardly be for you to blame me, if I could make anything of the shreds of my life which I had saved from yours. For that matter — you were free too. It was soon done, but why should I blame you for that? You were free — by the law — to go where you pleased, to love again, and to marry at once. You did. Oh no! I don't blame you for that!"

Both were silent for some time. But Mrs.

Bowring's eyes still had an indignant light in
them, and her fingers twitched nervously from
time to time. Sir Adam stared stolidly at the
white wall, without looking at his former
wife.

"I've been talking about myself," she said at
last. "I didn't mean to, for I need no justification. When you said that you wanted to say
something, I brought you here so that we could
be alone. What was it? I should have let you
speak first."

"It was this." He paused, as though choosing his words. "Well, I don't know," he continued presently. "You've been saying a good
many things about me that I would have said
myself. I've not denied them, have I? Well,
it's this. I wanted to see you for years, and
now we've met. We may not meet again, Lucy,
though I dare say we may live a long time. I
wish we could, though. But of course you don't
care to see me. I was your husband once, and
I behaved like a brute to you. You wouldn't
want me for a friend now that I am old."

He waited, but she said nothing.

"Of course you wouldn't," he continued. "I
shouldn't, in your place. Oh, I know! If I were
dying or starving, or very unhappy, you would
be capable of doing anything for me, out of sheer
goodness. You're only just to people who aren't

suffering. You were always like that in the old days. It's so much the worse for us. I have nothing about me to excite your pity. I'm strong, I'm well, I'm very rich, I'm relatively happy. I don't know how much I cared for my wife when I married her, but she has been a good wife, and I'm very fond of her now, in my own way. It wasn't a good action, I admit, to marry her at all. She was the beauty of her year and the best match of the season, and I was just divorced, and every one's hand was against me. I thought I would show them what I could do, winged as I was, and I got her. No; it wasn't a thing to be proud of. But somehow we hit it off, and she stuck to me, and I grew fond of her because she did, and here we are as you see us, and Brook is a fine fellow, and likes me. I like him too. He's honest and faithful, like his mother. There's no justice and no logic in this world, Lucy. I was a good-for-nothing in the old days. Circumstances have made me decently good, and a pretty happy man besides, as men go. I couldn't ask for any pity if I tried."

"No; you're not to be pitied. I'm glad you're happy. I don't wish you any harm."

"You might, and I shouldn't blame you. But all that isn't what I wished to say. I'm getting old, and we may not meet any more

after this. If you wish me to go away, I'll go.
We'll leave the place tomorrow."

"No. Why should you? It's a strange situation, as we were to-day at table. You with
your wife beside, and your divorced wife opposite
you, and only you and I knowing it. I suppose
you think, somehow — I don't know — that I
might be jealous of your wife. But twenty-
seven years make a difference, Adam. It's
half ₁a lifetime. It's so utterly past that I
sha'n't realise it. If you like to stay, then stay.
No harm can come of it, and that was so very
long ago. Is that what you want to say?"

"No." He hesitated. "I want you to say
that you forgive me," he said, in a quick, hoarse
voice.

His keen dark eyes turned quickly to her
face, and he saw how very pale she was, and
how the shadows had deepened under her eyes,
and her fingers twitched nervously as they
clasped one another in her lap.

"I suppose you think I'm sentimental," he
said, looking at her. "Perhaps I am; but it
would mean a good deal to me if you would just
say it."

There was something pathetic in the appeal,
and something young too, in spite of his grey
beard and furrowed face. Still Mrs. Bowring
said nothing. It meant almost too much to

her, even after twenty-seven years. This old
man had taken her, an innocent young girl, had
married her, had betrayed her while she dearly
loved him, and had blasted her life at the beginning. Even now it was hard to forgive. The
suffering was not old, and the sight of his face
had touched the quick again. Barely ten
minutes had passed since the pain had almost
wrung the tears from her.

" You can't," said the old man, suddenly. " I
see it. It's too much to ask, I suppose, and I've
never done anything to deserve it."

The pale face grew paler, but the hands were
still, and grasped each other, firm and cold.
The lips moved, but no sound came. Then a
moment, and they moved again.

" You're mistaken, Adam. I do forgive you."

He caught the two hands in his, and his face
shivered.

" God bless you, dear," he tried to say, and he
kissed the hands twice.

When Mrs. Bowring looked up he was sitting
beside her, just as before ; but his face was terribly drawn, and strange, and a great tear had
trickled down the furrowed brown cheek into
the grey beard.

CHAPTER XI

LADY JOHNSTONE was one of those perfectly
frank and honest persons who take no trouble
to conceal their anxieties. From the fact that
when she had met him on the way up to the
hotel Brook had been walking alone with Clare
Bowring, she had at once argued that a considerable intimacy existed between the two.
Her meeting with Clare's mother, and her sudden fancy for the elder woman, had momentarily
allayed her fears, but they revived when it became clear to her that Brook sought every possible opportunity of being alone with the young
girl. She was an eminently practical woman, as
has been said, which perhaps accounted for her
having made a good husband out of such a man
as Adam Johnstone had been in his youth. She
had never seen Brook devote himself to a young
girl before now. She saw that Clare was good
to look at, and she promptly concluded that
Brook must be in love. The conclusion was
perfectly correct, and Lady Johnstone soon grew
very nervous. Brook was too young to marry,
and even if he had been old enough his mother

217.

thought that he might have made a better
choice.   At all events he should not entangle
himself in an engagement with the girl ; and
she began systematically to interfere with his
attempts to be alone with her   Brook was as
frank as herself.   He charged her with trying
to keep him from Clare, and she did not deny
that he was right.   This led to a discussion on
the third day after the Johnstones' arrival.

" You mustn't make a fool of yourself, Brook,
dear," said Lady Johnstone.   " You are not old
enough to marry.   Oh, I know, you are five-and-
twenty, and ought to have come to years of
discretion.   But you haven't, dear boy.   Don't
forget that you are Adam Johnstone's son, and
that you may be expected to do all the things
that he did before I married him.   And he did
a good many things, you know.   I'm devoted to
your father, and if he were in the room I should
tell you just what I am telling you now.   Before
I married him he had about a thousand flirta-
tions, and he had been married too, and had
gone off with an actress—a shocking affair altogether !   And his wife had divorced him.   She
must have been one of those horrible women
who can't forgive, you know.   Now, my dear
boy, you aren't a bit better than your father,
and that pretty Clare Bowring looks as though
she would never forgive anybody who did any-

thing she didn't like. Have you asked her to marry you?"

"Good heavens, no!" cried Brook. "She wouldn't look at me!"

"Wouldn't look at you? That's simply ridiculous, you know! She'd marry you out of hand — unless she's perfectly idiotic. And she doesn't look that. Leave her alone, Brook. Talk to the mother. She's one of the most delightful women I ever met. She has a dear, quiet way with her — like a very thoroughbred white cat that's been ill and wants to be petted."

"What extraordinary ideas you have, mother!" laughed Brook. "But on general principles I don't see why I shouldn't marry Miss Bowring, if she'll have me. Why not? Her father was a gentleman, you like her mother, and as for herself —"

"Oh, I've nothing against her. It's all against you, Brook dear. You are such a dreadful flirt, you know! You'll get tired of the poor girl and make her miserable. I'm sure she isn't practical, as I am. The very first time you look at some one else she'll get on a tragic horse and charge the crockery — and there will be a most awful smash! It's not easy to manage you Johnstones when you think you are in love. I ought to know!"

"I say, mother," said Brook, "has anybody been telling you stories about me lately?"

"Lately? Let me see. The last I heard was that Mrs. Crosby — the one you all call Lady Fan — was going to get a divorce so as to marry you."

"Oh — you heard that, did you?"

"Yes — everybody was talking about it and asking me whether it was true. It seems that she was with that party that brought you here. She left them at Naples, and came home at once by land, and they said she was giving out that she meant to marry you. I laughed, of course. But people wouldn't talk about you so much, dear boy, if there were not so much to talk about. I know that you would never do anything so idiotic as that, and if Mrs. Crosby chooses to flirt with you, that's her affair. She's older than you, and knows more about it. But this is quite another thing. This is serious. You sha'n't make love to that nice girl, Brook. You sha'n't! I'll do something dreadful, if you do. I'll tell her all about Mrs. Leo Cairngorm or somebody like that. But you sha'n't marry her and ruin her life."

"You're going in for philanthropy, mother," said Brook, growing red. "It's something new. You never made a fuss before."

"No, of course not. You never were so foolish before, my dear boy. I'm not bad myself, I believe. But you are, every one of you, and I love you all, and the only way to do anything with you is to let you run wild a little first. It's the only practical, sensible way. And you've only just begun — how in the world do you dare to think of marrying? Upon my word, it's too bad. I won't wait. I'll frighten the girl to death with stories about you, until she refuses to speak to you! But I've taken a fancy to her mother, and you sha'n't make the child miserable. You sha'n't, Brook. Oh, I've made up my mind! You sha'n't. I'll tell the mother too. I'll frighten them all, till they can't bear the sight of you."

Lady Johnstone was energetic, as well as original, in spite of her abnormal size, and Brook knew that she was quite capable of carrying out her threat, and more also.

"I may be like my father in some ways," he answered. "But I'm a good deal like you too, mother. I'm rather apt to stick to what I like, you know. Besides, I don't believe you would do anything of the kind. And she isn't inclined to like me, as it is. I believe she must have heard some story or other. Don't make things any worse than they are."

"Then don't lose your head and ask her to marry you after a fortnight's acquaintance,

Brook, because she'll accept you, and you will make her perfectly wretched."

He saw that it was not always possible to argue with his mother, and he said nothing more. But he reflected upon her point of view, and he saw that it was not altogether unjust, as she knew him. She could not possibly understand that what he felt for Clare Bowring bore not the slightest resemblance to what he had felt for Lady Fan, if, indeed, he had felt anything at all, which he considered doubtful now that it was over, though he would have been angry enough at the suggestion a month earlier. To tell the truth, he felt quite sure of himself at the present time, though all his sensations were more or less new to him. And his mother's sudden and rather eccentric opposition unexpectedly strengthened his determination. He might laugh at what he called her originality, but he could not afford to jest at the prospect of her giving Clare an account of his life. She was quite capable of it, and would probably do it.

These preoccupations, however, were as nothing compared with the main point — the certainty that Clare would refuse him, if he offered himself to her, and when he left his mother he was in a very undetermined state of mind. If he should ask Clare to marry him now, she

would refuse him. But if his mother inter-
fered, it would be much worse a week hence.

At last, as ill-luck would have it, he came
upon her unexpectedly in the corridor, as he
came out, and they almost ran against each
other.

"Won't you come out for a bit?" he asked
quickly and in a low voice.

"Thanks — I have some letters to write,"
answered the young girl. "Besides, it's much
too hot. There isn't a breath of air."

"Oh, it's not really hot, you know," said
Brook, persuasively.

"Then it's making a very good pretence!"
laughed Clare.

"It's ever so much cooler out of doors. If
you'll only come out for one minute, you'll see.
Really — I'm in earnest."

"But why should I go out if I don't want to?"
asked the young girl.

"Because I asked you to —"

"Oh, that isn't a reason, you know," she
laughed again.

"Well, then, because you really would, if I
hadn't asked you, and you only refuse out of a
spirit of opposition," suggested Brook.

"Oh — do you think so? Do you think I
generally do just the contrary of what I'm asked
to do?"

"Of course, everybody knows that, who knows you." Brook seemed amused at the idea.

"If you think that — well, I'll come, just for a minute, if it's only to show you that you are quite wrong."

"Thanks, awfully. Sha'n't we go for the little walk that was interrupted when my people came the other day?"

"No — it's too hot, really. I'll walk as far as the end of the terrace and back — once. Do you mind telling me why you are so tremendously anxious to have me come out this very minute?"

"I'll tell you — at least, I don't know that I can — wait till we are outside. I should like to be out with you all the time, you know — and I thought you might come, so I asked you."

"You seem rather confused," said Clare gravely.

"Well, you know," Brook answered as they walked along towards the dazzling green light that filled the door, "to tell the truth, between one thing and another — " He did not complete the sentence.

"Yes?" said Clare, sweetly. "Between one thing and another — what were you going to say?"

Brook did not answer as they went out into the hot, blossom-scented air, under the spreading vines.

"Do you mean to say it's cooler here than indoors?" asked the young girl in a tone of resignation.

"Oh, it's much cooler! There's a breeze at the end of the walk."

"The sea is like oil," observed Clare. "There isn't the least breath."

"Well," said Brook, "it can't be really hot, because it's only the first week in June after all."

"This isn't Scotland. It's positively boiling, and I wish I hadn't come out. Beware of first impulses — they are always right!"

But she glanced sideways at his face, for she knew that something was in the air. She was not sure what to expect of him just then, but she knew that there was something to expect. Her instinct told her that he meant to speak and to say more than he had yet said. It told her that he was going to ask her to marry him, then and there, in the blazing noon, under the vines, but her modesty scouted the thought as savouring of vanity. At all events she would prevent him from doing it if she could.

"Lady Johnstone seems to like this place," she said, with a sudden effort at conversation. "She says that she means to make all sorts of expeditions."

"Of course she will," answered Brook, in a

half-impatient tone. "But, please — I don't want to talk about my mother or the landscape. I really did want to speak to you, because I can't stand this sort of thing any longer, you know."

"What sort of thing?" asked Clare innocently, raising her eyes to his, as they reached the end of the walk.

It was very hot and still. Not a breath stirred the young vine-leaves overhead, and the scent of the last orange-blossoms hung in the motionless air. The heat rose quivering from the sea to southward, and the water lay flat as a mirror under the glory of the first summer's day.

They stood still. Clare felt nervous, and tried to think of something to say which might keep him from speaking, and destroy the effect of her last question. But it was too late now. He was pale, for him, and his eyes were very bright.

"I can't live without you — it comes to that. Can't you see?"

The short plain words shook oddly as they fell from his lips. The two stood quite still, each looking into the other's face. Brook grew paler still, but the colour rose in Clare's cheeks. She tried to meet his eyes steadily, without feeling that he could control her.

"I'm sorry," she said, "I'm very sorry."

"You sha'n't say that," he answered, cutting

her words with his, and sharply.   " I'm tired of
hearing it.   I'm glad I love you, whatever you
do to me; and you must get to like me.   You
must.   I tell you I can't live without you."

" But if I can't—" Clare tried to say.

" You can—you must—you shall!" broke·
in Brook, hoarsely, his eyes growing brighter
and fiercer.   " I didn't know what it was to
love anybody, and now that I know, I can't
live without it, and I won't."

" But if—"

" There is no ' if,' " he cried, in his low strong
voice, fixing her eyes with his.   " There's no
question of my going mad, or dying, or anything
half so weak, because I won't take no.   Oh, you
may say it a hundred times, but it won't help
you.   I tell you I love you.   Do you understand
what that means?   I'm in God's own earnest.
I'll give you my life, but I won't give you up.
I'll take you somehow, whether you will or not,
and I'll hide you somewhere, but you sha'n't
get away from me as long as you live."

" You must be mad!" exclaimed the young
girl, scarcely above her breath, half-frightened,
and unable to loose her eyes from the fascination
of his.

" No, I'm not mad; only you've never seen
any one in earnest before, and you've been con-
demning me without evidence all along.   But it

must stop now. You must tell me what it is,
for I have a right to know. Tell me what it
all is. I will know — I will. Look at me; you
can't look away till you tell me."

Clare felt his power, and felt that his eyes
were dazzling her, and that if she did not escape
from them she must yield and tell him. She
tried, and her eyelids quivered. Then she raised
her hand to cover her own eyes, in a desperate
attempt to keep her secret. He caught it and
held it, and still looked. She turned pale suddenly. Then her words came mechanically.

"I was out there when you said ' good-bye '
to Lady Fan. I heard everything, from first to
last."

He started in surprise, and the colour rose
suddenly to his face. He did not look away yet,
but Clare saw the blush of shame in his face,
and felt that his power diminished, while hers
grew all at once, to overmaster him in turn.

"It's scarcely a fortnight since you betrayed
her," she said, slowly and distinctly, "and you
expect me to like you and to believe that you
are in earnest."

His shame turned quickly to anger.

"So you listened!" he exclaimed.

"Yes, I listened," she answered, and her words
came easily, then, in self-defence — for she had
thought of it all very often. "I didn't know

who you were. My mother and I had been sitting beside the cross in the shadow of the cave, and she went in to finish a letter, leaving me there. Then you two came out talking. Before I knew what was happening you had said too much. I felt that if I had been in Lady Fan's place I would far rather never know that a stranger was listening. So I sat still, and I could not help hearing. How was I to know that you meant to stay here until I heard you say so to her? And I heard everything. You are ashamed now that you know that I know. Do you wonder that I disliked you from the first?"

"I don't see why you should," answered Brook stubbornly. "If you do — you do. That doesn't change matters —"

"You betrayed her!" cried Clare indignantly. "You forgot that I heard all you said — how you promised to marry her if she could get a divorce. It was horrible, and I never dreamt of such things, but I heard it. And then you were tired of her, I suppose, and you changed your mind, and calmly told her that it was all a mistake. Do you expect any woman, who has seen another treated in that way, to forget? Oh, I saw her face, and I heard her sob. You broke her heart for your amusement. And it was only a fortnight ago!"

She had the upper hand now, and she turned
from him with a last scornful glance, and looked
over the low wall at the sea, wondering how he
could have held her with his eyes a moment
earlier.   Brook stood motionless beside her, and
there was silence.   He might have found much
in self-defence, but there was not one word of
it which he could tell her.   Perhaps she might
find out some day what sort of person Lady Fan
was, but his own lips were closed.   That was
his view of what honour meant.

Clare felt that her breath came quickly, and
that the colour was deep in her cheeks as she
gazed at the flat, hot sea.   For a moment she
felt a woman's enormous satisfaction in being
absolutely unanswerable.   Then, all at once, she
had a strong sensation of sickness, and a quick
pain shot sharply through her just below the
heart.   She steadied herself by the wall with
her hands, and shut her lips tightly.

She had refused him as well as accused him.
He would go away in a few moments, and never
try to be alone with her again.   Perhaps he
would leave Amalfi that very day.   It was impossible that she should really care for him, and
yet, if she did not care, she would not ask the
next question.   Then he spoke to her.   His
voice was changed and very quiet now.

"I'm sorry you heard all that," he said.   "I

don't wonder that you've got a bad opinion of
me, and I suppose I can't say anything just now
to make you change it. You heard, and you
think you have a right to judge. Perhaps I
shouldn't even say this — you heard me then,
and you have heard me now. There's a difference, you'll admit. But all that you heard then,
and all that you have told me now, can't change
the truth, and you can't make me love you less,
whatever you do. I don't believe I'm that sort
of man."

"I should have thought you were," said Clare
bitterly, and regretting the words as soon as
they were spoken.

"It's natural that you should think so. At
the same time, it doesn't follow that because a
man doesn't love one woman he can't possibly
love another."

"That's simply brutal!" exclaimed the young
girl, angry with him unreasonably because the
argument was good.

"It's true, at all events. I didn't love Mrs.
Crosby, and I told her so. You may think me
a brute if you like, but you heard me say it, if
you heard anything, so I suppose I may quote
myself. I do love you, and I have told you so
— the fact that I can't say it in choice language
doesn't make it a lie. I'm not a man in a book,
and I'm in earnest."

"Please stop," said Clare, as she heard the
hoarse strength coming back in his voice.

"Yes — I know. I've said it before, and you
don't care to hear it again. You can't kill it
by making me hold my tongue, you know. It
only makes it worse. You'll see that I'm in
earnest in time — then you'll change your mind.
But I can't change mine. I can't live without
you, whatever you may think of me now."

It was a strange wooing, very unlike anything she had ever dreamt of, if she had allowed
herself to dream of such things. She asked herself whether this could be the same man who
had calmly and cynically told Lady Fan that
he did not love her and could not think of
marrying her. He had been cool and quiet
enough then. That gave strength to the argument he used now. She had seen him with
another woman, and now she saw him with herself and heard him. She was surprised and
almost taken from her feet by his rough vehemence. He surely did not speak as a man
choosing his words, certainly not as one trying
to produce an effect. But then, on that evening at the Acropolis — the thought of that scene
pursued her — he had doubtless spoken just as
roughly and vehemently to Lady Fan, and had
seemed just as much in earnest. And suddenly
Lady Fan was hateful to her, and she almost

ceased to pity her at all. But for Lady Fan —
well, it might have been different. She should
not have blamed herself for liking him, for loving him perhaps, and his words would have had
another ring.

He still stood beside her, watching her, and
she was afraid to turn to him lest he should see
something in her face which she meant to hide.
But she could speak quietly enough, resting her
hands on the wall and looking out to sea. It
would be best to be a little formal, she thought.
The sound of his own name spoken distinctly
and coldly would perhaps warn him not to go
too far.

"Mr. Johnstone," she said, steadying her
voice, "this can't go on. I never meant to tell
you what I knew, but you have forced me to it.
I don't love you — I don't like a man who can
do such things, and I never could. And I can't
let you talk to me in this way any more. If we
must meet, you must behave just as usual. If
you can't, I shall persuade my mother to go
away at once."

"I shall follow you," said Brook. "I told
you so the other day. You can't possibly go to
any place where I can't go too."

"Do you mean to persecute me, Mr. Johnstone?" she asked.

"I love you."

"I hate you!"

"Yes, but you won't always. Even if you do, I shall always love you just as much."

Her eyes fell before his.

"Do you mean to say that you can really love a woman who hates you?" she asked, looking at one of her hands as it rested on the wall.

"Of course. Why not? What has that to do with it?"

The question was asked so simply and with such honest surprise that Clare looked up again. He was smiling a little sadly.

"But — I don't understand — " she hesitated.

"Do you think it's like a bargain?" he asked quietly. "Do you think it's a matter of exchange — 'I will love you if you'll love me'? Oh no! It's not that. I can't help it. I'm not my own master. I've got to love you, whether I like it or not. But since I do — well, I've said the rest, and I won't repeat it. I've told you that I'm in earnest, and you haven't believed me. I've told you that I love you, and you won't even believe that — "

"No — I can believe that, well enough, now. You do to-day, perhaps. At least you think you do."

"Well — you don't believe it, then. What's the use of repeating it? If I could talk well, it would be different, but I'm not much of a

talker, at best, and just now I can't put two
words together. But I — I mean lots of things
that I can't say, and perhaps wouldn't say, you
know. At least, not just now."

He turned from her and began to walk up
and down across the narrow terrace, towards
her and away from her, his hands in his pockets,
and his head a little bent. She watched him in
silence for some time. Perhaps if she had hated
him as much as she said that she did, she would '
have left him then and gone into the house.
Something, good or evil, tempted her to speak.

" What do you mean, that you wouldn't say
now? " she asked.

" I don't know," he answered gruffly, still
walking up and down, ten steps each way.
" Don't ask me — I told you one thing. I shall
follow you wherever you go."

" And then? " asked Clare, still prompted by
some genius, good or bad.

" And then? " Brook stopped and stared at
her rather wildly. " And then? If I can't get
you in any other way — well, I'll take you, that's
all! It's not a very pretty thing to say, is it? "

" It doesn't sound a very probable thing to
do, either," answered Clare. " I'm afraid you
are out of your mind, Mr. Johnstone."

" You've driven most things out of it since I
loved you," answered Brook, beginning to walk

again. " You've made me say things that I
shouldn't have dreamed of saying to any woman,
much less to you.   And you've made me think
of doing things that looked perfectly mad a
week ago."   He stopped before her.   " Can't
you see?   Can't you understand?   Can't you
feel how I love you?"

" Don't — please don't ! " she said, beginning
to be frightened at his manner again.

" Don't what ?   Don't love you?   Don't live,
then — don't exist — don't anything !   What
would it all matter, if I didn't love you?   Meanwhile, I do, and by the — no!   What's the use
of talking ?   You might laugh.   You'd make a
fool of me, if you hadn't killed the fool out of
me with too much earnest — and what's left
can't talk, though it can do something better
worth while than a lot of talking."

Clare began to think that the heat had hurt
his head.   And all the time, in a secret, shame-
faced way, she was listening to his incoherent
sentences and rough exclamations, and remembering them one by one, and every one.   And
she looked at his pale face, and saw the queer
light in his blue eyes, and the squaring of his
jaw — and then and long afterwards the whole
picture, with its memory of words, hot, broken,
and confused, meant earnest love in her thoughts.
No man in his senses, wishing to play a part and

produce an impression upon a woman, would
have acted as he did, and she knew it. It was
the rough, real thing — the raw strength of an
honest man's uncontrolled passion that she saw
— and it told her more of love in a few minutes
than all she had heard or read in her whole life.
But while it was before her, alive and throbbing
and incoherent of speech, it frightened her.

"Come," she said nervously, "we mustn't stay
out here any longer, talking in this way."

He stopped again, close before her, and his
eyes looked dangerous for an instant. Then he
straightened himself, and seemed to swallow
something with an effort.

"All right," he answered. "I don't want to
keep you out here in the heat."

He faced about, and they walked slowly
towards the house. When they reached the
door he stood aside. She saw that he did not
mean to go in, and she paused an instant on
the threshold, looked at him gravely, and nodded
before she entered. Again he bent his head, and
said nothing. She left him standing there, and
went straight to her room.

Then she sat down before a little table on
which she wrote her letters, near the window,
and she tried to think. But it was not easy, and
everything was terribly confused. She rested
her elbows upon the small desk and pressed

her fingers to her eyes, as though to drive away
the sight that would come back. Then she
dropped her hands suddenly and opened her
eyes wide, and stared at the wall-paper before
her. And it came back very vividly between
her and the white plaster, and she heard his
voice again — but she was smiling now.

She started violently, for she felt two hands
laid unexpectedly upon her shoulders, and some
one kissed her hair. She had not heard her
mother's footstep, nor the opening and shutting
of the door, nor anything but Brook Johnstone's
voice.

"What is it, my darling?" asked the elder
woman, bending down over her daughter's
shoulder. "Has anything happened?"

Clare hesitated a moment, and then spoke,
for the habit of her confidence was strong.
"He has asked me to marry him, mother — "

In her turn Mrs. Bowring started, and then
rested one hand on the table.

"You? You?" she repeated, in a low and
troubled voice. "You marry Adam Johnstone's
son?"

"No, mother — never," answered the young
girl.

"Thank God!"

And Mrs. Bowring sank into a chair, shiver-
ing as though she were cold.

CHAPTER XII

Brook felt in his pocket mechanically for his pipe, as a man who smokes generally takes to something of the sort at great moments in his life, from sheer habit. He went through the operation of filling and lighting with great precision, almost unconscious of what he was doing, and presently he found himself smoking and sitting on the wall just where Clare had leaned against it during their interview. In three minutes his pipe had gone out, but he was not aware of the fact, and sat quite still in his place, staring into the shrubbery which grew at the back of the terrace.

He was conscious that he had talked and acted wildly, and quite unlike the self with which he had been long acquainted; and the consciousness was anything but pleasant. He wondered where Clare was, and what she might be thinking of him at that moment. But as he thought of her his former mood returned, and he felt that he was not ashamed of what he had done and said. Then he realised, all at once, for the second time, that Clare had been on the platform on that first night, and he tried to

recall everything that Lady Fan and he had
said to each other.

No such thing had ever happened to him
before, and he had a sensation of shame and
distress and anger, as he went over the scene,
and thought of the innocent young girl who had
sat in the shadow and heard it all. She had
accidentally crossed the broad, clear line of
demarcation which he drew between her kind
and all the tribe of Lady Fans and Mrs. Cairn-
gorms whom he had known. He felt somehow
as though it were his fault, and as though he
were responsible to Clare for what she had heard
and seen. The sensation of shame deepened,
and he swore bitterly under his breath. It was
one of those things which could not be undone,
and for which there was no reparation possible.
Yet it was like an insult to Clare. For a man
who had lately been rough to the girl, almost to
brutality, he was singularly sensitive perhaps.
But that did not strike him. When he had
told her that he loved her, he had been too much
in earnest to pick and choose his expressions.
But when he had spoken to Lady Fan, he might
have chosen and selected and polished his
phrases so that Clare should have understood
nothing — if he had only known that she had
been sitting up there by the cross in the dark.
And again he cursed himself bitterly.

It was not because her knowing the facts had spoilt everything and given her a bad impression of him from the first: that might be set right in time, even now, and he did not wish her to marry him believing him to be an angel of light. It was that she should have seen something which she should not have seen, for her innocence's sake — something which, in a sense, must have offended and wounded her maidenliness. He would have struck any man who could have laughed at his sensitiveness about that. The worst of it — and he went back to the idea again and again —was that nothing could be done to mend matters, since it was all so completely in the past.

He sat on the wall and pulled at his briar-root pipe, which had gone out and was quite cold by this time, though he hardly knew it. He had plenty to think of, and things were not going straight at all. He had pretended indifference when his mother had told him how Lady Fan meant to get a divorce and how she was telling her intimate friends under the usual vain promises of secrecy that she meant to marry Adam Johnstone's son as soon as she should be free. Brook had told her plainly enough that he would not marry her in any case, but he asked himself whether the world might not say that he should, and whether in that case it might

not turn out to be a question of honour. He had
secretly thought of that before now, and in the
sudden depression of spirits which came upon
him as a reaction he cursed himself a third
time for having told Clare Bowring that he
loved her, while such a matter as Lady Fan's
divorce was still hanging over him as a possibility.

Sitting on the wall, he swung his legs angrily,
striking his heels against the stones in his perplexed discontent with the ordering of the universe. Things looked very black. He wished
that he could see Clare again, and that, somehow, he could talk it all over with her. Then
he almost laughed at the idea. She would tell
him that she disliked him — he was sick of the
sound of the word — and that it was his duty to
marry Lady Fan. What could she know of Lady
Fan ? He could not tell her that the little lady
in the white serge, being rather desperate, had
got herself asked to go with the party for the
express purpose of throwing herself at his head,
as the current phrase gracefully expresses it,
and with the distinct intention of divorcing her
husband in order to marry Brook Johnstone.
He could not tell Clare that he had made love
to Lady Fan to get rid of her, as another common expression put it, with a delicacy worthy
of modern society. He could not tell her that

Lady Fan, who was clever but indiscreet, had unfolded her scheme to her bosom friend Mrs. Leo Cairngorm, or that Mrs. Cairngorm, unknown to Lady Fan, had been a very devoted friend of Brook's, and was still fond of him, and secretly hated Lady Fan, and had therefore unfolded the whole plan to Brook before the party had started; or that on that afternoon at sunset on the Acropolis he had not at all assented to Lady Fan's mad proposal, as she had represented that he had when they had parted on the platform at Amalfi; he could not tell Clare any of these things, for he felt that they were not fit for her to hear. And if she knew none of them she must judge him out of her ignorance. Brook wished that some supernatural being with a gift for solving hard problems would suddenly appear and set things straight.

Instead, he saw the man who brought the letters just entering the hotel, and he rose by force of habit and went to the office to see if there were anything for him.

There was one, and it was from Lady Fan, by no means the first she had written since she had gone to England. And there were several for Sir Adam and two for Lady Johnstone. Brook took them all, and opened his own at once. He did not belong to that class of people who put off reading disagreeable correspond-

ence. While he read he walked slowly along
the corridor.

Lady Fan was actually consulting a firm of
solicitors with a view to getting a divorce. She
said that she of course understood his conduct
on that last night at Amalfi — the whole plan
must have seemed unrealisable to him then —
she would forgive him. She refused to believe
that he would ruin her in cold blood, as she must
be ruined if she got a divorce from Crosby, and
if Brook would not marry her; and much more.

Why should she be ruined? Brook asked
himself. If Crosby divorced her on Brook's account, it would be another matter altogether.
But she was going to divorce Crosby, who was
undoubtedly a beast, and her reputation would
be none the worse for it. People would only
wonder why she had not done it before, and so
would Crosby, unless he took it into his head
to examine the question from a financial point
of view. For Crosby was, or had been, rich,
and Lady Fan had no money of her own, and
Crosby was quite willing to let her spend a good
deal, provided she left him in peace. How in
the world could Clare ever know all the truth
about such people? It would be an insult to
her to think that she could understand half of
it, and she would not think the better of him
unless she could understand it all. The situa-

tion did not seem to admit of any solution in that way. All he could hope for was that Clare might change her mind. When she should be older she would understand that she had made a mistake, and that the world was not merely a high-class boarding-school for young ladies, in which all the men were employed as white-chokered professors of social righteousness. That seemed to be her impression, he thought, with a resentment which was not against her in particular, but against all young girls in general, and which did not prevent him from feeling that he would not have had it otherwise for anything in the world.

He stuffed the letter into his pocket, and went in search of his father. He was strongly inclined to lay the whole matter before him, and to ask the old gentleman's advice. He had reason to believe that Sir Adam had been in worse scrapes than this when he had been a young man, and somehow or other nobody had ever thought the worse of him. He was sure to be in his room at that hour, writing letters. Brook knocked and went in. It was about eleven o'clock.

Sir Adam, gaunt and grey, and clad in a cashmere dressing-jacket, was extended upon all the chairs which the little cell-like room contained, close by the open window. He had a very thick cigarette between his lips, and a half-emptied glass of brandy and soda stood on the corner of a table at his elbow. He had not failed to drink one brandy and soda every morning at eleven o'clock for at least a quarter of a century.

His keen old eyes turned sharply to Brook as the latter entered, and a smile lighted up his furrowed face, but instantly disappeared again; for the young man's features betrayed something of what he had gone through during the last hour.

"Anything wrong, boy?" asked Sir Adam quickly. "Have a brandy and soda and a pipe with me. Oh, letters! It's devilish hard that the post should find a man out in this place! Leave them there on the table."

Brook relighted his pipe. His father took one leg from one of the chairs, which he pushed towards his son with his foot by way of an invitation to sit down.

"What's the matter?" he asked, renewing his question. "You've got into another scrape, have you? Mrs. Crosby — of all women in the world. Your mother told me that ridiculous story. Wants to divorce Crosby and marry you, does she? I say, boy, it's time this sort of nonsense stopped, you know. One of these days you'll be caught. There are cleverer women in the world than Mrs. Crosby."

"Oh! she's not clever," answered Brook thoughtfully.

"Well, what's the foundation of the story? What the dickens did you go with those people for, when you found out that she was coming? You knew the sort of woman she was, I suppose? What happened? You made love to her, of course. That was what she wanted. Then she talked of eternal bliss together, and that sort of rot, didn't she? And you couldn't exactly say that you only went in for bliss by the month, could you? And she said, 'By Jove, as you don't refuse, you shall have it for the rest of your life,' and she said to herself that you were richer than Crosby, and a good deal younger, and better-looking, and better socially, and that if you were going to make a fool of yourself she might as well get the benefit of it as well as any other woman. Then she wrote to a solicitor — and now you are in the devil of a scrape. I fancy that's the history of the case, isn't it?"

"I wish you wouldn't talk about women in that sort of way, Governor!" exclaimed Brook, by way of answer.

"Don't be an ass!" answered Sir Adam. "There are women one can talk about in that way, and women one can't. Mrs. Crosby is one of the first kind. I distinguish between

'women' and 'woman.' Don't you? Woman
means something to most of us — something a
good deal better than we are, which we treat
properly and would cut one another's throats
for. We sinners aren't called upon to respect
women who won't respect themselves. We are
only expected to be civil to them because they
are things in petticoats with complexions.
Don't be an ass, Brook. I don't want to know
what you said to Mrs. Crosby, nor what she
said to you, and you wouldn't be a gentleman
if you told me. That's your affair. But she's
a woman with a consumptive reputation that's
very near giving up the ghost, and that would
have departed this life some time ago if Crosby
didn't happen to be a little worse than she is.
She wants to get a divorce and marry my son
— and that's my affair. Do you remember
the Arab and his slave? 'You've stolen my
money,' said the sheikh. 'That's my business,'
answered the slave. 'And I'm going to beat
you,' said the sheikh. 'That's your business,'
said the slave. It's a similar case, you know,
only it's a good deal worse. I don't want to
know anything that happened before you two
parted. But I've a right to know what Mrs.
Crosby has done since, haven't I? You don't
care to marry her, do you, boy?"

　"Marry her! I'd rather cut my throat."

"You needn't do that. Just tell me whether all this is mere talk, or whether she has really been to the solicitor's. If she has, you know, she will get her divorce without opposition. Everybody knows about Crosby."

"It's true," said Brook. "I've just had a letter from her again. I wish I knew what to do!"

"You can't do anything."

"I can refuse to marry her, can't I?"

"Oh — you could. But plenty of people would say that you had induced her to get the divorce, and then had changed your mind. She'll count on that, and make the most of it, you may be sure. She won't have a penny when she's divorced, and she'll go about telling everybody that you have ruined her. That won't be pleasant, will it?"

"No — hardly. I had thought of it."

"You see — you can't do anything without injuring yourself. I can settle the whole affair in half an hour. By return of post you'll get a letter from her telling you that she has abandoned all idea of proceedings against Crosby."

"I'll bet you she doesn't," said Brook.

"Anything you like. It's perfectly simple. I'll just make a will, leaving you nothing at all, if you marry her, and I'll send her a copy to-day. You'll get the answer fast enough."

"By Jove!" exclaimed Brook, in surprise. Then he thoughtfully relighted his pipe and threw the match out of the window. "I say, Governor," he added after a pause, "do you think that's quite — well, quite fair and square, you know?"

"What on earth do you mean?" cried Sir Adam. "Do you mean to tell me that I haven't a perfect right to leave my money as I please? And that the first adventuress who takes a fancy to it has a right to force you into a disgraceful marriage, and that it would be dishonourable of me to prevent it if I could? You're mad, boy! Don't talk such nonsense to me!"

"I suppose I'm an idiot," said Brook. ".Things about money so easily get a queer look, you know. It's not like other things, is it?"

"Look here, Brook," answered the old man, taking his feet from the chair on which they rested, and sitting up straight in the low easy chair. "People have said a lot of things about me in my life, and I'll do the world the credit to add that it might have said twice as much with a good show of truth. But nobody ever said that I was mean, nor that I ever disappointed anybody in money matters who had a right to expect something of me. And that's pretty conclusive evidence, because I'm a Scotch-

man, and we are generally supposed to be a close-
fisted tribe. They've said everything about me
that the world can say, except that I've told
you about my first marriage. She — she got
her divorce, you know. She had a perfect
right to it."

The old man lit another cigarette, and sipped
his brandy and soda thoughtfully.

"I don't like to talk about money," he said
in a lower tone. "But I don't want you to
think me mean, Brook. I allowed her a thousand a year after she had got rid of me. She
never touched it. She isn't that kind. She
would rather starve ten times over. But the
money has been paid to her account in London
for twenty-seven years. Perhaps she doesn't
know it. All the better for her daughter, who
will find it after her mother's death, and get it
all. I only don't want you to think I'm mean,
Brook."

"Then she married again — your first wife?"
asked the young man, with natural curiosity.
"And she's alive still?"

"Yes," answered Sir Adam, thoughtfully.
"She married again six years after I did —
rather late — and she had one daughter."

"What an odd idea!" exclaimed Brook.
"To think that those two people are somewhere
about the world. A sort of stray half-sister of

mine, the girl would be — I mean — what would
be the relationship, Governor, since we are talking about it?"

"None whatever," answered the old man, in
a tone so extraordinarily sharp that Brook
looked up in surprise. "Of course not! What
relation could she be? Another mother and
another father — no relation at all."

"Do you mean to say that I could marry
her?" asked Brook idly.

Sir Adam started a little.

"Why — yes — of course you could, as she
wouldn't be related to you."

He suddenly rose, took up his glass, and
gulped down what was left in it. Then he
went and stood before the open window.

"I say, Brook," he began, his back turned to
his son.

"What?" asked Brook, poking his knife into
his pipe to clean it. "Anything wrong?"

"I can't stand this any longer. I've got to
speak to somebody — and I can't speak to your
mother. You won't talk, boy, will you? You
and I have always been good friends."

"Of course! What's the matter with you,
Governor? You can tell me."

"Oh — nothing — that is — Brook, I say,
don't be startled. This Mrs. Bowring is my
divorced wife, you know."

"Good God!"

Sir Adam turned on his heels and met his son's look of horror and astonishment. He had expected an exclamation of surprise, but Brook's voice had fear in it, and he had started from his chair.

"Why do you say 'Good God' — like that?" asked the old man. "You're not in love with the girl, are you?"

"I've just asked her to marry me."

The young man was ghastly pale, as he stood stock-still, staring at his father. Sir Adam was the first to recover something of equanimity, but the furrows in his face had suddenly grown deeper.

"Of course she has accepted you?" he asked.

"No — she knew about Mrs. Crosby." That seemed sufficient explanation of Clare's refusal. "How awful!" exclaimed Brook hoarsely, his mind going back to what seemed the main question just then. "How awful for you, Governor!"

"Well — it's not pleasant," said Sir Adam, turning to the window again. "So the girl refused you," he said, musing, as he looked out. "Just like her mother, I suppose. Brook" — he paused.

"Yes?"

"So far as I'm concerned, it's not so bad as

you think. You needn't pity me, you know. It's just as well that we should have met — after twenty-seven years."

"She knew you at once, of course?"

"She knew I was your father before I came. And, I say, Brook — she's forgiven me at last."

His voice was low and unsteady, and he resolutely kept his back turned.

"She's one of the best women that ever lived," he said. "Your mother's the other."

There was a long silence, and neither changed his position. Brook watched the back of his father's head.

"You don't mind my saying so to you, Brook?" asked the old man, hitching his shoulders.

"Mind? Why?"

"Oh — well — there's no reason, I suppose. Gad! I wish — I suppose I'm crazy, but I wish to God you could marry the girl, Brook! She's as good as her mother."

Brook said nothing, being very much astonished, as well as disturbed.

"Only — I'll tell you one thing, Brook," said the voice at the window, speaking into space. "If you do marry her — and if you treat her as I treated her mother — " he turned sharply on both heels and waited a minute — "I'll be damned if I don't believe I'd shoot you!"

"I'd spare you the trouble, and do it myself," said Brook, roughly.

They were men, at all events, whatever their faults had been and might be, and they looked at the main things of life in very much the same way, like father like son. Another silence followed Brook's last speech.

"It's settled now, at all events," he said in a decided way, after a long time. "What's the use of talking about it? I don't know whether you mean to stay here. I shall go away this afternoon."

Sir Adam sat down again in his low easy chair, and leaned forward, looking at the pattern of the tiles in the floor, his wrists resting on his knees, and his hands hanging down.

"I don't know," he said slowly. "Let us try and look at it quietly, boy. Don't do anything in a hurry. You're in love with the girl, are you? It isn't a mere flirtation? How the deuce do you know the difference, at your age?"

"Gad!" exclaimed Brook, half angrily. "I know it! that's all. I can't live without her. That is — it's all bosh to talk in that way, you know. One goes on living, I suppose — one doesn't die. You know what I mean. I'd rather lose an arm than lose her — that sort of thing. How am I to explain it to you? I'm in earnest about it. I never asked any girl to marry me

till now. I should think that ought to prove
it. You can't say that I don't know what
married life means."

"Other people's married life," observed Sir
Adam, grimly. "You know something about
that, I'm afraid."

"What difference does it make?" asked Brook.
"I can't marry the daughter of my father's
divorced wife."

"I never heard of a case, simply because such
cases don't arise often. But there's no earthly
reason why you shouldn't. There is no relationship whatever between you. There's no mention of it in the table of kindred and affinity, I
know, simply because it isn't kindred or affinity
in any way. The world may make its observa-
tions. But you may do much more surprising
things than marry the daughter of your father's
divorced wife when you are to have forty thousand pounds a year, Brook. I've found it out in
my time. You'll find it out in yours. And it
isn't as though there were the least thing about
it that wasn't all fair and square and straight
and honourable and legal — and everything
else, including the clergy. I supposed that
the Archbishop of Canterbury wouldn't have
married me the second time, because the Church
isn't supposed to approve of divorces. But I
was married in church all right, by a very good

man. And Church disapproval can't possibly extend to the second generation, you know. Oh no! So far as its being possible goes, there's nothing to prevent your marrying her."

"Except Mrs. Crosby," said Brook. "You'll prove that she doesn't exist either, if you go on. But all that doesn't put things straight. It's a horrible situation, no matter how you look at it. What would my mother say if she knew? You haven't told her about the Bowrings, have you?"

"No," answered Sir Adam, thoughtfully. "I haven't told her anything. Of course she knows the story, but — I'm not sure. Do you think I'm bound to tell her that — who Mrs. Bowring is? Do you think it's anything like not fair to her, just to leave her in ignorance of it? If you think so, I'll tell her at once. That is, I should have to ask Mrs. Bowring first, of course."

"Of course," assented Brook. "You can't do that, unless we go away. Besides, as things are now, what's the use?"

"She'll have to know, if you are engaged to the daughter."

"I'm not engaged to Miss Bowring," said Brook, disconsolately. "She won't look at me. What an infernal mess I've made of my life!"

"Don't be an ass, Brook!" exclaimed Sir Adam, for the third time that morning.

s

"It's all very well to tell me not to be an ass," answered the young man gravely. "I can't mend matters now, and I don't blame her for refusing me. It isn't much more than two weeks since that night. I can't tell her the truth — I wouldn't tell it to you, though I can't prevent your telling it to me, since you've guessed it. She thinks I betrayed Mrs. Crosby, and left her — like the merest cad, you know. What am I to do? I won't say anything against Mrs. Crosby for anything — and if I were low enough to do that I couldn't say it to Miss Bowring. I told her that I'd marry her in spite of herself — carry her off — anything! But of course I couldn't. I lost my head, and talked like a fool."

"She won't think the worse of you for that," observed the old man. "But you can't tell her — the rest. Of course not! I'll see what I can do, Brook. I don't believe it's hopeless at all. I've watched Miss Bowring, ever since we first met you two, coming up the hill. I'll try something — "

"Don't speak to her about Mrs. Crosby, at all events!"

"I don't think I should do anything you wouldn't do yourself, boy," said Sir Adam, with a shade of reproval in his tone. "All I say is that the case isn't so hopeless as you seem to

think. Of course you are heavily handicapped,
and you are a dog with a bad name, and all the
rest of it. The young lady won't change her
mind to-day, nor to-morrow either, perhaps.
But she wouldn't be a human woman if she
never changed it at all."

"You don't know her!" Brook shook his
head and began to refill his refractory pipe.
"And I don't believe you know her mother
either, though you were married to her once.
If she is at all what I think she is, she won't
let her daughter marry your son. It's not as
though anything could happen now to change
the situation. It's an old one— it's old, and set,
and hard, like a cast. You can't run it into a
new mould and make anything else of it. Not
even you, Governor — and you are as clever
as anybody I know. It's a sheer question of
humanity, without any possible outside incident.
I've got two things against me which are about
as serious as anything can be — the mother's
prejudice against you, and the daughter's prejudice against me — both deuced well founded, it
seems to me."

"You forget one thing, Brook," said Sir Adam,
thoughtfully.

"What's that?"

"Women forgive."

Neither spoke for some time.

"You ought to know," said Brook in a low tone, at last. "They forgive when they love — or have loved. That's the right way to put it, I think."

"Well — put it in that way, if you like. It will just cover the ground. Whatever that young lady may say, she likes you very much. I've seen her watch you, and I'm sure of it."

"How can a woman love a man and hate him at the same time?"

"Why do jealous women sometimes kill their husbands? If they didn't love them they wouldn't care; and if they didn't hate them, they wouldn't kill them. You can't explain it, perhaps, but you can't deny it either. She'll never forgive Mrs. Crosby — perhaps — but she'll forgive you, when she finds out that she can't be happy without you. Stay here quietly, and let me see what I can do."

"You can't do anything, Governor. But I'm grateful to you all the same. And — you know — if there's anything I can do on my side to help you, just now, I'll do it!"

"Thank you, Brook," said the old man, leaning back, and putting up his feet again.

Brook rose and left the room, slowly shutting the door behind him. Then he got his hat and went off for a solitary walk to think matters over. They were grave enough, and all that

his father had said could not persuade him that
there was any chance of happiness in his future.
There was a sort of horror in the situation, too,
and he could not remember ever to have heard
of anything like it. He walked slowly, and
with bent head.

CHAPTER XIII

SIR ADAM sat still in his place and smoked another thick cigarette before he moved. Then he roused himself, got up, sat down at his table, and took a large sheet of paper from a big leather writing-case.

He had no hesitation about what he meant to put down. In a quarter of an hour he had written out a new will, in which he left his whole fortune to his only son Brook, on condition that Brook did not marry Mrs. Crosby. But if he married her before his father's death he was to have nothing, and if he married her afterwards he was to forfeit the whole, to the uttermost farthing. In either of these cases the property was to go to a third person. Sir Adam hesitated a moment, and then wrote the name of one of his sisters as the conditional legatee. His wife had plenty of money of her own, and besides, the will was a mere formality, drawn up and to be executed solely with a view to checking Lady Fan's enthusiasm. He did not sign it, but folded it smoothly and put it into his pocket. He also took his own pen, for he was particular in matters appertaining to the mechanics of writing, and very neat in all he did.

He went out and wandered up and down the terrace in the heat, but no one was there. Then he knocked at his wife's door, and found her absorbed in an interesting conversation with her maid in regard to matters of dress, as connected with climate. Lady Johnstone at once appealed to him, and the maid eyed him with suspicion, fearing his suggestions. He satisfied her, however, by immediately suggesting that she should go away, whereat she smiled and departed.

Lady Johnstone at once understood that something very serious was in the air. A wonderful good fellowship existed between husband and wife; but they very rarely talked of anything which could not have been discussed, figuratively, on the housetops.

"Brook has got himself into a scrape with that Mrs. Crosby, my dear," said Sir Adam. "What you heard is all more or less true. She has really been to a solicitor, and means to take steps to get a divorce. Of course she could get it easily enough. If she did, people would say that Brook had let her go that far, telling her that he would marry her, and then had changed his mind and left her to her fate. We can't let that happen, you know."

Lady Johnstone looked at her husband with anxiety while he was speaking, and then was silent for a few seconds.

"Oh, you Johnstones! You Johnstones!" she cried at last, shaking her head. "You're perfectly incorrigible!"

"Oh no, my dear," answered Sir Adam; "don't forget me, you know."

"You, Adam!"

Her tone expressed an extraordinary conflict of varying sentiment — amusement, affection, reproach, a retrospective distrust of what might have been, but could not be, considering Sir Adam's age.

"Never mind me, then," he answered. "I've made a will cutting Brook off with nothing if he marries Mrs. Crosby, and I'm going to send her a copy of it to-day. That will be enough, I fancy."

"Adam!"

"Yes — what? Do you disapprove? You always say that you are a practical woman, and you generally show that you are. Why shouldn't I take the practical method of stopping this woman as soon as possible? She wants my money — she doesn't want my son. A fortune with any other name would smell as sweet."

"Yes — but —"

"But what?"

"I don't know — it seems — somehow — "
Lady Johnstone was perplexed to express what
she meant just then. "I mean," she added
suddenly, "it's treating the woman like a mere
adventuress, you know — "

"That's precisely what Mrs. Crosby is, my
dear," answered Sir Adam calmly. "The fact
that she comes of decent people doesn't alter
the case in the least. Nor the fact that she
has one rich husband, and wishes to get another
instead. I say that her husband is rich, but
I'm very sure he has ruined himself in the last
two years, and that she knows it. She is not
the woman to leave him as long as he has
money, for he lets her do anything she pleases,
and pays her well to leave him alone. But he
has got into trouble — and rats leave a sinking
ship, you know. You may say that I'm cynical,
my dear, but I think you'll find that I'm telling
you the facts as they are."

"It seems an awful insult to the woman to
send her a copy of your will," said Lady Johnstone.

"It's an awful insult to you when she tries
to get rid of her husband to marry your only
son, my dear."

"Oh — but he'd never marry her ! "

"I'm not sure. If he thought it would be
dishonourable not to marry her, he'd be quite

capable of doing it, and of blowing out his brains afterwards."

" That wouldn't improve her position," observed the practical Lady Johnstone.

" She'd be the widow of an honest man, instead of the wife of a blackguard," said Sir Adam. " However, I'm doing this on my own responsibility. What I want is that you should witness the will."

" And let Mrs. Crosby think I made you do this? No — "

" Nonsense. I sha'n't copy the signatures — "

" Then why do you need them at all?"

" I'm not going to write to her that I've made a will, if I haven't," answered Sir Adam. " A will isn't a will unless it's witnessed. I'm not going to lie about it, just to frighten her. So I want you and Mrs. Bowring to witness it."

" Mrs. Bowring?"

" Yes — there are no men here, and Brook can't be a witness, because he's interested. You and Mrs. Bowring will do very well. But there's another thing — rather an extraordinary thing — and I won't let you sign with her until you know it. It's not a very easy thing to tell you, my dear."

Lady Johnstone shifted her fat hands and folded them again, and her frank blue eyes gazed at her husband for a moment.

"I can guess," she said, with a good-natured smile. " You told me you were old friends — I suppose you were in love with her somewhere!" She laughed and shook her head. "I don't mind," she added. " It's one more, that's all — one that I didn't know of. She's a very nice woman, and I've taken the greatest fancy to her!"

"I'm glad you have," said Sir Adam, gravely. "I say, my dear — don't be surprised, you know — I warned you. We knew each other very well — it's not what you think at all, and she was altogether in the right and I was quite in the wrong about it. I say, now — don't be startled — she's my divorced wife — that's all."

"She! Mrs. Bowring! Oh, Adam — how could you treat her so!"

Lady Johnstone leaned back in her chair and slowly turned her head till she could look out of the window. She was almost rosy with surprise — a change of colour in her sanguine complexion which was equivalent to extreme pallor in other persons. Sir Adam looked at her affectionately.

"What an awfully good woman you are!" he exclaimed, in genuine admiration.

"I! No, I'm not good at all. I was thinking that if you hadn't been such a brute to her I could never have married you. I don't suppose that is good, is it? But you were a brute, all the same, Adam, dear, to hurt such a woman as that!"

"Of course I was! I told you so when I told you the story. But I didn't expect that you'd ever meet."

"No, it is an extraordinary thing. I suppose that if I had any nerves I should faint. It would be an awful thing if I did; you'd have to get those porters to pick me up!" She smiled meditatively. "But I haven't fainted, you see. And, after all, I don't see why it should be so very dreadful, do you? You see, you've rather broken me in to the idea of lots of other people in your life, and I've always pitied her sincerely. I don't see why I should stop pitying her because I've met her and taken such a fancy to her without knowing who she was. Do you?"

"Most women would," observed Sir Adam. "It's lucky that you and she happen to be the two best women in the world. I told Brook so this morning."

"Brook? Have you told him?" .

"I had to. He wants to marry her daughter."

"Brook! It's impossible!"

Lady Johnstone's tone betrayed so much more surprise and displeasure than when her husband had told her of Mrs. Bowring's identity that he stared at her in surprise.

"I don't see why it's impossible," he said, "except that she has refused him once. That's nothing. The first time doesn't count."

"He sha'n't!" said the fat lady, whose vivid colour had come back. "He'll make her miserable — just as you — no, I won't say that! But they are not in the least suited to one another — he's far too young; there are fifty reasons."

"Brook won't act as I did, my dear," said Sir Adam. "He's like you in that. He'll make as good a husband as you have been a good wife — "

"Nonsense!" interrupted Lady Johnstone. "You're all alike, you Johnstones! I was talking to him this morning about her — I knew there was the beginning of something — and I told him what I thought. You're all bad, and I love you all; but if you think that Clare Bowring is as practical as I am, you're very much mistaken, Adam, dear! She'll break her heart — "

"If she does, I'll shoot him," answered the old man with a grim smile. "I told him so."

"Did you? Well, I am glad you take that view of it," said Lady Johnstone, thoughtfully, and not at all realising what she was saying. "I'm glad I'm not a nervous woman," she added, beginning to fan herself. "I should be in my grave, you know."

"No — you are not nervous, my dear, and

I'm very glad of it. I suppose it really is
rather a trying situation. But if I didn't know
you, I wouldn't have told you all this. You've
spoiled me, you know — you really have been so
tremendously good to me — always, dear.''

There was a rough, half unwilling tenderness
in his voice, and his big bony hand rested
gently on the fat lady's shoulder, as he spoke.
She bent her head to one side, till her large red
cheek touched the brown knuckles. It was, in
a way, almost grotesque. But there was that
something in it which could make youth and
beauty and passion ridiculous — the outspoken
truthful old rake and the ever-forgiving wife.
Who shall say wherein pathos lies? And yet
it seems to be something more than a mere hack-
writer's word, after all. The strangest acts of
life sometimes go off in such an oddly quiet
humdrum way, and then all at once there is
the little quiver in the throat, when one least
expects it — and the sad-eyed, faithful, loving
angel has passed by quickly, low and soft, his
gentle wings just brushing the still waters of
our unwept tears.

Sir Adam left his wife to go in search of Mrs.
Bowring. He sent a message to her, and she
came out and met him in the corridor. They
went into the reading-room together, and he
shut the door. In a few words he told her all

that he had told his wife about Mrs. Crosby,
and asked her whether she had any objection to
signing the document as a witness, merely in
order that he might satisfy himself by actually
executing it.

"It is high handed," said Mrs. Bowring.
" It is like you—but I suppose you have a right
to save your son from such trouble. But there
is something else — do you know what has happened? He has been making love to Clare —
he has asked her to marry him, and she has
refused. She told me this morning — and I
have told her the truth — that you and I were
once married."

She paused, and watched Sir Adam's furrowed
face.

"I'm glad of that," he said. "I'm glad that
it has all come out on the same day. He knows
everything, and he has told me everything. I
don't know how it's all going to end, but I want
you to believe one thing. If he had guessed the
truth, he would never have said a word of love
to her. He's not that kind of boy. You do
believe me, don't you?"

"Yes, I believe you. But the worst of it is
that she cares for him too — in a way I can't
understand. She has some reason, or she thinks
she has, for disliking him, as she calls it. She
wouldn't tell me. But she cares for him all the

same. She has told him, though she won't tell
me. There is something horrible in the idea of
our children falling in love with each other."

Mrs. Bowring spoke quietly, but her pale face
and nervous mouth told more than her words.

Sir Adam explained to her shortly what had
happened on the first evening after Brook's
arrival, and how Clare had heard it all, sitting
in the shadow just above the platform. Mrs.
Bowring listened in silence, covering her eyes
with her hands. There was a long pause after
he had finished speaking, but still she said
nothing.

"I should like him to marry her," said Sir
Adam at last, in a low voice.

She started and looked at him uneasily, remembering how well she had once loved him,
and how he had broken her heart when she was
young. He met her eyes quietly.

"You don't know him," he said. "He loves
her, and he will be to her — what I wasn't to
you."

"How can you say that he loves her? Three
weeks ago he loved that Mrs. Crosby."

"He? He never cared for her — not even at
first."

"He was all the more heartless and bad to
make her think that he did."

"She never thought so, for a moment. She

wanted my money, and she thought that she could catch him."

"Perhaps — I saw her, and I did not like her face. She had the look of an adventuress about her. That doesn't change the main facts. Your son and she were — flirting, to say the least of it, three weeks ago. And now he thinks himself in love with my daughter. It would be madness to trust such a man — even if there were not the rest to hinder their marriage. Adam — I told you that I forgave you. I have forgiven you — God knows. But you broke my life at the beginning like a thread. You don't know all there has been to forgive — indeed, you don't. And you are asking me to risk Clare's life in your son's hands, as I risked mine in yours. It's too much to ask."

"But you say yourself that she loves him."

"She cares for him — that was what I said. I don't believe in love as I did. You can't expect me to."

She turned her face away from him, but he saw the bitterness in it, and it hurt him. He waited a moment before he answered her.

"Don't visit my sins on your daughter, Lucy," he said at last. "Don't forget that love was a fact before you and I were born, and will be a fact long after we are dead If these two love each other, let them marry I hope that Clare

is like you, but don't take it for granted that
Brook is like me. He's not. He's more like
his mother."

"And your wife?" said Mrs. Bowring suddenly. "What would she say to this?"

"My wife," said Sir Adam, "is a practical
woman."

"I never was. Still — if I knew that Clare
loved him — if I could believe that he could love
her faithfully — what could I do? I couldn't
forbid her to marry him. I could only pray
that she might be happy, or at least that she
might not break her heart."

"You would probably be heard, if anybody is.
And a man must believe in God to explain your
existence," added Sir Adam, in a gravely medi-
tative tone. "It's the best argument I know."

CHAPTER XIV

BROOK JOHNSTONE had gone to his room when
he had left his father, and was hastily packing
his belongings, for he had made up his mind to
leave Amalfi at once without consulting anybody. It is a special advantage of places where
there is no railway that one can go away at a
moment's notice, without waiting tedious hours
for a train. Brook did not hesitate, for it
seemed to him the only right thing to do, after
Clare's refusal, and after what his father had
told him. If she had loved him, he would have
stayed in spite of every opposition. If he had
never been told her mother's history, he would
have stayed and would have tried to make her
love him. As it was, he set his teeth and said
to himself that he would suffer a good deal
rather than do anything more to win the heart
of Mrs. Bowring's daughter. He would get over
it somehow in the end. He fancied Clare's horror if she should ever know the truth, and his
fear of hurting her was as strong as his love.
He made no phrases to himself, and he thought

of nothing theatrical which he should like to say. He just set his teeth and packed his clothes alone. Possibly he swore rather unmercifully at the coat which would not fit into the right place, and at the starched shirt-cuffs which would not lie flat until he smashed them out of shape with unsteady hands.

When he was ready, he wrote a few words to Clare. He said that he was going away immediately, and that it would be very kind of her to let him say good-bye. He sent the note by a servant, and waited in the corridor at a distance from her door.

A moment later she came out, very pale.

"You are not really going, are you?" she asked, with wide and startled eyes. "You can't be in earnest?"

"I'm all ready," he answered, nodding slowly. "It's much better. I only wanted to say good-bye, you know. It's awfully kind of you to come out."

"Oh — I wouldn't have — " but she checked herself, and glanced up and down the long corridor. "We can't talk here," she added.

"It's so hot outside," said Brook, remembering how she had complained of the heat an hour earlier.

"Oh no — I mean — it's no matter. I'd rather go out for a moment."

She began to walk towards the door while she was speaking. They reached it in silence, and went out into the blazing sun. Clare had Brook's note still in her hand, and held it up to shield the glare from the side of her face as they crossed the platform. Then she realised that she had brought him to the very spot whereon he had said good-bye to Lady Fan. She stopped, and he stood still beside her.

"Not here," she said.

"No — not here," he answered.

"There's too much sun — really," said she, as the colour rose faintly in her cheeks.

"It's only to say good-bye," Brook answered sadly. "I shall always remember you just as you are now — with the sun shining on your hair."

It was so bright that it dazzled him as he looked. In spite of the heat she did not move, and their eyes met.

"Mr. Johnstone," Clare began, "please stay. Please don't let me feel that I have sent you away." There was a shade of timidity in the tone, and the eyes seemed brave enough to say something more. Brook hesitated.

"Well — no — it isn't that exactly. I've heard something — my father has told me something since I saw you —"

He stopped short and looked down.

"What have you heard?" she asked. "Something dreadful about us?"

"About us all — about him, principally. I can't tell you. I really can't."

"About him — and my mother? That they were married and separated?"

The steady innocent eyes had waited for him to look up again. He started as he heard her words.

"You don't mean to say that you know it too?" he cried. "Who has dared to tell you?"

"My mother — she was quite right. It's wrong to hide such things — she ought to have told me at once. Why shouldn't I have known it?"

"Doesn't it seem horrible to you? Don't you dislike me more than ever?"

"No. Why should I? It wasn't your fault. What has it to do with you? Or with me? Is that the reason why you are going away so suddenly?"

Brook stared at her in surprise, and the dawn of returning gladness was in his face for a moment.

"We have a right to live, whatever they did in their day," said Clare. "There is no reason why you should go away like this, at a moment's notice."

With an older woman he would have understood the first time, but he did not dare to understand Clare, nor to guess that there was anything to be understood.

"Of course we have a right to live," he answered, in a constrained tone. "But that does not mean that I may stay here and make your life a burden. So I'm going away. It was quite different before I knew all this. Please don't stay out here — you'll get a sun-stroke. I only wanted to say good-bye."

Man-like, having his courage at the striking-point, he wished to get it all over quickly and be off. The colour sank from Clare's face again, and she stood quite still for a moment, looking at him. "Good-bye," he said, holding out his hand, and trying hard to smile a little.

Clare looked at him still, but her hand did not meet his, though he waited, holding it out to her. Her face hardened as though she were making an effort, then softened again, and still he waited.

"Won't you say good-bye to me?" he asked unsteadily.

She hesitated a moment longer.

"No!" she answered suddenly. "I—I can't!"

And here the story comes to its conclusion, as many stories out of the lives of men and women seem to end at what is only their turn-ing-point. For real life has no conclusion but real death, and that is a sad ending to a tale, and one which may as well be left to the imagi-nation when it is possible.

Stories of strange things, which really occur, very rarely have what used to be called a "moral" either. All sorts of things happen to people who afterwards go on living just the same, neither much better nor much worse than they were in the beginning. The story is a slice, as it were, cut from the most interesting part of a life, generally at the point where that life most closely touches another, so that the future of the two momentarily depends upon each separately, and upon both together. The happiness or unhappiness of both, for a long time to come, is founded upon the action of each just at those moments. And sometimes, as in the tale here told, the least promising of all the persons concerned is the one who helps matters out. The only logical thing about life is the certainty that it must end. If there were any logic at all about what goes between birth and death, men would have found it out long ago, and we should all know how to live as soon as we leave school; whereas we spend our lives under Fate's ruler, trying to understand, while she raps us over the knuckles every other minute because we cannot learn our lesson and sit up straight, and be good without being prigs, and do right without sticking it through other people's peace of mind as one sticks a pin through a butterfly.

A ROSE OF YESTERDAY

A ROSE OF YESTERDAY

CHAPTER I

"I wonder what he meant by it," said Sylvia, turning again in her chair, so that the summer light, softened and tinted by the drawn blinds, might fall upon the etching she held.

" My dear," answered Colonel Wimpole, stretching out his still graceful legs, leaning back in his chair, and slowly joining his nervous but handsome hands, " nobody knows."

He did not move again for some time, and his ward continued to scrutinize Dürer's Knight. It was the one known as ' The Knight, Death, and the Devil,' and she had just received it from her guardian as a birthday present.

" But people must have thought a great deal about it," said Sylvia, at last. " There must be stories about what it means. Do tell me. I'm sure you know."

She laid the unframed print upon her knees, still holding it by the edges, lest the fitful breeze

that came in through the blinds should blow it
to the floor.   At the same time she raised her
eyes till they met the colonel's.

Her earnest young face expressed something
like veneration as she gazed at him, and perhaps
he thought that it was undeserved, for he soon
looked away, with a faint sigh.   She sighed, too,
but more audibly, as though she were not ashamed
of it.   Possibly she knew that he could not guess
what the sigh meant, and the knowledge added
a little pain to what she felt just then, and had
felt daily of late.   She began to study the etching again.

" To me," she said softly, " the Knight is a
hero.   He is making Death show him the way,
and he has made the Devil his squire and servant.   He will reach the city on the hill in
time, for there is still sand enough in the hour-
glass.   Do you see ? "   She held out the print
to the colonel.   " There is still sand enough,"
she repeated.   " Don't you think so ? "

Again, as she asked the question, she looked
at him ; but he was bending over the etching,
and she could only see his clear profile against
the shadows of the room.

" He may be just in time," he answered
quietly.

" I wonder which house they lived in, of those
one can see," said Sylvia.   .

"Who are 'they'? Death, the Devil, and the Knight?"

"No. The Knight and the lady, of course, —the lady who is waiting to see whether he will come in time."

The colonel laughed a little at her fancy, and looked at her as the breeze stirred her brown hair. He did not understand her, and she knew that he did not. His glance took in her brown hair, her violet eyes, her delicately shaded cheek, and the fresh young mouth with its strange little half-weary smile that should not have been there, and that left the weariness behind whenever it faded for a time. He wondered what was the matter with the girl.

She was not ill. That was clear enough, for they had travelled far, and Sylvia had never once seemed tired. The colonel and Miss Wimpole, his elderly maiden sister, had taken Sylvia out to Japan to meet her father, Admiral Strahan, who had been stationed some time with a small squadron in the waters of the far East. He had been ordered home rather suddenly, and the Wimpoles were bringing the girl back by way of Europe. Sylvia's mother had been dead three years, and had left her a little fortune. Mrs. Strahan had been a step-sister, and no blood relation, of the Wimpoles; but they had been as a real brother and a real sister to her,

and she had left her only child to their care
during such times as her husband's service
should keep him away from home. The girl
was now just eighteen.

Colonel Wimpole wondered whether she could
be destined for suffering, as some women are,
and the thought linked itself to the chain of
another life, and drew it out of his heart that
he might see it and be hurt, for he had known
pain in himself and through one he loved. He
could not believe that Sylvia was forefated to
sorrow, and the silent weariness that of late was
always in her face meant something which he
feared to learn, but for which he felt himself
vaguely responsible, as though he were not
doing his duty by her.

He was a man of heart, of honour, and of
conscience. Long ago, in his early youth, he
had fought bravely in a long and cruel war, and
had remained a soldier for many years afterwards, with an old-fashioned attachment for
arms that was dashed with chivalry, till at last
he had hung up his sword, accepting peace as
a profession. Indeed he had never loved anything of war, except its danger and its honour;
and he had loved one woman more than either,
but not against honour nor in danger, though
without any hope.

He had lived simply, as some men can and

as a few do live, in the midst of the modern
world, parting with an illusion now and then,
and fostering some new taste in its place, in a
sort of innocent and simple consciousness that
it was artificial, but in the certainty that it was
harmless. He was gentle in his ways, with the
quiet and unaffected feeling for other people
which not seldom softens those who have fought
with their hands in the conviction of right, and
have dealt and received real wounds. War
either brutalizes or refines a man; it never
leaves him unchanged. Colonel Wimpole had
travelled from time to time, more for the sake
of going to some one place which he wished to
see, than of passing through many places for the
sake of travelling. There is a great difference
between the two methods. Wherever he went,
he took with him his own character and his
slightly formal courtesy of manner, not leaving
himself at home, as some people do, nor assum-
ing a separate personality for Europe, like a
disguise; for, such as he was, he was incapable
of affectation, and he was sure that the manners
which had been good enough for his mother
were good enough for any woman in the world,
as indeed they were, because he was a gentleman, that is, a man, and gentle at all points,
excepting for his honour. But no one had ever
touched that.

He looked what he was, too, from head to foot. He was a tall, slender man, of nervous strength, with steady grey eyes, high features, smooth, short and grizzled hair; simple and yet very scrupulous in his dress; easy in his movements; not old before his time, but having already something of the refinement of age upon the nobility of his advanced manhood; one of whom a woman would expect great things in an extremity, but to whom she would no longer turn for the little service, the little fetching and carrying, which most women expect of men still in prime. But he did such things unasked, and for any woman, when it seemed natural to do them. After all, he was only fifty-three years old, and it seems to be established that sixty is the age of man's manumission from servitude, unless the period of slavery be voluntarily extended by the individual. That leaves ten years of freedom if one live to the traditional age of mankind.

But Sylvia saw no sign of age in Colonel Wimpole. In connexion with him the mere word irritated her when he used it, which he sometimes did quite naturally, and he would have been very much surprised could he have guessed how she thought of him, and what she was thinking as she sat looking from him to Dürer's Knight and from the etched rider to the

living man again. For she saw a resemblance
which by no means existed, except, perhaps,
between two ideals.

The Knight in the picture is stern and strong
and grim, and sits his horse like the incarnation
of an unchanging will, riding a bridled destiny
against Death and Evil to a good end. And
Death's tired jade droops its white head and
sniffs at the skull in the way, but the Knight's
charger turns up his lip and shows his teeth at
the carrion thing and arches his strong neck,
while the Knight looks straight before him, and
cares not, and his steel-clad legs press the great
horse into the way, and his steel-gloved hand
holds curb and snaffle in a vise. As for the
Devil, he slinks behind, an evil beast, but subdued, and following meanly with a sort of mute,
animal astonishment in his wide eyes.

And beside Sylvia sat the colonel, quiet, gentle, restful, suggesting just then nothing of desperate determination, and not at all like the
grim Knight in feature. Yet the girl felt a
kinship between the two, and saw one and the
same heroism in the man and in the pictured
rider. In her inmost heart she wished that she
could have seen the colonel long ago, when he
had fought, riding at death without fear. But
the thought that it had been so very long ago
kept the wish down, below the word-line in her

heart's well.   Youth clothes its ideals with
the spirit of truth and hides the letter out of
sight.

But in the picture, Sylvia looked for herself,
since it was for a lady that the Knight was
riding, and all she could find was the big old
house up in the town, on the left of the tallest
tower.   She was waiting somewhere under the
high-gabled roof, with her spinning-wheel or her
fine needlework, among her women.   Would he
ever come?   Was there time before the sand in
Death's hour-glass should run out?

"I wish the horse would put his fore foot
down, and go on!" she said suddenly.

Then she laughed, though a little wearily.
How could she tell the colonel that he was
the Knight, and that she was waiting in the
tall house with the many windows?   Perhaps
he was never to know, and forever the charger's
fore foot would be lifted, ready for the step that
was never to fall upon the path.

But Colonel Wimpole did not understand.
It was unlike her to wish that an old print
should turn into a page from a child's movable
picture-book.

"Why do you wish that the horse would go
on?" he asked half idly.

"Because the sand will not last, if he waits,"
said Sylvia, quietly; and as she spoke a third

time of the sand in the hour-glass, she felt a little chill at her heart.

"There will always be time," answered the colonel, enigmatically.

"As there will always be air, I suppose; and that will not matter to us, when we are not here to breathe it any more."

"That is true. Nothing will matter very much a hundred years hence."

"But a few years matter much more than a hundred." Her voice was sad.

"What are you thinking of?" asked Colonel Wimpole, changing his position so as to see her face better.

He resented her sadness a little, for he and his sister were doing their best to make her happy. But Sylvia did not answer him. She bent her white forehead to the faint breeze that came through the closed green blinds, and she looked at the etching. The colonel believed that she was thinking of her dead mother, whom she had loved. He hesitated, choosing his words, for he hated preaching, and yet it seemed to him that Sylvia mourned too long.

"I was very fond of your mother, too, my dear," he said gently, after a time. "She was like a real sister to us. I wish I could have gone instead, and left her to you."

"You?" Sylvia's voice startled him; she

was suddenly pale, and the old print shook in
her hands. "Oh, no!" she cried half passionately. "Not you—not you!"

The colonel was surprised for a moment.
Then he was grateful, for he felt that she
was very fond of him. He thought of the
woman he loved, and that he might have had
such a daughter as Sylvia, but with other
eyes.

"I am glad you are fond of me," he said.
"You are very good to me, and I know I am
a tiresome old man."

At that word, one beat of the girl's heart sent
resentful blood to her face.

"You are not old at all!" she cried. "And
you could not be tiresome if you tried! And
I am not good to you, as you call it!"

The girl's young anger made him think of
summer lightning, and of the sudden flashing
of new steel drawn silently and swiftly from
the sheath into the sunshine.

"Goodness may be a matter of opinion, my
dear," said he. "But age is a matter of fact.
I was fifty-three years old on my last birthday."

"Oh, what do years matter?" Sylvia rose
quickly and turned from him, going towards the
window.

The colonel watched her perfectly graceful

movements. She wore grey, with a small black band at her throat, and the soft light clung to the lovely outline of her figure and to her brown hair. He thought again of the daughter that might have been born to him, and even of a daughter's daughter. It seemed to him that his own years might be a greater matter than Sylvia would admit. Yet, as their descending mists veiled hope's height, he was often glad that there should not be as many more as there had been. He said nothing, and there was a dream in his eyes.

"You are always saying that you are old. Why?" Sylvia's voice came from the window, but she did not turn. "It is not kind," she said, still more softly.

"Not kind?" He did not understand.

"It is not kind to me. It is as though I did not care. Besides, it is not true!"

Just then the conviction had come back to her voice, stronger than ever, strengthening the tone just when it was breaking. She had never spoken to him in this way. He called her.

"Sylvia! Will you come here, my dear?" She came, and he took her fresh young hands. "What is it? Has anything happened? Are you unhappy? Tell me."

At his question the violet eyes slowly filled,

and she just bent her head once or twice, as though assenting.

" You are unhappy?" He repeated his question, and again she nodded sadly.

" But happy, too, — often."

There was not room for happiness and sorrow together in her full eyes. The tear fell, and gladness took its place at his touch. But he looked, and remembered other hands, and began to know the truth. Love's unforgotten spirit came, wafting a breath of older days.

He looked, and wondered whom the girl had chosen, and was glad for her happiness while he grew anxious for its life. She was so young that she must have chosen lately and quickly. In a rush of inward questioning his mind ran back through the long journey they had made together, and answers came in many faces of men that glided before him. One of them stopped him and held his thought, as a fleeting memory will. A young officer of her father's flagship, lean, brown, bright-eyed, with a strong mouth and a rare smile. Sylvia had often talked with him, and the boy's bright eyes used to watch her from the distance when he was not beside her. Quiet of speech he was, and resolute, bred in the keen air of a northern sea, of the few from among whom fate may choose the one. That was the man.

The colonel spoke, then, as though he had said much, glad and willing to take the girl's conclusion.

"I know who it is," he said, as if all had been explained. "I am glad, very glad."

His hands pressed hers more tightly, for he was a man of heart, and because his own life had failed strangely, he knew how happy she must be, having all he had not. But the violet eyes grew wide and dark and surprised, and the faint colour came and went.

"Do you really, really know at last?" she asked, very low.

"Yes, dear, I know," he said, for he had the sure conviction out of his sympathy for the child.

"And you are glad? Even as I am?"

"Indeed I am! I love you with all my heart, my dear."

She looked at him a moment longer, and then her sight grew faint, and her face hid itself against his coat.

"Say it! Say it again!" she repeated, and her white fingers closed tightly upon his sleeve. "I have waited so long to hear you say it!"

An uneasy and half-distressed look came to his face instantly, as he looked down at the brown hair.

"What?" he asked. "What have you waited to hear me say?"

"That — the words you said just now." Her face still hidden, she hesitated.

"What did I say? That I loved you, my dear?"

She nodded silently, against his coat.

"That I have always loved you, Sylvia dear," he said, while a wondering fear stole through him.

"You never told me. And I did not dare tell you — how could I? But now you understand. You know that the years mean nothing, after all, and that there is still sand in the hour-glass, and you and I shall reach the end of the road together —"

"Sylvia!" His voice rang sharply and painfully as he interrupted her.

He was a little pale, and his grey eyes were less steady than usual, for he could not be mistaken any longer. He had faced many dangers bravely, but the girl frightened him, clinging to his sleeve, and talking of her half-childish love for him. Then came the shock to his honour, for it seemed as though it must somehow have been his fault.

She looked up and saw his face, but could not understand it, though she had a prevision of evil, and the stealing sickness of disappointment made her faint.

"I did not know what you meant, my child,"

he said, growing more pale, and very gently
pushing her back a little. "I was thinking of
young Knox. I thought you loved him. I was
so sure that he was the man."

She drew back, now, of her own will, staring.

"Knox? Mr. Knox?" She repeated the
name, hardly hearing her own words, half
stunned by her mistake. "But you said — you
said you loved me — "

"As your father does," said Colonel Wimpole,
very gravely. "Your father and I are just of
the same age. We were boys together. You
know it, my dear."

She was a mere child, and he made her feel
that she was. Her hands covered her face in
an instant as she fled, and before the door had
closed behind her, the colonel heard the first
quick sob.

He had risen to his feet, and stood still, looking at the door. When he was alone, he might
have smiled, as some men might have done, not
at Sylvia, indeed, though at the absurdity of the
situation. But his face was sad, and he quietly
sat down again by the table, and began to think
of what had happened.

Sylvia was very foolish, he said to himself,
as he tried to impose upon his mind what he
thought should have been his conviction. Yet
he was deeply and truly touched by her half-

childish love, and its innocence seemed pathetic
to him, while he was hurt for her pain, and most
of all for her overwhelming confusion.

At the same time came memories and visions,
and his head sank forward a little as he sat in
his chair by the table.   The vision of hope was
growing daily more dim, but the remembrance
of the past was as undying as what has been
is beyond recall.

Sylvia would wake from her girlish dream,
and, in the fulness of young womanhood, would
love a man of her own years.   The colonel knew
that.   She would see that he was going in under
the gateway of old age, while she was on the
threshold of youth's morning.   A few days, or
a few months, or, at most, a few years more,
and she must see that he was an old man.   That
was certain.

He sighed, not for Sylvia, but because age is
that deadly sickness of which hope must perish
at last.   Time is a prince of narrow possessions,
absolute where he reigns at all, cruel upon his
people, and relentless; for, beyond his scanty
principality, he is nothing, and his name is not
known in the empire of eternity.   Therefore
while he rules he raises the dark standard of
death, taking tribute of life, and giving back a
slow poison in return.

Colonel Wimpole was growing old, and, though

the woman he still loved was not young, she was far younger than he, and he must soon seem an old man even in her eyes. And then there would not be much hope left. Sadly he wondered what Sylvia saw in him which that other woman, who had known him long, seemed to have never quite seen. But such questioning could find no satisfaction.

He might have remained absorbed in his reflexions for a long time had he been left alone, but the door opened behind him, and he knew by the steady and precise way in which it was opened and shut that his sister had entered the room.

"Richard," she said, "I am surprised." Then she stood still and waited.

Miss Wimpole was older than her brother, and was an exaggeration of him in petticoats. Her genuine admiration for him was curiously tempered by the fact that, when they had been children, she, as the elder, had kept him out of mischief, occasionally by force, often by authority, but never by persuasion. When in pinafores the colonel had been fond of sweets. Miss Wimpole considered that he owed his excellent health to her heroic determination to save him from destruction by jam. Since those days she had been obliged to yield to him on other points, but the memory of victory in the matter of preserves still made her manner authoritative.

She was very like him, being tall, thin, and not ungraceful, though as oddly precise in her movements and gestures as she was rigid in her beliefs, faithful in her affections, and just in her judgments. She had loved a man who had been killed in the civil war, and, being what she was, she had never so much as considered the possibility of marrying any one else. She was much occupied in good works and did much good, but she was so terribly accurate about it as to make Sylvia say that she was like a public charity that had been brought up in good society.

The colonel rose as she spoke.

" What is the matter ? " he asked. " Why are you surprised ? "

'· What have you been saying to Sylvia, Richard ? " enquired Miss Wimpole, not moving.

It would have been hard to hit upon a question more certain to embarrass the colonel. He felt the difficulty of his position so keenly that, old as he was, a faint colour rose in his cheeks. No answer occurred to him, and he hesitated.

" She has locked herself up in her room," continued Miss Wimpole, with searching severity, " and she is crying as though her heart would break. I heard her sobbing as I passed the door, and she would not let me in."

" I am very sorry," said the colonel, gravely.

" You do not seem much concerned," retorted

his sister. "I insist upon knowing what is the matter."

"Girls often cry," observed Colonel Wimpole, who felt obliged to say something, though he did not at all know what to say.

"Sylvia does not often cry, Richard, and you know it. You must have said something very unkind to her."

"I hope not," answered the colonel, evasively.

"Then why is she sobbing there, all by herself? I should like you to answer that question."

"I am very sorry that I cannot. When she is herself again you had better ask her."

Colonel Wimpole thought this good diplomacy. Since he meant not to tell his sister the truth, and was incapable of inventing a falsehood, he saw no means of escape except by referring Miss Wimpole directly to Sylvia.

"Richard," said the maiden lady, impressively, "I am surprised at you." And she turned away rather stiffly. "I thought you had more confidence in me," she added, as she reached the door.

But Colonel Wimpole made no further answer, for he saw that she had accepted his silence, which was all he wanted. When he was quite sure that she was in her own room, he went and got his hat and stick and slipped quietly out of the hotel.

CHAPTER II

COLONEL WIMPOLE did not like Lucerne, and
as he strolled along the shady side of the street,
he unconsciously looked up at the sky or down
at the pavement rather than at the houses and
the people. He disliked the tourists, the buildings, the distant scenery and the climate, and
could give a reason for each separate aversion.
Excepting the old tower, which was very much
like a great many other old towers, he main-
tained that the buildings were either flat and
dull, or most modernly pretentious. The tourists were tourists, and that alone condemned
them beyond redemption. The climate was de-
testable, and he was sure that every one must
think so. As for the scenery, with its prim
lake, its tiresome snow mountains, and its toy
trees, he said that it was little better than a
perpetual chromolithograph, though at sunset
it occasionally rose to the dignity of a transparent 'landscape' lamp-shade. The colonel's
views of places were not wholly without prejudice. Being a very just man, where men and

women were concerned, he allowed himself to
be as unfair as he chose about inanimate things,
from snow mountains to objects of art.

It was the pretension of Switzerland, he said,
to please and to attract. Since it neither attracted him nor pleased him, he could not see
what harm there could be in saying so. The
Rigi's feelings could not be hurt by a sharp
remark, nor could Mount Pilatus be supposed
to be sensitive. He never abused Switzerland
where any Swiss person could hear him. The
same things, he said, were true of objects of art.
If they failed to please, there could be no reason
for their existence, or for not saying so, provided
that the artist were not present. As for the latter, the charitable colonel was always willing
to admit that he had done his best. It was
gratuitous to suppose that any man should wil-
fully do badly what he could do well.

The colonel strolled slowly through the back
streets, keeping in the shade. The day was hot,
and he felt something like humiliation at having
allowed himself to yield to circumstances and
come out of the house earlier than usual. He
would certainly not have acknowledged that he
had been driven from the hotel by the fear of
his sister's curiosity, but he would have faced a
hotter sun rather than be obliged to meet her
inquisitive questions again.

It was true that, being alone, he had to meet himself, and discuss with himself the painful little scene which had taken place that afternoon, for he was not one of those people who can get rid of unpleasant difficulties simply by refusing to think about them. And he examined the matter carefully as he went along, staring alternately at the sky and at the pavement, while his stick rang sharply in time with his light but still military step. He did not see the people who passed, but many of them looked at him, and noticed his face and figure, and set him down for a gentleman and an old soldier, as he was.

At first sight it seemed ridiculous that Sylvia should be in love with him; then it seemed sad, and then it seemed childish. He remembered the tragedy of Ninon de l'Enclos and her son, and it was horrible until he recalled an absurd story of a short-sighted young man who had fallen in love with his grandmother because his vanity would not allow him to wear spectacles. At this recollection, Colonel Wimpole smiled a little, though he was obliged to admit that Sylvia's eyes had always been very good. He wished, for a moment, that he were quite old already, instead of being only on the edge of old age. It would have been more easy to laugh at the matter. He was glad that he was not ten

years younger, for in that case he might have
been to blame. As he was turning into the
main street, he caught sight of his own reflexion
in the big plate glass window of a shop. He
stopped short, with a painful sensation.

Had the image been that of a stranger, he
should have judged the original to be a young
man. The figure he saw was tall and straight
and active, dressed in the perfection of neatness
and good taste. The straw hat shaded the upper
part of the face, but the sunlight caught the well-
cut chin and gilded the small, closely trimmed
moustache.

The colonel was extremely annoyed, just then,
by his youthful appearance. He stopped and
then went close to the plate glass window, till
he could see his face distinctly in it, against the
shadows of the darkened shop. He was positively relieved when he could clearly distinguish
the fine lines and wrinkles and grey hairs, which
he saw every morning in his mirror when he
shaved. It was the sunshine playing with
shadow that had called up the airy reflexion of
his departed youth for a moment. Sylvia could
never have seen him as he had appeared to
himself in the window.

He looked a little longer. A lady in black
was talking with the shopkeeper, and a short
young man stood beside her. Colonel Wim-

pole's fingers tightened suddenly upon the familiar silver knob of his stick, his face grew a little pale, and he held his breath.

The lady turned quietly, walked to the window, followed by the shopkeeper and the young man, and pointed to a miniature which lay among a great number of more or less valuable antiquities and objects of art, all of them arranged so as to show them to an undue advantage. She stood quite still, looking down at the thing she wanted, and listening to what the shopkeeper said. The colonel, just on the other side of the thick plate glass, could hear nothing, though he could have counted the heavy lashes that darkly fringed the drooping lids as the lady kept her eyes upon the miniature. But his heart was standing still, for she was the woman he had loved so long and well, and he had not known that she was to pass through Lucerne. The short young man beside her was her son, and Colonel Wimpole knew him also, and had seen him from time to time during the nineteen years of his life. But he scarcely noticed him now, for his whole being was intent upon the face of the woman he loved.

She was dark, though her hair had never been jet black, and her complexion had always reminded the colonel of certain beautiful roses of which the smooth cream-coloured leaves are

very faintly tinged with a warm blush that
bears no relation to pink, but which is not red
either, a tint without which the face was like
marble, which could come in a moment but was
long in fading as a northern sunset, and which
gave wonderful life to the expression while it
lasted. The lady's features were bold and well
cut, but there were sad lines of lifelong weariness about the curved mouth and deep-set eyes;
and there was a sort of patient but not weak
sadness in all her bearing, the look of those who
have tired but have not yielded, who have borne
a calm face against a great trouble from without
and a true heart against a strong temptation
from within.

She was neither tall nor short, neither heavy
nor light in figure, a woman of good and strong
proportion, and she was dressed in black, though
one small jewelled ornament and a coloured
ribbon in her hat showed that she was not in
mourning.

The elderly man at the window did not move
as he watched her, for he felt sure that she
must presently look up and meet his eyes. Then
he would go in. But it did not happen just in
that way, for her son recognized him first, a
dark youth, very squarely built, with a heavy
face and straight eyebrows that met over his
nose. When he saw the colonel he smiled,

lifted his hat, and spoke to his mother. The
lady started perceptibly and seemed to press
the handle of her black parasol to her side.
Several seconds passed after that, before the
fringed lids were lifted, and the two looked at
each other fixedly through the thick glass. A
soft, slow smile smoothed and illuminated the
lady's face, but Colonel Wimpole felt that he
was paler than before, and his lips moved, unconsciously pronouncing a name which he had
never spoken carelessly during two and twenty
years. Nor, in that long time, had he ever met
Helen Harmon suddenly, face to face, without
feeling that his cheeks grew pale and that his
heart stood still for a moment.

But his pulse beat quite regularly again when
he had entered the shop and stood before her,
extending his hand to meet hers, though he felt
that he was holding out his heart to meet her
heart, and he was full of unexpected happiness.
So, in dim winter days, the sun shines out in a
sudden glory, and spring is in the air before
her time, for an hour; but afterwards it is cold
again, and snow falls before night. Many a far
glimpse of the flower-time had gladdened the
colonel's heart before now, but the promised
summer had never come.

The two stood still for a moment, hand in
hand, and their eyes lingered in meeting, just a

second or two longer than if they had been mere friends. That was all that a stranger could have seen to suggest that Richard Wimpole had loved Helen Harmon for twenty-two years, and the young man at her side did not even notice it. He shook hands with the colonel in his turn, and was the first to speak.

" One meets everybody in Lucerne," he observed, in a tactless generalization.

" I certainly did not hope to meet you," answered the colonel, smiling. "It is true that the cross-roads of Europe are at Lucerne if they are anywhere. My sister and I are taking Sylvia Strahan home from Japan. Of course we stopped here."

" Oh, of course ! " laughed young Harmon. " Everybody stops here. We have been here ever so long, on our way to Carlsbad, I believe."

His mother glanced at him nervously before she spoke, as though she were not sure of what he might say next.

" I am thinking of buying a miniature," she said. " Will you look at it for me ? You know all about these things. I should like your advice."

The dealer's face fell as he stood in the background, for he knew the colonel, and he understood English. But as she spoke, Mrs. Harmon was thinking more of Wimpole than of the miniature; and he, when he answered, was wondering how he could succeed in being alone with her for one half-hour — one of those little half-hours on which he lived for weeks and months after they were past.

Mrs. Harmon's manner was very quiet, and there was not often very much change in her expressions. Her laugh was low, regretful, and now and then a little bitter. Sometimes, when one might have expected a quick answer, she said nothing at all, and then her features had a calm immobility that was almost mysterious. Only now and then, when her son was speaking, she was evidently nervous, and at the sound of his voice her eyes turned quickly and nervously towards his face, while the shadows about the corners of her mouth deepened a little, and her lips set themselves. When he said anything more witless than usual, she was extraordinarily skilful and quick to turn his saying to sense by a clear explanation. At other times she generally spoke rather slowly and even indolently, as though nothing mattered very much. Yet she was a very sensible woman, and not by any means unpractical in daily life. Her tragedy, if it were one, had been slow and long drawn out.

First, a love which had been real, silent, and so altogether unsuspected, even by its object,

that Richard Wimpole had never guessed it even
to this day. Then a marriage thrust upon her
by circumstances, and which she had accepted at
last in the highest nobility of honest purpose.
After that, much suffering, most scrupulously
covered up from the world, and one moment of
unforgotten horror. There was a crooked scar
on her forehead, hidden by the thick hair which
she drew down over it. When she was angry
it turned red, though there was no other change
in her face. Then a little while, and her husband's mind had gone. Even then she had tried
to take care of him, until it had been hopeless,
and he had become dangerous. The mercy of
death seemed far from him, and he still lived,
for he was very strong. And all along there
had been the slowly increasing certainty of another misfortune. Her son, her only child, had
been like other children at first, then dull and
backward, and in the end, as compared with
grown men, deficient. His mind had not developed much beyond a boy's; but he was
unusually strong, he had learned to apply his
strength, and had always excelled in athletic
sports. One might have been deceived at first
by the sharp glance of his eyes, but they were
not bright with intelligence. The young man's
perfect physical health alone made them clear
and keen as a young animal's; but what they

saw produced little reaction of understanding or thought.

Nor was that all that Helen Harmon had borne. There was one other thing, hardest of any to bear. By an accident she had learned at last that Richard Wimpole had loved her, and she had guessed that he loved her still. He had fancied her indifferent to him; and Harmon had been his friend in young days. Harmon had been called fast, even then, but not vicious, and he had been rich. Wimpole had stood aside and had let him win, being diffident, and really believing that it might be better for Helen in the end. He thought that she could make anything she chose of Harmon, who was furiously in love with her.

So the two had made the great mistake, each meaning to do the very best that could be done. But when Harmon had gone mad at last, and was in an asylum without prospect of recovery, and Helen found herself the administrator of his property for her son, it had been necessary to go through all his disordered papers, and she had found a letter of Wimpole's to her husband, written long ago. Had it been a woman's letter, she would have burned it unread. But it was a duty to read every paper which might bear upon business matters, from the beginning, and she naturally supposed that Harmon must have had some reason for keeping this one. So she read it.

It had been written in the early days of her husband's courtship. He, too, had been generous, then, with impulses of honour in which there had been, perhaps, something of vanity, though they had impelled him to do right. There had been some conversation between the friends, and Harmon had found out that Wimpole loved Helen. Not being yet so far in love as he was later, he had offered to go away and let the young colonel have a chance, since the latter had loved her first. Then Wimpole had written this letter which she found twenty years later.

It was simple, grateful, and honourably conceived. It said what he had believed to be the truth, that Helen did not care for him, that Harmon was quite as good as he in all ways, and much richer, and it finally and definitely refused the offer of 'a chance.' There was nothing tragic about it, nor any high-flown word in its short, clear phrases. But it had decided three lives, and the finding of it after such a long time hurt Helen more than anything had ever hurt her before.

In a flash she saw the meaning of Wimpole's life, and she knew that he loved her still, and had always loved her, though in all their many meetings, throughout those twenty years, he had

never said one word of it to her. In one sudden
comprehension, she saw all his magnificent generosity of silence. For he had partly known how
Harmon had treated her. Every one knew something of it, and he must have known more than
any one except the lawyer and the doctor whom
she had been obliged to consult.

And yet, in that quick vision, she remembered,
too, that she had never complained to him, nor
ever said a word against Harmon. What Wimpole knew, beyond some matters of business in
which he had helped her, he had learned from
others or had guessed. But he had guessed
much. Little actions of his, under this broad
light of truth, showed her now that he had often
understood what was happening when she had
thought him wholly in ignorance.

But he, on his side, found no letter, nor any
unexpected revelation of her secret; and still,
to him, she seemed only to have changed indifference for friendship, deep, sincere, lasting and
calm.

She kept the old letter two days, and then,
when she was alone, she read it again, and her
eyes filled, and she saw her hands bringing the
discoloured page towards her lips. Then she
started and looked at it, and she felt the scar on
her forehead burning hot under her hair, and the
temptation was great, though her anger at her-

self was greater. Harmon was alive, and she was a married woman, though he was a madman. She would not kiss the letter, but she laid it gently upon the smouldering embers, and then turned away, that she might not see it curling and glowing and blackening to ashes on the coals. That night a note from the director of the asylum told her that her husband was in excellent bodily health, without improvement in his mental condition. It was dated on the first of the month.

After that she avoided the colonel for some time, but when she met him her face was again like marble, and only the soft, slow smile and the steady, gentle voice showed that she was glad to see him. Two years had passed since then, and he had not even guessed that she knew.

He often sought her, when she was within reach of him, but their meeting to-day, in the fashionable antiquary's shop, at the cross-roads of Europe, was altogether accidental, unless it were brought about by the direct intervention of destiny. But who believes in destiny nowadays? Most people smile at the word 'fate,' as though it had no meaning at all. Yet call 'fate' the 'chemistry of the universe' and the sceptic's face assumes an expression of abject credulity, because the term has a modern ring

and smacks of science. What is the difference
between the two? We know a little chemistry:
we can get something like the perfume of spring
violets out of nauseous petroleum, and a flavour
of strawberries out of stinking coal-tar; but we
do not know much of the myriad natural laws
by which our bodies are directed hither and
thither, mere atoms in the everlasting whirl-
pool of all living beings. What can it matter
whether we call those rules chemistry or fate?
We shall submit to them in the end, with our
bodies, though our souls rebel against them ever
so eternally. The things that matter are quite
different, and the less they have to do with our
bodies, the better it is for ourselves.

Colonel Wimpole looked at the miniature and
saw that it was a modern copy of a well-known
French one, ingeniously set in an old case, to fit
which it had perhaps been measured and painted.
He looked at the dealer quickly, and the man
expressed his despair by turning up his eyes a
very little, while he bent his head forward and
spread out his palms, abandoning the contest,
for he recognized the colonel's right to advise a
friend.

"What do you think of it?" asked Mrs.
Harmon.

"That depends entirely on what you mean to
do with it, and how much you would give for

it," answered the colonel, who would not have let her buy an imitation under any circumstances, but was far too kind-hearted to ruin the shopkeeper in her estimation.

"I rather liked it," was the answer. "It was for myself. There is something about the expression that pleases me. The lady looks so blindly happy and delighted with herself. It is a cheerful little thing to look at."

The colonel smiled.

"Will you let me give it to you?" he asked, putting it into her hand. "In that way I shall have some pleasure out of it, too."

Mrs. Harmon held it for a moment, and looked at him thoughtfully, asking herself whether there was any reason why she should not accept the little present. He was not rich, but she had understood from his first answer that the thing was not worth much, after all, and she knew that he would not pay an absurd price for it. Her fingers closed quietly upon it.

"Thank you," she said. "I wanted it."

"I will come back this afternoon and pay for it," said the colonel to the dealer, as the three went out of the shop together a few moments later.

During the little scene, young Harmon had looked on sharply and curiously, but had not spoken.

"How are those things made, mother?" he asked, when they were in the street.

"What things?" asked Mrs. Harmon, gently.

"Those things — what do you call them? Like what Colonel Wimpole just gave you. How are they made?"

"Oh, miniatures? They are painted on ivory with very fine brushes."

"How funny! Why do they cost so much money, then?"

His questions were like those of a little child, but his mother's expression did not change as she answered him, always with the same unvarying gentleness.

"People have to be very clever to paint them," she said. "That is why the very good ones are worth so much. It is like a good tailor, my dear, who is paid well because he makes good coats, whereas the man who only knows how to make workmen's jackets earns very little."

"That's not fair," said young Harmon. "It isn't the man's fault if he is stupid, is it?"

"No, dear, it isn't his fault, it's his misfortune."

It took the young man so long to understand this that he said nothing more, trying to think over his mother's words, and getting them by heart, for they pleased him. They walked along in the hot sun and then crossed the street opposite the Schweizerhof to reach the shade of the foolish-looking trees that have been stuck about like Nuremberg toys, between the lake and the highway. The colonel had not spoken since they had left the shop.

"How well you are looking," he said suddenly, when young Harmon had relapsed into silence. "You are as fresh as a rose."

"A rose of yesterday," said Helen Harmon, a little sadly.

Quite naturally, Colonel Wimpole sighed as he walked along at her elbow; for though he did not know that she had ever loved him, he remembered the letter he had written to the man she had afterwards married, and he was too much a man himself not to believe that all might have been different if he had not written it.

"Where are you stopping?" he asked, when they had gone a few steps in silence.

Mrs. Harmon named a quiet hotel on the other side of the river.

"Close to us," observed the colonel, just as they reached the new bridge.

They were half-way across when an exclamation from young Harmon interrupted their conversation, which was, indeed, but a curiously stiff exchange of dry information about them-

selves and their movements, past, planned, and
probable. For people who are fond of each
other and meet rarely are first of all anxious
to know when they may meet again. But the
boy's cry of surprise made them look round.

"Jukes!" he exclaimed loudly. "Jukes!"
he repeated, more softly but very emphatically,
as though solely for his own benefit.

'Jukes' was his only expression when pleased
and surprised. No one knew whether he had
ever heard the word, or had invented it, and
no one could ever discover what it meant nor
from what it was derived. It seemed to be
what Germans call a 'nature-sound,' by which
he gave vent to his feelings. His mother hated
it, but had never been able to induce him to
substitute anything else in its place. She followed the direction of his eager glance, for she
knew by his tone that he wanted what he
saw.

She expected to see a pretty boat, or a big
dog, or a gorgeous posted bill. Archie had a
passion for the latter, and he often bought them
and took them home with him to decorate his
own particular room. He loved best the ones
printed in violent and obtrusive colours. The
gem of his collection was a purple woman on
a red ground with a wreath of yellow flowers.

But Mrs. Harmon saw neither advertisement

nor dog, nor boat. She saw Sylvia Strahan. She knew the girl very well, and knew Miss Wimpole, of course. The two were walking along on the other side of the bridge, talking together. Against the blaze of the afternoon sun, reflected from the still lake, they could hardly have recognized the colonel and the Harmons, even if they had looked that way.

"It's Sylvia, mother," said Archie, glaring at the girl. "But isn't she grown! And isn't she lovely? Oh, Ju-u-ukes!"

His heavy lips thickened outwards as he repeated the mysterious ejaculation, and there was more colour than usual in his dark face. He was but little older than Sylvia, and the two had played together as small children, but he had never shown any special preference for her as a playmate. What struck him, now, was evidently her beauty. There was a look in his eyes, and a sort of bristling of the meeting eyebrows that reminded Helen of his father, and her white lids quivered for an instant at the recollection, while she felt a little chill run through her.

The colonel also saw.

"Shall we cross over and speak to them?" he asked in a low voice. "Or shall we just go on?"

"Let us go on," answered Helen. "I will

go and see them later. Besides, we have passed
them now. Let us go on and get into the
shade; it is dreadfully hot here."

"Won't you stop and speak to them, mother?"
asked Archie Harmon, in a tone of deep disappointment. "Why, we have not seen them for
ever so long!"

"We shall see them by and by," answered
his mother. "It's too hot to go back now."

The young man turned his head and lagged
a little, looking after the girl's graceful figure,
till he stumbled awkwardly against a curbstone.
But he did not protest any more. In his dull
way, he worshipped his mother as a superior
being, and hitherto he had always obeyed her
with a half-childish confidence. His arrested
intelligence still saw her as he had seen her
ten years earlier, as a sort of high and protecting wisdom incarnate for his benefit, able
to answer all questions and to provide him
with unlimited pocket-money wherewith to buy
bright-coloured posters and other gaudy things
that attracted him. Up to a certain point, he
could be trusted to himself, for he was almost
as far from being an idiot as he was from being
a normally thinking man. He was about as
intelligent and about as well informed as a
rather unusually dull schoolboy of twelve years
or thereabouts. He did not lose his way in the

streets, nor drop his money out of his pockets, and he could speak a little French and German which he had learned from a foreign nurse, - enough to buy a ticket or order a meal. But he had scarcely outgrown toys, and his chief delight was to listen to the stories his mother told him. She was not very inventive, and she told the same old ones year after year. They always seemed to be new to him. He could remember faces and names fairly well, and had an average recollection of events in his own life; but it was impossible to teach him anything from books, his handwriting was the heavy, unformed scrawl of a child, and his spelling was one long disaster.

So far, at least, Helen had found only his intellectual deficiency to deal with, and it was at once a perpetual shame to her and a cause of perpetual sorrow and sympathy. But he was affectionate and docile enough, not cruel as some such beings are, and certainly not vicious, so far as she could see. Dull boys are rarely mischievous, though they are sometimes cruel, for mischief implies an imagination which dulness does not possess.

Archie Harmon had one instinct, or quality, which redeemed him from total insignificance and raised him above the level of an amiable and harmless animal. He had a natural horror of taking life, and felt the strongest possible impulse to save it at any risk to himself. His mother was never quite sure whether he made any distinction between the value of existence to a man, and its worth to an animal, or even to an insect. He seemed not to connect it with its possessor, but to look upon it as something to be preserved for its own sake, under all circumstances, wherever it manifested itself. At ordinary times he was sufficiently cautious for his own safety, and would hesitate to risk a fall or scratch in climbing, where most boys would have been quite unaware of such possibilities. But at the sight of any living thing in danger, a reckless instinct to save it took possession of him, and his sluggish nature was roused to sudden and direct activity, without any intermediate process of thought. He had again and again given proof of courage that might have shamed most men. He had saved a child from drowning in the North River, diving after it from a ferryboat running at full speed, and he had twice stopped bolting horses — once, a pair with a heavy brougham in the streets of New York, and once, in the park, a dog-cart driven by a lady. On the first of these two occasions he had been a good deal cut and bruised, and had narrowly escaped with his life. His mother was too brave not to be proud of his deeds, but with each one her fears for his own daily safety increased.

He was never violent, but he occasionally showed a strength that surprised her, though he never seemed to care about exhibiting it. Once, she had fallen and hurt her foot, and he had carried her up many stairs like a child. After that, she had felt now and then as men must feel who tame wild beasts and control them.

He worshipped her, and she saw that he looked with a sort of pity on other women, young or old, as not worthy to be compared with her in any way. She had begun to hope that she might be spared the humiliation of ever seeing him in love, despised or pitied, as the case might be, by some commonplace, pretty girl with white teeth and pink cheeks. She feared that, and she feared lest he should some day taste drink, and follow his father's ways to the same ruin. But as yet he had been like a child.

It was no wonder that she shuddered when, as he looked at Sylvia Strahan, she saw something in his face which had never been there before and heard that queer word of his uttered in such a tone. She wondered whether Colonel Wimpole had heard and seen, too, and for some time the three walked on in silence.

"Will you come in?" asked Mrs. Harmon, as they reached the door of her hotel.

The colonel followed her to her little sitting-room, and Archie disappeared; for the conversation of those whom he still, in his own thoughts, regarded as 'grown-up people' wearied him beyond bearing.

"My dear friend," said Colonel Wimpole, when they were alone, "I am so very glad to see you!"

He held one of her hands in his while he spoke the conventional words, his eyes were a little misty, and there was a certain tone in his voice which no one but Helen Harmon had ever heard.

"I am glad, too," she said simply, and she drew away her hand from his with a sort of deprecation which he only half understood, for he only knew that half of the truth which was in himself.

They sat down as they had sat many a time in their lives, at a little distance from each other, and just so that each had to turn the head a little to face the other. It was easier to talk in that position because there was a secret between them, besides many things which were not secrets, but of which they did not wish to speak.

"It is terribly long since we last met," said the colonel. "Do you remember? I went to see you in New York the day before we started for Japan. You had just come back from the country, and your house was in confusion."

"Oh yes, I remember," replied Mrs. Harmon. "Yes, it is terribly long; but nothing is changed."

"Nothing?" The colonel meant to ask her about Harmon, and she understood.

"Nothing," she answered gravely. "There was no improvement when the doctor wrote, on the first of last month. I shall have another report in a day or two. But they are all exactly alike. He will just live on, as he is now, to the end of his life."

"To the end of his life," repeated the colonel, in a low voice, and the two turned their heads and looked at each other.

"He is in perfect health," said Mrs. Harmon, looking away again.

She drew out a long hat-pin and lifted her hat from her head with both hands, for it was a hot afternoon, and she had come into the sitting-room as she was. The colonel noticed how neatly and carefully she did the thing. It seemed almost unnecessary to do it so slowly.

"It is so hot," she said, as she laid the hat on the table.

She was pale now, perhaps with the heat of which she complained, and he saw how tired her face was.

"Is this state of things really to go on?" he asked suddenly.

She moved a little, but did not look at him.

"I am not discontented," she said. "I am not—not altogether unhappy."

"Why should you not be released from it all?" asked the colonel.

It was the first time he had ever suggested such a possibility, and she looked away from him.

"It is not as if it had all been different before he lost his mind," he went on, seeing that she did not answer at once. "It is not as if you had not had fifty good reasons for a divorce before he finally went mad. What is the use of denying that?"

"Please do not talk about a divorce," said Mrs. Harmon, steadily.

"Please forgive me, if I do, my dear friend," returned the colonel, almost hotly; for he was suddenly convinced that he was right, and when he was right it was hard to stop him. "You have spent half your life in sacrificing all of yourself. Surely you have a right to the other half. There is not even the excuse that you might still do him some good by remaining his wife in name. His mind is gone, and he could not recognize you if he saw you."

"What should I gain by such a step, then?" asked Helen, turning upon him rather suddenly. "Do you think I would marry again?" There was an effort in her voice. "I hate to talk in this way, for I detest the idea of divorce, and the principle of it, and all its consequences. I believe it is going to be the ruin of half the world, in the end. It is a disgrace, in whatever way you look at it!"

"A large part of the world does not seem to think so," observed the colonel, rather surprised by her outbreak, though in any case excepting her own he might have agreed with her.

"It would be better if the whole world thought so," she observed with energy. "Do you know what divorce means in the end? It means the abolition of marriage laws altogether; it means reducing marriage to a mere experiment which may last a few days, a few weeks, or a few months, according to the people who try it. There are men and women, already, who have been divorced and married again half a dozen times. Before the next generation is old that will be the rule and not the exception."

"Dear me!" exclaimed Colonel Wimpole. "I hope not!"

"I know you agree with me," said Mrs. Harmon, with conviction. "You only argue on the other side because — " She stopped short.

"Why?" He did not look at her as he asked the question.

"Because you are my best friend," she answered, after a moment's hesitation, "and be-

cause you have got it into your head that I
should be happier. I cannot imagine why. It
would make no difference at all in my life —
now."

The last word fell from her lips with a regretful tone and lingered a little on the air like the
sad singing of a bell's last note, not broken by
a following stroke. But the colonel was not
satisfied.

"It may make all the difference, even now,"
he said. "Suppose that Harmon were to recover."

Helen did not start, for the thought had been
long familiar to her, but she pressed her lips
together a little and let her head rest against
the back of her chair, half closing her eyes.

"It is possible," continued the colonel. "You
know as well as I do that doctors are not always
right, and there is nothing about which so little
is really certain as insanity."

"I do not think it is possible."

"But it is, nevertheless. Imagine what it
would be, if you began to hear that he was
better and better, and finally well, and, at last,
that there was no reason for keeping him in
confinement."

Mrs. Harmon's eyes were quite closed now, as
she leaned back. It was horrible to her to wish
that her husband might remain mad till he died,

yet she thought of what her own life must be if
he should recover. She was silent, fighting it
out in her heart. It was not easy. It was hard
even to see what she should wish, for every
human being has a prime right of self-preser-
vation, against which no argument avails, save
that of a divinely good and noble cause to be
defended. Yet the moral wickedness of praying that Harmon might be a madman all the
rest of his life frightened her. Throughout
twenty years and more she had faced suffering and shame without flinching and without
allowing herself one thought of retaliation or
hatred. She had been hardened to the struggle
and was not a woman to yield, if it should begin
again, but she shrank from it, now, as the best
and bravest may shrink at the thought of torture, though they would not groan in slow fire.

"Just think what it might be," resumed
Colonel Wimpole. "Why not look the facts
in the face while there is time? If he were let
out, he would come back to you, and you would
receive him, for I know what you are. You
would think it right to take him back because
you promised long ago to love, honour, and obey
him. To love, to honour, and to obey — Henry
Harmon!"

The colonel's steady grey eyes flashed for an
instant, and his gentle voice was suddenly thick

E

and harsh as he pronounced the last words. They meant terribly much to the woman who heard them, and in her distress she leaned forward in her seat and put up her hands to her temples, as though she had pain, gently pushing back the heavy hair she wore so low on her forehead. Wimpole had never seen her so much moved, and the gesture itself was unfamiliar to him. He did not remember to have ever seen her touch her hair with her hands, as some women do. He watched her now, as he continued to speak.

"You did all three," he said. "You honoured him, you loved him, and you obeyed him for a good many years. But he neither loved, nor honoured, nor cherished you. I believe that is the man's part of the contract, is it not? And marriage is always called a contract, is it not? Now, in any contract, both parties must do what they have promised, so that if one party fails, the other is not bound. Is not that true? And, Heaven knows, Harmon failed badly enough!"

"Don't! Please don't take it that way! No, no, no! Marriage is not a contract; it is a bond, a vow — something respected by man because it is sacred before God. If Henry failed a thousand times more, I should be just as much bound to keep my promise."

Her head sank still more forward, and her hands pushed her hair straight back from the temples.

"You will never persuade me of that," answered the colonel. "You will never make me believe —" He stopped short, for as he watched her, he saw what he had never seen before, a deep and crooked scar high on her forehead. "What is that?" he asked suddenly, leaning towards her, his eyes fixed on the ugly mark.

She started, stared at him, dropping her hands, realized what he had seen, and then instantly turned away. He could see that her fingers trembled as she tried to draw her hair down again. It was not like her to be vain, and he guessed at once that she had some reason other than vanity for hiding the old wound.

"What is that scar?" he asked again, determined to have an answer. "I never saw it before."

"It is a — I was hurt long ago —" She hesitated, for she did not know how to lie.

"Not so very long ago," said the colonel. "I know something about scars, and that one is not many years old. It does not look as though you had got it in a fall either. Besides, if you had, you would not mind telling me, would you?"

"Please don't ask me about it! I cannot tell you about it."

The colonel's face was hardening quickly. The lines came out in it stern and straight, as when, at evening, a sudden frost falls upon a still water, and the first ice-needles shoot out, clear and stiff. Then came the certainty, and Wimpole looked as he had looked long ago in battle.

"Harmon did that," he said at last, and the wrathful thought that followed was not the less fierce because it was unspoken.

Helen's hands shook now, for no one had ever known how she had been wounded. But she said nothing, though she knew that her silence meant her assent. Wimpole rose suddenly, straight as a rifle, and walked to the window, turning his back upon her. He could say things there, under his breath, which she could not understand, and he said them, earnestly.

"He did not know what he was doing," Helen said, rather unsteadily.

The colonel turned on his heels at the window, facing her, and his lips still moved slowly, though no words came. Helen looked at him and knew that she was glad of his silent anger. Not real-izing what she was thinking of, she wondered what sort of death Harmon might have died if Richard Wimpole had seen him strike her to the ground with a cut-glass decanter. For a moment the cloak of mercy and forgiveness was rent from head to heel. The colonel would have killed the man with those rather delicate looking hands of his, talking to him all the time in a low voice. That was what she thought, and perhaps she was not very far wrong. Even now, it was well for Harmon that he was safe in his asylum on the other side of an ocean.

It was some time before Wimpole could speak. Then he came and stood before Helen.

"You will stay a few days? You do not mean to go away at once?" he said, with a question.

"Yes."

"Then I think I shall go away now, and come and see you again later."

He took her hand rather mechanically and left the room. But she understood and was grateful.

CHAPTER III

WHEN Archie Harmon disappeared and left the colonel and his mother together, she supposed that he had gone to his room to sleep, for he slept a great deal, or to amuse himself after his fashion, and she did not ask him where he was going. She knew what his favourite amusement was, though he did his best to keep it a secret from her.

There was a certain mysterious box, which he had always owned, and took everywhere with him, and of which he always had the key in his pocket. It took up a good deal of space, but he could never be persuaded to leave it behind when they went abroad.

To-day he went to his room, as usual, locked the door, took off his coat, and got the box out of a corner. Then he sat down on the floor and opened it. He took out some child's building-blocks, some tin soldiers, much the worse for wear, for he was ashamed to buy new ones, and a small and gaudily painted tin cart, in which an impossible lady and gentleman of papier-mâché, dressed in blue, grey, and yellow, sat leaning back with folded arms and staring, painted eyes. There were a few other toys besides, all packed away with considerable neatness, for Archie was not slovenly.

He sat cross-legged on the floor, a strong grown man of nearly twenty years, and began to play with his blocks. His eyes fixed themselves on his occupation, as he built up a little gateway with an arch and set red-legged French soldiers on each side of it for sentinels. He had played the same game a thousand times already, but the satisfaction had not diminished. One day in a hotel he had forgotten to lock the door, and his mother had opened it by mistake, thinking it was that of her own room. Before he could look round she had shut it again, but she had seen, and it had been like a knife-thrust. She kept his secret, but she lost heart from that day. He was still a child, and was always to be one.

Yet there was perhaps something more of intelligence in the childish play than she had guessed. He was lacking in mind, but not an idiot; he sometimes said and did things which were certainly far beyond the age of toys. Possibly the attraction lay in a sort of companionship which he felt in the society of the blocks, and the tin soldiers, and the little papier-mâché lady and gentleman. He felt that they understood what he meant and would answer him if they could speak, and would expect no more of him than he could give. Grown people always seemed to expect a great deal more, and looked at him strangely when he called Berlin the capital of Austria and asked why Brutus and Cassius murdered Alexander the Great. The toy lady and gentleman were quite satisfied if their necks were not broken in the cunningly devised earthquake which always brought the block house down into a heap when he had looked at it long enough and was already planning an ther.

Besides, he did all his best thinking among his toys, and had invented ways of working out results at which he ould not possibly have arrived by a purely mental process. He could add and subtract, for instance, with the bits of wood, and, by a laborious method, he could even do simple multiplication, quite beyond him with paper and pencil. Above all, he could name the tin soldiers after people he had met, and make them do anything he pleased, by a sort of rudimentary theatrical instinct that was not altogether childish.

To-day he built a house as usual, and, as usual, after some reflexion as to the best means of ruining it by taking out a single block, he

pulled it down with a crash. But he did not
at once begin another. On the contrary, he sat
looking at the ruins for a long time in a rather
disconsolate way, and then all at once began to
pack all the toys into the box again.

"I don't suppose it matters," he said aloud.
"But of course Sylvia would think me a baby if
she saw me playing with blocks."

And he made haste to pack them all away,
locking the box and putting the key into his
pocket. Then he went and looked through the
half-closed blinds into the sunny street, and he
could see the new bridge not far away.

"I don't care what mother thinks!" he exclaimed. "I'm going to find her again."

He opened his door softly, and a moment
later he was in the street, walking rapidly
towards the bridge. At a distance he looked
well. It was only when quite near to him that
one was aware of an undefinable ungainliness
in his face and figure — something blank and
meaningless about him, that suggested a heavy
wooden doll dressed in good clothes. In military countries one often receives that impression. A fine-looking infantry soldier, erect,
broad shouldered, bright eyed, spotless, and
scrupulously neat, comes marching along and
excites one's admiration for a moment. Then,
when close to him, one misses something which

ought to go with such manly bearing. The fellow is only a country lout, perhaps, hardly able to read or write, and possessed of an intelligence not much beyond the highest development of instinct. Drill, exercise, and the fear of black bread and water under arrest, have produced a fine piece of military machinery, but they could not create a mind, nor even the appearance of intelligence, in the wooden face. In a year or two the man will lay aside his smart uniform and go back to the class whence he came. One may give iron the shape and general look of steel, but not the temper and the springing quality.

Archie Harmon looked straight ahead of him as he crossed the bridge and followed the long street that runs beside the water, past the big hotels and the gaudy awnings of the provincially smart shops. At first he only looked along the pavement, searching among the many people who passed. Then as he remembered how Colonel Wimpole had seen him through a shop window, he stopped before each of the big plate glass ones and peered curiously into the shadows within.

At last, in a milliner's, he saw Sylvia and Miss Wimpole, and his heavy face grew red, and his eyes glared oddly as he stood motionless outside, under the awning, looking in. His lips went out a little, as he pronounced his own especial word very softly.

"Jukes!"

He stood first on one foot and then on the other, like a boy at a pastry cook's, hesitating, while devouring with his eyes. He could see that Sylvia was buying a hat. She turned a little each way as she tried it on before a big mirror, putting up her hands and moving her arms in a way that showed all the lines of her perfect figure.

Archie went in. He had been brought up by his mother, and chiefly by women, and he had none of that shyness about entering a women's establishment, like a milliner's, which most boys and many men feel so strongly. He walked in boldly and spoke as soon as he was within hearing.

"Miss Sylvia! I say! Miss Sylvia — don't you know me?"

The question was a little premature, for Sylvia had barely caught sight of him when he asked it. When she had recognized him, she did not look particularly pleased.

"It's poor Archie Harmon, my dear," said Miss Wimpole, in a low voice, but quite audibly.

"Oh, I have not forgotten you!" said Sylvia, trying to speak pleasantly as she gave her hand. "But where in the world did you come

from ?   And what are you doing in a milliner's
shop ? "

" I happened to see you through the window,
so I just came in to say how do you do.   There's
no harm in my coming in, is there ?   You look
all right.   You're perfectly lovely."

His eyes were so bright that Sylvia felt oddly
uncomfortable.

" Oh no," she answered, with an indifference she did not feel.   " It's all right — I
mean — I wish you would go away now, and
come and see us at the hotel, if you like, by
and by."

" Can't I stay and talk to you ?   Why can't
I stay and talk to her, Miss Wimpole ? " he
asked, appealing to the latter.   " I want to
stay and talk to her.   We are awfully old
friends, you know ; aren't we, Sylvia ?   You
don't mind my calling you Sylvia, instead of
Miss Sylvia, do you ? "

" Oh no !   I don't mind that ! " Sylvia
laughed a little.   " But do please go away
now ! "

" Well — if I must — " he broke off, evidently
reluctant to do as she wished.   " I say," he
began again with a sudden thought, " you like
that hat you're trying on, don't you ? "

Instantly Sylvia, who was a woman, though
a very young one, turned to the glass again,

settled the hat on her head and looked at herself critically.

"The ribbons stick up too much, don't they?"
she asked, speaking to Miss Wimpole, and quite
forgetting Archie Harmon's presence. "Yes,
of course they do! The ribbons stick up too
much," she repeated to the milliner in French.

A brilliant idea had struck Archie Harmon.
He was already at the desk, where a young
woman in black received the payments of passing customers with a grieved manner.

"She says the ribbons stick up too much," he
said to the person at the desk. "You get
them to stick up just right, will you? The
way she wants them. How much did you say
the hat was? Eighty francs? There it is. Just
say that it's paid for, when she asks for the bill."

The young woman in black raked in the note
and the bits of gold he gave her, catching them
under her hard, thin thumb on the edge of the
desk, and counting them as she slipped them
into her little drawer. She looked rather curiously at Archie, and there was still some surprise in her sour face when he was already on
the pavement outside. He stopped under the
awning again, and peered through the window
for a last look at the grey figure before the
mirror, but he fled precipitately when Sylvia
turned as though she were going to look at

him. He was thoroughly delighted with himself. It was just what Colonel Wimpole had
done about the miniature, he thought; and
then, a hat was so much more useful than a
piece of painted ivory.

In a quarter of an hour he was in his own
room again, sitting quite quietly on a chair by
the window, and thinking how happy he was,
and how pleased Sylvia must be by that time.

But Sylvia's behaviour when she found out
what he had done would have damped his innocent joy, if he had been looking through the
windows of the shop, instead of sitting in his
own room. Her father, the admiral, had a hot
temper, and she had inherited some of it.

"Impertinent young idiot!" she exclaimed,
when she realized that he had actually paid for
the hat, and the angry blood rushed to her face.
"What in the world —" She could not find
words.

"He is half-witted, poor boy," interrupted
Miss Wimpole. "Take the hat, and I will
manage to give his mother the money."

"Betty Foy and her idiot boy over again!"
said Sylvia, with all the brutal cruelty of extreme
youth. "'That all who view the idiot in his
glory' —" As the rest of the quotation was not
applicable, she stopped and stamped her little
foot in speechless indignation.

"The young gentleman doubtless thought to give Mademoiselle pleasure," suggested the milliner, suavely. "He is doubtless a relation—"

"He is not a relation at all!" exclaimed Sylvia in English, to Miss Wimpole. "My relations are not idiots, thank Heaven! And it's the only one of all those hats that I could wear! Oh, Aunt Rachel, what shall I do? I can't possibly take the thing, you know! And I must have a hat. I've come all the way from Japan with this old one, and it isn't fit to be seen."

"There is no reason why you should not take this one," said Miss Wimpole, philosophically. "I promise you that Mrs. Harmon shall have the money by to-night, since she is here. Your Uncle Richard will go and see her at once, of course, and he can manage it. They are on terms of intimacy," she added rather primly, for Helen Harmon was the only person in the world of whom she had ever been jealous.

"You always use such dreadfully correct language, Aunt Rachel," answered the young girl. "Why don't you say that they are old friends? 'Terms of intimacy' sounds so severe, somehow."

"You seem impatient, my dear," observed Miss Wimpole, as though stating a fact about nature.

"I am," answered Sylvia. "I know I am.

You would be impatient if an escaped lunatic rushed into a shop and paid for your gloves, or your shoes, or your hat, and then rushed off again, goodness knows where. Wouldn't you? Don't you think I am right?"

"You had better tell them to send the hat to the hotel," suggested Aunt Rachel, not paying the least attention to Sylvia's appeal for justification.

"If I must take it, I may as well wear it at once, and look like a human being," said Sylvia. "That is, if you will really promise to send Mrs. Harmon the eighty francs at once."

"I promise," answered Miss Wimpole, solemnly, and as she had never broken her word in her life, Sylvia felt that the difficulty was at an end.

The milliner smiled sweetly, and bowed them out.

"All the same," said Sylvia, as she walked up the street with the pretty hat on her head, "it is an outrageous piece of impertinence. Idiots ought not to be allowed to go about alone."

"I should think you would pity the poor fellow," said Miss Wimpole, with a sort of severe kindliness, that was genuine but irritating.

"Oh yes! I will pity him by and by, when I'm not angry," answered the young girl. "Of course — it's all right, Aunt Rachel, and I'm not depraved nor heartless, really. Only, it was very irritating."

"You had better not say anything about it to your Uncle Richard, my dear. He is so fond of Archie's mother that he will feel very badly about it. I will break it to him gently."

"Would he?" asked Sylvia, in surprise. "About herself, I should understand — but about that boy! I can't see why he should mind."

"He 'minds,' as you call it, everything that has to do with Mrs. Harmon."

Sylvia glanced at her companion, but said nothing, and they walked on in silence for some time. It was still hot, for the sun had not sunk behind the mountains; but the street was full of people, who walked about indifferent to the temperature, because Switzerland is supposed to be a cold country, and they therefore thought that it was their own fault if they felt warm. This is the principle upon which nine people out of ten see the world when they go abroad. And there was a fine crop of European and American varieties of the tourist taking the air on that afternoon, men, women, and children. The men who had huge field-glasses slung over their shoulders by straps predominated, and one, by whom Sylvia was particularly struck, was arrayed in

F

blue serge knickerbockers, patent-leather walk-
ing-boots, and a very shiny high hat. But there
were also occasional specimens of what she
called the human being — men in the ordinary
garments of civilization, and not provided with
opera-glasses. There were, moreover, young and
middle-aged women in short skirts, boots with
soles half an inch thick, complexions in which
the hue of the boiled lobster vied with the
deeper tone of the stewed cherry, bearing alpenstocks that rang and clattered on the pavement;
women who, in the state of life to which Heaven
had called them, would have gone to Margate
or Staten Island for a Sunday outing, but who
had rebelled against providence, and forced the
men of their families to bring them abroad.
And the men generally walked a little behind
them and had no alpenstocks, but carried shawls
and paper bundles, badges of servitude, and
hoped that they might not meet acquaintances
in Lucerne, because their women looked like
angry cooks and had no particular luggage.
Now and then a smart old gentleman with an
eyeglass, in immaculate grey or white, threaded
his way along the pavement, with an air of
excessive boredom; or a young couple passed
by, in the recognizable newness of honeymoon
clothes, the young wife talking perpetually, and
evidently laughing at the ill-dressed women,

while the equally young husband answered in
monosyllables, and was visibly nervous lest his
bride's remarks should be overheard and give
offence.

Then there were children, obtrusively English
children, taken abroad to be shown the miserable inferiority of the non-British world, and to
learn that every one who had not yellow hair
and blue eyes was a 'nasty foreigner,' — unless,
of course, the individual happened to be English, in which case nothing was said about hair
and complexion. And also there were the vulgar little children of the not long rich, repul-
sively disagreeable to the world in general, but
pathetic in the eyes of thinking men and
women. They are the sprouting shoots of the
gold-tree, beings predestined never to enjoy, because they will be always able to buy what
strong men fight for, and will never learn to
enjoy what is really to be had only for money;
and the measure of value will not be in their
hands and heads, but in bank-books, out of
which their manners have been bought with
mingled affection and vanity. Surely, if anything is more intolerable than a vulgar woman,
it is a vulgar child. The poor little thing is
produced by all nations and races, from the
Anglo-Saxon to the Slav. Its father was happy
in the struggle that ended in success. When it

grows old, its own children will perhaps be happy
in the sort of refined existence which wealth can
bring in the third generation.   But the child of
the man grown suddenly rich is a living misfortune between two happinesses : neither a worker
nor an enjoyer; having neither the satisfaction of the one, nor the pleasures of the other;
hated by its inferiors in fortune, and a source of
amusement to its ethic and æsthetic betters.

Sylvia had never thought much about the
people she passed in a crowd.   Thought is generally the result of suffering of some kind, bodily
or intellectual, and she had but little acquaintance with either.   She had travelled much, and
had been very happy until the present time,
having been shown the world on bright days
and by pleasant paths.   But to-day she was
not happy, and she began to wonder how many
of the men and women in the street had what
she had heard called a ' secret care.'   Her eyes
had been red when she had at last yielded to
Miss Wimpole's entreaties to open the door,
but the redness was gone already, and when
she had tried on the hat before the glass she
had seen with a little vanity, mingled with
a little disappointment, that she looked very
much as usual, after all.   Indeed, there had
been more than one moment when she had
forgotten her troubles because the ribbons on

the new hat stuck up too much. Yet she was really unhappy, and sad at heart. Perhaps some of the people she passed, even the women with red faces, dusty skirts, and clattering alpenstocks, were unhappy too.

She was not a foolish girl, nor absurdly romantic, nor full of silly sentimentalities, any more than she was in love with Colonel Wimpole in the true sense of the word. For she knew nothing of its real meaning, and, apart from that meaning, what she felt for him filled all the conditions proposed by her imagination. If one could classify the ways by which young people pass from childhood to young maturity, one might say that they are brought up by the head, by the imagination, or by the heart, and one might infer that their subsequent lives are chiefly determined by that one of the three which has been the leading-string. Sylvia's imagination had generally had the upper hand, and it had been largely fed and cultivated by her guardian, though quite unintentionally on his part. His love of artistic things led him to talk of them, and his chivalric nature found sources of enthusiasm in lofty ideals, while his own life, directed and moved as it was by a secret, unchanging and self-sacrificing devotion to one good woman, might have served as a model for any man. Modest, and not much inclined

to think of himself, he did not realize that
although the highest is quite beyond any one's
reach, the search after it is always upward, and
may lead a good man very far.

Sylvia saw the result, and loved it for its own
sake with an attachment so strong that it made
her blind to the more natural sort of humanity
which the colonel seemed to have outgrown,
and which, after all, is the world as we inherit
it, to love it, or hate it, or be indifferent to it,
but to live with it, whether we will or not.   He
fulfilled her ideal, because it was an ideal which
he himself had created in her mind, and to
which he himself nearly approached.   Logically
speaking, she was in a vicious circle, and she
liked what he had taught her to like, but liked
it more than he knew she did.

Sylvia glanced at Miss Wimpole sideways.
She knew her simple story, and wondered
whether she herself was to live the same sort
of life.   The idea rather frightened her, to tell
the truth, for she knew the aridity of the elderly
maiden lady's existence, and dreaded anything
like it.   But it was very simple and logical and
actual.   Miss Wimpole had loved a man who
had been killed.   Of course she had never married, nor ever thought of loving any one else.
It was perfectly simple.   And Sylvia loved,
and was not loved, as she told herself, and

she also must look forward to a perpetually
grey life.

Then, suddenly, she felt how young she was,
and she knew that the colonel was almost an
old man, and her heart rebelled. But this
seemed disloyal, and she blushed at the word
'unfaithful,' which spoke itself in her sensitive
conscience with the cruel power to hurt which
such words have against perfect innocence.
Besides, it was as if she were quarrelling with
what she liked, because she could not have it,
and she felt as though she were thinking child-
ishly, which is a shame in youth's eyes.

Also, she was nervous about meeting him
again, for she had not seen him since she had
fled from the room in tears, though he had seen
her on the bridge. She wished that she might
not see him at all for a whole day, at least,
and that seemed a very long time.

Altogether, when she went into the hotel
again, she was in a very confused state of mind
and heart, and was beginning to wish that she
had never been born. But that was childish,
too.

CHAPTER IV

HELEN HARMON was glad when the colonel
was gone. She went to a mirror, fixed to the
wall between the two windows of the room, and
she carefully rearranged her hair. She could
not feel quite herself until she knew that the
scar was covered again and hidden from curious
eyes. Then she sat down, glad to be alone.
It had been a great and unexpected pleasure to
see Wimpole, but the discovery he had made,
and the things he had said, had disturbed and
unnerved her.

There had been conviction in his voice when
he had said that Harmon might recover, and the
possibility of a change in her husband's condition had crossed her mind more than once.
She felt that a return to such a state of things
as had made up her life before he had become
insane, would kill her by slow torture. It was
of no use any longer to tell herself that recovery
was impossible, and to persuade herself that it
was so by the mere repetition of the words.
Words had no more weight, now.

72

She thought of her freedom since that merciful deliverance. It was not happiness, for there were other things yet to be suffered, but it was real freedom. She had her son's affliction to bear, but she could bear it alone and go and come with him as she pleased. She contrasted this liberty with what she had borne for years.

The whole history of their married life came back to her, the gradual progress of it from first to last, if indeed it had yet reached the end and was not to go back to the beginning again.

First there had been the sort of half-contented resignation which many young women feel during the early months of married life, when they have made what is called by the world a good match, simply because they saw no reason for not marrying and because they were ashamed to own that they cared for a man who did not seem to be attached to them. Sometimes the state lasts throughout life, a neutral, passionless, negative state, in which the heart turns flat and life is soon stale, a condition in which many women, not knowing what pain is, grow restless and believe that it must be pleasanter to be hurt than to feel nothing.

Henry Harmon had been handsome, full of life and nerve and enthusiasm for living, a rider, a sportsman, more reckless than brave and more brave than strong-minded, with a gift for being, or seeming to be, desperately in love, which had ultimately persuaded Helen to marry him in spite of her judgment. He turned pale when he was long near her, his eyes flashed darkly, his hands shook a little, and his voice trembled. An older woman might have thought it all rather theatrical, but he seemed to suffer, and that moved Helen, though it did not make her really love him. Women know that weakness of theirs and are more afraid of pitying an importunate suitor than of admiring him. So Helen married Harmon.

Disillusionment came as daylight steals upon dancers in a ballroom. At first it was not so painful as might have been imagined, for Helen was not excessively sensitive, and she had never really loved the man in the least. He grew tired of her and left her to herself a good deal. That was a relief, at first, for after she had realized that she did not love him, she shrank from him instinctively, with something very like real shame, and to be left alone was like being respected.

"Mrs. Blank's husband is neglecting her," says one.

"She does not seem to care; she looks very happy," answers another.

And she is temporarily happy, because Mr. Blank's neglect gives her a sense of bodily relief, for she knows that she has made a mistake in marrying him. It was so with Helen, and as she was not a changeable nor at all a capricious person, it might have continued to be so. But Harmon changed rapidly in the years that followed. From having been what people called fast, he became dissipated. He had always loved the excitement of wine. When it failed him, he took to stronger stuff, which presently became the essential requisite of his being. He had been said to be gay, then he was spoken of as wild, then as dissipated. Some people avoided him, and every one pitied Helen. Yet although he ruined his constitution, he did not wreck his fortunes, for he was lucky in all affairs connected with money. There remained many among his acquaintances who could not afford to disapprove of him, because he had power.

He drank systematically, as some men do, for the sake of daily excitement, and Helen learned to know tolerably well when he was dangerous and when he might be approached with safety. But more than once she had made horrible mistakes, and the memories of them were like dreams out of hell. In his drunkenness her face recalled other days to him, and forgotten words of passion found thick and indistinct utterance. Once she had turned on

him, white and desperate in her self-defence.
He struck her on the forehead with a cut-glass
decanter, snatched from her toilet table. When
she came to herself hours afterwards, it was
daylight. Harmon was in a drunken sleep, and
the blood on his face was hers.

She shuddered with pain from head to foot
when she thought of it. Then had come
strange lapses of his memory, disconnected
speech, even hysterical tears, following senseless anger, and then he had ceased to recognize any one, and had almost killed one of the
men who took care of him, so that it was necessary to take him to an asylum, struggling like a
wild beast. Twice, out of a sense of duty, she
had been to see whether he knew her, but he
knew no one, and the doctors said it was a
hopeless case. Since then she had received
a simple confirmation of the statement every
month, and there seemed to be no reason for
expecting any change, and she felt free.

Free was the only word she could find, and
she applied it to herself in a sense of her own,
meaning that she had been liberated from the
thraldom in which she had lived so many years
face to face with his brutality, and hiding it
from the world as best she could, protecting and
defending his name, and refusing pity as she
would have refused money had she been poor.

People might guess what she suffered, but no one should know it from her, and no one but herself could tell the half of what she underwent.

Yet, now that it was all over, Wimpole suggested that it might begin again, unless she took measures to defend herself. But her heart revolted at the idea of a divorce. She wondered, as she tried to test herself, whether she could be as strong if the case really arose. It never occurred to her to ask whether her strength might not be folly, for it lay in one of those convictions by which unusual characters are generally moved, and conviction never questions itself.

It was not that in order to be divorced she must almost necessarily bring up in public and prove by evidence a certain number of her many wrongs. The publicity would be horrible. Every newspaper in the country would print the details, with hideous head-lines. Even her son's deficiency would be dragged into the light. She should have to explain how she had come by the scar on her forehead, and much more that would be harder to tell, if she could bring her lips to speak the words.

Nevertheless, she could do that, and bear everything, for a good cause. If, for instance, Archie's future depended upon it, or even if it could do him some good, she could do all that for his

sake. But even for his sake, she would not be
divorced, not even if Harmon were let out of
the asylum and came back to her.

Some people, perhaps many, could not understand such a prejudice, or conviction, now that
all convictions are commonly spoken of as rela-
tive. But will those who do not understand
Helen Harmon consider how the world looked
upon divorce as recently as five and twenty
years ago? Nothing can give a clearer idea
of the direction taken by social morality than
the way in which half the world has become
accustomed to regard marriage as a contract,
and not as a bond, during the lifetime of people
now barely in middle age.

Twenty-five or thirty years ago divorces were
so rare as to be regarded in the light of very
uncommon exceptions to the general rule. The
divorce law itself is not yet forty years old in
England, nor twenty years old in France. In
Italy there is no civil divorce whatever at the
present day, and the Catholic Church only grants
what are not properly divorces, but annullations
of marriage, in very rare cases, and with the
greatest reluctance.

Even in America, every one can remember how
divorce was spoken of and thought of until very
recently. Within a few years it was deemed
to be something very like a disgrace, and cer-

tainly a profoundly cynical and immoral pro-
ceeding. To-day we can most of us count in
our own acquaintance half a dozen persons who
have been divorced and have married again.
Whatever we may think of it in our hearts, or
whatever our religious convictions may be on
the subject, it has become so common that when
we hear of a flagrant case of cruelty or unfaithfulness, by which a man or woman suffers, the
question at once rises to our lips, 'Why does
he not divorce his wife?' or 'Why does she
not divorce her husband?' We have grown
used to the idea, and, if it does not please us,
it certainly does not shock us. It shocked our
fathers, but we are perfectly indifferent.

Of course there are many, perhaps a majority,
who, though not Roman Catholics, would in their
own lives put up with almost anything rather
than go to the divorce court for peace. Some
actually suffer much and ask for no redress.
But there are very many who have not suffered
anything at all, excepting the favourite 'incom-
patibility of temper,' and who have taken advantage of the loose laws in certain states to try
a second matrimonial experiment. In what
calls itself society, there seems still to be a
prejudice against a third marriage for divorced
persons, but at the present rate of so-called
progress this cannot last long, and the old

significance of the word marriage will be quite
lost before our great grandchildren are dead;
in other words, by the end of the next century,
at the furthest.

There are various forms of honourable political
dreaming and of dishonourable political mischief-
making nowadays, which we are accustomed to
call collectively ' socialism.'   Most of these rely
for their hope of popular success upon their
avowed intention of dividing property and pre-
venting its subsequent accumulation.   Marriage
is an incentive of such accumulation, because it
perpetuates families and therefore keeps property
together by inheritance.   Therefore most forms
of socialism are at present in favour of divorce,
as a means of ultimately destroying marriage
altogether.   A proverb says that whosoever
desires the end, desires also the means.   There
is more truth in the saying than morality in the
point of view it expresses.   But there are those
who desire neither the means nor the end to
which they lead, and a struggle is coming, the
like of which has not been seen since the beginning of the world, and of which we who are
now alive shall not see the termination.

The Civil War in the United States turned
upon slavery incidentally, not vitally.   The cause
of that great fight lay much deeper.   In the same
way the Social War, which is coming, will turn

incidentally upon religion, and be perhaps called
a religious war hereafter, but it will not be de-
clared for the sake of faith against unbelief, nor
be fought at first by any church, or alliance of
churches, against atheism. It will simply turn
out that the men who fight on the one side will
have either the convictions or the prejudices of
Christianity, or both, and that their adversaries
will have neither. But the struggle will be at
its height when the original steady current of
facts which led to inevitable strife has sunk into
apparent insignificance under the raging storm
of conflicting belief and unbelief. The disad-
vantage of the unbelievers will lie in the fact
that belief is positive and assertive, whereas unbelief is negative and argumentative. It is
indeed easier to deny than to prove almost anything. But that is not the question. In life
and war it is generally easier to keep than to
take, and besides, those who believe 'care,' as
we say, whereas those who deny generally 'care'
very little. It is probable, to say the least of it,
that so long as the socialists of the near future
believe assertively that they have discovered the
means of saving humanity from misery and
poverty, and fight for a pure conviction, they
will have the better of it, but that when they
find themselves in the position of attacking half
of mankind's religious faith, having no idea, but

G

only a proposition, to offer in its place, they will
be beaten.

That seems far from the question of divorce,
but it is not. Before the battle, the opposing
forces are encamped and intrenched at a little
distance from each other, and each tries to un-
dermine the other's outworks. Socialism, collectively, has dug a mine under Social Order's
strongest tower, which is called marriage, and
the edifice is beginning to shake from its foun-
dations, even before the slow-match is lighted.

To one who has known the world well for a
quarter of a century, it seems as though the
would-be destroyers of the existing order had
forgotten, among several other things, the existence of woman, remembering only that of the
female. They practically propose to take away
woman's privileges in exchange for certain more
or less imaginary 'rights.' There is an apparent
justice in the 'conversion,' as it would be called
in business. If woman is to have all the rights
of man, which, indeed, seem reducible to a political vote now and then, why should she keep all
the privileges which man is not allowed? But
tell her that when she is allowed to vote for the
president of the United States once in four years,
no man shall be expected to stand up in a public
conveyance to give her a seat, nor to fetch and
carry for her, nor to support her instead of being

supported by her, nor to keep her for his wife any longer than he chooses, and the 'conversion' looks less attractive.

The reason why woman has privileges instead of rights is that all men tacitly acknowledge the future of humanity to be dependent on her from generation to generation. Man works or fights, and takes his rights in payment therefor, as well as for a means of working and fighting to greater advantage. And while he is fighting or working, his wife takes care of his children almost entirely. There is not one household in a hundred thousand, rich or poor, where there is really any question about that. It sounds insignificant, perhaps, and it looks as though anybody could take care of two or three small children. Those who have tried it know better, and they are women. Now and then rich mothers are too lazy to look after their children themselves. To do them such justice as one may, they are willing to spend any amount of money in order to get it well done for them, but the result is not encouraging to those who would have all children brought up 'by the state.' Even if it were so, who would bring them up? Women, of course. Then why not their own mothers? Because mothers sometimes — or often, for the sake of argument — do not exactly know how. Then educate the mothers, give them

chances of knowing how, let them learn, if you
know any better than they, which is doubtful,
to say the least of it.

Moreover, does any man in his senses really
believe that mothers, as a whole, would submit and let their children be taken from them
to a state rearing-house, to be brought up
under a number on a ticket by professional
baby-farmers, in exchange for the 'right' to
vote at a presidential election, and the 'right'
to put away their husbands and take others
as often as they please, and the 'right' to run
for Congress?   Yet the plan has been proposed
gravely.

There seems to be a good deal to be said in
favour of the existing state of things, after all,
and particularly in favour of marriage, and
therefore against divorce ; and it is not surprising that woman, whose life is in reality far
more deeply affected by both questions than
man's life is, should have also the more profound convictions about them.

Woman brings us into the world, woman is
our first teacher, woman makes the world what
it is, from century to century.   We can no more
escape from woman, and yet continue to live our
lives as they should be lived, than we can hide
ourselves from nature.   We are in her care or
in her power during more than half our years,

and often during all, from first to last. We are
born of her, we grow of her, as truly as trees
and flowers come of the mother earth and draw
their life from the soil in which they are planted.
The man who denies his mother is a bad man,
and the man who has not loved woman is a
man in darkness.

Man is not really unjust to woman in his
thoughts of her either, unless he be a lost soul,
but he has not much reason in respect of her
nor any justice in his exactions. Because within
himself he knows that she is everything and all
things for the life and joy of men, therefore he
would seem perfect in her eyes; and he rails
against whatsoever in her does not please him,
as a blot upon the lustre of his ideal, which
indeed he would make a glorified reflexion of
his own faults. When he is most imperfect,
he most exacts her praise; when he is weak-
est, she must think him most strong; when he
fails, she must call failure victory, or at the
least she must name it honourable defeat; she
must not see his meanness, but she must mag-
nify the smallest of his generosities to the great
measure of his immeasurable vanity therein;
she must see faith in his unfaithfulness, honour
in his disgrace, heroism in his cowardice, for his
sake; she must forgive freely and forgettingly
such injury as he would not pardon any man;

in one word, she must love him, that in her love
he may think and boast himself a god.

It is much to ask. And yet many a woman
who loves a man with all her heart has done
and daily does every one of those things, and
more; and the man knows it, and will not think
of it lest he should die of shame. And, moreover, a woman has borne him, a woman has
nursed him, a woman taught him first; a
woman gives him her soul and her body when
he is a man; and when he is dead, if tears are
shed for him, they are a woman's.

If we men are honest, we shall say that we
do not give her much for all that, not much
honour, not much faith. We think we do
enough if we give her life's necessities and lux-
uries in fair share to the limit of our poverty
or wealth; that we give much, if we love her;
too much, if we trust her altogether.

It is a wonder that women should love, seeing
what some men are and what most men may be
when the devil is in them. It is a wonder that
women should not rise up in a body and demand
laws to free them from marriage, for one-half
the cause that so many of them have.

But they do not. Even in this old age of
history they still believe in marriage, and cling
to it, and in vast majority cry out against its
dissolution. No man ever believes in anything

as a woman who loves him believes in him.
Men have stronger arms, and heads for harder
work, but they have no such hearts as women.
And the world has been led by the heart in all
ages.

Even when the great mistake is made, many
a woman clings to the faith that made it, for
the sake of what might have been, in a self-
respect of which men do not dream. Even
when she has married with little love, and taken
a man who has turned upon her like a brute
beast, her marriage is still a bond which she
will not break, and the vow made is not void
because the promise taken has been a vain lie.
Its damnation is upon him who spoke it, but
she still keeps faith.

So, when her fair years of youth lay scattered
and withered as blown leaves along the desert
of her past, Helen Harmon, wisely or unwisely,
but faithfully and with a whole heart, meant to
keep that plighted word which is not to be
broken by wedded man and woman 'until death
shall them part.'

CHAPTER V

MISS WIMPOLE was walking up and down the little sitting-room in considerable perplexity. When she was greatly in doubt as to her future conduct, she puckered her elderly lips, frowned severely, and talked to herself with an occasional energetic shaking of the head. She always did up her hair very securely and neatly, so that this was quite safe. Women who are not sure of their hairpins carry their heads as carefully as a basket of eggs and do not bend them if they have to stoop for anything.

Talking to oneself is a bad habit, especially when the door is open, whether one be swearing at something or examining one's own conscience. But Miss Wimpole could not help it, and the question of returning the price of the hat to Archie Harmon's mother was such a very difficult one, that she had forgotten to shut the door.

"Most impossible situation!" she repeated aloud. "Most terrible situation! Poor boy! Half idiotic — father mad. Most distressing

88

situation! If I tell his mother, I shall hurt her
feelings dreadfully. If I tell Richard, I shall
hurt his feelings dreadfully. If I tell nobody,
I shall break my promise to Sylvia, besides
putting her in the position of accepting a hat
from a young man. Ridiculous present, a hat!
If it had only been a parasol! Parasols are not
so ridiculous as hats. I wonder why! Perfectly impossible to keep the money, of course.
Even Judas Iscariot — dear me! Where are
my thoughts running to? Shocking! But a
terrible situation. It was dear, too — eighty
francs! We must get it into Mrs. Harmon's
hands somehow — "

"Why must you get eighty francs into Mrs.
Harmon's hands?" enquired the colonel, laying
his hat upon a chair.

The door had been open, and he had heard
her talking while he was in the corridor. She
uttered an exclamation as she turned and saw
him.

"Oh — well — I suppose you heard me. I
must really cure myself of talking when I am
alone! But I was not saying anything in particular."

"You were saying that you must manage to
pay Mrs. Harmon eighty francs. It is very
easy, for she happens to be here and I have just
seen her."

"Oh, I know she is here!" cried Miss Wimpole. "I know it to my cost! She and that — and her son, you know."

"Yes, I know. But what is the matter? What is the trouble?"

"Oh, Richard! You are so sensitive about anything that has to do with Mrs. Harmon!"

"I?" The colonel looked at her quietly.

"Yes. Of course you are, and it is quite natural and I quite understand, and I do not blame you in the least. But such a dreadful thing has happened. I hardly know how I can tell you about it. It is really too dreadful for words."

Wimpole sat down and fanned himself slowly with the Paris *Herald*. He was still rather pale, for his nerves had been shaken.

"Rachel, my dear," he said mildly, "don't be silly. Tell me what is the matter."

Miss Wimpole walked slowly once round the room, stopped at the window and looked through the blinds, and at last turned and faced her brother with all the energy of her seasoned character.

"Richard," she began, "don't call me silly till you hear. It's awful. That boy suddenly appeared in a shop where Sylvia was buying a hat, and paid for it and vanished."

"Eh? What's that?" asked Wimpole, opening his eyes wide. "I don't think I quite understood, Rachel. I must have been thinking of something else, just then."

"I daresay you were," replied his sister, severely. "You are growing dreadfully absent-minded. You really should correct it. I say that when Sylvia was buying a hat, just now, Archie Harmon suddenly appeared in the shop and spoke to us. Then he asked Sylvia whether she liked the hat she was trying on, and she said she did. Then he went off, and when we wished to pay we were told that the hat had been paid for by the young gentleman. Now — "

The colonel interrupted and startled his sister by laughing aloud at this point. · He could not help it, though he had not felt in the least as though he could laugh at anything for a long time, when he had entered the room. Miss Wimpole was annoyed.

"Richard," she said solemnly, "you surprise me."

"Does it not strike you as funny?" asked the colonel, recovering.

"No. It is — it is almost tragic. But perhaps," she continued, with a fine point of irony, "since you make so light of the matter, you will be good enough to return to Mrs. Harmon the price of the hat purchased by her half-witted boy for your ward."

"Don't call him half-witted, Rachel," said the colonel. "It's not so bad as that, you know."

"I cannot agree with you," replied his sister. "Only an idiot would think of rushing into a shop where a lady is buying something, and suddenly paying for it. You must admit that, Richard. Only an idiot could do such a thing."

"I have done just such a thing myself," observed Wimpole, thoughtfully, for he remembered the miniature he had bought for Helen that afternoon. "I suppose I was an idiot, since you say —"

"I said nothing of the kind, my dear! How can you accuse me of calling you an idiot? Really, Richard, you behave very strangely to-day! I don't know what can be the matter with you. First, you manage to make Sylvia cry her eyes out — Heaven knows what dreadful thing you said to her! And now you deliberately accuse me of calling you an idiot. If this sort of thing goes on much longer, there will be an end of our family happiness."

"This is not one of my lucky days," said the colonel, resignedly, and he laid down the folded newspaper. "How much did the hat cost? I will return the money to Mrs. Harmon, and explain."

Miss Wimpole looked at him with gratitude and admiration in her face.

"It was eighty francs," she answered. "Richard, I did not call you an idiot. In the first place, it would have been totally untrue, and in the second place, it would have been — what shall I say? It would have been very vulgar to call you an idiot, Richard. It is a vulgar expression."

"It might have been true, my dear, but I certainly never knew you to say anything vulgar. On the other hand, I really did not assert that you applied the epithet to me. I applied it to myself, rather experimentally. And poor Archie Harmon is not so bad as that, either."

"If he is not idiotic — or — or something like it, why do you say 'poor' Archie?"

"Because I am sorry for him," returned the colonel. "And so are you," he added presently.

Miss Wimpole considered the matter for a few seconds; then she slowly nodded, and came up to him.

"I am," she said. "Richard, kiss me."

That was always the proclamation of peace, not after strife, for they never quarrelled, but at the close of an argument. It was done in this way. The colonel rose, and stood before his sister; then both bent their heads a little, and as their cool grey cheeks touched, each kissed the air somewhere in the neighbourhood of the other's ear. They had been little chil-

dren together, and their mother had taught
them to 'kiss and make friends,' as good
children should, whenever there had been any
difference; and now they were growing old
together, but they had never forgotten, in
nearly fifty years, to 'kiss and make friends'
when they had disagreed. What is childlike
is not always childish.

The colonel resumed his seat, and there was
silence for a few minutes. The folded newspaper lay on the table unread, and he looked
at it, scarcely aware that he saw it.

"I think Archie Harmon must have fallen
in love with Sylvia," he said at last. "That
is the only possible explanation. She has grown
up since he saw her last, and so has he, though
his mind has not developed much, I suppose."

"Not at all, I should say," answered Miss
Wimpole. "But I wish you would not suggest such things. The mere idea makes me
uncomfortable."

"Yes," assented the colonel, thoughtfully.
"We will not talk about it."

Suddenly he knew what he was looking at,
and he read the first head-lines on the paper,
just visible above the folded edge. The words
were 'Harmon Sane,' printed in large capitals.
In a moment he had spread out the sheet.

The big letters only referred to a short tele-

gram, lower down. "It is reported on good
authority that Henry Harmon, who has been
an inmate of the Bloomingdale Insane Asylum
for some years, is recovering rapidly, and will
shortly be able to return to his numerous friends
in perfect mental health."

That was all. The colonel searched the paper
from beginning to end, in the vain hope of finding something more, and read the little paragraph over and over again. There was no
possibility of a mistake. There had never been
but one Henry Harmon, and there could certainly be but one in the Bloomingdale asylum.
The news was so sudden that Wimpole felt his
heart stand still when he first read it, and as he
thought of it he grew cold, and shivered as
though he had an ague.

It had been easier to think of Harmon's possible recovery before he had seen that scar on
Helen's forehead. For many years he had borne
the thought that the woman he had silently loved
so long was bound to a man little better than a
beast; but it had never occurred to him that
she might have had much to bear of which he
had known nothing, even to violence and physical danger. The knowledge had changed him
within the last hour, and the news about Harmon now hardened him all at once in his anger,
as hot steel is chilled when it has just reached

the cutting temper, and does not change after
that.

The colonel was as honourable a man as ever
shielded a woman's good name, or rode to meet
an enemy in fair fight.   He was chivalrous with
all the world, and quixotic with himself.   He
had charity for the ways of other men, for he
had seen enough to know that many things
were done by men whom no one would dare to
call dishonourable, which he would not have done
to save his own life.   He understood that such a
lasting love as his was stronger than himself, yet
he himself had been so strong that he had never
yielded even to its thoughts, nor ever allowed
the longing for a final union with Helen at all
costs to steal upon his unguarded imagination.

He was not tempted beyond his strength,
indeed, and in his apparent perfection, that
must be remembered.   In all those years of
his devoted friendship Helen had never let him
guess that she could have loved him once, much
less that she loved him now, as he did her, with
the same resolution to hide from her inward
eyes what she could not tear from her inmost
heart.   But it is never fair to say that if a man
had been placed in a certain imaginary position,
he might have been weak.   So long as he has
not broken down under the trials and burdens
of real life, he has a right to be called strong.

The colonel set no barrier, however, against the devotion to Helen's welfare which he might honourably feel and show. In day-dreams over old books he had envied those clean knights of a younger time, who fought for wives not theirs so openly and bravely, and so honestly that the spotless women for whom they faced death took lustre of more honour from such unselfish love. And for Helen's sake he had longed for some true circumstance of mortal danger in which to prove once more how well and silently an honest man can die to save an innocent woman.

But those were dreams. In acts he had done much, though never half of what he had always wished to do. The trouble had all come little by little in Helen's existence, and there had not been one great deciding moment in which his hand or head could have saved her happiness.

Now it seemed as though the time were full, and as if he might at last, by one deed, cast the balance by the scale of happiness. He did not know how to do it, nor whither to turn, but he felt, as he sat by the table with the little newspaper in his hand, that unless he could prevent Harmon from coming back to his wife, his own existence was to turn out a miserable failure, his love a lie, and his long devotion but a worthless word.

His first impulse was to leave Lucerne that

night and reach home in the shortest possible time. He would see Harmon and tell him what he thought, and force from him a promise to leave Helen in peace, some unbreakable promise which the man should not be able to deny, some sort of bond that should have weight in law.

The colonel's nostrils quivered, and his steady grey eyes fixed themselves and turned very light as he thought of the interview and of the quiet, hard words he would select. Each one of them should be a retribution in itself. He was the gentlest of men, but under great provocation he could be relentless.

What would Harmon answer? The colonel grew thoughtful again. Harmon would ask him, with an intonation that would be an insult to Helen, what right Wimpole had acquired to take Helen's part against him, her lawful husband. It would be hard to answer that, having no right of his own to fight her battles, least of all against the man she had married.

He might answer by reminding Harmon of old times. He might say that he at least resigned the hope of that right, when Harmon had been his friend, because he had believed that it was for Helen's happiness.

That would be but a miserably unsatisfactory answer, though it would be the truth. The colonel did not remember that he had ever wished to strike a man with a whip until the present moment. But the sight of the cut on Helen's forehead had changed him very quickly. He was not sure that he could keep his hands from Harmon if he should see him. And slowly a sort of cold and wrathful glow rose in his face, and he felt as though his long, thin fingers were turning into steel springs.

Miss Wimpole had taken up a book and was reading. She heard him move in his chair, and looked up and saw his expression.

"What is the matter with you, Richard?" she enquired, in surprise.

"Why?" He started nervously.

"You look like the destroying angel," she observed calmly. "I suppose you are gradually beginning to be angry about Sylvia's hat, as I was. I don't wonder."

"Oh yes — Sylvia's hat; yes, yes, I remember." The colonel passed his hand over his eyes. "I mean, it is perhaps the heat. It's a warm day. I'll go to my room for a while."

"Yes, do, my dear. You behave so strangely to-day — as if you were going to be ill."

But the colonel was already gone, and was stalking down the corridor with his head high, his eyes as hard as polished grey stones, and his nervous hands clenched as they swung a little with his gait.

His sister shook her head energetically, then slowly and sadly, as she watched him in the distance.

"How much more gracefully we grow old than men!" she said aloud, and took up her book again.

CHAPTER VI

HELEN had not seen the paragraph about Harmon. She rarely read newspapers, and generally trusted to other people to learn what they contained. The majority read papers for amusement, or for the sort of excitement produced on nervous minds by short, strong shocks often repeated. There are persons who ponder the paper daily for half an hour in absorbed silence, and then lift up their voices and cackle out all they have read, as a hen runs about and cackles when she has laid an egg. They fly at every one they see, an unnatural excitement in every tone and gesture, and ask in turn whether each friend has heard that this one is engaged to be married, and that another is dead and has left all his money to a hospital. When they have asked all the questions they can think of, without waiting for an answer, they relapse into their normal condition, and become again as other men and women are. Very few really read the papers in order to follow the course of events for the mere sake of information. Mrs.

Harmon was more or less indifferent to things that neither directly concerned her nor appealed to her tastes and sympathies.

Her letters were brought to her before she had left the sitting-room after the colonel had gone away, and she looked at the addresses on them carelessly, passing them from one hand to the other as one passes cards. One arrested her attention, among the half-dozen or so which she had received. It was the regular report from the asylum, posted on the first of the month. But it was thicker than usual; and when she tore open the envelope, rather nervously and with a sudden anticipation of trouble, a second sealed letter dropped from the single folded sheet contained in the first. But even that one sheet was full, instead of bearing only the few lines she always received to tell her that there was no change in her husband's condition.

There had been a change, and a great one. Since last writing, said the doctor, Harmon had suddenly begun to improve. At first he had merely seemed more quiet and patient than formerly; then, in the course of a few days, he had begun to ask intelligent questions, and had clearly understood that he had been insane for some time and was still in an asylum. He had rapidly learned the names of the people about him, and had not afterwards confused them, but remembered them with remarkable accuracy. Day by day he had improved, and was still improving. He had enquired about the state of his affairs, and had wished to see one or two of his old friends. More than once he had asked after his wife, and had evidently been glad to hear that she was well. Then he had written a letter to her, which the doctor immediately forwarded. So far as it was possible to form a judgment in the case, the improvement seemed to promise permanent recovery; though no one could tell, of course, whether a return to the world might not mean also a return to the unfortunate habit which had originally unbalanced Harmon's mind, but from which he was safe as long as he remained where he was.

It was not easy for Helen to read to the end of such a letter: it shook in her hands as she went on from one sentence to the next, and the sealed envelope slipped from her knees to the floor while she was reading. When she had got to the end, she stared a moment at the signature, and then folded the sheet, almost unconsciously, and drew her nail sharply along the folds, as though she would make the paper feel what she felt, and suffer as she suffered, in every nerve of her body, and in every secret fibre of her soul.

She had not believed a recovery possible. Now that it was a fact, she knew how utterly beyond probability she had thought it; and immediately the great problem rose before her, confusing, vast, terrifying. But before she faced it she must read Harmon's letter.

It had fallen to the floor, and she had to look for it and find it and pick it up. The handwriting was large, somewhat ornamental, yet heavy in parts and not always regular. As she glanced at the address, she remembered how she had disliked the writing when she had first seen it, at a time when she had seen much to admire in Harmon himself. Now she did not like to touch the envelope on which he had written her name, and she unreasoningly feared the contact of the sheet it held, as of something that might defile her and must surely hurt her cruelly. The hand that had traced the characters on the paper was the hand that had struck her and left its mark for all her life. And as she remembered the rest, an enormous loathing of the man who was still her husband took possession of her, so that she could not open the letter for a few moments.

It was at once a loathing of bodily disgust, like a sickness, and a mental horror of a creature who was so far from her natural nobility that it frightened her to know how she hated him, and she began to fear the letter itself, lest it should make some great change in her for which she should at last hate herself also. The spasm ran all through her, as the sight of some very disgusting evil thing violently disturbs body and mind at the same time.

The temptation to destroy the letter unread came upon her with all possible force, and the vision of a return to peace was before her eyes, as though the writing were already burned and beyond her power to recover. But that would be cowardly, and she was brave. With drawn lips, pale cheeks, and knitted brows she opened it, took out the folded contents, and began to read. As though to remind her of the place where he was, and of all the circumstances from first to last, the name of the asylum was printed at the head of each sheet in small, businesslike letters.

She began to read:

My Dear Helen, — You will be surprised to hear directly from me, I suppose, and I can hardly expect that you will be pleased, though you are too good not to be glad that I am better after my long illness. I have a great many things to write to you, and no particular right to hope that you will read them. Will you? I hope so, for I do not mean to write again until I get an answer to this letter. But if you do read this one, please believe that I am quite in my right senses again, and that I mean all I say. Besides, the doctor has written

to you. He considers me almost 'safe' now. I mean,
safe to remain as I am.

It is not easy for me to write to you. You must hate
me, of course. God knows, I have given you reason
enough to wish that I might stay here for the rest of my
life. You are a very good woman, and perhaps you will
forgive me for all I have done to hurt you. That is the
main thing I wanted to say. I want to ask your pardon
and forgiveness for everything, from beginning to end.

'Everything' is a big word, I know. There has been
a great deal during these many years, — a great deal
more than I like to think of; for the more I think of it,
the less I see how you can forgive even the half, much
less forget it.

I was not myself, Helen. You have a right to say
that it was my fault if I was not myself. I drank hard.
That is not an excuse, I know; but it was the cause of
most of the things I did. No woman can ever understand how a man feels who drinks, and has got so far
that he cannot give it up. How should she? But you
know that most men cannot give it up, and that it is a
sort of disease, and can be treated scientifically. But I do
not mean to make excuses. I only ask your forgiveness,
and in order to forgive me you will find better excuses
for me than I could invent for myself. I throw myself
upon your kindness, for that is the only thing I can do.

They say that it would not be quite safe for me to
leave the asylum for another month or two, and I am
quite resigned to that; for the life is quiet here, and I
feel quiet myself and hate the idea of excitement. I suppose I have had too much of it.

But by and by they will insist upon my leaving, when
I am considered quite cured; and then I want to go back
to you, and try to make you happy, and do my best to
make up to you for all the harm I have done you.

Perhaps you think it is impossible, but I am very much changed since you saw me.

I know what I am asking, dear Helen. Do not think I ask it as though it were a mere trifle. But I know what you are and what you have done. You could have got a divorce over and over again, and I believe you could now if you liked. It is pretty easy in some states, and I suppose I could not find much to say in defence. Yet you have not done it. I do not know whether you have ever thought of it.

If you think of it now that I want to come back to you and try to do better, and make you happy, for God's sake give me another chance before you take any step. Give me one more chance, Helen, for the sake of old times. You used to like me once, and we were very happy at first. Then — well, it was all my fault, it was every bit of it my fault, and I would give my soul to undo it. If you will forgive me, we can try together and begin over again, and it shall all be different, for I will be different.

Can we not try? Will you try? It will be easy if you will only let us begin. It is not as if we should have other troubles to deal with, for we have plenty of friends and plenty of money, and I will do the rest. I solemnly promise that I will, if you will forgive me and begin over again. I know it must seem almost impossi-ble. It would be quite impossible for any other woman, though you can do it if you will.

I shall wait for your answer, before I write again, though it will seem a very long time, and I am very anxious about it. If it is what I hope it will be, perhaps you will cable a few words, even one word. 'Forgiven' is only one word. Will you not say it? Will you not give me one chance more? Oh, Helen dear, for God's sake, do!   H.

Helen read the letter to the end, through every phrase and every repetition. Then the fight began, and it was long and bitter, a battle to death, of which she could not see the issue.

The man wrote in earnest, and sincerely meant what he said. No one could read the words and doubt that. Helen believed all he had written, so far as his intention was concerned, but she could not cut his life in two and leave out of the question the man he had been, in order to receive without fear or disgust the man he professed himself to be. That was too much to ask of any woman who had suffered what she had of neglect, of violence, of shame.

'No one could tell,' the doctor wrote, 'whether a return to the world might not mean also a return to the unfortunate habit' — no one could tell that. And Harmon himself wrote that most men could not give it up, that it was a disease, and that no woman could understand it. What possible surety could he give that it should never get hold of him again? None. But that was only a small matter in the whole question.

If she had ever loved him, perhaps if she could have felt that he had ever loved her truly, it would have been different. But she could not. Why had he married her? For her beauty. The shame of it rose in her eyes as she sat alone, and she could not help turning her face from the light.

For love's sake, even for an old love, outraged long ago and scarred past recognizing, she could have forgiven much. Old memories, suddenly touched, are always more tender than we have thought they were, till the tears rise for them, and the roots of the old life stir in the heart.

Helen had nothing of that. She had made the great mistake of marrying a man whom she had not loved, but whom she had admired, and perhaps believed in, more than she understood. She had married him because he seemed to love her very much, and the thought of being so loved was pleasant. She had soon found out what such love meant, and by and by she had seen how traces of it survived in Henry Harmon, when all thought of honouring her, or even of respecting her, was utterly gone.

A bitter laugh rang through the quiet room, and she started, for it was her own voice. She was to forgive! Did he know what he was asking, and for what things he was praying forgiveness? Yet when he was sober he had generally remembered what he had done when he had been drunk. That is to say, he had seemed to have the faculty of remembering what he chose to recall, and of forgetting

everything else. She was to forgive what he
chose to remember!

'Oh, Helen dear, for God's sake, do!' She
could see the last written words of his letter
before her eyes, though the sheet was folded and
bent double in her tightly closed hand. He
meant it, and it was an appeal for mercy. She
hated herself for having laughed so cruelly a
moment earlier. There was a cry in the words,
quite different from all he had written before
them. It did not touch her, it hardly appealed
to her at all, but somehow it gave him the right
to be heard, for it was human.

Then she went over all he said, though it
hurt her. She was not a woman of quick impulses, and she knew that what was left of her
life was in the balance. Even he seemed to
acknowledge that, for he spoke of a possibility
of freedom for her by divorce. To speak so
easily of it, he must have thought of it often,
and that meant that it was really an easy
matter, as Colonel Wimpole had said. It was
in her power, and she had free will. He knew
that she had a choice, and that she could either
take him back, now that he was cured, or make
it utterly out of the question for him to approach
her. He said as much, when he implored her
to give him one more chance 'before taking any
step.' She went over and over it all, for hours.

In the cool of the evening she opened the blinds, collected her letters, and then sat down again, no nearer to a decision than she had been at first. A servant came and told her that Colonel Wimpole was downstairs. He had written a word on his card, asking to see her again.

Her first impulse was the natural one. She would let him come in and she would lay the whole matter before him, as before the best friend she had in the world, and ask him how she should act. There was not in all the world a man more honourable and just. She would let him come to her.

The words were on her lips, while the servant stood in the open door, waiting for her answer. She checked herself with an effort. She wrote a line and gave it to the man.

She would not see Wimpole just then, for it would not be fair to him nor perhaps quite just to Harmon. Wimpole loved her, though he was quite unaware that she knew it. She believed firmly that when he had advised her that very afternoon to divorce her husband, he was thinking only of her happiness; but he had advised it, all the same, just because he believed that Harmon might recover. He could not change his mind now that what he feared for her was taking place. How could he? He would use

every argument in his power, and he would find
many good ones, against her returning to her
husband.   He could influence her against her
free will, and far more than he could guess,
because she loved him secretly as much as he
loved her.   It was bitter not to see him, and
tell him, and ask his help; it was desperately
hard, but as soon as she saw that it was right,
she wrote the words that must send him away,
before she could have time to hesitate.   Deep in
her heart, too, there was a thought for him.
Loving her as he did, it would not be easy for
him, either, to go into the whole matter.   His
honour and his love would have to fight it out.
So she sent him away.

Then Archie came into the room, vague and
childish at first, but with an odd look in his
eyes, and he began to talk to her about Sylvia
Strahan in a way that frightened her, little by
little, as he went on.

"Marry me to her, mother," he said at last,
as though asking for the simplest thing.   "I
want to be married, and I want Sylvia.   I
never saw any other girl whom I wanted."

CHAPTER VII

THERE are times when trouble accumulates
as an avalanche, or like water in one of those
natural intermittent springs that break out
plentifully, and dry up altogether in a sort of
alternation. But the spring has its regular
period, and trouble has not, and in an avalanche
of disasters it is impossible to say at any moment whether the big boulders have all passed
in the sliding drift of smaller stuff, or whether
the biggest of all may not be yet coming.

There are days in a lifetime which decide all
the rest, and sometimes explain all that has
gone before, happy days, or days of tears, as the
case may be. Perhaps they are the most interesting days to describe, after all, for they are the
ones which generally terminate a period in existence. But many say that in real life sit-
uations, as they are called, never have any
satisfactory termination, and that the story
which is most true of men and women is that
one which has neither beginning nor end. The
fact is that what appears to be the beginning is

often in reality the termination of a long series
of events. Novels often end in marriage, yet
real life frequently begins there. There is a
very old proverb to that effect.

On such days all sorts of things happen that
never occurred before and perhaps never occur
again, and every one who has had one or two
such short and eventful periods of confusion
can remember how a host of unforeseen trifles
thrust themselves forward to disturb him. It
was as though nothing could turn out right, as
if nobody could take a message without a mistake, as if the post and the telegraph had con-
spired together to send letters and telegrams
to wrong addresses, and altogether all things,
including the most sober and reliable institu-
tions, seem to work backwards against results
instead of for them. Those are bad times.
When they last long, people come to grie.'.
When they are soon over, people laugh at
them. When they decide a whole life, as they
sometimes do, people can afterwards trace the
causes of happiness or disaster to some very
small lucky coincidence or unfortunate mistake
over which they themselves had no control.

When Colonel Wimpole had left Helen so
abruptly, he had looked upon his going away as
a mere interruption of his visit, necessary, because he could not be sure of controlling himself

just then, but not meant to last any length of time. But after so suddenly learning the change in Harmon's condition, he would have waited till the evening before going back, if his sister had not been so absurdly nervous about the price of the hat, insisting that he should go at once and return the money. He had gone to his own room in a disturbed state of mind and had stayed there an hour, after which Miss Wimpole, judging that he must be sufficiently rested, had knocked at his door and urged him to go at once to see Mrs. Harmon. As he had no very good reason to give for refusing to do so, he had made the attempt and had been refused admittance. He went for a walk along the lake and came back again after an hour, and wrote on his card a special request.

" May I see you now ? It is about a rather awkward little matter."

It was growing late. Helen reflected that he could not stay long before his own dinner time and hers, that he evidently had something especial to say, and that she was certainly strong enough to keep her own counsel for a quarter of an hour if she made up her mind to do so. Besides, it must seem strange to him to be refused a second time; he would infer that something was wrong and would ask questions when they next met. She decided to see him.

His face was grave, and he was quite calm
again.   As he took her hand and spoke, there
was a sort of quiet tenderness in his manner
and tone, a little beyond what he usually
showed, perceptible to her, who longed for it,
though it could hardly have been noticed by
any one else.

"It is rather an awkward little matter," he
said, repeating the words he had written.

Then he saw her face in the twilight, and he
guessed that she had seen the newspaper.

"You are in trouble," he said quickly.

She hesitated and turned from him, for she
had forgotten that her face must betray her
distress.

"Yes," she answered, but she said no more
than that.

"Can I help you?" he asked after a short
pause.

"Please do not ask me."

She sat down, and Wimpole sighed audibly as
he took his seat at a little distance from her.
He knew that she must have seen the paragraph
about Harmon's recovery.

"Then I will explain my errand," he said.
"May I?"

It seemed rather a relief to have so small a
matter ready to hand.

"Yes.   It will not take long, will it?" she

asked rather nervously, for she felt how his presence tempted her to confidence. "It — it will soon be dinner time, you know."

"I shall not stay long," said the colonel, quietly. "It is rather an awkward little matter. You know Archie was with you this morning when I saw you in the shop and got that miniature."

Helen looked at him suddenly with a change of expression, expecting some new trouble.

"Yes, Archie was with us. What is it?" Her voice was full of a new anxiety.

"It is nothing of any great importance," answered Wimpole, quickly, for he saw that she was nervous. "Only, he went out by himself afterwards, and came across my sister and Sylvia in a milliner's shop — "

"What was he doing in a milliner's shop?" interrupted Helen, in surprise.

"I don't know," said the colonel. "I fancy he saw them through the window and went in to speak to them. Sylvia was trying on a hat, you know, and she liked it, and Archie, without saying anything, out of pure goodness of heart, I suppose — "

He hesitated. On any other day he would have smiled, but just now he was as deeply disturbed as Helen herself, and the absurd incident of the hat assumed a tremendous importance.

"Well? What did he do?" Helen's nerves were on edge, and she spoke almost sharply.

"He paid for the hat," answered Wimpole, with an air of profound sorrow, and even penitence, as if it had been all his fault. "And then he went off, before they knew it."

Helen bit her lip, for it trembled. He had not told the story very clearly or connectedly, but she understood. Archie had just been talking to her strangely about Sylvia, and she had seen that he had fallen in love with his old playmate, and she was afraid. And now, she was horribly ashamed for him. It was so stupid, so pitifully stupid.

The colonel, guessing what greater torment was tearing at her heart, sat still in a rather dejected attitude, waiting for her to speak, but not watching her.

The matter which had brought him was certainly not very terrible in itself, but it stirred and quickened all the ever-growing pain for her son which was a part of her daily life. It knitted its strength to that of all the rest, to hurt her cruelly, and the torture was more than she could bear.

She turned suddenly in her seat and half buried her face against the back of the chair, so that Wimpole could not see it, and she bit the coarse velvet savagely, trying to be silent and tearless till he should go away. But he knew what she was doing. If he had not spoken, she could still have kept back the scalding tears awhile. But he did speak, and very gently.

"Helen — dear Helen — what is it?"

"My heart is breaking," she said, almost quietly.

But then the tears came, and she shook once or twice, like an animal that has a deep wound but cannot die. The tears came slowly, and burned her like drops of fire. She kept her face turned away.

Wimpole was beside her and held her passive hand. It twitched painfully as it lay in his, and every agonized movement of it shot through him, but he could not say anything at first. Besides, she knew he was there and would help her if he could. At last he spoke his thought.

"I will keep him from you," he said. "He shall not come near you."

Her hand tightened upon his, instantly, and she sat up in her chair, turning her face to him, quite white in the dusk, by the open window.

"Then you know?" she asked.

"Yes. It is in the Paris paper to-day. But it is only a report. I do not believe it is true."

She rose, mastering herself, as she withdrew her hand, and steadied herself a moment against the chair beside him.

"It is true," she said. "He has recovered. He has written to me."

Wimpole felt as if he had been condemned to death without warning.

"When?" he managed to ask.

"I got the letter this afternoon."

Their voices answered each other, dull and colourless in the gloom, and for some moments neither spoke. Helen went to the window and leaned upon the broad marble sill, breathing the evening air from the lake, and Wimpole followed her. The electric lamps were lighted in the street, glaring coldly out of the grey dusk, and many people were moving slowly along the pavement below, in little parties, some gay, some silent.

"That is why I did not let you come up," said Helen, after a long time. "But now — since you know — " She stopped, still hesitating, and he tried to see her expression, but there was not enough light.

"Yes?" he said, with a question, not pressing her, but waiting.

"Since you know," she answered at last, "you can guess the rest."

A spasm of pain half choked her, and Wimpole put out his hand to lay it gently upon her arm, but drew it back again. He had never done even that much in all those years, and he would not do it now.

"I will keep him from you," he said again.

"No. You must not do that." Her voice was steady again. "He will not come to me against my will."

Wimpole turned sharply as he leaned on the window-sill beside her, for he did not understand.

"You cannot possibly be thinking of writing to him, of letting him come back?"

"Yes," she said. "That is what I am thinking of doing."

She hardly dared think that she still could hesitate, now that Wimpole was beside her. If he had not come, it might have been different. But he was close to her now, and she knew how long and well he had loved her. Alone, she could have found reasons for refusing ever to see Harmon again, but they lost their look of honour now that this man, who was everything to her, was standing at her elbow. Exaggerating her danger, she feared lest Wimpole should influence her, even unintentionally, if she left the question open. And he, for her own happiness and honourably setting all thoughts of himself aside, believed that he ought to use whatever influence he had, to the utmost.

"You must not do it," he said. "I implore you not to think of it. You will wreck your life."

She did not move, for she had known what he would say.

"If you are my friend," she answered, after a pause, "you should wish me to do what is right."

It was a trite commonplace, but she never tried to be original, at any time, and just then the words exactly expressed her thought. He resented it.

"You have done more than enough of that sort of right already. It is time you thought a little of yourself. I do not mean only of your happiness, but of your safety. You are not safe with that man. He will drink again, and he may kill you."

She turned her white face deliberately towards him in the gloom.

"And do you think I am afraid of that?" she asked slowly.

There was a sort of reproach in the tone, and a great good pride with it. Wimpole did not know what to say, and merely bent his head gravely.

"Besides," she added, "he is in earnest. He is sorry. He was mad then, and he asks me to forgive him now. How can I refuse? He was really mad, really insane. No one can deny it. Shall I?"

"You can forgive him without going back to him. Why should you risk your life?"

"It is the only way of showing him that I forgive him, and my life will not be in danger."

"Do you think that you can ever be happy again, if you go back to him?" asked Wimpole.

"My happiness is not the question. The only thing that matters is to do right."

"It seems to me that right is more or less dependent on its results —"

"Never!" cried Helen, almost fiercely, and drawing back a little against the side of the window. "If one syllable of that were true, then we could never know whether we were doing right or not, till we could judge the result. And the end would justify the means, always, and there would be no more right and wrong at all in the world."

"But when you know the results?" objected Wimpole. "It seems to me that it may be different."

"Then it is fear! Then one is afraid to do right because one knows that one risks being hurt! What sort of morality would that be? It would be contemptible."

"But suppose that it is not only yourself who may be hurt, but some one else? One should think of others first. That is right, too." He could not help saying that much.

Helen hesitated a moment.

"Yes," she answered presently. "But no one else is concerned in this case."

"I will leave your friends out of the question," said Wimpole. "Do you think it will do Archie any good to live under the same roof with his father?"

Helen started perceptibly.

"Oh, why did you say that!" she exclaimed in a low voice, and as she leaned over the window-sill again she clasped her hands together in a sort of despairing way. "Why did you say that!" she repeated.

Wimpole was silent, for he had not at first realized that he had found a very strong argument. As yet, being human, she had thought only of herself, in the first hours of her trouble. He had recalled all her past terrors for her unfortunate son, and the memory of all she had done to keep him out of his father's way in old days. He had been a mere boy, then, and it had been just possible, because his half-developed mind was not suspicious. Now that he was grown up, it would be another matter. The prospect was hideous enough, if Harmon should take a fancy to the young man, and make him his companion, and then fall back into his old ways.

"Why did you say it? Why did you make me think of that?" Helen asked the questions

almost piteously. "I should have to send Archie
away — somewhere, where he would be safe."

"How could he be safe without you?" The
argument was pitilessly just.

But, after all, her life and happiness were at
stake. Wimpole saw right in everything that
could withhold her from the step to which she
had evidently made up her mind.

"And if I refuse to go back to my husband,
what will become of him?" she asked, still clasp-
ing her hands hard together.

"He could be properly taken care of," suggested Wimpole.

"And would that be forgiveness?" Helen
turned to him again energetically.

"It would be wisdom, at all events."

"Ah, now you come back to your argument!"
Her voice changed. "You are pressing me to
do what is wise, not what is right. Don't do
that! Please don't do that!"

"Do you forgive him?" asked the colonel,
very gravely.

Again she paused before answering him.

"Why should you doubt it?" she asked in
her turn. "Don't you see that I wish to go
back to him?"

"You know what I mean. It is not the same
thing. You are a very good woman, and by
sheer force of goodness you could make an

enormous sacrifice for the sake of what you thought right."

" And would not that be forgiveness?"

" No. If you freely forgave him, it would be no sacrifice, for you would believe in him again. You would have just the same faith in Harmon which you had on the day you married him. If forgiveness means anything, it means that one takes back the man who has hurt one, on the same real, inward terms with oneself on which one formerly lived with him. You cannot do that, for it would not be sane."

" No, I cannot quite do that," Helen answered, after a moment's thought. " It would not be true to say that I had even thought I could. But then, if you put it in that way, it would be hard to forgive any one, and it would generally be foolish. There is something wrong about your way of looking at it."

" I am not a woman," said Wimpole, simply. " That is what is the matter. At the same time, I do not see how you, as a woman, are ever going to reconcile what you believe to be your duty to Harmon with what is certainly your duty to your son."

" I must," said Helen. " I must."

" Then you must do it before you write to Harmon, for afterwards it will be impossible. You must decide first what you will do with

Archie to keep him out of danger. When you have made up your mind about that, if you choose to sacrifice yourself, nobody can prevent you. At least you will not be ruining him, too."

He saw no reason for not putting the case plainly, since what he said was true. Yet as he felt his advantage, he knew that by pressing it he was increasing her perplexity. In all his life he had never been in so difficult a position. She stood close beside him, her arm almost touching his, and he had loved her all his life, as few men love, with an honesty and purity that were more than quixotic. What there was left, he could have borne for her sake, even to seeing her united again with Henry Harmon. But the thought of the risk she was running was more than he could bear. He would use argument, stratagem, force, anything, to keep her out of such a life; and when he had succeeded in saving her, he would be capable of denying himself even the sight of her, lest his conscience should accuse him of having acted for himself rather than for her alone.

He remembered Harmon's face as he had last seen it, coarse, cunning, seamed with dissipation, and he looked sideways at Helen, white, weary, bruised, a fast fading rose of yesterday, as she had called herself. The thought of Harmon's touch was more than he could bear.

"You shall not do it!" he exclaimed, after a long silence. "I will make it impossible."

Almost before he spoke the last words, he had repented them. Helen drew herself up and faced him, one hand on the window-sill.

"Colonel Wimpole," she said, "I know that you have always been my best friend. But you must not talk in that way. I cannot allow even you to come between me and what I think is right."

He bent his head a little.

"I beg your pardon," he answered, in a low voice. "I should have done it — not said it."

"I hope you will never think of it again," said Helen.

She left the window, and felt in the dark for matches, on the table, to light a small candle she used for sealing letters. It cast a faint light up to her sad face. Wimpole had stayed by the window, and watched her now, while she looked towards him over the little flame.

"Please go, now," she said gravely. "I cannot bear to talk about this any longer."

CHAPTER VIII

AFTER the door had closed, Helen stood a moment by the table, motionless. Then she sat down by the feeble light of the taper and wrote upon a sheet of paper her husband's address and one word — 'forgiven.' She looked at the writing fixedly for a minute or two, and then rang the bell.

"Have this telegram sent at once, please, and bring me a lamp and dinner," she said to the servant.

With the lamp came Archie, following it with a sort of interest, as children do.

"You must have been in the dark ever so long, mother," he said, and just then he saw her white face. "You are not looking all right," he observed.

Helen smiled, from force of habit, rather wearily. The servant began to set the table, moving stealthily, as though he were meditating some sudden surprise which never came. He was a fairly intelligent Swiss, with an immense pink face and very small blue eyes.

Helen watched him for a moment, and sighed. The man was intellectually her son's superior, and she knew it. Any one else might have smiled at the thought, as grotesque, but it had for her the cruel vividness of a misfortune that had saddened all of her life which her husband had not embittered. She envied, for her son, the poor waiter's little powers of mental arithmetic and memory.

"What's the matter, mother?" asked Archie, who sat looking at her.

"Nothing, dear," she answered, rousing herself, and smiling wearily again. "I am a little tired, perhaps. It has been a hot day."

"Has it? I didn't notice. I never do — at least, not much. I say, mother, let's go home! I'm tired of Europe, and I know you are. Let's all go home together — we and the Wimpoles."

"We shall be going home soon," said Helen.

"I thought you meant to go to Carlsbad first. Wasn't it to Carlsbad we were going?"

"Yes, dear. But — here comes dinner — we will talk about it by and by."

They sat down to table. In hotels abroad Helen always dined in her rooms, for she was never quite sure of Archie. He seemed strangely unconscious of his own defect of mind, and was always ready to enter boldly into conversation with his neighbours at a foreign hotel dinner table. His childish ignorance had once or twice caused her such humiliation as she did not feel called upon to bear again.

"I don't know why we shouldn't talk about it now," began Archie, when he had eaten his soup in silence, and the servant was changing his plate.

"We shall be alone, after dinner," answered his mother.

"Oh, the waiter doesn't care! He'll never see us again, you know, so why shouldn't we say anything we like before him?"

Mrs. Harmon looked at her son and shook her head gravely, which was an admonition he always understood.

"Did you see anything you liked, to-day?" she asked incautiously, by way of changing the conversation.

"Rather!" exclaimed Archie, promptly. "I met Sylvia Strahan — jukes!"

Helen shuddered, as she saw the look in his face and the glitter in his eyes.

"I wish you could remember not to say 'jukes' every other minute, Archie," she said, for the thousandth time.

"Do you think Sylvia minds when I say 'jukes'?" asked the young man, suddenly.

"I am sure she thinks it a very ugly and senseless word."

"Does she? Really?" He was silent for a few moments, pondering the question. "Well," he resumed at last, in a regretful tone, "I've always said it, and I like it, and I don't see any harm in it. But, of course, if Sylvia doesn't like it, I've got to give it up, that's all. I'm always going to do what Sylvia likes, now, as long as I live. And what you like, too, mother," he added as an apologetic and dutiful after-thought. "But then, you're pretty sure to like the same things, after all."

"You really must not go on in this way about Sylvia, my dear," said Helen. "It is too absurd."

Archie's heavy brows met right across his forehead as he looked up with something like a glare in his eyes, and his voice was suddenly thick and indistinct, when he answered.

"Don't call it absurd, mother. I don't under-stand what it is, but it's stronger than I am. I don't want anything but Sylvia. Things don't amuse me any more. It was only to-day — "

He stopped, for he was going to tell her how he had found no pleasure in his toys, neither in the blocks, nor in the tin soldiers, nor in the little papier-mâché lady and gentleman in the painted cart. But he thought she did not know about them, and he checked himself in a sudden shame which he had never felt before. A deep **red**

blush spread over his dark face, and he looked
down at his plate.

"I'm a man, now," he said, through his teeth,
in a rough voice.

After that, he was silent for a time, but Helen
watched him nervously. She, too, saw that he
was a man, with almost less than a boy's mind,
and her secret terror grew. She could not
eat that evening, but he did not notice her.
They dined quickly and then they sat down together, as they usually did, quite near to each
other and side by side. She could sometimes
teach him little things which he remembered,
when everything was quiet. He generally began to talk of something he had seen, and she
always tried to make him understand it and
think about it. But this evening he said nothing for a long time, and she was glad of his
silence. When she thought of the telegram she
had sent, she had a sharp pain at her heart, and
once or twice she started a little in her chair.
But Archie did not notice her.

"I say, mother," he began, looking up, "what
becomes of all the things one forgets? Do they
— do they go to sleep in one's head?"

Mrs. Harmon looked at him in surprise, for
it was by far the most thoughtful question he
had ever asked. She could not answer it at
once, and he went on.

"Because you always tell me to try and remember, and you think I could remember if I tried hard enough. Then you must believe the things are there. You wouldn't expect me to give you what I hadn't got, would you? That wouldn't be fair."

"No, certainly not," answered his mother, considerably puzzled.

"Then you really think that I don't forget. You must think I don't remember to remember. Something like that. I can't explain what I mean, but you understand."

"I suppose so, my dear. Something like that. Yes, perhaps it is just as you say, and things go to sleep in one's head and one has to wake them up. But I know that I can often remember things I have forgotten if I try very hard."

"I can't. I say, mother, I suppose I'm stupid, though you never tell me so. I know I'm different from other people, somehow. I wish you would tell me just what it is. I don't want to be different from other people. Of course I know I could never be as clever as you, nor the colonel. But then you're awfully clever, both of you. Father used to call me an idiot, but I'm not. I saw an idiot once, and his eyes turned in, and he couldn't shut his mouth, and he couldn't talk properly."

"Are you sure that your father ever called you an idiot, Archie?"

Helen's lips were oddly pale, and her voice was low. Archie laughed in a wooden way.

"Oh, yes! I'm quite sure," he said. "I remember, because he hit me on the back of the head with the knob of his stick when he said so. That was the first time. Then he got into the way of saying it. I wasn't very big then."

Helen leaned back and closed her eyes, and in her mind she saw the word 'forgiven' as she had written it after his name, — 'Henry Harmon, New York. Forgiven.' It had a strange look. She had not known that he had ever struck the boy cruelly.

"Why did you never tell me?" she asked slowly.

"Oh, I don't know. It would have been like a cry-a-baby to go running to you. I just waited."

Helen did not guess what was coming.

"Did he strike you again with the knob of his stick?" she asked.

"Lots of times, with all sorts of things. Once, when you were off somewhere for two or three days on a visit, he came at me with a poker. That was the last time. I suppose he had been drinking more than usual."

"What happened?" asked Helen.

"Oh, well, I'd grown big then, and I got sick of it all at once, you know. He never tried to touch me again, after that."

Helen recalled distinctly that very unusual occasion when she had been absent for a whole week, at the time of a sister's death. Harmon had seemed ill when she had returned, and she remembered noticing a great change in his manner towards the boy only a few months before he had become insane.

"What did you do?" she asked.

"I hit him. I hit him badly, a good many times. Then I put him to bed. I knew he wouldn't tell."

Archie smiled slowly at the recollection of beating his father, and looked down at his fist. Helen felt as though she were going mad herself. It was all horribly unnatural,—the father's cruel brutality to his afflicted son, the son's ferocious vengeance upon his father when he had got his strength.

"You see," continued Archie, "I knew exactly how many times he had hit me altogether, and I gave all the hits back at once. That was fair, anyhow."

Helen could not remember that he had ever professed to be sure of an exact number from memory.

"How could you know just how many

times —" She spoke faintly, and stopped, half sick.

"Blocks," answered Archie. "I dropped a little blot of ink on one of my blocks every time he hit me. I used to count the ones that had blots on them every morning. When they all had one blot each, I began on the other side, till I got round again. Some had blots on several sides at last. I don't know how many there were, now; but it was all right, for I used to count them every morning and remember all day. There must have been forty or fifty, I suppose. But I know it was all right. I didn't want to be unfair, and I hit him slowly and counted. Oh," — his eyes brightened suddenly, — "I've got the blocks here. I'll go and get them, and we can count them together. Then you'll know exactly."

Helen could not say anything, and Archie was gone. She only half understood what the blocks were, and did not care to know. There was an unnatural horror in it all, and Archie spoke of it quite simply and without any particular resentment. She was still half dazed when he came back with the mysterious box in which he kept his toys.

He set it down on the floor at her feet and knelt beside it, feeling for the key in his pocket.

"I don't care if you see all the things now,"
he said. "They don't amuse me any more."

Nevertheless, she saw the blush of shame rising to his forehead as he bent down and put the
key into the lock.

"I don't care, after all," he said, before he
lifted the lid. "It's only you, mother, and you
won't think I was a baby just because they
amused me. I don't care for them any more,
mother. Indeed I don't; so I may as well
make a clean breast of it and tell you. Besides,
you must see the blocks. All the blots are there
still, quite plain, and we can count them, and
then you'll always remember, though I shan't.
Here they are. I've carried them about a long
time, you know, and they're getting pretty old,
especially the soldiers. There isn't much paint
left on them, and the captain's head's gone."

Helen leaned forward, her elbow on her knees,
her chin resting on her hand, her eyes dim, and
her heart beating oddly. It seemed as though
nothing were spared her on that day.

Archie unpacked the toys in silence, and arranged the blocks all on one side in a neat pile,
while on the other he laid the soldiers and the
little cart, with the few remaining toys. Helen's
eyes became riveted on the bits of wood. There
were about twenty of them, and she could plainly
distinguish on them the little round blots which

Archie had made, one for each blow he had received. He began to count, and Helen followed him mechanically. He was very methodical, for he knew that he was easily confused. When he had counted the blots on each block, he put it behind him on the floor before he took another from the pile. He finished at last.

"Sixty-three — ju — ! " He checked himself. "I forgot. I won't say 'jukes' any more. I won't. There were sixty-three in all, mother. Besides, I remember now. Yes; there were sixty-three. I remember that it took a long time, because I was afraid of not being fair."

Again he smiled at the recollection, with some satisfaction, perhaps, at his conscientious rectitude. With those hands of his, it was a wonder that he had not killed his father. Helen sat like a stone figure, and watched him unconsciously, while her thoughts ground upon each other in her heart like millstones, and her breath half choked her.

He swept all the blocks back in front of him, and, by force of habit, he began to build a little house before he put them away. She watched his strong hands, that could do such childish things, and the bend of his athletic neck. His head was not ill-shaped nor defective under the thick short hair.

"Did he always strike you on the head, Archie?" she asked suddenly.

He knocked the little house over with a sweep of his hand and looked up.

"Generally," he said quietly. "But it doesn't matter, you know. He generally went for the back of my head because it didn't make any mark, as I have such thick hair, so I hit him in the same place. It's all right. It was quite fair. I say, mother, I'm going to throw these things away, now that you know all about them. What's the good of keeping them, anyway? I'm sure I don't know why I ever liked them."

"Give them to me," answered Helen. "Perhaps some poor child might like them."

But she knew that she meant to keep them.

"Well, there isn't much paint on those tin soldiers, you know. I don't believe any child would care for them much. At least not so much as I did, because I was used to them. Of course that made a difference. But you may have them, if you like. I don't want them any more. They're only in the way."

"Give them to me, for the present."

"All right, mother." And he began to pack the toys into the box.

He did it very carefully and neatly, for the habit was strong, though the memory was weak.

Still Helen watched him, without changing her attitude. He sighed as he put in the last of the tin soldiers.

"I suppose I shall really never care for them again," he said.

He looked at them with a sort of affection and touched some of the things lightly, arranging them a little better. Then he shut the lid down, turned the key, and held it out to his mother.

"There you are," he said. "Anyhow, the blocks helped me to remember. Sixty-three, wasn't it, mother?"

"Sixty-three," repeated Helen, mechanically.

Then, for the second time on that evening, she turned her face to the cushion of her chair, and shook from head to foot, and sobbed aloud. She had realized what the number meant. Sixty-three times, in the course of years, had Henry Harmon struck his son upon the head. It was strange that Archie should have any wits at all, and it was no wonder that they were not like those of other men. And it had all been a secret, kept by the child first, then by the growing boy, then by the full-grown man, till his thews and sinews had toughened upon him and he had turned and paid back blow for blow, all at once. And last of all the father had struck her, with a thought of revenge, perhaps, as well as in passion, because he dared not raise his hand against his strong son.

Again she saw the words of her telegram, 'Henry Harmon, New York. Forgiven,' and they were in letters of fire that her tears could not quench. She had not known how much she was forgiving. Archie knelt beside her in wonder, for he had never seen her cry in his life. He touched her arm lovingly, trying to see her face, and his own softened strangely, growing more human as it grew more childlike.

"Don't, mother! Please don't cry like that! If I had thought you would cry about it, I'd never have told you. Besides, it couldn't have hurt him so very much—"

"Him!"

Helen's voice rang out, and she turned, with a fierce light in her angry eyes. In a quick movement her arms ran round Archie's neck and drew him passionately to her breast, and she kissed his head, again and again, always his head, upon the short, thick hair, till he wondered, and laughed.

When they were quiet again, sitting side by side, her battle began once more, and she knew that it must all be fought over on different ground. She had forgiven Henry Harmon, as well as she could, for her own wrongs; but there were others now, and they seemed worse to her than anything she had suffered. It was just to think so, too, for she knew that at any time she could have left Harmon without blame or stain. It had been in her power, but she had chosen not to do it.

But the boy had been powerless and silent through long years. She had never even guessed that his father had ever struck him cruelly. At the merest suspicion of such a thing she would have turned upon her husband as only mothers do turn, tigresses or women. But Archie had kept his secret, while his strength quietly grew upon him, and then he had paid the long score with his own hands. Out of shame, Harmon had kept the secret, too.

Yet she had said in one word that she forgave him, and the word determined the rest of her life. A suffering, a short, sad respite, and then suffering again; that was to sum the history of her years. She must suffer to the end, more and more.

And all at once it seemed to her that she could not bear it. For herself she might have forgiven anything. She had pardoned all for herself, from the first neglect to the scar on her forehead. But it was another matter to forgive for Archie. Why should she? What justice could there be in that? What right had she

to absolve Harmon for his cruelty to her
child?

She must ask Archie if he forgave his father.
She could no longer decide the question alone,
and Archie had the best of rights to be con-
sulted. Wimpole's words came back to her,
asking whether it could do Archie any good
to be under the same roof with his father; and
all at once she saw that her whole married life
had been centred in her son much more than
in herself.

Besides, he must be told that his father had
recovered, for every one must know it soon, and
people would speak of it before him, and think
it very strange if he were ignorant of it. She
hid from herself the underthought that Archie
must surely refuse to live with his father, after
all that had passed, and the wild hope of escape
from what she had undertaken to do, which the
suggestion raised.

She sat silent and thoughtful, her tears drying
on her cheeks, while her son still knelt beside
her. But without looking at him, she laid her
hand on his arm, and her grasp tightened while
she was thinking.

"What is it, mother? What is it?" he asked
again and again.

At last she let her eyes go to his, and she
answered him.

"Your father is well again. By this time he must have left the asylum. Shall we go back to him?"

"I suppose we must, if he's all right," answered Archie, promptly.

Helen's face fell suddenly, for she had expected a strong refusal.

"Can you forgive him for all he did to you?" she asked slowly.

"I don't see that there's much to forgive. He hit me, and I hit him just as often; so we're square. He won't hit me now, because he's afraid of me. I hate him, of course, and he hates me. It's quite fair. He thinks I'm stupid, and I think he's mean; but I don't see that there's anything to forgive him. I suppose he's made so. If he's all right again, I don't see but what we shall have to go and live with him again. I don't see what you're going to do about it, mother."

Helen buried her face in her hands, not sobbing again, but thinking. She did not see 'what she was going to do about it,' as Archie expressed the situation. If she had not already sent the telegram, it would have been different. The young man's rough phrases showed that he had not the slightest fear of his father, and he was ignorant of what she herself had suffered. Much she had hidden from him altogether, and his dulness had seen nothing of the rest. He supposed, if he thought anything about it, that his mother had been unhappy because Harmon drank hard, and stayed away from home unaccountably, and often spoke roughly and rudely when he had been drinking. To his unsensitive nature and half-developed mind these things had seemed regrettable, but not so very terrible, after all. Helen had been too loyal to hold up Harmon as an example of evil to his son, and the boy had grown up accustomed to what disgusted and revolted her, as well as ignorant of what hurt her; while his own unfinished character was satisfied with a half-barbarous conception of what was fair so far as he himself was concerned. He had given blow for blow and bruise for bruise, and on a similar understanding he was prepared to return to similar conditions. Helen saw it all in a flash, but she could not forgive Harmon.

"I can't! I can't!" she repeated aloud, and she pressed Archie's arm again.

"Can't — what, mother?" he asked. "Can't go back?"

"How can I, after this? How can I ever bear to see him, to touch his hand, — his hand that hurt you, Archie, — that hurt you so much more than you ever dream of?"

There were tears in her voice again, and again

she pressed him close to her. But he did not understand.

"Oh, that's all right, mother," he answered. "Don't cry about me! I made it all right with him long ago. And I don't suppose he hurt me more than I dreamed of, either. That's only a way of talking, you know. It used to make me feel rather stupid. But then, I'm stupid anyway; so even that didn't matter much." And Archie smiled indifferently.

"More than you think, more than you know!" She kissed his hair. "It was that — it may have been that — it must have been — I know it was — "

She was on the point of breaking down again.

"What?" he asked with curiosity. "What do you mean? I don't understand."

Helen's voice sank low, and she hardly seemed to be speaking to her son.

"Your father made you what you are," she said, and her face grew cold and hard.

"What? Stupid?" asked Archie, cheerfully. Then his face changed, too. "I say, mother," he went on, in another voice, "do you think I'm so dull because he hit me on the head?"

Helen repented her words, scarcely knowing why, but sure that it would have been better not to speak them. She did not answer the question.

"That's what you think," said Archie. "And it's because I'm not like other people that you say it's absurd of me to want to marry Sylvia Strahan, isn't it? And that's my father's doing? Is that what you think?"

He waited for an answer, but none came at once. Helen was startled by the clear sequence of ideas, far more logical than most of his reasonings. It seemed as if his sudden passion for Sylvia had roused his sluggish intelligence from its long torpor. She could not deny the truth of what he said, and he saw that she could not.

"That's it," he continued. "That's what you think. I knew it."

His brows knitted themselves straight across his forehead, and his eyes were fixed upon his mother's face, as he knelt beside her. She had not been looking at him, but she turned to him slowly now.

"And that's why you ask whether I can forgive him," he concluded.

"Can you?"

"No."

He rose to his feet from his knees easily, by one movement, and she watched him. Then there was a long silence and he began to walk up and down.

Helen felt as if she had done something dis-

loyal, and that he had given the answer for
which she had been longing intensely, as an
escape from her decision, and as a means of
freedom from bondage to come. She could ask
herself now what right she had to expect that
Archie should forgive his father. But, instead,
she asked what right she could have had to give
Archie so good a reason for hating him, when
the boy had not suspected that which, after all,
might not be the truth. She had made an enormous sacrifice in sending the message of forgiveness for her own wrongs, but it seemed to her,
all at once, that in rousing Archie's resentment
for his own injuries she had marred the purity
of her own intention.

Indeed she was in no state to judge herself,
for what Archie had told her was a goad in her
wound, with a terror of new pain.

"You cannot forgive him," she said mechanically and almost to herself.

"Why should I?" asked Archie. "It means
Sylvia to me. How can I forgive him that?"

And suddenly, without waiting for any answer,
he went out and left her alone.

After a long time, she wrote this letter to her
husband:

DEAR HENRY,—I am very glad to hear of your recovery, and I have received your letter to-day, together with
the doctor's. I have telegraphed the one word for which

you asked, and you have probably got the message already. But I must answer your letter as well as I can, and say a great many things which I shall never say again. If we are to meet and try to live together, it is better that I should speak plainly before I see you.

You asked a great deal of me, and for myself I have done what you asked. I do not say this to make it seem as though I were making a great sacrifice and wished you to admit it. We were not happy together; you say that it was your fault, and you ask me to forgive you. If I believed that you had been in full possession of your senses till you were taken ill, I do not think that forgiveness could be possible. You see, I am frank. I am sure that you often did not know what you said and did, and that when you did know, you could not always weigh the consequences of your words and actions. So I will try to forget them. That is what you mean by being forgiven, and it is the only meaning either you or I can put upon the word. I will try to forget, and I will bear no malice for anything in the past, so far as I am concerned. Never speak of it, when we meet, and I never will. If you really wish to try the experiment of living together again, I am willing to attempt it, as an experiment.

But there is Archie to be considered, and Archie will not forgive you. By a mere chance, to-day, after I had sent my telegram, he told me that you used to strike him cruelly and often because his dulness irritated you. You struck him on the head, and you injured his brain, so that his mind has never developed fully and never can.

I do not think that if I were a man, as he is, I could forgive that. Could you? Do you expect that I should, being his mother? You cannot. You and he can never live under the same roof again. It would perhaps be

harder for you, feeling as you must, than for him; but
in any case it is not possible, and there is only one
arrangement to be made. We must put Archie in some
place where he shall be safe and healthy and happy,
and I will spend a part of the year with you and a part
with him. I will not give him up for you, and I am not
willing to give you up for him. Neither would be right.
You are my husband, whatever there may have been in
the past; but Archie is my child. It will be harder for
me than for him, too.

You say that I might have got a divorce from you,
and you do me the justice to add that you believe I have
never thought of it. That is true, but it is not a proof
of affection. I have none for you. I told you that I
should speak plainly, and it is much better. It would
be an ignoble piece of comedy on my part to pretend to
be fond of you. I was once. I admired you, I suppose,
and I liked you well enough to marry you, being rather
ignorant of the world and of what people could feel. If
you had really loved me and been kind to me, I should
have loved you in the end. But, as it turned out, I could
not go on admiring you long, and I simply ceased to like
you. That is our story, and it is a sad one. We made
the great mistake, for we married without much love on
either side, and we were very young.

But it was a marriage, just the same, and a bond
which I never meant to break and will not break now.
A promise is a promise, whatever happens, and a vow
made before God is ten times a promise. So I always
mean to keep mine to you, as I have kept it. I will do
my best to make you happy, and you must do your part
to make it possible.

After all, that is the way most people live. True
love, lasting lifetimes and not changing, exists in the
world, and it is the hope of it that makes youth lovely

and marriage noble. Few people find it, and the many
who do not must live as well as they can without it.
That is what we must do. Perhaps, though the hope of
love is gone, we may find peace together. Let us try.

But not with Archie. There are things which no
woman can forgive nor forget. I could not forgive you
this if I loved you with all my heart, and you must not
expect it of me, for it is not in my power. The harm
was not done to me, but to him, and he is more to me
than you ever were, and far more to me than myself.
I will only say that. There can be no need of ever
speaking about it, but I want you to understand; and
not only this, but everything. That is why I write
such a long letter.

It must all be perfectly clear, and I hope I have made
it so. It was I who suffered for the great mistake we
made in marrying, but you are sorry for that, and I say,
let us try the experiment and see whether we can live
together in peace for the rest of our lives. You are
changed since your illness, I have no doubt, and you
will make it as easy as you can. At least, you will do
your best, and so shall I.

Have I repeated myself in this letter? At least, I
have tried to be clear and direct. Besides, you know
me, and you know what I mean by writing in this way.
I am in earnest.

God bless you, Henry. I hope this may turn out
well.   HELEN.

It was ten o'clock when she had finished.
She laid her hand upon the bell, meaning to
send her letter to the post office by a servant;
but just then the sound of laughing voices came
up to her through the open window, and she

did not ring. Looking out, she saw that there
were still many people in the street, for it was
a warm evening. It was only a step from her
hotel to the post office, and if she went herself
she should have the satisfaction of knowing
positively that the letter was safe. She put
on a hat with a thick veil, and went out.

CHAPTER IX

COLONEL WIMPOLE looked positively old that
evening when he went down to dinner with his
sister and Sylvia. His face was drawn and
weary and the lids hung a little, in small
wrinkles; but down in his grey eyes there was
a far-off gleam of danger-light.

Sylvia looked down when she met him, and
she was very silent and grave at first. At
dinner she sat between him and Miss Wimpole,
and for some time she scarcely dared to glance
at him. He, on his part, was too much preoccupied to speak much, and she thought he
was displeased. Nevertheless, he was more
than usually thoughtful for her. She understood by the way he sat, and even by the half-
unconscious shrinking of the elbow next to her,
that he was sorry for her. At table, seated
close together, there is a whole language in
one's neighbour's elbow and an unlimited power
of expression in its way of avoiding collisions.
Very perceptive people understand that. Pri-
marily, in savage life, the bold man turns his

154

elbows out, while the timid one presses them,
to his sides, as though not to give offence with
them. Society teaches us to put on some little
airs of timidity as a substitute for the modesty
that few feel, and we accordingly draw in our
elbows when we are near any one. It is ridiculous enough, but there are a hundred ways of
doing it, a hundred degrees of readiness, unwill-
ingness, pride, or consideration for others, as
well as sympathy for their troubles or in their
successes, all of which are perfectly natural to
refined people, and almost entirely unconscious.
The movement of a man's jaws at dinner shows
much of his real character, but the movement of
his elbows shows with fair accuracy the degree
of refinement in which he has been brought up.

Sylvia was sure that the colonel was sorry for
her, and the certainty irritated her, for she hated
to be pitied, and most of all for having done
something foolish. She glanced at Wimpole's
tired face, just when he was looking a little
away from her, and she was startled by the
change in his features since the early afternoon.
It needed no very keen perception to see that
he was in profound anxiety of some kind, and
she knew of nothing which could have disturbed
him deeply but her own conduct.

Under the vivid light of the public dining
table, he looked old. That was undeniable, and

it was really the first time that Sylvia had definitely connected the idea of age with him. Just
beyond him sat a man in the early prime of
strength, one of those magnificent specimens
of humanity such as one sees occasionally in
travelling but whom one very rarely knows in
acquaintance. He could not have been more
than twenty-eight years old, straight in his seat,
broad-shouldered, with thick, close, golden hair
and splendid golden beard, white forehead and
sunburned cheeks, broad, well-modelled brows
and faultless nose, and altogether manly in
spite of his beauty. As he leaned forward a
little, his fresh young face appeared beside the
colonel's tired profile, in vivid contrast.

For the first time, Sylvia realized the meaning
of Wimpole's words, spoken that afternoon. He
might almost have been her grandfather, and he
was in reality of precisely the same age as her
father. Sylvia looked down again and reflected
that she must have made a mistake with herself.
Youth can sometimes close its eyes to grey hair,
but it can never associate the idea of love with
old age, when clearly brought to its percep-
tions.

For at least five minutes the world seemed
utterly hollow to Sylvia, as she sat there. She
did not even wonder why she had thought the
colonel young until then. The sudden dropping

out of her first great illusion left a void as big
and as hollow as itself.

She turned her head, and looked once more,
and there, again, was the glorious, unseamed
youth of the stranger, almost dazzling her and
making the poor colonel look more than ever
old, with his pale, furrowed cheeks and wrinkled
eyelids. She thought a moment, and then she
was sure that she could never like such a terribly handsome young man; and at the same
instant, for the first time in her life, she felt
that natural, foolish, human pity which only
extreme youth feels for old age, and she wondered why she had not always felt it, for it
seemed quite natural, and was altogether in
accordance with the rest of her feelings for the
colonel, with her reverence for his perfect character, her admiration for his past deeds, her
attachment to his quiet, protective, wise, and
all-gentle manliness. That was her view of his
qualities, and she had to admit that though he
had them all, he was what she called old. She
had taken for love what was only a combination
of reverence and attachment and admiration.
She realized her mistake in a flash, and it
seemed to her that the core had withered in
the fruit of the universe.

Just then the colonel turned to her, holding
his glass in his hand.

"We must not forget that it is your birthday, my dear," he said, and his natural smile came back. "Rachel," he added, speaking to his sister across the young girl, "let us drink Sylvia's health on her eighteenth birthday."

Miss Wimpole usually took a little thin Moselle with the cold water she drank. She solemnly raised the glass, and inclined her head as she looked first at Sylvia and then at the colonel.

"Thank you," said Sylvia, rather meekly.

Then they all relapsed into silence. The people at the big table talked fast, in low tones, and the clattering of dishes and plates and knives and forks went on steadily and untunefully all around. Sylvia felt lonely in the unindividual atmosphere of the Swiss hotel. She hated the terribly handsome young man, with a mortal hatred, because he made the colonel look old. She could not help seeing him whenever she turned towards Wimpole. At last she spoke softly, looking down at her plate.

"Uncle Richard," she said, to call his attention.

He was not really her uncle, and she almost always called him 'colonel,' half playfully, and because she had hated the suggestion of age that is conveyed by the word 'uncle.' Wimpole turned to her quietly.

"Yes, my dear," he said. "What is it?"

"I suppose I was very foolish to-day, wasn't I?" asked Sylvia, very low indeed, and a bright blush played upon her pretty face.

The colonel was a courteous man, and was also very fond of her.

"A woman need never be wise when she is lovely," he said in his rather old-fashioned way, and he smiled affectionately at the young girl. "It is quite enough if she is good."

But she did not smile. On the contrary, her face became very grave.

"I am in earnest," she said, and she waited a moment before saying more. "I was very foolish," she continued, thoughtfully. "I did not understand — or I did not realize — I don't know. You have been so much to me all my life, and there is nobody like you, of course. It seemed to me — I mean, it seems to me — that is very much like really caring for some one, isn't it? You know what I mean. I can't express it."

"You mean that it is a good deal like love, I suppose," answered the colonel, speaking gravely now. "Yes, I suppose that love is better when people believe each other to be angels. But it is not that sort of thing which makes love what it is."

"What is it, then?" Sylvia was glad to

ask any question that helped to break through the awkwardness and embarrassment she felt towards him.

"There are a great many kinds of love," he said; "but I think there is only one kind worth having. It 'is the kind that begins when one is young, and lasts all one's life."

"Is that all?" asked Sylvia, innocently, and in a disappointed tone.

"All!" The colonel laughed softly, and a momentary light of happiness came into his face, for that all was all he had ever had. "Is not that enough, my dear?" he asked. "To love one woman or man with all one's heart for thirty or forty years? Never to be disappointed? Never to feel that one has made a mistake? Never to fear that love may grow old because one grows old oneself? Is not that enough?"

"Ah, yes! That would be, indeed. But you did not say all those other things at first."

"They are just what make a life-long love," answered the colonel. "But then," he added, "there are a great many degrees, far below that. I am sure I have seen people quite really in love with each other for a week."

Sylvia suddenly looked almost angry as she glanced at him.

"That sort of thing ought not to be called love at all!" she answered energetically. "It is nothing but a miserable flirtation, — a miserable, wretched, unworthy flirtation."

"I quite agree with you," said Wimpole, smiling at her vehemence.

."Why do you laugh?" she asked, almost offended by his look. His smile disappeared instantly.

"You hit the world very hard, my dear," he answered.

"I hate the world!" cried Sylvia.

She was just eighteen. Wimpole knew that she felt an innocent and instinctive repulsion for what the world meant to him, and for all the great, sinful unknown. He disliked it himself, with the steady, subdued dislike which is hatred in such natures as his, both because it was contrary to his character, and for Sylvia's sake, who must surely one day know something of it. So he did not laugh at her sweeping declaration. She hated the world before knowing it, but he hated it in full knowledge. That was a bond of sympathy like any other. To each of us the world means both what we know, and what we suspect, both what we see and the completion of it in the unseen, both the outward lives of our companions which we can judge, and their inward motives, which we dimly guess.

But on this evening Sylvia felt that the world was particularly odious, for she had suffered a

first humiliation in her own eyes.   She thought
that she had lowered herself in the colonel's estimation, and she had discovered that she had
made a great mistake with herself about him.

"I hate the world!" she repeated, in a lower
tone, almost to herself, and her eyes gleamed
with young anger, while her delicate, curving
lips just showed her small white teeth.

Wimpole watched her face.

"That is no reason for hating yourself," he
said gently.

She started and turned her eyes to him.   Then
she blushed and looked away.

"You must not guess my thoughts," she
answered.   "It is not kind."

"I did not mean to.   I am sorry."

"Oh — you could not help it, of course.   I
was so foolish to-day."

The blush deepened, and she said nothing
more.   The colonel returned to his own secret
trouble, and on Sylvia's other side Miss Wimpole
was silently planning a charitable institution of
unusual severity, while she peeled an orange with
the most scrupulous neatness and precision.

CHAPTER X

SYLVIA went to her own room after dinner, still wondering what had happened to her on her birthday. There is an age at which most of us unexpectedly come across the truth about ourselves, and sometimes about others, and it generally happens that in our recollection the change turns upon one day, or even one hour.

The shock is sudden and unexpected. Floating down a quick smooth stream in a boat, a man is aware of motion, as he watches the bank without realizing the strength of the flowing water; but when the skiff is suddenly checked by any obstacle in midstream, the whole force of the river rushes upon it, and past it, and perhaps over it, in an instant. Something of the same sort happens now and then in our lives. The great illusion of childhood carries us along at a speed of which we have no idea, in the little boat which is the immediate and undeniable reality of near surroundings, the child's cradle afloat upon a fiction which is wide and deep and strong, and sometimes we are grown

men and women before our small craft strikes
upon a shoal of truth, with a dash that throws
us from the thwart, and frightens the bravest of
us.　There we stick fast upon the rough fact for
a while, and the flood that was so smooth and
pleasant rushes past us, foaming and seething
and breaking against the boat's side and threatening to tear her to pieces.　And if the tide is
ebbing at the river's mouth, we may be left high
and dry upon the sharp reality for a long time;
but if not, the high water will presently float us,
and off we shall spin again, smoothly and safely,
on the bosom of the sweet untrue.

Such accidents happen more than once to
most people, and almost every one resents them
bitterly.　Even in daily living, few men can
bear to be roughly roused from sleep.　Much
more is the waking rude from year-long dreams
of fancy.

Sylvia sat at her table and stared at the lamp,
as if it were her own heart which she could look
into, and watch, and study, and criticise.　For
most of all, she was in a humour to find fault
with it, as having played her false when she
least expected that it could deceive her.　She
had built on it, as it dictated; she had trusted
it, as it suggested; she had lived, and loved to
live, for its sake; and now it had betrayed her.
It had not been in earnest, all the time, but had

somehow made her think that she herself was
all earnestness. It was a false and silly little
heart, and she hated it, as she looked at it in
the lamp, and she wished that it would frizzle
and burn like the poor moth that had gone too
near the hot glass while she had been downstairs.

It was positively laughing at her, now, and she
set her small mouth angrily. To think that she
should ever have fancied herself in love with a
man who might have been her grandfather!
And it wickedly showed her the colonel as he
would be in another ten years, a picture founded
upon the tired look she had just seen in his face.
She was ashamed of herself, and furious against
herself for being ashamed, and she suddenly
wished that she were dead, because that would
give people a real reason for being sorry for her.
It would be very pathetic to die so young! If
she did, her heart could not laugh at her.

She thought about it for a while, and among
other reflexions she suddenly found herself wondering whether young Knox, the officer on her
father's ship, would be very sorry. He had
written her a letter from Japan which she had
not answered. Indeed, she was not sure that
she had read every word of it, for it had only
come this morning. Life had been too short
for reading letters on that day. But there it

was, on the table.   She had the evening before
her, and though it was a long letter, it could
not take more than a quarter of an hour to
go through it.   She put out her hand to take
it and then looked at the lamp again.

A lean, brown young face was suddenly there,
and bright eyes that looked straight at her, without anything vastly superior in them, but full of
something she liked and understood and instantly
longed for.   Her heart was not laughing at her
any more, for she had forgotten all about it,
which is generally the best thing one can do in
such cases.

Even the expression of her face changed and
softened as she laid her hand upon the letter.
For Wimpole's sake, as she had made herself
think a few hours earlier, she would gladly have
doubled her age, and the forced longing for
equality of years between herself and her ideal
had fleetingly expressed itself in her face by
shadows, where there could not yet be lines.
But as the illusion sank down into the store-
house of all impossibilities and all mistakes, the
light of early youth fell full and unscreened
upon her face again, and she revived unconsciously, as day-flowers do at sunrise, when the
night-flowers fold their leaves.

It was surely no thought of love which made
the change; or if that were its cause, it was but

love's fore-lightening in a waking dream. Much
rather it must have been the consciousness of living roused by the thought of youth. For youth
is the elixir of life, and the touch of old age
is a blight on youth, when youth is longing to
be old; but youth that is willingly young has
power to give the old a breath of itself again,
before the very end. In their children men live
again, and in their children's children they remember the loveliness of childhood.

From a very far country, across half a world
of land and water, the letter had come to Sylvia
on her birthday, as Harmon's had come to
Helen. There is something strange and terrible, if we realize it, in man's power to harm
or help by written words from any distance.
The little bit of paper leaves our hand with its
wishing-carpet in the shape of a postage stamp,
and swiftly singles out the one man or woman,
in two thousand millions, for whom it is meant,
going straight to its mark with an aim far more
unerring than steel or ball. A man may much
more probably miss his enemy with a pistol at
ten paces, than with a letter at ten thousand
miles. If the fabled inhabitant of Mars could
examine our world under an imaginary glass, as
we study a drop of water under a microscope, he
would surely be profoundly interested in the
movements of the letter-bacillus, as he might

call it.   He might question whether it is gener-
ated spontaneously, or is the result of an act of
will, more or less aggressive, but he would mar-
vel at the rapidity of its motion and at the
strength of its action upon the human animal
through the eye.   It would be very inexplicable
to him; least of all could he understand the
instant impulse of man to tear off the shell
of the bacillus as soon as it reaches him, for
he would no doubt notice that in a vast number
of cases the sight of it produces discontent and
pain, and he might even find a few instances in
which death followed almost immediately.   In
others the bacteria produce amazingly exhila-
rating results, such as laughter and the undigni-
fied antics of joy, and even sudden improvements
in the animal's health and appearance.   He
would especially notice that these bacilli are
almost perpetually in motion, from the time
they leave one human being until they fasten
themselves upon another, and that in parts of
the world where they are not found at all, or
only sporadically, the animals behave in a very
different way, are healthier, and are less exposed
to the fatal results of their own inventions.   If
the inhabitant of Mars were given to jumping
at conclusions, he would certainly announce to
his fellow-beings that he had discovered in Earth
the germ of a disease called by Terrenes 'Civ-

ilization.' And perhaps that is just what the letter is.

Young Knox wrote to Sylvia because he was in love with her, which is the best of all reasons for writing when love is right, and the worst imaginable when it is wrong. He was so much in love that as soon as she was out of his sight his first impulse was to set down on paper all sorts of things which had very little sense in them, but made up for a famine of wisdom by a corresponding plenty of feeling. There is something almost pathetic in the humbleness of a young man's strength before the object of his first true love. It is the abasement of the real before the ideal; but if the ideal fails, the real takes vengeance of the man for having trodden it under.

Young women rarely understand their power; older ones too often overrate what they have. The girl who first breathes the air of the outer world and first sees in a man's eyes that he loves her, knows that he is stronger, better taught, more experienced than she is, and compares herself with him by a measure which he rates as nothing. Man is much more real to woman, when both are very young, than woman is to man; and being real he represents to her a sort of material force. But to him she is an imaginary being, strong with a mystic influence

from which he cannot escape when he has come
within the pentagram of the spell.   It is bad
for a man if she comes to know her strength
before he has learned his weakness.   Then she
riots in it, recklessly, for a time, until she has
hurt him.   She says, 'Do this,' and he does it,
like the Centurion's servant; or 'Say this,' and
he says it, be the words wise or foolish, and she
reckons his wisdom to herself and his folly to
him, frankly, and without the least doubt of
her own perfection, for a while, rejoicing sense-
lessly in driving him.   But by and by, as in a
clock, the mainspring feels the gentle regulation
of the swaying balance, and the balance takes
its motion from the spring, till both together
move in perfect time, while each without the
other would be but a useless bit of machinery.

Sylvia did not know all that, and if she had,
she would perhaps not have reasoned about it
much.   She did not understand why young
Knox wrote that he would live for her, die for
her, and, if necessary, convulse the solar system
for her exclusive pleasure and benefit.   It seemed
a great deal to promise under the circumstances,
and her moderate maiden vanity could not make
her appear, in her own eyes, as an adequate
cause of such serious disturbance in the order
of things; yet it was not displeasing to be
magnified into a possible source of astronomical

miracles, though the idea was slightly ridiculous and she was glad that she had it entirely to herself and beyond carping criticism.

She was not in the least in love with the man who wrote to her, and she had not been in love with him when they had parted. That very morning, when she had received the letter, she had been a little inclined to smile at the writer's persistence, and had laid the letter aside, half read, in no great hurry to finish it. But since then, her life had changed. She had gone aground on the shoal of truth and she was already longing for the waters of illusion to rise and float her away.

So she let the breezy memories come back to her, and they brought her a sweet forewarning of her growing life. All at once, she knew that she had never met any one so young who had pleased her so much, any one with such clear eyes and manly ways, frank smile and honest voice, as the young officer who had hated this hollow world with such grave conviction because Sylvia Strahan could not go home in her father's ship. She read on, and felt an unexpected thrill of pleasure when the words told her what she had already known; namely, that the squadron would be far on its way to San Francisco by the time the letter reached her, that Knox was to come to the capital with her

father, and that she was quite certain to meet
him there before very long.   She was unconscious of looking round at her things just then
and wishing that they were already packed for
the homeward journey.

She wrote to him before she went to bed.   It
was a duty of civility to answer him, though
she felt herself under no obligation to reply to
his numerous questions.   On the contrary, she
said nothing at all about them, but she gave
him her impressions of Lucerne and told him
that Aunt Rachel had taken cold, but was now
quite well, a piece of information which, though
satisfactory in its way, was not calculated to
affect her correspondent's happiness in any
marked degree.   'It would be nice to see each
other again,' she said at the end, with which
mild sentiment she signed herself 'sincerely'
his.

The only odd thing about it all was that
when the letter was finished she had not the
slightest idea where to send it, a fact which had
not crossed her mind when she had unscrewed
her travelling inkstand, but which sufficiently
proved that she had acted under an impulse of
some sort.   She said to herself that it did not
matter, but she was disappointed, and the smile
faded from her face for a little while.

When she was asleep it came back in the

dark and lingered on her lips all night, waning and waxing with her maiden dreams.

Her eighteenth birthday had been a good day in her life, after all. There are few indeed who fall asleep happily when the first illusion has gone down into darkness with the evening sun.

CHAPTER XI

HELEN HARMON went out alone to mail her
letter. She would not have done such a thing
in any great city of Europe, but there is a sense
of safety in the dull, impersonal atmosphere of
Lucerne, and it was a relief to her to be out in
the open air alone; it would be a still greater
relief to have dropped the letter into the mysterious slit which is the first stage on the road to
everywhere.

No one ever thinks of the straight little cut,
with its metal cover, as being at all tragical.
And yet it is as tragic as the jaws of death, in
its way. Many a man and woman has stood
before it with a letter and hesitated; and every
one has, at some time or other, felt the sharp
twist at the heart, which is the wrench of the
irrevocable, when the envelope has just slipped
away into darkness. The words cannot be un-
written any more, after that, nor burned, nor
taken back. A telegram may contradict them,
or explain them, or ask pardon for them, but the
message will inevitably be read, and do its work

of peace or war, of challenge or forgiveness, of cruelty, or kindness, or indifference.

Helen did not mean to hesitate, for she hastened towards the moment of looking back upon a deed now hard to do. It was not far to the post office, either, and the thing could soon be done. Yet in her·brain there was a surging of uncertainties and a whirling of purposes, in the midst of which she clung hard to her determination, though it should cost ever so dear to carry it out. She had not half thought of all the consequences yet, nor of all it must mean to her to be separated from her son. The results of her action sprang up now, like sudden dangers, and tried to frighten her from her purpose, tried to gain time against her to show themselves, tried to terrify her back to inaction and doubt. Something asked her roughly whence she had got the conviction that she was doing right at all. Another something, more subtle, whispered that she was sacrificing Archie for the sake of her own morbid conscience, and making herself a martyr's crown, not of her own sufferings only, but of her son's loss in losing her. It told her that the letter she held in her hand was a mistake, but not irrevocable until it should have slipped into the dark entrance of the road to everywhere.

She had still a dozen steps to make before

reaching the big white building that stands across the corner of the street, and she was hurrying on, lest she should not reach the door in time. Then she almost ran against Colonel Wimpole, walking slowly along the pavement where there was a half shadow. Both stopped short, and looked at each other in surprise. He saw the letter in her hand, and guessed that she had written to her husband.

"I was only going to the post office," she said, half apologetically, for she thought that he must wonder why she had come out alone at such an hour.

"Will you let me walk with you?" he asked.

"Yes."

He made a step forwards, as though expecting her to turn back from her errand and go with him.

"Not that way," she said. "I must go to the post office first."

"No. Please don't." He placed himself in her way.

"I must."

She spoke emphatically and stood still, facing him, while their eyes met again, and neither spoke again for a few seconds.

"You are ruining your life," he said, after the pause. "When that letter is gone, you will never be able to get it back."

"I know. I shall not wish to."

"You will." His lips set themselves rather firmly as he opposed her, but her face darkened.

"Is this a trial of strength between us?" she asked.

"Yes. I mean to keep you from going back to Henry Harmon."

"I have made up my mind," Helen answered.

"So have I," said Wimpole.

"How can you hinder me? You cannot prevent me from sending this letter, nor from going to him if I choose. And I have chosen to go. That ends it."

"You are mistaken. You are reckoning without me, and I will make it impossible."

"You? How? Even if I send this letter?"

"Yes. Come and walk a little, and we can talk. If you insist upon it, drop your letter into the box. But it will only complicate matters, for you shall not go back to Harmon."

Again she looked at him. He had never spoken in this way, during all the years of their acknowledged friendship and unspoken love. She felt that she resented his words and manner, but at the same time that she loved him better and admired him more. He was stronger and more dominant than she had guessed.

"You have no right to say such things to

me," she answered. "But I will walk with
you for a few minutes. Of course you can
hinder me from sending my letter now. I
can take it to the post office by and by."

"You cannot suppose that I mean to prevent
you by force," said Wimpole, and he stood aside
to let her pass if she would.

"You said that it was a trial of strength,"
she answered.

She hesitated one moment, and then turned
and began to walk with him. They crossed the
street to the side by which the river runs, away
from the hotels and the houses. It was darker
there and more quiet, and they felt more alone.
It would seem easier, too, to talk in the open
air, with the sound of the rushing water in their
ears. He was the first to speak then.

"I want to explain," he said quietly.

"Yes." She waited for him to go on.

"I suppose that there are times in life when
it is better to throw over one's own scruples, if
one has any," he began. "I have never done
anything to be very proud of, perhaps, but I
never did anything to be ashamed of either.
Perhaps I shall be ashamed of what I am going
to say now. I don't care. I would rather com-
mit a crime than let you wreck your whole existence, but I hope you will not make me **do**
that."

They had stopped in their walk, and were leaning against the railing that runs along the bank.

"You are talking rather desperately," said Helen, in a low voice.

"It is rather a desperate case," Wimpole answered. "I talk as well as I can, and there are things which I must tell you, whatever you think of me; things I never meant to say, but which have made up most of my life. I never meant to tell you."

"What?"

"That I love you. That is the chief thing."

The words did not sound at all like a lover's speech, as he spoke them. He had drawn himself up and stood quite straight, holding the rail with his hands. He spoke coolly, with a sort of military precision, as though he were facing an enemy's fire. There was not exactly an effort in his voice, but the tone showed that he was doing a hard thing at that moment. Then he was silent, and Helen said nothing for a long time. She was leaning over the rail, trying to see the running water in the dark.

"Thank you," she said at last, very simply, and there was another pause.

"I did not expect you to say that," he answered presently.

"Why not? We are not children, you and I. Besides — I knew it."

"Not from me!" Wimpole turned almost sharply upon her.

"No. Not from you. You wrote Henry a letter, many years ago. Do you remember? I had to read everything when he went to the asylum, so I read that, too. He had kept it all those years."

"I am sorry. I never meant you to know. But it does not matter now, since I have told you myself."

He spoke coldly again, almost indifferently, looking straight before him into the night.

"It matters a great deal," said Helen, almost to herself, and he did not hear her.

She kept her head bent down, though he could not have seen her face clearly if she had looked up at him. Her letter burned her, and she hated herself, and loved him. She despised herself, because in the midst of the greatest sacrifice of her life, she had felt the breath of far delight in words that cost him so much. Yet she would have suffered much, even in her good pride, rather than have had them unspoken, for she had unknowingly waited for them half a lifetime. Being a good woman, she was too much a woman to speak one word in return, beyond the simple thanks that sounded so strangely to him, for women exaggerate both good and evil as no man can.

"I know, I know!" he said, suddenly continuing. "You are married, and I should not speak. I believe in those things as much as you do, though I am a man, and most men would laugh at me for being so scrupulous. You ought never to have known, and I meant that you never should. But then, you are married to Harmon still, because you choose to be, and because you will not be free. Does not that make a difference?"

"No, not that. That makes no difference." She raised her head a little.

"But it does now," answered Wimpole. "It is because I do love you, just as I do, with all my heart, that I mean to keep you from him, whether it is right or wrong. Don't you see that right and wrong only matter to one's own miserable self? I shall not care what becomes of my soul if I can keep you from all that unhappiness — from that real danger. It does not matter what becomes of me afterwards — even if I were to go straight to New York and kill Harmon and be hanged for the murder, it would not matter, so long as you were free and safe."

The man had fought in honourable battles, and had killed, and knew what it meant.

"Is that what you intend to do?" asked Helen, and her voice shook.

"It would mean a great deal, if I had to do it," he answered quietly enough. "It would show that I loved you very much. For I have been an honourable man all my life, and have never done anything to be ashamed of. I should be killing a good deal, besides Henry Harmon, but I would give it to make you happy, Helen. I am in earnest."

"You could not make me happy in that way."

"No. I suppose not. I shall find some other way. In the first place, I shall see Harmon and talk to him — "

"How? When?" Helen turned up her face in surprise.

"If you send what you have written, I shall leave to-night," said the colonel. "I shall reach New York as soon as your letter and see Harmon before he reads it, and tell him what I think."

"You will not do that?" She did not know whether she was frightened, or not, by the idea.

"I will," he answered. "I will not stay here tamely and let you wreck your life. If you mail your letter, I shall take the midnight train to Paris. I told you that I was in earnest."

Helen was silent, for she saw a new difficulty and more trouble before her, as though the last few hours had not brought her enough.

"I think," said Wimpole, "that I could persuade Harmon not to accept your generosity."

"I am not doing anything generous. You are making it hard for me to do what is right. You are almost threatening to do something violent, to hinder me."

"No. I know perfectly well that I should never do anything of that sort, and I think you know it, too. To treat Harmon as he deserves would certainly make a scandal which must reflect upon you."

"Please remember that he is still my husband —"

"Yes," interrupted Wimpole, bitterly, "and that is his only title to consideration."

Helen was on the point of rebuking him, but reflected that what he said was probably true.

"Please respect it, then, if you think so," she said quietly. "You say that you care for me — no, I won't put it so — you do care for me. You love me, and I know you do. Let us be perfectly honest with each other. As long as you help me do right, it is not wrong to love me as you do, though I am another man's wife. But as soon as you stand between me and my husband, it is wrong — wicked! It is wicked, no matter what he may have been to me. That has nothing to do with it. It is coming between man and wife —"

"Oh — really — that is going too far!" Wimpole raised his head a little higher, and seemed to breathe the night air angrily through his nostrils.

"No," answered Helen, persistently, for she was arguing against her heart, if not against her head, "it is not going at all too far. Such things should be taken for granted, or at least they should be left to the man and wife in question to decide. No one has any right to interfere, and no one shall. If I can forgive, you can have nothing to resent; for the mere fact of your liking me very much does not give you any sort of right to direct my life, does it? I am glad that you are so fond of me, for I trust you and respect you in every way, and even now I know that you are interfering only because you care for me. But you have not the right to interfere, not the slightest, and although you may be able to, yet if I beg you not to, it will not be honourable of you to come between us."

Colonel Wimpole moved a little impatiently.

"I will take my honour into my own hands," he said.

"But not mine," answered Helen.

They looked at each other in the gloom, as they leaned upon the railing.

"Yours shall be quite safe," said the colonel slowly. "But if you will drop that letter into the river, you will make things easier in every way."

"I should write it over again. Besides, I have telegraphed to him already."

"What? Cabled?"

"Yes. You see that you can do nothing to hinder me. He has my message already. The matter is decided."

She bent her head again, looking down into the rushing water as though tired of arguing.

"You are a saint," said the colonel. "I could not have done that."

"Perhaps I could not, if I had waited," answered Helen, in a voice so low that he could hardly hear the words. "But it is done now," she added, still lower, so that he could not hear at all.

Wimpole had been a man of quick decisions so long as he had been a soldier, but since then he had cultivated the luxury of thinking slowly. He began to go over the situation, trying to see what he could do, not losing courage yet, but understanding how very hard it would be to keep Helen from sacrificing herself.

And she peered down at the black river, that rushed past with a cruel sound, as though it were tearing away the time of freedom, second by second. It was done, now, as she had said. She knew herself too well to believe that even

if she should toss the letter into the stream, she
would not write another in just such words.
But the regret was deep, and thrilled with a
secret, aching pulse of its own, all through her,
and she thought of what life might have been,
if she had not made the great mistake, and of
what it still might be if she did not go back to
her husband. The man who stood beside her
loved her, and was ready to give everything,
perhaps even to his honour, to save her from
unhappiness. And she loved him, too, next to
honour. In the tranquil life she was leading,
there could be a great friendship between them,
such as few people can even dream of. She knew
him, and she knew herself, and she believed it
possible, for once in the history of man and
woman. In a measure, it might subsist, even
after she had gone back to Harmon, but not in
the same degree, for between the two men there
would be herself. Wimpole would perhaps refuse
altogether to enter Harmon's door or to touch
Harmon's hand. And then, in her over-scrupu-
lousness, during the time she was to spend with
Archie, she knew that she should hesitate to
receive freely a man who would not be on
speaking terms with the husband whom she
had taken back, no matter how she felt towards
Wimpole.

Besides, he had told her that he loved her,

and that made a difference, too. So long as the word had never been spoken, there had been the reasonable doubt to shield her conscience. His old love might, after all, have turned to friendship, which is like the soft, warm ashes of wood when the fire is quite burned out. But he had spoken at last, and there was no more doubt, and his quiet words had stirred her own heart. He had begun by telling her that he had many things to say; but, after all, the one and only thing he had said which he had never said before was that he loved her.

It was enough, and too much, and it made everything harder for her. We speak of struggles with ourselves. It would really be far more true to talk of battles between our two selves, or even sometimes between our threefold natures, — our good, our bad, and our indifferent personalities.

To Helen, the woman who loved Richard Wimpole was not the woman who meant to go back to Henry Harmon; and neither, perhaps, was quite the same individual as the mother of poor Archie. The three were at strife with one another, though they were one being in suffering. For it is true that we may be happy in part, and in part be indifferent; but no real pain of the soul leaves room for any happiness at all, or indifference, while it lasts.

So soon as we can be happy again, even for a
moment, the reality of the pain is over, though
the memory of it may come back now and then
in cruel little day-dreams, after years. Happiness is composite; pain is simple. It may take
a hundred things to make a man happy, but it
never needs more than one to make him suffer.
Happiness is, in part, elementary of the body;
but pain is only of the soul, and its strength
is in its singleness. Bodily suffering is the opposite of bodily pleasure; but true pain has no
true opposite, nor reversed counterpart, of one
unmixed composition, and the dignity of a great
agony is higher than all the glories of joy.

"Promise me that you will not do anything
to hinder me," said Helen at last.

"I cannot." There was no hesitation in the
answer.

"But if I ask you," she said; "if I beg you,
if I entreat you — "

"It is of no use, Helen. I should do my best
to keep you away from Harmon, even if I were
sure that you would never speak to me nor see
me again. I have said almost all I can, and so
have you. You are half a saint, or altogether
one, or you could not do what you are doing.
But I am not. I am only a man. I don't like
to talk about myself much, but I would not have
you think that I care a straw for my own hap-

piness compared with yours. I would rather
know that you were never to see Harmon again
than —" He stopped short.

"Than what?" asked Helen, after a pause.

He did not answer at once, but stood upright
again beside her, grasping the rail.

"No matter, if you do not understand," he
said at last. "Can I give you any proof that it
is not for myself, because I love you, that I want
to keep you from Harmon? Shall I promise you
that when I have succeeded I will not see you
again as long as I live?"

"Oh, no! No!" The cry was sudden, low,
and heartfelt.

Wimpole squeezed the cold railing a little
harder in his hands, but did not move.

"Is there any proof at all that I could give
you? Try and think."

"Why should I need proof?" asked Helen.
"I believe you, as I always have."

"Well, then —" he began, but she interrupted
him.

"That does not change matters," she continued. "You are right merely because you are
perfectly disinterested for yourself, and altogether interested for me alone. I am not the
only person to be considered."

"I think you are. And if any one else has
any right to consideration, it is Archie."

"I know," Helen answered, "and you hurt me again when you say it. But besides all of us, there is Henry."

"And what right has he?" asked Wimpole, almost fiercely. "What right has he to any sort of consideration from you, or from any one? If you had a brother, he would have wrung Harmon's neck long ago! I wish I had the right!"

"I never heard you say anything brutal before," said Helen.

"I never had such good cause," retorted Wimpole, a little more quietly. "Put yourself in my position. I have loved you all my life, — God knows I have loved you honestly, too, — and held my tongue. And Harmon has spent his life in ruining yours in every way, — in ways I know and in ways I don't know, but can more than half guess. He neglected you, he was unfaithful to you, he insulted you, and at last he struck you. I have found that out to-day, and that blow must have nearly killed you. I know about those things. Do you expect me to have any consideration for the brute who has half killed the woman I love? Do you expect me to keep my hands off the man whose hands have struck you and wounded you? By the Lord, Helen, you are expecting too much of human nature! Or too little — I don't know which!"

He had controlled his temper long, keeping down the white heat of it in his heart, but he could not be calm forever. The fighting instinct was not lost yet, and must have its way.

"He did not know what he was doing," said Helen, shrinking a little.

"You have a right to say that," answered the colonel, "if you can be forgiving enough. But only a coward could say it for you, and only a coward would stand by and see you go back to your husband. I am not a coward, and I won't. Since you have cabled to him, I shall leave to night, whether you send that letter or not. Can't you understand?"

"But what can you do? What can you say to him? How can you influence him? Even if I admit that I have no power to keep you from going to him, what can you do when you see him?"

"I can think of that on the way," said Wimpole. "There will be more than enough time. I don't know what I shall say or do yet. It does not matter, for I have made up my mind."

"Will nothing induce you to stay here?" asked Helen, desperately.

"Nothing," answered Wimpole, and his lips shut upon the word.

"Then I will go, too," answered Helen.

"You!" Wimpole had not thought of such a possibility, and he started.

"Yes. My mind is made up, too. If you go, I go. I shall get there as soon as you, and I will prevent you from seeing him at all. If you force me to it, I will defend him from you. I will tell the doctors that you will drive him mad again, and they will help me to protect him. You cannot get there before me, you know, for we shall cross in the same steamer, and land at the same moment."

"What a woman you are!" Wimpole bent his head, as he spoke the words, leaning against the railing. "But I might have known it," he added; "I might have known you would do that. It is like you."

Helen felt a bitter sort of triumph over herself, in having destroyed the last chance of his interference.

"In any case," she said, "I should go at once. It could be a matter of only a few days at the utmost. Why should I wait, since I have made up my mind?"

"Why indeed?" The colonel's voice was sad. "I suppose the martyrs were glad when the waiting was over, and their turn came to be torn to pieces."

He felt that he was annihilated, and he suffered keenly in his defeat, for he had been deter-

mined to save her at all risks. She was making
even risk impossible. If she went straight to her
husband and took him back, and protected him,
as she called it, what could any one do? It
was a hopeless case. Wimpole's anger against
Harmon slowly subsided, and above it rose his
pity for the woman who was giving all the life
she still had left for the sake of her marriage vow,
who was ready, and almost eager, to go back to
a state full of horror in the past, and of danger
in the future, because she had once solemnly
promised to be Henry Harmon's wife, and could
not find in all the cruel years a reason for taking back her word. He bowed his head, and he
knew that there was something higher in her
than he had ever dreamt in his own honourable
life, for it was something that clung to its belief,
against all suggestion or claim of justice for
itself.

It was not only pity. A despair for her
crept nearer and grew upon him every moment.
Though he had seen her rarely, he had felt
nearer to her since Harmon had been mad, and
now he was to be further from her than ever
before. He would probably not go so far as she
feared, and would be willing to enter her husband's house for her sake, and in the hope of
being useful to her. But he could never be so
near to her again as he was now, and his last

chance of protecting her had vanished before
her unchangeable resolution. He would almost
rather have known that she was going to her
death, than see her return to Harmon. He
made one more attempt to influence her. He
did it roughly, but his voice shook a little.

"It seems to me," he said, "that if I were a
woman, I should be too proud to go back to
a man who had struck me."

Helen moved and stood upright, trying to
look into his face clearly in the dimness as she
spoke.

" Then you think I am not proud?"

He could see her white features and dark eyes,
and he guessed her expression.

" You are not proud for yourself," he answered
rather stubbornly. " If you were, you could not
do this."

She turned from him again, and looked down
at the black water.

"I am prouder than you think," she said.
"That does not make it easier."

"In one way, yes. When you have determined to do a thing, you are ashamed to change
your mind, no matter what your decision may
cost yourself and others."

" Yes, when I am right. At least, I hope I
should be ashamed to break down now."

" I wish you would!"

It was a helpless exclamation, and Wimpole knew it, for he was at the end of all argument and hope, and his despair for her rose in his eyes in the dark.   He could neither do nor say anything more, and presently when he had left her at the door of her hotel, she would do what she meant to do, to the letter.   For the second time on that day he wished that he had acted, instead of speaking, and that he had set out on his journey without warning her.   But in the first place he had believed that she would take more time to consider her action; and again, he had a vague sense that it would not have been loyal and fair to oppose her intention without warning her.   And now she had utterly defeated him, and upheld her will against him, in spite of all he could do.   He loved her the better for her strength, but he despaired the more.   He felt that he was going to say good-bye to her, as though she were about to die.

He put out his hand to take hers, and she met it readily.   In her haste to come out with her letter she had not even taken the time to put on gloves, and her warm, firm fingers closed upon his thin hand as though they were the stronger.

"I must go," she said.   "It is very late."

"Is it?"

"Yes.   I want to thank you, for wishing to

help me — and for everything. I know that
you would do anything for me, and I like to
feel that you would. But there is nothing to
be done. Henry will answer my cable, and
then I shall go to him."

"It is as though you were dying, and I were
saying good-bye to you, Helen."

"That would be easier," she answered, "for
you and me."

She pressed his hand with a frank, unaffected
pressure, and then withdrew her own. He
sighed as he turned from the dark water to
cross the quiet street with her. The people
who had been walking about had gone home
suddenly, as they do in provincial places, and
the electric light glared and blinked upon the
deserted, macadamized road. There was something unwontedly desolate, even the air, for the
sky was cloudy, and a damp wind came up from
the lake.

Without a word the two walked to the post
office, and as Wimpole saw the irrevocable message dropped into the slit, his heart almost
stopped beating. A faint smile that was cruelly
sad to see crossed Helen's white face ; a reflexion
of the bitter victory she · had won over herself
against such great odds.

CHAPTER XII

THE two walked slowly and silently along
the pavement to the hotel, the damp wind following them in fitful gusts and chilling them
as they went. They had no words, for they
had said all to each other; each knew that
the other was suffering, and both knew that
their lives had led them into a path of sadness
from which they could not turn back. They
walked wearily and unwillingly, side by side,
and the way seemed long, and yet too short,
as it shortened before them.

At the lighted porch of the hotel they paused,
reluctant to part.

"May I see you to-morrow?" asked Wimpole,
in a dull voice.

"Yes, I must see you before I go," Helen
answered.

In the light of the lamps he saw how pale
she was, and how very tired, and she looked
at him and knew from his face how he was
suffering for her. They joined hands and forgot
to part them when their eyes had met. But they

197

had nothing to say, and they had only to bid each other a good night which meant good-bye to both, though they should meet ever so often again.

The porter of the hotel stood in the doorway a few steps above them and watched them with a sort of stolid interest. The lamplight gleamed upon his gilt buttons, and the reflexion of them made Helen aware of his presence. Then he went into the entrance, and there was nobody else about. Voices came with broken laughter from the small garden adjacent to the hotel, where there was a café, and far away, at the end of the entrance hall, the clerk pored over his books.

Still Wimpole held Helen's hand.

"It is very hard," he said.

"It is harder than you know," she answered.

For she loved him, though he did not know it, and she felt as well as he did that she was losing him. But because she was Harmon's wife and meant to stand by her husband, she would not call it love in her heart, though she knew her own secret. She would hardly let herself think that it was much harder for her than for Wimpole, though she knew it. Temptation is not sin. She had killed her temptations that day, and in their death had almost killed herself.

The sacrifice was perfect and whole-hearted, brave as true faith, and final as death itself.

"Good night," said Wimpole, and his voice broke.

Helen still had strength to speak.

"Neither you nor I shall ever regret this," she answered, but she looked long at him, as though she were not to see him again.

He pressed her hand hard and dropped it. Once more she looked at him and then turned slowly and left him standing there.

The porter of the hotel was facing her on the steps. Neither she nor Wimpole had noticed that he had come back and was waiting for them to part. He held a telegram in his hand, and Helen started slightly as she saw it, for she knew that it must be Harmon's answer to her word of forgiveness.

"Already!" she exclaimed faintly, as she took it.

She turned back to Wimpole, and met his eyes again, for he had not moved.

"It is Henry's answer," she said.

She opened the envelope, standing with her back to the light and to the porter. Wimpole breathed hard, and watched her face, and knew that nothing was to be spared to either of them on that day. As she read the words, he thought she swayed a little on her feet, and her eyes

opened very wide, and her lips were white.
Wimpole watched them and saw how strangely
they moved, as if she were trying to speak and
could not. He set his teeth, for he believed
that even the short message had in it some
fresh insult or injury for her.

She reeled visibly, and steadied herself against
one of the pillars of the porch, but she was able
to hold out the thin scrap of paper to Wimpole
as he moved forwards to catch her. He read
it. It was a cable notice through the telegraph
office from Brest.

" Your message number 731 Henry Harmon
New York not delivered owing to death of the
person addressed."

Wimpole read the words twice before their
meaning stunned him. When he knew where
he was, his eyes were still on the paper, and
he was grasping Helen's wrist, while she stood
stark and straight against the pillar of the
porch. She lifted her free hand and passed it
slowly across her forehead, opening and shutting
her eyes as if waking. The porter stared at
her from the steps.

" Come," said Wimpole. " Let us go out
again. We can't stay here."

Helen looked at him, only half comprehend-
ing. Even in the uncertain light he could see
the colour returning to her face, and he felt it

in his own.   Then her senses came back all at once with her own clear judgment and decision, and the longing to be alone, which he could not understand, as he tried to draw her away with him.

"No, no!" she cried, resisting.   "Let me go, please let me go!   Please!"

He had already dropped her wrist.

"Come to-morrow," she added quickly.

And all her lost youth was in her as she lightly turned and went from him up the steps. Again he stood still, following her with his eyes, but an age had passed, with Harmon's life, between that time and this.

He understood better, when he himself was alone, walking far on, through the damp wind, by the shore of the lake, past the big railway station, just then in one of its fits of silence, past the wooden piers built out into the lake for the steamers, and out beyond, not counting his steps, nor seeing things, with bent head, and one hand catching nervously at the breast of his coat.

He understood Helen, for he also had need of being alone to face the tremendous contrast of the hour and to digest in secret the huge joy he was ashamed to show to himself, because it was for the death of a man whose existence had darkened his own.   Because Harmon was

suddenly dead, the sleeping hope of twenty
years had waked with deep life and strength.
Time and age were rolled away like a mist
before the morning breeze, the world was young
again, and the rose of yesterday was once more
the lovely flower of to-day.

Yet he was too brave a man, and too good, to
let himself rejoice cruelly in Harmon's death,
any more than he would have gloried, in his
younger days, over an enemy fallen in fight.
But it was hard to struggle against this instinct,
deep rooted and strong in humanity ages before Achilles dragged Hector round the walls of
Troy. Christianity has made it mean to insult
the dead and their memory. For what we call
honour comes to us from chivalry and knighthood, which grew out of Christian doings when
men believed; and though non-Christian people
have their standards of right and wrong, they
have not our sort of honour, nor anything like
it, and cannot in the least understand it.

But Wimpole was made happy by Harmon's
death, and he himself could not deny it. That
was another matter, and one over which he had
no control. His satisfaction was in the main
disinterested, being on Helen's behalf; for though
he hoped, he was very far from believing that
she would marry him, now that she was a
widow. He had not even guessed that she had

loved him long. It was chiefly because his
whole nature had been suffering so sincerely for
her sake during the long hours since he had read
the paragraph in the paper, that he was now so
immensely happy. He tried to call up again
the last conversation in the dark, by the river;
but though the words both he and she had
spoken came back in broken echoes, they seemed
to have no meaning, and he could not explain to
himself how he could possibly have stood there,
wrenching at the cold iron rail to steady his
nerves, less than half an hour ago. It was in-
credible. He felt like a man who has been in
the delirium of a fever, in which he has talked
foolishly and struck out wildly at his friends,
and who cannot believe such things of himself
when he is recovering, though he dimly remem-
bers them, with a sort of half-amused shame for
his weakness.

Wimpole did not know how long he wandered
by the lake in the windy darkness, before he felt
that he had control of speech and action again
and found himself near the bridge, going towards
his hotel. It was less than half an hour, perhaps, but ever afterwards, when he thought of
it, he seemed to have walked up and down all
night, a hundred times past the railway station,
a hundred times along the row of steamboat.
piers, struggling with the impression that he

had no right to be perfectly happy, and fighting
off the instinct to rejoice in Harmon's death.

But Helen had fled to her own room and had
locked the door upon the world. To her, as to
Wimpole, it would have seemed horrible to be
frankly glad that her husband was dead. But
she had no such instinct. She had been dazed
beyond common sense and speech by the sudden
relief from the strain she had borne so strongly
and bravely. She had been dazzled by the light
of freedom as a man let out of a dark prison
after half a lifetime of captivity. She had been
half stunned by the instant release of all the
springs of her nature, long forced back upon
themselves by the sheer strength of her conscience. And yet she was sorry for the dead
man.

Far away in her past youth she remembered
his handsome face, his bright eyes, his strong
vitality, his pleasant voice, and the low ringing
tone of it that had touched her and brought her
to the ruin of her marriage, and she remembered that for a time she had half loved him and
believed love whole. She is a hard and cruel
woman who has not a little pitiful tenderness
left for a dead past, — though it be buried under
a hideous present, — and some kind memory of
the man she has called dear.

Helen thought of his face as he was lying

dead now, white and stony, but somehow, in her kindness, it became the face of long ago, and was not like him as when she had seen him last. The touch of death is strangely healing. She had no tears, but there was a dim softness in her eyes, for the man who was gone; not for the man who had insulted her, tortured her, struck her, but for the husband she had married long ago.

The other, the incarnate horror of her mature life, had dropped from existence, leaving his place full of the light in which she was thereafter to live, and in the bright peace she saw Wimpole's face, as he waited for her.

In the midst of her thoughts was the enigmatic spectre of the world, the familiar tormentor of those with whom the world has anything to do — a vast, disquieting question-mark to their actions. What would the world say, when she married Wimpole?

What could it say? It knew, if it knew anything of her, that her husband had been little better than a beast — no better; worse, perhaps. It knew that Wimpole was a man in thousands, and perhaps it knew that he had been faithful to her mere name in his heart during the best of his years. She had no enemies to cast a shadow upon her future by slurring her past.

Yet she had heard the world talk, and the
names of women who had married old friends
within the first year of widowhood were rarely
untouched by scandal. She did not fear that,
but in her heart there was a sort of unacknow-
ledged dread lest Wimpole, who was growing
old in patience, should be patient to the end
out of some over-fine scruple for her fair
name.

Then came the thought of her new widowhood and rebuked her, and with the old habit
of fighting battles against her heart for her
conscience, she turned fiercely against her long-
silent love that was crying freedom so loudly
in her ears. Harmon just dead, not buried yet,
perhaps, and she already thinking of marriage !
Said in those words, it seemed contemptible,
though all her loyalty to her husband had been
for a word's sake, almost since the beginning.

But then, again, as she closed her eyes to
think sensibly, she set her lips to stay the
smile at her scruples. Her loyalty had been
all for the vow, for the meaning of the bond,
for the holiness of marriage itself. It had not
been the loyalty of love for Harmon, and Harmon being dead, its only object was gone. The
rest, the mourning for the unloved dead, was a
canon of the world, not a law of God. For
decency, she would wear black for a short time,

but in her heart she was free, and free in her conscience.

To the last, she had borne all, and had been ready to bear more. Her last word had gone at once, with the message of forgiveness he had asked, and though he had been dead before it reached him he could not have doubted her answer, for he knew her. If she had been near him, she would have been with him to the end, to help him, and to comfort him if she could. She had been ready to go back to him, and the letter that was to have told him so was already gone upon its fruitless journey, to return to her after a long time as a reminder of what she had been willing to bear. She could not reproach herself with any weakness or omission, and her reason told her plainly that although she must mourn outwardly to please the world, it would be folly to refuse her heart the thought of a happiness for which she had paid beforehand with half a lifetime of pain.

When that was all at once and unmistakably clear to her, she let her head sink gently back upon the cushion of the chair, her set lips parted, and she softly sighed, as though the day were done at last and her rest had come. As she sat there, the lines of sorrow and suffering were smoothed away and the faint colour crept slowly and naturally to her cheeks, as her eyes closed by slow degrees under the shaded light of the lamp. One more restful sigh, her sweet breath came slower and more evenly, one hand fell upon her knee with upward palm and loosened fingers that did not move again; she was asleep.

CHAPTER XIII

So ends the history of a day unforgotten in the memories of the men and women, young and old, for whom it chanced to be life's turning-point. Looking back into the full, past years through which the fight has been fought, most of us still know one day and hour in which the tide of battle turned; we see the faces that rose up against us, and those that stood beside us in the struggle; we hear the words spoken which cheered us to the great charge, or turned our hearts cold and our daring to fear; even our bodily hearts, handfuls of wandering atoms of which not one is left in us from those times, answer the deep memory and beat loud, or fail, as those other atoms did in the decisive instant when one blow more meant victory, and one blow less, defeat.

Helen's last letter to her husband came back to her like a ghost, after many weeks, when she was going over Harmon's papers. There it lay, unopened, as she had sealed it, full of the words that had seemed to cost her life — the promise to pay a debt not justly owed, which no man could claim now. She burned it unread, for she knew every line of it by heart. To read it, even to glance at the writing, she thought, would rouse some pride in her for what she had done and stir a sort of gladness in her soul, because the man was dead and she was safe from him forever. She would not let herself feel such things. Unconsciously she had fought with herself for a principle, not, as most of us do, for the intimate satisfaction of having done right, which is in itself a reward, an object, and an aim for ambition, and therefore not wholly unselfish, not wholly noble, though often both high and worthy.

Right, as we understand it, is the law for each individual, the principle is for all mankind; and as the whole is greater than any of its parts, so is the principle greater than the law. The law says, " Whosoever sheddeth man's blood, by man shall his blood be shed." But the Blood which was shed for all men required of man no lawful avenging.

Moreover, law and all forms of law are only deductions made by the intelligence from the right instincts of the people's heart. Laws which are evolved out of existing circumstances, backwards, as it were, to correct bad results, are rarely anything more than measures of expedi-

ency and have not much lasting power. They
are medicines, not nourishment for humanity —
a cure for the sick, not a rule of life for the
sound and whole.

When such enactments of law-givers tend
against those impulses which spring from the
roots of human feeling, taking into consideration the happiness of the few and not the good
of the many, they are bad medicines for the
world. The instant, quick release by divorce
from all troubles, great and small, between man
and wife, is no better than that other instant,
quick relief from bodily pain, which is morphia,
a material danger no longer at all dim or
shadowy.

We are a cowardly generation, and men shrink
from suffering now, as their fathers shrank from
dishonour in rougher times. The Lotus hangs
within the reach of all, and in the lives of many
" it is always afternoon," as for the Lotus Eaters.
The fruit takes many shapes and names; it is
called Divorce, it is called Morphia, it is called
Compromise, it is designated in a thousand ways
and justified by ten thousand specious arguments,
but it means only one thing : Escape from Pain.

Soft-hearted and weak-nerved people ask why
humanity should suffer at all, and they hail every
invention, moral or material, which can make
life easier for the moment, as a heaven-sent bless-

ing. Why should we be uncomfortable, even an
hour, when a little dose of poison can create a
lazy oblivion?   That is the drunkard's reasoning,
the opium-eater's defence, the invalid's excuse.
It is no argument for men who call themselves
the world's masters.

Civilization and Progress are not the same
thing. We have too much progress and too
little civilization nowadays. Progress is omnivo-
rous, eager after new things, seeking above all
to save trouble and get money. Civilization is
eclectic, slow, painstaking, wise, willing to buy
good at the price it is worth. Civilization gave
us marriage, in respecting which we are above
animals. Progress is giving us divorce, wholesale, cheap, immoral, a degradation beneath that
of those primitive peoples, who make no promises and break none, who do not set up right as
a fashion and wrong as a practice, the truth for
the ensign and the lie for the course.

Helen Harmon's existence turned out happily
in the end. She was fortunate at last, before
the love of life was gone. But for the accident
of her husband's sudden death, she would have
had to face her cruel difficulties to death's solution; and with her character she would not have
been defeated, for she had on her side the accu-
mulated force of all womanliness against the
individual evil that was her familiar enemy.

Far should it be from the story-teller to draw
a moral; furthest of all, that false moral that
makes faith and truth and courage get worldly
pay for their services — servants to be hired as
guides and porters to happiness. In Helen's
case it chanced that she got what she wanted.
Fate had spent its force against her, and peace
was with her thereafter.

Even "poor Archie" found his vocation at
last. The day that had meant so much to many
had brought him a sort of awakening of mind,
an increase of reason and a growth of character.
His one strong instinct became a dominating
force. He would save life, many lives, so long
as he had strength. Sylvia would never care
for him, of course; he said to himself that she
should at least see what he could do. He remembered with constant longing the wild delight
he had felt when he had brought the little child
safely to the deck of the ferryboat on the North
River, and when, bruised and bleeding, he had
stopped the bolting horses in the New York street.

He unfolded his plan to the colonel first, because he was a man, and must understand; then
he told his mother. There was nothing to be
said against it, except that it was dangerous.
He had made up his mind to join a Life-Saving
Station on the coast. It was the one thing he
could do, and he knew it.

"Of course," he said, with his elementary philosophy, "if I get drowned the first time, there won't be anything gained. But if I can help to save a few people before that, it won't matter so much, you know. It'll be like money, when you get something for it."

The rude bravery of the argument brought a look into Wimpole's eyes which had not been there for a long time. Helen had a lump in her throat.

"But if anything should happen to you —" she began, and stopped.

"Well, then," answered Archie, "I suppose I'd go to heaven, shouldn't I? And that would be all right, just the same."

And thereupon he began to whistle thoughtfully. It was very simple in his eyes, and very desirable. Life seemed to him to be man's first and greatest possession, as it is. For him, its possibilities were small, but he had a dim perception of its value to others, whom he called "clever" in wholesale distinction from himself. It was worth having, worth keeping, and worth saving, for them, at the risk of his own.

As for Miss Rachel Wimpole, as soon as she heard of Harmon's death, she knew that her brother would marry Helen. She had systematically disapproved of his life-long devotion to a woman beyond his reach, while she had

involuntarily respected in him the same unchanging faithfulness which had guarded her
own heart against everything else for so many
years, a little stronghold of no great importance
to the rest of the world, but which held all that
was most dear and precious to her. So here and
there, in the chaos of the middle ages, some
strong, poor gentleman, a mere atom in the
wide Holy Empire, may have kept his small
castle and his narrow acres of meagre land
against all comers.

When Harmon was dead and gone, Miss Wimpole's disapprobation instantly disappeared, and
she never at any time afterwards seemed to remember how she had felt about the matter during so many years. Wimpole approached her
with some diffidence, and she met him with
genuine enthusiasm. She was one of those rare
people who can make others vicars of their happiness, so to say, whose place has been long
darkened by sad clouds, but who see the sunshine far away on another's land and are glad
for that other one's sake.

It is a sign of our times that a man whose
fancy leads him now and then to make a story
of characters almost ideal, should feel as if he
owed his reader a sort of apology for so far dis-
regarding the common fashion. There must
always be a conflict between the real and the

ideal, between what we are told is knowledge
and what our hearts tell us is truth, between
the evil men do and the good which is beyond
their strength, but not above their aspiration.
And therefore the old question stands unanswered : Do most people wish to be shown what
they are, or what they might be ?   In order to
avoid the difficulty of replying, fashion comes
forward and says to-day that art is truth, and
infers that art must be accurate and photo-
graphic and closely imitative.

What has art to do with truth ?   Is not truth
the imagination's deadly enemy ?   If the two
meet, they must fight to the death.   It is therefore better, in principle, to keep them apart,
and let each survive separately with their uses.
Two and two make four, says Truth.   Never
mind facts, says Art, let us imagine a world in
which two and two make five, and see whether
we can get anything pleasant, or amusing, out
of the supposition.   Let us sometimes talk about
men and women who are unimaginably perfect,
and let us find out what they would do with the
troubles that make sinners of most of us, and
puzzle us, and turn our hair grey.

Matter, says the mystic, is the inexhaustible
source and active cause of all harm.   Imagination can be altogether free from matter.   That
is what we mean by the ideal, and men may say

what they will, it is worth having. A man must know the enemy against whom he is matched, if he hopes to win; he must know his adversary's fence, his thrusts and feints and parries. Truth will give him that knowledge. But beyond the enemy, and beyond victory over him, there is the aspiration, the hope, the aim of all life — and that is the ideal, if it is anything at all worth hoping; it is transcendent, outside of all facts and perhaps of any attainment, and only the imagination can ever tell us what it may be.

Yet those who guess at it, dwell on it and love it, and it comes to be the better part of their lives. The world holds two great classes of mankind, artists and truth-seekers. There are millions of artists, there always have been, and there always will be. One in each million, perhaps, is born with the gift of creation and knows the tools of his trade by instinct, and works with them, as soon as he is old enough to think. The rest are not less artists, because they are not producers. They have the same aspirations, the same longings, the same tastes, though they are not makers, as he is; and when he has finished his work, they look at it with eyes like his, and enjoy even more perfectly than he, for they see the expression of a thought like their own, while all that he could not express is hidden from them and does not disturb their satisfaction.   Art for art's sake, if such a thing could be, would mean that the one man would work just as hard to give his imagination a shape, even if the rest of the million were not there to understand him. But he knows that they are all living and that the ideal for which he labours is divine to them all, whether he fail or whether he succeed.

THE END